THE PROTECTOR'S RESOLVE

BOOK SIX OF THE TALES OF CALEDONIA

PETER WACHT

The Protector's Resolve
By Peter Wacht

Book 6 of The Tales of Caledonia

ISBN: 978-1-950236-28-2

eBook ISBN: 978-1-950236-29-9

Library of Congress Control Number: 9781950236282

❀ Created with Vellum

The Makings of a Warrior

The Lord of the Highlands

The Lost Kestrel Found

The Claiming of the Highlands

The Fight Against the Dark

The Defender of the Light

THE RISE OF THE SYLVAN WARRIORS

*Through the Knife's Edge (short story)**

* Free short stories can be downloaded from my author website at
www.kestrelmg.com

YOUR FREE SHORT STORY IS WAITING

THE DIAMOND THIEF

This short story is a prelude to the events in my series *The Tales of Caledonia* and is free to readers who receive my newsletter.

Join Peter's newsletter and get your FREE short story.
www.kestrelmg.com

SETTING THE STAGE

The Protector's Resolve, Book Six of *The Tales of Caledonia*, is set more than one thousand years before the events that occur in *The Sylvan Chronicles* and takes place in a separate land of *The Realms of the Talent and the Curse*. Caledonia, though a monarchy, functions more like a loose confederation of Duchies, even more so now that the King of Caledonia, Marden Beleron, has met his end in the Pit at the hands of the Volkun.

During this time some of the more adventurous and grasping members of the Caledonian nobility accepted King Corinthus Beleron's territorial grants and begin to colonize the Territories far to the west on the other side of the Burnt Ocean. These Territories will eventually become the Kingdoms of *The Sylvan Chronicles*.

In Caledonia, as in the other realms, the ability to use the Talent sets apart the person gifted with this unique skill. But being able to use the Talent is only part of the dynamic. For if a Magus chooses to follow a darker path, the Talent becomes the Curse.

PROLOGUE

"He's stronger than I ever imagined possible."

"That's good, Sirius. He needs to be strong if he's to have any chance of rebuilding the Weir."

Sirius and Rafia stood on the parapet of the Library of the Magii, looking out over the glacial lake currently linked to the far shore by a span of the Curse set there by the Ghoule Overlord. It was still dark, the sun the faintest of glows behind the towering peaks encircling the hidden valley.

"Yes, but you felt what happened when he removed those Elders from the fight, didn't you?"

"How could I not, Sirius," Rafia replied with just a hint of exasperation.

The Ghoules had been pressing the Company of Blood hard, threatening to break through to the tower upon which she and Sirius now observed the lake and the surrounding environs. The Elders had joined the fight, seeking to tip the balance, and it was Bryen who stopped them, using the Seventh Stone to drain them of their corrupt power as well as their very essences. With the Elders no longer a threat, the

Magii and the gladiators forced the Ghoules to retreat from the island.

For the time being.

They would be back.

Soon. Very soon.

The Ghoule Overlord did not manage defeat well.

The Ghoule Overlord needed the Seventh Stone, needed the Protector, and Bryen's latest display of power most assuredly had caught his attention, had intensified his craving for the artifact reclaimed from him so long ago.

"He was close to going over the edge, Rafia. You know that just as well as I do. If he does that, he doesn't come back. We lose him, and he loses himself."

Sirius' voice revealed his worry. There was something else there as well.

Fear.

Whether for the lost opportunity to repair the Weir or for Bryen or for what he and Rafia might need to do if Bryen actually touched the Curse ... she wasn't sure. It could be a combination of all three.

"Yes, but he didn't, Sirius. That's what matters." Rafia motioned toward the end of the dock where Bryen stood, the Lady of the Southern Marches right at his side. "Aislinn was there. She brought him back before it was too late. She helped him even though she probably didn't know she was doing it. She kept him with us."

"And what if she's not there next time, Rafia? What if there is no one there to stop him from going over the edge?"

Rafia understood Sirius' concerns. Much of it was driven by what was required of the Protector. Because the Seventh Stone had joined with him, he was the only Magus with a chance, slim though it might be, to rebuild the Weir and prevent the Ghoule Legions from flooding into the Kingdom.

She sensed, though, that there was a great deal more to

Sirius' concern than just that. His relationship with Bryen was much more complicated than he was willing to let slip, and he was struggling to come to grips with what that actually meant. For Bryen and for himself.

"Sirius, you need to let this go for now. We have enough to deal with as it is. If we don't get off Haven, then everything else will be moot."

"I know you're right, Rafia. It's just that with Bryen I ..."

Sirius' words trailed off, not knowing how to express what he wanted to say, needing to start again.

"Bryen means more to me than ..." The old Magus stopped himself again, at a loss for how to explain what he was feeling.

Rather than making fun of him, which was her initial instinct, because it was such a rare occurrence when the old Magus' words didn't flow, she gripped his arm strongly.

"I know, Sirius. I understand your fears. That you want to be there in case he needs you. However, the reality is that the Protector is quite competent on his own. If he is to succeed in the task we've set before him, we must trust him. Even when we fear that he might be making a mistake, even when we fear that he might be too close to the edge, we must trust that in the end he will do what is required no matter how much it might cost him."

1

ALL YOU CAN DO

"You did all that you could."

Bryen stood at the end of the pier that jutted out into the lake, staring down at the molded Curse that resembled black ice, the span that would give the Ghoule Overlord and his creatures the opportunity to attack the island once again. He was certain that this time the Master of the Lost Land would be directing the fight, because the beast couldn't afford another failure.

That likely would lead to one result. A result that would doom the Company of Blood.

Aislinn could tell by the spark in his eyes and his grim expression that Bryen was angry, even though as usual he kept his emotions hidden well. She wanted to help him, to ease his burden, understanding the other pressures that he was facing.

She couldn't, however. This wasn't her struggle. It was his. All she could do was try to give him a path that took him away from the dark thoughts and self-recrimination that plagued him.

"I should have done more."

"You healed as many gladiators as you could."

"Yes, but we still lost too many fighters. It seems that even with the Seventh Stone I can't bring my friends back from the dead."

Aislinn reached for Bryen's arm and squeezed warmly, her sympathy flowing through her touch. She understood what Bryen was going through.

The gladiators had pledged their lives to him, and he felt responsible for them. He wanted to help his friends, to keep them from harm.

He was discovering on this quest to reach the Sanctuary, however, that sometimes despite putting forth your best effort, that simply wasn't enough. That you couldn't control all that you wanted to control.

"All you can do is the best that you can do," Aislinn said quietly, leaning her head against his shoulder. "Beating yourself up about your perceived failures doesn't help anyone. You do the best that you can do, and then you move on to what you have to do next. That stricture applies here just as it did in the Pit. Any gladiator of the Blood Company would tell you exactly that."

"I think you've been spending too much time with Declan," grumbled Bryen. "That sounds like something that he would say. In fact, I think he has said it. Many times."

"That might be the case," Aislinn admitted with a small smile. "Still, it's good advice, and I hope that you will listen to it."

Bryen reached across and squeezed Aislinn's arm in silent thanks. She was right. He didn't have to like it. He did have to accept the reality that she had just pointed out to him because it wasn't going to change.

More of his friends were going to die before all this was over. He couldn't escape that fact, no matter how much he might try.

"I hate this. I hate that so many people have to die for me. I wish there was another way."

Bryen stared more intently at the black ice linking the island to the mainland. He couldn't save the gladiators who had died defending Haven, though maybe he could help those who still lived, an idea percolating in the back of his brain.

Perhaps there was a way that he could make the Ghoule Overlord's pursuit more difficult and give the Blood Company more time to recuperate from the last battle. It might even improve their odds of escaping.

"I wish there was as well. But you know as well as I that ..."

"Hoping doesn't make it real," finished Bryen.

"You've been spending too much time with Sirius," chastised Aislinn with a gentle smile.

"I agree with you on that," confirmed Bryen. "I really haven't had much of a choice." He motioned down toward the black ice. "You know, I think there is something that I can do. That will help us now."

Bryen had just used the Talent to search around them, having sensed several more Ghoule packs coming their way. The Ghoule Overlord's reinforcements would arrive by dusk. Soon after that, his forces replenished, the Master of the Curse would lead his beasts against them.

Although the gladiators would give everything they had against the beasts, the Blood Company could not defeat the Ghoules who were hunting them. They could only delay them. There were too many. For every Ghoule they eliminated from the fight, another soon appeared to take the place of the fallen beast.

He and his gladiators were on the wrong end of a battle of attrition. Yet Bryen believed that he could at least increase the level of difficulty for their pursuers.

Neither Sirius nor Rafia had enjoyed any success when attempting to break apart the sheet of Dark Magic the Ghoules used to cross the lake, so clearly the Talent wasn't the answer to his dilemma. That being the case, he did have another tool at his disposal that might work.

Just as he did only a few hours before, Bryen reached for the Talent, this time also opening himself to the Seventh Stone. He used the Spear of the Magii as a focal point, the twin blades of the weapon glowing brightly as the energy surged into him.

"Bryen, what are you doing?" asked Aislinn, squeezing his arm with a stronger grip, not knowing if she should be worried or curious or both.

"I want to test a theory," he replied. "There's something that I might be able to do that Sirius and Rafia can't."

Aislinn nodded, her eyes betraying her slight trepidation, already having an idea of what he had in mind. "Just be careful."

Nodding in response to Aislinn's demand that masqueraded as a request, he applied the same approach that had been so effective in draining the Elders of their power to the span that connected Haven to the lakeshore, sending a hollow tube of the Talent down toward the shining surface. The cord latched on when the Dark Magic contained within the Seventh Stone surged out and joined with the hardened Curse.

Bryen was certain that the principles he was applying were sound, the primary difference compared to what he did to the Elders being the scale of his effort since the Ghoule Overlord had used so much of the Curse to construct the bridge. So he took his time, working slowly and cautiously. He checked, and then checked again, making sure that when he connected the cord of Dark Magic to the black ice that there was no way that the Curse could corrupt him.

For several heartbeats nothing happened. Bryen worried that he might have misjudged. Maybe he couldn't manage this much of the Curse at one time.

His eyes brightened just a moment later, his concern fading

away. He had been right. His calculated gamble was about to pay off.

The transformation began slowly, the black ice shimmering, taking on an almost liquid appearance before switching back to a rigid form, that transition between states accelerating as Bryen used the Seventh Stone to pull on the Ghoule Overlord's Dark Magic with greater insistence. The shiny, solid black surface flashed several times, from solid to liquid to a foggy gas, and then back again, faster and faster, before it finally shifted permanently into a hazy mist, Bryen drawing in the Curse, adding it to the Dark Magic the Seventh Stone already contained. After only just a few more heartbeats, it was done, the span dissolving entirely, the Ghoule Overlord's creation destroyed.

Having taken in a huge amount of Dark Magic, Bryen needed a moment to regain his bearings. He confirmed again, just to make certain, that he had protected himself properly, the Curse never breaking free from the constraints he had set around that corrosive power.

For the first time in days, he smiled broadly. Now the Ghoule Overlord would need to work a little bit harder to attack the island. After what Bryen had just done, his adversary would begin to wonder, perhaps even doubt, which likely would unsettle the beast. It might even affect his thinking, leading to some bad decisions, which was fine with Bryen. If the Ghoule Overlord began to second guess himself that was all to the good.

The soft and subtle voice in the back of his head that was always there and that he wasn't sure was entirely his own was cackling with glee at his success.

He had done it, the voice was saying. He had made the Curse his own.

With those thoughts drifting through his mind, several

questions joined them, and he wasn't certain that these questions belonged to him.

If he was the Seventh Stone, did he really need to fear the Curse? If he could make the Curse his own, was he bound by the strictures of the past? By rules that might not apply to him? Could he not become more than even the Ghoule Overlord?

"Bryen."

He heard a voice just at the edge of his consciousness. He tried to ignore it, wanting to think more on those questions. The answers could be crucial to the larger task set for him. But he couldn't, the voice becoming more insistent.

"Bryen!"

"Sorry," he said sheepishly, struggling to come back to himself.

"Show off," said Aislinn teasingly, giving Bryen a nudge with her shoulder, finally breaking his train of thought, those troublesome questions fading away.

She was clearly pleased by what he had just accomplished. She also seemed worried, though he couldn't tell for sure, as he couldn't understand why she would be.

"Just doing what needed to be done."

"Another of Declan's sayings?" asked Aislinn, that trace of concern in the back of her eyes fading away.

"Either one of his or Sirius'. It's hard to keep track of them all."

"You all right, lad?" asked Sirius.

He and Rafia had rushed down to join them at the end of the dock when they realized what Bryen was doing with the Seventh Stone. The looks on the faces of the two Magii told Bryen that they weren't as impressed or pleased by his action as he thought that they might be. Rather, they were anxious. Maybe even a little afraid.

Because of that, they were both on edge.

"Fine," Bryen replied evenly after several seconds had

passed, deciding to keep his thoughts to himself. Deciding the two Magii didn't need to know everything. "It just took a bit more out of me than I thought it would after today's fight."

"So nothing for us to worry about?"

Bryen studied dispassionately the similar looks that Rafia and Sirius were giving him, both obviously worried that he might have touched the Curse. Bryen's gaze sharpened, his voice coming out as a challenge.

"Would you like to check yourself just to make sure?"

Both Magii were somewhat taken aback by the intensity of his tone, neither expecting it. Sirius' eyes narrowed, his brow furrowing. He was about to accept Bryen's challenge, to reach for the Talent to confirm that the Protector indeed was free of the Curse, when Rafia placed a hand on his arm to stop him.

"No, no need," she said, her gaze appraising. "We trust you. We just wanted to make sure that you were all right."

Bryen nodded, then watched with a hint of distrust as the two Magii walked back down the pier toward the Library of the Magii, their heads together, deep in conversation. He needed to remember that Sirius and Rafia were there to help him if he required their assistance, but their greater loyalty was to the Kingdom, to protecting against the Ghoule Overlord and the Curse, and not to him.

He hoped that it didn't reach a point where the two Magii would need to make a decision between the two. For their sakes, not his. He hoped that they did, indeed, trust him.

Because he feared that if they tried to kill him, he might try to stop them. Then his training as a gladiator would take over, and even if the two Magii combined their power, even with their greater experience and knowledge, he knew that he was much stronger in the Talent than the both of them. Particularly when he made use of the Seventh Stone. So he had no doubt as to how that combat would end.

THE GHOULE OVERLORD GROWLED ANGRILY, furious at his Ghoules' latest setback. He had only a few packs left, and the Protector who had become the Seventh Stone had eliminated all his Elders. He would have to wait until the additional packs coming toward him from the north arrived before trying for a third time to conquer the island.

He believed that he could defeat the Protector in a combat. He just didn't want to have to deal with the distraction of the Magii joining that fight, so better to allow his Elders to deal with them, better to control all the variables that he could before taking that risk.

Gurzen and the Ghoules who had survived the failed incursion had found a spot to wait farther down the beach, unwilling to be too close to him, unwilling to risk his wrath.

They were right to be afraid, because all he wanted to do in that moment was lash out, to release the fury building up within him.

Struggling to contain his rage, he stared across the lake with death in his eyes.

The Ghoule Overlord had watched what the Protector had done, following what he was doing as he did it, astounded by what the human had achieved. Most frustrating was the fact that he had no good way to stop him.

He could have tried to use his Dark Magic to maintain the bridge at the same time that the Protector drained the Curse from it. He had stopped himself the instant before he did just that, a rare caution coming into play. He worried about what might happen if the Seventh Stone grasped not onto the Curse but onto him.

He held few concerns when it came to fighting the Protector, but the artifact was a variable that he could not control.

Could the artifact empty him of his immense power just as

it had emptied his Elders? Just as it drained the span he crafted of the Curse?

He didn't know, and that bothered him, although not as much as the touch of fear that had settled within him as he considered what the result might be if the Protector did, indeed, turn the Seventh Stone directly against him.

That disturbing thought wasn't even the most worrisome that passed through the Ghoule Overlord's mind.

The Protector had become the Seventh Stone. Just a host for the artifact, he believed. However, he was beginning to realize that there was more to it than that.

Because now the Protector was mastering the Seventh Stone.

And if he could master the Seventh Stone, what else could he master?

The Ghoule Overlord growled again as he considered that question.

He didn't like the possibilities that came to mind.

He needed to stop this before it became more than a challenge, before it became a threat.

He needed to take the Protector.

Before the Protector became even more powerful than he already was. Before he learned more about what he could really do with the potency that had joined with him.

2

TIME TO MOVE

Bryen and Aislinn strode down the pier, stepping around the large holes scattered around the dock and avoiding the cracked and splintered posts.

"You're certain?"

"Yes," nodded Aislinn. "By late afternoon. They're moving fast. Faster than we expected."

"Then we'll need to move faster than they are," replied Bryen. "I just wish that we had more time."

"So do I, but we're not going to get it. The Ghoule Overlord hasn't demonstrated much patience during this hunt."

"That he hasn't," agreed Bryen. He and Aislinn stopped where the pier met the shore, a small group having gathered there to discuss what to do before the Ghoule Overlord attacked again, the conversation pausing when they saw the two young Magii approach. "How many did we lose?"

"Seventeen," Declan replied sadly. "All good men and women."

"Could I have helped them?" Bryen asked, his frustration evident in his tired voice and sad eyes.

"You couldn't have. I can say that they left us as the gladiators they were. They fought until they couldn't fight anymore."

He sympathized with Bryen, and Declan was glad that despite fighting in the Pit for ten years he hadn't lost his humanity. Nevertheless, this was a reality of war. People died no matter how hard you fought to keep them alive. It was terrible, it was heartbreaking, and it was inevitable.

Declan shook his head grimly. They could mourn the dead later. Now, they needed to focus on the living and ensure that they didn't follow those who had already gone to the other side.

"There's nothing that you could have done to help them," explained Declan. "They were killed before you destroyed the Elders. Lock away the sorrow for now and don't allow the guilt to stay with you. You did all that you could. We need to shift our focus to how we stay ahead of the Ghoule Overlord."

"You're right," nodded Bryen, pushing aside his anger at how many of his friends had to sacrifice themselves so that he could live. He would deal with his grief later, because he didn't want to waste the gift that the fallen gladiators had given him. "We need to get moving again. The Ghoule Overlord will begin to recreate the black ice soon. Once he's done with his latest construction, we won't be able to stop him this time, even if we applied the same strategy that worked so effectively for us during the last attack. He'll be coming across at the head of his packs. Of that, I'm certain."

"Why are you so sure about all of that?" asked Rafia with a raised eyebrow, her natural curiosity coming to the forefront.

"I can sense the Ghoule Overlord through the Dark Magic of the Seventh Stone. I imagine that my ability to do this is similar to how he can sense the Seventh Stone within me."

"You can do what?" demanded Sirius, his eyes a bit wild at Bryen's declaration, the fears and concerns he had been discussing with Rafia just moments before returning with a vengeance.

"I can sense the Ghoule Overlord and, roughly -- no more than a few pieces here and there -- what he might be thinking through the Dark Magic of the Seventh Stone."

"That shouldn't be possible," protested Sirius, at a complete loss, which surprised everyone around him. The old Magus always seemed to have an answer for every question. "How can that be?"

"I don't know."

"You haven't touched the Curse, have you?" Sirius stepped right up to Bryen, his fears getting the better of him, his eyes becoming flintier when he asked the question.

The old Magus' personality shifted in a heartbeat. He was no longer the somewhat befuddled tutor. Instead, he was the powerful Master of the Magii, his intensity as he focused on Bryen almost suffocating. And, in Rafia's opinion, although she hoped desperately that she was wrong, he was a man who appeared to be about to reach for the Talent and strike down Bryen if he gave the answer that Sirius didn't want to hear.

"No, I haven't. You're welcome to check if you like, if you don't believe me."

Bryen's voice came out through gritted teeth in a quiet, emotionless tone, matching the hardheartedness that had settled within his eyes. The same challenge that he had voiced just minutes before. The Volkun stood in front of the Master of the Magii now, and he clearly did not like what Sirius was insinuating.

Even more telling, he wasn't frightened or intimidated. The thought of a combat with the Master of the Magii didn't appear to faze Bryen in the least. Rafia didn't know if she should be impressed or worried by that conclusion.

"Sirius, calm down, please," requested Rafia. "We've been through this before. Just because Bryen now has certain unexpected and unexplained capabilities because of his close connection to the Seventh Stone does not mean that he's become corrupted by the Curse. If we are going to achieve our larger goal, we must trust one another. There is no reason not to trust Bryen, and there is no reason for Bryen not to trust you, at least when you're thinking clearly." Rafia added that comment at the end hoping that it would grab Sirius' attention.

Declan watched as Rafia's words washed over both Sirius and Bryen, although neither man appeared ready or willing to back down just yet. The behavior of the two resembled the stare downs that frequently occurred in the Colosseum before the start of a combat, one gladiator trying to get the better of the other before steel met steel. It was impressive and it was dangerous. He prepared himself to push between the two if it proved necessary to separate them.

"We can talk about this later, although I see no need to do so," Aislinn interjected, having adopted the commanding tone reserved for the Lady of the Southern Marches. "We've got other issues to deal with at the moment, and we're losing time. We need to counter what the Ghoules are going to do next."

Even with Aislinn's admonition, Sirius and Bryen continued to glare at one another, neither willing to look away. Sirius' fingers flexed, as if he were itching to reach for the Talent. Bryen stood there calmly, his gaze strong, his body relaxed, his hands gripping the Spear of the Magii comfortably.

Neither had grasped the natural power of the world. Yet. How much longer that would prove to be the case was anyone's guess as the tension between the two intensified.

Bryen had been in circumstances such as this more times than he could count. The only question that passed through his mind in that moment was whether this confrontation would progress to the next step. The drawing of blood.

If so, he was ready. He would do what was necessary to protect himself. But he would allow Sirius to make the decision as to whether there would be a next step.

Just when Bryen thought that the combat was about to

begin, the old Magus' eyes narrowed sharply, Sirius letting out a deep breath and nodding. Finally, he turned away from Bryen, apparently agreeing with both Rafia and Aislinn.

"Lady Winborne is correct," said Declan. "The Ghoule Overlord needs more fighters. By winning this battle, we've bought some additional time. Even so, we don't have much of that left. We can't afford to waste what we've earned."

"We can't stay here," said Tarin, the Captain of the Battersea Guard having watched the encounter between Sirius and Bryen with a great deal of interest. The tension increasing with each passing second, he wondered which of the two would win the combat if it came to it. And then he had thought about whether he would observe the combat or try to step in, because although he knew both Sirius and Bryen quite well, only one had earned his allegiance. "Declan is right. We'll be overrun during the next attack when that black ice appears again."

"Rafia and I tried to destroy it with the Talent but we couldn't," said Sirius, almost as if he were apologizing for their failure to do so. "As you saw, only Bryen has the capacity to do anything to hinder the Ghoule Overlord's Dark Magic when applied in such a way."

"It was a difficult thing to do," Bryen admitted, recoiling somewhat at the thought of taking in so much of the Curse into the Seventh Stone so soon after his last effort ... and the growing temptation to actually use that power, a temptation that he feared was becoming more seductive. "If the Ghoule Overlord expands the size of the span he's going to build to give his Ghoules more avenues to attack, I don't know that I'd be able to handle that much of his Dark Magic or would want to take that risk. Even with the Spear of the Magii, I'd be too worried about losing control." He then gave the old Magus a pointed look. "And I wouldn't want to worry Sirius any more than I already have."

Bryen meant for his last remark to lighten the mood,

attempting to ease the strain between them. Based on Sirius' expression, Bryen could tell that it hadn't worked.

Sirius ignored the Protector's comment, lost in thought. If Bryen was learning how to use the Seventh Stone, if he was connecting more profoundly with the artifact within him, which clearly seemed to be the case based on how he destroyed the span of Dark Magic, then Sirius wasn't certain that he could kill Bryen if it became necessary to do so, his rising doubts in that respect becoming more real.

He would try if it came to it, though *try* was now the critical term. The Protector might be too strong an adversary, even with Rafia and Aislinn aiding him, and that was a conclusion that he didn't want to contemplate.

"The Ghoule Overlord will never admit his mistakes," said Sirius, finally pushing to the side his burgeoning concerns, at least for the present. "He will learn from them, however. I expect that Bryen is right. He will work with his Elders to expand the spread of his Dark Magic. Rather than create a span a few hundred yards wide, he will do it in a way so that the Curse encircles the island. The Ghoules can then attack from any direction that they choose. Our fates will be sealed before the beasts even set foot on Haven again."

"That's the bad news," said Aislinn. "I've got even worse news."

"There's worse news than that?" asked Jerad with a grin and raised eyebrow, trying to interject some humor into a somber discussion and not having much luck with his attempt.

"Unfortunately so. I've been using the Talent to search around us. In addition to the half dozen that should be here by late afternoon, there are a dozen more Ghoule packs coming from the northeast. I'm assuming that there is at least one Elder with each pack."

"The Ghoule Overlord summoned them from the Winter Pass," murmured Rafia.

"I expect so," agreed Sirius.

"We're not in a position to handle that many reinforcements," said Declan. "Not now. Not with so many Elders coming this way."

"It's time to take the next step in our plan," said Tarin. "We need to get Bryen off the island. If it proves necessary, the Company of Blood can serve as a rear guard and delay the Ghoules for as long as possible."

"I won't leave the Blood Company here to fight my battles for me," protested Bryen. "And I don't think ..."

"Lad, I don't question your bravery," interrupted Sirius, his voice sharper than he intended, blaming it on his fears, which still colored his perspective. "No one questions your bravery. But as several have said, you are more important than the rest of us. Only you can do what needs to be done with respect to the Weir. No matter the cost, you need to get to the Sanctuary. Not us. So if the only option is to sacrifice ourselves so that you can do that, then so be it. That's the price we have to pay."

"I was going to say," said Bryen with a grin, unsurprised by Sirius' reaction and strangely grateful for it despite the strain existing between them, "that I don't think that we'll have to leave a guard in place, not with what Rafia has in mind."

"I'll start getting the Company in order," said Declan. "It won't take us long to get ready. I just want to go through the storerooms one more time to see if there's anything still there that we might want to take with us that could prove useful."

"We'll help you with that," offered Tarin, who nodded to Jerad, the two soldiers of the Battersea Guard following Declan.

"Wait, what are we talking about here?" asked Sirius. "I feel like I've missed an important conversation."

"You haven't missed anything, Sirius," Rafia stated matter of factly. "It's time to brave the tunnel that leads to the Trench, and if we're fast enough we won't need to leave anyone to guard our backs. It will take the Ghoule Overlord quite some time to break into the tower and find where we've gone. Even better, we can leave a few surprises along the way that should delay him further."

"Wait," said Sirius, holding up his hands. "I thought that tunnel was destroyed centuries ago."

"That was the rumor," said Rafia. "From what I was able to determine through my explorations while serving as Keeper of Haven, most of the tunnel still should be intact."

"Most of the tunnel should be intact? You're not certain? We're going to risk the success of a mission that will determine the fate of Caledonia on an assumption?"

Sirius sounded as if he couldn't quite believe his ears. Rafia just ignored him.

"Well, I wasn't able to get all the way to the Trench," said Rafia. "I didn't have the time. From what I discovered, though, we should be able to make use of the passageway. We'll just need to be cautious. Structurally, there are some parts of the tunnel we'll have to negotiate very carefully, as well as some unanticipated dangers we'll need to avoid if we can. But those worries can wait until after we've gained some distance on the Ghoule Overlord."

"Why didn't you tell me it was passable?" demanded Sirius. "Wait a moment. What do you mean by unanticipated dangers?"

"I assumed that you knew," said Rafia. "You're the Master of the Magii, after all." She shook her head as if she couldn't quite believe that he had never obtained the information from the previous Keeper of Haven. "Some portions of the tunnel may be difficult to traverse, but we should be able to make it through, particularly with Bryen as part of our group. I'm sorry. I thought that you were aware. And as I said, let's deal with the more immediate threat first before worrying about what we might find in the tunnel." Rafia's contrition appeared to be genuine, which mollified Sirius to a certain extent, though not completely. "Besides, I didn't want to tell everyone else because I feared that would reduce the incentive to fight as would be required of them."

"That was a mistake and an insult," said Bryen softly. "You saw how my gladiators handled themselves. It doesn't matter if they have an escape route or not. We only know one way to fight, so you had nothing to worry about in that regard."

"I'm sorry," replied Rafia, acknowledging that error. Bryen was right. She had made a mistake. It wasn't her first and it wouldn't be her last. "I know that now. I don't trust easily, and I allowed that to affect my thinking."

Bryen nodded, accepting her apology, because he was much like her just as he had demonstrated in his confrontation with Sirius. Trust remained an issue for him. "Besides, the Blood Company already knew that there was an escape route. We wouldn't have come to Haven otherwise."

"You told them?"

"Of course I did," replied Bryen. "We're a free company, Magus. We don't keep secrets from one another." With that statement, Bryen's gaze brushed over both Rafia and Sirius, hoping that they understood the point that he was trying to make. "My gladiators fought as they did because that's what they do. They only know one way to fight."

"So everyone knew about the tunnel's functionality but me?" cut in Sirius, still perturbed that he had no idea that the proposed escape route was passable, not yet willing to let the perceived slight go.

"Sirius, I told you that I thought you already knew about the tunnel and that it could still be used. I wasn't trying to keep it from you. As I said, you're the Master of the Magii, so I assumed that you of all people would be aware of this option for leaving Haven."

"Apparently being the Master of the Magii doesn't guarantee that I know everything I need to know," grumbled Sirius, still miffed at not being privy to this essential information.

"I couldn't agree with you more, Sirius."

"You're not helping, Bryen," chastised Aislinn, her expression suggesting that she wasn't amused by his quick wit.

"Sorry, I couldn't resist."

"Can we move on to more pressing issues, please?" requested Rafia, fearing that they were about to slide off onto a tangent that would waste even more time that they didn't have.

"I still don't understand how I didn't know," complained Sirius.

"Sirius, would you just let this go," pleaded Rafia with a touch of pique. "No one was withholding information from you intentionally. I simply had assumed that you were aware that the tunnel was passable, at least the section that I negotiated myself."

"All right," replied Sirius, shaking his head angrily. "But we're going to talk more about this later."

"I can't wait," replied Rafia, her sarcasm plain. "Now even though we can use the tunnel, we will still need a head start. Perhaps instead of being angry because you didn't know about the burrow that you could have found yourself if you had used the Talent, you could think up some ways to prevent the Ghoules from immediately following after us."

"I can probably do that," replied Sirius, his devious mind already turning toward this new task.

"Good, then start thinking," said Rafia. "Because we need to leave Haven before the sun sets and the Ghoule Overlord gets here."

3

UNDER THE GROUND

"How was this constructed? Why was this constructed?"

Declan stared down the dark path, only the first hundred feet that stretched out from the base of the steps illuminated by the small globe of light that sparked just above Rafia's hand. He and the Magus had climbed down a steep, winding staircase at the back of the Library of the Magii that was just beyond the storeroom they had scavenged for supplies.

They were at least a hundred feet down into the earth, although even with the lake around them the passage was dry and musty. So far a good sign. They hadn't gone any farther yet, Declan simply wanting to get a look at the shaft before the Blood Company made its way down later that afternoon to take the next step in their journey.

From what Declan could determine, the tunnel, ten feet in height, twenty feet in width, arced gradually to about fifteen feet at the center of the ceiling. A thin coating of dirt covered the rough stone floor and massive spiderwebs that reached down from the ceiling and in some places blocked the passage extended off into the distance.

When Declan ran his hand across the stone wall, much to

his surprise it was perfectly smooth. He assumed that when the Magii first built the tunnel they had used the Talent, which was why the rock was burnished and scoured clean. An incredible construction. Even so, he could tell after taking just a few steps into the passage that one thousand years of disuse and neglect was beginning to take its toll.

The walls of the tunnel were no longer perfectly flat and even. Bulges were visible, showing where the stone had shifted over time, the walls and ceiling straining and failing to keep back the thousands upon thousands of tons of dirt and rock that pressed against it.

Just a bit farther down where the dim light faded into the gloom he glimpsed a rather large pile of dirt and rock that covered the floor, cutting the passage in half. Looking up, the jagged crack in the ceiling ran for several yards, expanding naturally as time passed.

In some places the walls and the ceiling had failed. Or were failing. And if it was happening here at the beginning of the tunnel, it was happening elsewhere. That suggested the need to be wary of the potential for more cave ins, particularly where it was obvious that the walls and ceiling were buckling, a larger collapse just a matter of time.

"The Talent, of course, for the how," replied Rafia, "although clearly you've already figured that out. The why you've probably already guessed as well. The Ten Magii needed a safe, easy, and hidden way to get to and from the Sanctuary while they built it. Remember, they did the work during the height of the First Ghoule War. There were Ghoule packs hunting in the Shattered Peaks for Magii and Caledonian soldiers, although for obvious reasons the Magii were the bigger prize of the two. So they constructed this tunnel to give them the protection and secrecy that they needed. If the Ghoules had found out what they were doing, the Ten Magii never would have succeeded in creating the Weir."

"The Weir was the why?"

"It was."

"And this path runs all the way to the Trench?"

"It does," confirmed Rafia. "Or at least it did. I have faith that it still does."

"How far down have you braved the tunnel?" asked Declan, concerned by the slight hitch in the Magus' voice. He didn't want to think about what might occur if the Blood Company reached a point farther along the tunnel and deep beneath the Shattered Peaks where a more devastating collapse blocked the passage entirely.

"About a dozen leagues."

"That would take us farther into the mountains," said Declan. "We'd still have a long way to go from there."

"True, but it was as far as I could go at the time."

"More examples of that along the way?" asked Declan, gesturing to the pile of dirt and debris farther down the passageway.

"Yes, unfortunately. Though I didn't come across anything that we can't get past with a little effort."

"So no collapsed walls or ceilings?"

"Not completely collapsed, so nothing to worry about," replied Rafia with a grin that she hoped would instill greater confidence within Declan. The Master of the Gladiators appeared to be unconvinced as to the utility and safety of the only path open to them for escaping Haven and the Ghoule Overlord.

"That makes me feel so much better," Declan replied with a hint of sarcasm. "So we don't know if we'll have a relatively clear path all the way through to the Trench."

"It should be. I can't make any promises, though. I searched all the way to the Trench with the Talent and didn't find any additional hazards that I didn't think we could get by. Still, we won't really know until we try." Rafia shrugged her shoulders, wishing that she could provide more helpful information but not wanting to get Declan's hopes up unnecessarily. "Hope for the best, expect the worse."

"Hoping doesn't make it real," grumbled Declan.

"That it doesn't," agreed Rafia, pleased by his comment. "That's one of Sirius' favorite sayings, although I'm actually the one who came up with it."

"Well, whoever deserves the credit for it, I like it. It's a good way of looking at the world. At what's really in front of us rather than what we want in front of us."

"You know, you're not at all what I expected," Rafia said, her crafty gaze fixed on the Sergeant of the Blood Company.

"Really?" he asked, his thoughts still on the possible obstructions in the tunnel as he turned toward her. "How so?"

Declan regretted asking the question as soon as he voiced it. He should have kept his mouth shut, the sparkle in the Magus' eyes making him uncomfortable.

"I assumed that you were no more than a ruffian at best, a thug, when I learned that you were the Master of the Gladiators for almost ten years and before that you fought in the Pit for another ten, the ten years in the Royal Guard preceding that only reinforcing my estimation of you."

"I'm not sure how I'm supposed to take that," replied Declan, eyebrows raised. "It sounds almost like an insult."

"I don't mean any offense as it's not intended as such," said Rafia. "As you may have noticed, I tend to speak bluntly, and I don't hide what I'm thinking. That tends to ruffle a few feathers."

"I hadn't noticed," Declan replied wryly.

"And there's the sarcasm that I was anticipating," said Rafia. "Bryen blamed his own dry wit on you."

"I do my best."

"That you do," replied Rafia, her grin now matching

Declan's. "Then I learned from Bryen that you're much more than a trained killer."

"I guess I should take that as a compliment," said Declan, his thoughts still on the path they would be taking to leave Haven. There was some other aspect of this tunnel that bothered him, but he couldn't figure out what. "What else did Bryen tell you?" The Magus obviously had done her research on him, perhaps his challenging her on the Breakwater Plateau the cause.

"How you took him under your wing and then did everything that you could to ensure that he received a good education, and that you did the same for several others sentenced to the Colosseum."

"I was only doing what was right," Declan replied, almost as if it was of little matter that he spent so much time looking out for the interests and well-being of the young men and women slated to die in the Pit. "Bryen, Davin, Lycia, a few others, they all came to the Colosseum as children. I wanted them to survive. I also didn't want them to do just that. If the only thing they learned while under my tutelage was how to kill ... well, that was something I just couldn't allow. They needed more than that. I needed more than that."

"I understand," Rafia said, placing her hand gently on his forearm. Declan was stoic, she knew. She hoped that eventually he might reveal more of himself to her than he was willing to do so now. Of course, there was no guarantee that would happen. Life rarely played out as you expected or wanted. A fact that she well knew. "When you've lived as long as I have people tend to be easy to read. You can decipher their intentions, their desires, their goals in an instant. What they want from life and what they're willing to share with others tends to be quite obvious. But I can't do that with you. Every time I learn something new about you, my view of you changes, and I have to start over with my assessment. I find it quite irritating."

"Glad to be of service," said Declan with another hint of sarcasm. "I guess you could say that I'm a riddle wrapped in a mystery inside an enigma."

"Where did you learn that?" asked Rafia, her obvious surprise suggesting to Declan that he had just pushed her perspective of him off kilter once again.

"Just like Bryen, I like to read. If I recall correctly that statement was made by Winson the Elder after his visit with the Giants of the Rime who live just north of the Ice Forest on the Frozen Steppe."

For just a moment, Rafia stared at Declan as if she were seeing him for the first time. Then she gave him a broad smile that sent a bolt of unexpectedly pleasant heat up his spine.

"A soldier. A gladiator. A principled man. A learned man. A good man. The mystery only deepens."

"And also a trained killer as you said."

"I did say that, yes."

"I think you're making more out of me than I truly deserve," objected Declan, his natural modesty and humility revealing itself. "I'm really no different than anyone else."

"You do yourself a grave disservice, Sergeant of the Blood Company," said Rafia, ignoring Declan's protest. "All this leads to the dilemma that I face."

"What would that be?" asked Declan, who didn't really want to ask yet for some strange reason couldn't stop himself.

"I'm not sure what to do about you."

"Why would you need to do anything about me?"

"Because you're a soldier, a gladiator, a teacher, a leader, a friend to those gladiators despite your gruff exterior, a father to Bryen. I could continue adding to the list, but we have only so much time. Putting all those pieces together ... all I can say is that you intrigue me."

"You make me sound much more complicated, interesting, and adept than I actually am."

"Maybe," admitted Rafia. "I doubt it, though. I'm rarely wrong about things such as this."

"You're quite confident, you know that?" challenged Declan. "Perhaps overconfident. Maybe even arrogant."

"Perhaps. I've been accused of worse. With respect to you, Declan, I know that I'm right. So I believe that my confidence is justified."

"Better to call it arrogance," Declan muttered, though Rafia ignored him.

"The problem is that there is something else about you that has captured my attention. I just can't put my finger on it."

"But you feel the need to do that? To put your finger on it?"

Rafia stared at Declan in the dim light, mulling what he had just said. Bryen was so much like Declan in so many ways, his dry sense of humor and sarcastic wit chief among them.

"I do need to put my finger on it," Rafia replied, staring straight into Declan's eyes, challenging him, giving him a wink that made him rethink his attempt to engage with the Magus in this way. "I don't like not knowing what I don't know."

"Another of Sirius' sayings," commented Declan, not sure how to respond to Rafia's latest statement, "or one of yours?"

"One of Sirius'. Despite his many other failings, he does have a way with words."

The spark that flashed behind Rafia's eyes was beginning to make Declan more than just uncomfortable, although not in the way that he expected. So he tried to bring their conversation back to its initial course.

"Perhaps we can get back to discussing the tunnel," suggested Declan. "Anything else I need to know before I start bringing everyone down here?"

Rafia stared at Declan a moment longer, realizing that she wouldn't get any more conversation out of him. At least not the conversation that she wanted. He was done sharing. It was time to get to work.

"As I said, I only explored the tunnel to a certain distance, not having the time to go any farther. I didn't see any signs of a major collapse, just more spots than I cared to count along the way where the walls and ceiling are weakening because of the passage of time and the natural pressures within the earth pushing against the construction. My greatest fear, of course, was that the section beneath the lake would be flooded. Thankfully, we have nothing to worry about in that regard. Even so, that's not to say that there won't be problems the farther along we go. In fact, I'd be surprised if there weren't."

"If the path is blocked and we can't clear it, then the Ghoules will take us easily. We'll have little chance to defend ourselves in the tunnel."

"I can't disagree with you," replied Rafia, acknowledging Declan's concern with a brief nod. "All I can say is that we will be traveling with three other Magii. If we run into any areas where the tunnel has collapsed, I believe that we should be able to manage them without too much difficulty, and perhaps we could even leave a few surprises and obstacles along the way that will slow down the Ghoules."

"I like how you think," commented Declan, his gaze turning malevolent at the thought of Ghoules and Elders becoming trapped in the shaft, unable to dig themselves out.

"You know just what to say to a woman, don't you, Declan," Rafia said with a broad smile, the Magus giving Declan's arm another squeeze, this one stronger than the first. She had yet to release his forearm, a fact that he had noticed and had said nothing about, clearly not minding.

"I'm just speaking the truth, Magus," challenged Declan, hoping his use of her honorific would pull her thoughts away from the road they were traveling.

"And another reason I find you so intriguing," confirmed Rafia, ignoring his attempt to divert her attention. "So few are willing to do so." She squeezed his arm a third time, then patted it gently, before her gaze became serious once more. "Now back to the path that we will be taking. Keep in mind that there are other dangers in the tunnel that we'll need to take into account."

"More dangerous than the Ghoules?" asked Declan.

Rafia took a moment to consider Declan's question, longer, in fact, than Declan would have preferred, which in his mind could only mean that she needed to balance the risk and hazards of the tunnel that they were not aware of against the risk and hazards that they were.

"No, probably not," she said finally, her shrewd mind having completed its work. "Although I really can't say with complete certainty."

"What are some of these other dangers that we'll need to navigate?" asked Declan, his voice calm. It seemed to Rafia that there was little that could rattle the Sergeant of the Blood Company.

"Traps set by the Magii," Rafia replied with a wave of her hand. "Sirius and I should be able to manage those without any difficulty, assuming they're still even functioning. They were set a thousand years ago, and the Talent does degrade over time. I didn't come across any when I scouted the path."

"You're not giving me the full answer, Magus," said Declan, his sharp gaze locked onto Rafia.

"I'm not trying to be coy or hide information. The truth is that I'm just not sure. The last time that I came down here I found the skin of a snake stretched out along the floor."

"What kind of snake?"

"I wasn't sure," replied Rafia. "At least not one that I've ever come across before. The skin must have been at least forty feet long. Maybe fifty. And it was quite wide, suggesting an animal with a very large girth."

"Anything else you can remember?"

"When I looked at it with the Talent, the skin sparkled a bit in the light."

"What color?"

"Red," Rafia replied confidently. Then she amended her answer. "Actually more like blood red."

Declan nodded. He should have known. Nothing was ever straightforward or simple in life, so what was another complication? He had thought that the animal that Rafia described preferred the southern tip of the Northern Spine, but why wouldn't these creatures expand their territory into the Shattered Peaks if they could find plentiful game here?

"What you're describing sounds like a bloodsnake. Probably just a juvenile. I fought one on the white sand when I first was thrown into the Pit."

"That makes sense now that I think on it," said Rafia, her eyes taking on a faraway look as she remembered her discovery. "That makes a great deal of sense, actually. There's no prey in the tunnel, yet a bloodsnake entered, which might support a theory that my mentor had."

"What would that be?"

"That certain creatures, such as a bloodsnake, might be attracted to the Talent or the Curse."

"Why would that be the case?"

"I have no idea. Again, just a theory. There would be no cause for a bloodsnake to be here otherwise. Other than the fact that the animals might have been attracted by the residue of the Talent that runs through the entire length of this passage." Rafia shrugged, as if to say she wished that she could offer Declan greater clarity, but she simply couldn't. "How dangerous is a bloodsnake?"

"It's only dangerous if it attacks," replied Declan. "It might, or it might not. Bloodsnakes usually lie in wait for their prey, and they move based on sound. They try to mimic the movement of whatever they're stalking. You move, they move, until they're close enough to strike. If this bloodsnake is still alive and as large as you say, it could kill a soldier easily. One hundred soldiers are a different matter entirely. They're dangerous animals, so the trick is to recognize that they could be close and keep a keen eye and an even keener ear. Often you'll hear them before you see them."

"That doesn't sound promising, though it's good to know."

"No, but we'll have a good number of soldiers down here. Bloodsnakes, even one the size that we're talking about, might choose to avoid us, thinking we're too big a target. We'll just have to wait and see, and of course be ready."

"I'll spread the word," said Rafia. "I'll make sure that Aislinn, Sirius, and I are checking regularly for the animals, though carefully. No need to prove my mentor's theory correct if we can avoid it. I would hate to attract them by using the Talent."

"That's a start."

"You're still concerned," suggested Rafia.

"I am," replied Declan. "Just think of it as a natural wariness. It's why I've been able to live for as long as I have."

"What do you mean exactly?"

"Well, if one bloodsnake could find its way into this tunnel, what's to say there aren't more? I'd really hate to come up against a nest of these animals. That would not be fun, Magii or no."

"You certainly know how to fill a woman with hope."

"I do my best," replied Declan laconically.

"Not too large a fire," said Kollea as she watched her partner throw more and more pieces of wood onto the growing blaze. "Just big enough so that it stays alight until the wee hours of the morning. We don't want to make it seem like we're burning the place down. That will only get the Ghoules' attention all the faster."

"I'm not burning the place down," grunted Dorlan as he threw a few more pieces of split wood onto the burgeoning flames. "I just want to make sure that the fire lasts for most of the night. The longer the Ghoules see the light, the better."

"Just a few more logs should do the trick then," agreed Kollea, who started passing him several large pieces of driftwood that once they caught ablaze would burn for hours and then smolder for several more. "Then we should be done."

Dorlan accepted without complaint the wood that she handed him and then he picked out the three largest blocks of timber that he had cut from a tree that he judged had fallen the winter before, adding them to the fire as well. When he was given a task, Dorlan liked to be thorough, and he believed that his last additions to the conflagration satisfied that need.

His partner was right. They were done.

He gave Kollea a nod to suggest that he was content with his work before he peered down the shore that faced the beach the Ghoules were using as their staging point. A dozen more fires illuminated the rapidly falling darkness along the coast of the island, and he knew that much the same was happening on the other side as well. The Ghoules watching them from across the lake likely would assume that they were settling in for the night, just as Declan wanted.

The Vedra had reported earlier that evening that more Ghoule packs were coming their way, called by their Master, though the beasts were still hours away. The Magii believed that the Ghoule Overlord would not attack again until those packs arrived. The beast needed to replenish his losses.

Dorlan smiled at that thought. That was thanks to the efficient and vicious work conducted by him and the other gladiators. Many of his friends had died during the last clash, and he believed that all of them would go to the other side with honor.

They had done what was required of them. They had earned their passage. Based on his experience in the Pit, no one could ask for any more than that.

And now it was time for those who had survived the fight to continue on their journey. The illusion that the Blood Company was continuing with its regular evening activity should aid their efforts to escape, hopefully lulling the Ghoules into a sense of complacency, making them believe that the Company was trapped on Haven.

Dorlan almost wanted to be here to see the look of surprise on the beasts' faces when they realized that they had been tricked. Almost. Though not quite.

Better to be long gone before the Ghoules attacked again. They were the deadliest adversaries that he had ever faced, and he had spent several years fighting on the white sand before the Volkun freed him.

"That should do the trick," Kollea said, her approval clear in her voice. "Well done, Dorlan."

"Then it's time to get out of here," rumbled Dorlan. "Let's get going." The gladiator offered a beefy arm to Kollea as they navigated the felled and fallen trees that littered the shore, carefully making their way through the maze and then up the gentle grassy slope to the Library of the Magii, the tower gleaming dimly as the rising full moon struck the translucent stone.

Dorlan and Kollea greeted Sirius, who kept the entrance open with the Talent.

"Are you the last?" asked the Magus. "No stragglers?"

"No stragglers," confirmed Dorlan. "We're the last ones."

Sirius nodded then stepped into the tower after the two gladiators. As Dorlan and Kollea followed the other gladiators tasked with starting the fires through the wide hallway that curved around the periphery of the tower, Sirius remained at the door, taking his time, wanting to make sure that he did everything correctly.

Using the Talent he ensured that the defenses of the Library of the Magii were activated. He then added a few more surprises to the mix to aggravate and hopefully slow down even more the Ghoule Overlord and his Elders when they attempted to break into the tower.

"Everyone here?" asked Rafia when she thought that the last of the gladiators had appeared. She stood at the base of the winding staircase, the Company of Blood stretching off into the distance down the hidden pathway that ran beneath the island to the west.

"Yes, Magus," replied Declan, who had just completed his count now that Dorlan and Kollea had joined them. The Blood Company's Sergeant had no desire to leave anyone behind. "Lead the way."

"Good," nodded Rafia, who began to walk toward the front of the column, smiling and offering a greeting to each gladiator as she passed them. These men and women had not only impressed her because of their bravery and tenacity, but they also had grown on her. Why they had been thrown into the Colosseum didn't matter to her. They had remained standing even when the misfortunes of life tried to knock them down, a necessary quality for the challenge they faced now. She couldn't say the same for many of the people she had come across during her many centuries who had enjoyed the benefits granted to them by power and privilege yet when struck by misfortune failed to stay on their feet. "Then it's time to get moving. Make sure that you don't get too far behind."

"Have no fear about that, Magus," replied Declan in a low grumble that failed to mask his small smile. "I'll be right behind you, step for step, just like a bloodsnake. Probably closer than you would like, in fact."

Rafia stopped and turned back toward Declan with a raised eyebrow, her eyes sparking in the dim light.

"Was that a joke, Declan?"

"It was, Magus," Declan replied, "though admittedly a poor one."

"Don't worry about following too closely, Declan," called Rafia over her shoulder in a mischievous tone as she started walking toward the front of the line, the Magus adding more Talent to the small globe of light that danced across her palm so that the tunnel became as bright as a cloudy day. "The closer the better, in my opinion. Oh, and Declan?"

"Yes, Magus?" replied Declan, realizing that Rafia had called his bluff, a slight tinge of red coloring his cheeks.

"Call me Rafia."

"Of course, Magus," answered Declan, still feeling the need to make a point.

"Are you ready, Aislinn?" asked Rafia as she strode past the Lady of the Southern Marches, intent on her task of leading the Company of Blood through the tunnel of the Ten Magii.

"Yes, Rafia." Aislinn balanced a ball of light above her palm that she released as soon as the Magus walked by so that it floated up to the top of the tunnel's ceiling. The light would move with her, keeping the path lit for a hundred feet in every direction.

Rafia would lead the Company through the tunnel, Aislinn would stay near the middle of the column, while Sirius remained at the back, charged with tracking the Ghoule pursuit and providing whatever defense might be necessary if the beasts got too close, short of collapsing a section of the burrow.

She had been quite adamant with Sirius about that. Rafia feared that any effort to do so might prove to be much like a tsunami. Unstoppable. She didn't want him to bring the rock and dirt down on them as well.

So other measures would be needed, because they all understood that the Ghoules would find them eventually. It was just a question of when. All three of the Magii would keep the path lit with the Talent, Bryen staying near the front with Rafia to help with any unexpected and hidden threats, such as the one she and Declan discussed.

Not too far behind Bryen walked Davin and Lycia, the two gladiators having agreed through the unspoken communication of twins that they would be staying as close to Bryen as they could. Along with being their friend, the Protector was the key to this expedition, so they would do all that they could to protect him.

Davin found the entire concept somewhat amusing. They had tasked themselves with protecting the Protector. Very ironic in his opinion. Besides, knowing Bryen's proclivity for rushing into danger without thinking things through, they understood the assignment that they had given themselves would be difficult at best and potentially impossible. But what was the point of life without a challenge?

"I'd much prefer fighting in the Pit to this," said Davin, Bryen and Rafia no more than a few feet to their front as the long column got underway.

"Not enjoying the experience of walking beneath hundreds of tons of rock and soil that could come crashing down on us at any time?" asked Lycia.

She tried to say the words with a smirk, sensing her brother's unease at traveling within the constricted space. Her attempt to do so failed. She was just as uncomfortable in the passageway as he was. The piles of dirt and stone that they had to walk around or climb over every so often that suggested that the tunnel could cave in with barely any warning only made her more nervous, so she did her best to not look too closely at the gaping holes in the ceiling and along the wall.

"Thanks for pointing that out," said Davin drily, not appreciating his sister's humor. "At least in the Pit I don't have to worry about that, about something over which I have no control."

"Always looking on the bright side, aren't you?" Lycia asked with a touch of sarcasm.

"I'm just telling you how I feel." Davin couldn't tell if his sister was irritated with him because of his fear of being in an enclosed space or because she might be feeling much the same as he was and she was simply doing a better job of hiding her unease and trying to distract herself by needling him. "I just don't like it down here. It's too restricting."

"Even so, it's better to be here than up above. I have no desire to be eaten by a Ghoule."

"A good point," Davin grudgingly admitted, scanning the smooth stone wall as they strode down the tunnel, searching for large cracks in the surface or other evidence that the walls or the ceiling were about to collapse, or perhaps that there were other surprises or dangers waiting for them, "but that doesn't mean I have to like it."

4

BLOOD-RED SKIN

After spending most of the night in the tunnel, the Company of Blood already had traveled more than eight leagues down the path that led away from Haven and the Ghoules. They had faced no major obstructions yet that caused much of a delay, although it was quite clear that the walls of the tunnel were weakening, rocks and rubble cascading down to the floor in a multitude of places.

A handful of times they had to climb over a large blockage. With the last the space between the top of the pile of debris and the ceiling was so tight that Majdi needed to be pulled through the gap. After that Rafia slowed their pace, exercising more caution.

Dorlan learned the need for greater care the hard way shortly thereafter when he grabbed onto a stone that protruded into the tunnel so that he could climb over a pile of dirt that blocked much of the path. The stone came loose and with it a steady stream of gritty earth and rock that resembled the flow of sand through an hourglass. If not for Asaia and Majdi's quick thinking, the gladiator would have been buried alive.

After that episode, only once did the Company find their

way blocked, a large section of the roof having collapsed. The gladiators worked quickly to dig a way through the obstruction, no one having any desire to stand any longer than necessary in a location where the likelihood of another cave in increased exponentially thanks to the damage already caused to the tunnel.

"So far so good," said Rafia. "I was expecting much worse."

"I'm glad you're being so positive. That last obstacle was quite a challenge."

"Just being realistic. Your friend Declan is rubbing off on me."

"Let's hope it stays that way," agreed Bryen, focusing on her original comment and not the unintended image she had placed in his mind with the second. "The farther we can get before the chase begins again, the better."

They all understood that the Ghoule Overlord would attack Haven as soon as his reinforcements arrived, probably before the sun rose. It wouldn't take the Master of the Curse long to gain control of the island without any defenders to slow him down. The traps constructed of the Talent would delay him for only so long, and eventually he would discover the tunnel.

But he wouldn't find breaking into the Library of the Magii an easy task. In the time the beast spent to do that, Rafia hoped that they could make it all the way to the Trench. It was that objective that pushed Bryen and the Blood Company to move as fast as they could and put as much distance between themselves and the Ghoules as possible.

"I'm surprised at how dry the tunnel is," said Bryen. "I would have assumed that with the passage of time we'd see at least some evidence of water. Based on how far we've come, we've passed beneath at least two other lakes besides the one encircling Haven."

"Yes, that's definitely a good sign," agreed Rafia. "I was worried about that as well. It's a testament to the skill of the Ten

Magii that their work remains in such good condition after the passage of a thousand years."

"What else do we have to look forward to from the Ten Magii?" asked Bryen. "You mentioned that they left some traps and other protections along the way, but you were never very specific about what those might be."

"Yes, I'm rather curious about that myself," said Tarin, who had moved to the front of the column and had walked with Bryen and Rafia for the last hour.

"Nothing that we really need to worry about with respect to that," replied Rafia, her eyes always to the front. They were coming upon the section of the tunnel that had concerned her the most the last time she was down here. Not because of structural issues. Rather, her worries centered on the blood-red skin she had come upon. "There's not too much written about the tunnel. From what I was able to piece together during the last few years, only creatures touched by the Curse have anything to fear from the snares and other defenses the Ten Magii set in the tunnel when they were using it to get to the Sanctuary. Keeping in mind, of course, that those snares may no longer be functioning because of the degradation of the Talent over time."

"So we have nothing to fear even if these traps are still in place?" asked Tarin.

"Correct, we shouldn't have anything to fear," Rafia replied, although some of her customary confidence was lacking in her voice. "What the Ten Magii put in place should remain dormant as we pass through, recognizing the Talent that Bryen, Sirius, Aislinn, and I have at our disposal. Most likely just ignoring us. As I may have mentioned, a few years ago I traveled about ten leagues down the path we are on without coming across anything to be concerned about, at least in that respect."

"You said *shouldn't*, not *won't*."

"I can't offer any guarantees, Captain," said Rafia with a grin.

"Yes, such is the way of life," agreed Tarin with a smile of his own.

"And the fact that the Seventh Stone and what it contains has joined with me will not set off these traps," prodded Bryen, referencing the fact that the artifact within him contained a large quantity of the Curse.

"That's why I said *shouldn't*," confirmed Rafia. "I'm hoping your use of the Talent will negate that concern."

"Wonderful," murmured Bryen. To distract himself from that worry, he shifted his focus to another topic that he had been thinking about.

"Any ideas about what some of the protections the Ten Magii prepared could be?" He was always interested in learning something new, particularly if he could put it to use to the detriment of the Ghoule Overlord and his beasts. "I'd love to know what's waiting for the Ghoules once they enter the tunnel."

"As would I," confirmed Tarin.

"From what I could gather based on my research, there appear to be several of the same traps that you and Aislinn set on Haven to slow down the Ghoules. I also read about one in which darts of light shoot out from the sides of the tunnel to puncture the flesh, and then after a delay, I'm assuming so that the trap caught the beasts again when they believed that the initial onslaught was over, the same thing would happen from floor to ceiling."

"That sounds quite final," said Tarin. "Almost dastardly."

"Yes, it was," agreed Rafia, "and I believe you have your fore-bear Viktor Keldragan to thank for that one, Bryen."

"I knew there was a reason I felt a kinship toward him," Bryen replied with a grin. "I like how he thinks."

"That and the fact that he poked the Ghoule Overlord in

the eye by stealing the Seventh Stone and the black diamond from right under his nose."

"That as well. You'll need to tell me more about that when there's time."

Rafia nodded that she would. "Mikayla Benewyn, Master of the Magii at the time and a woman of great interest to your uncle, also wrote of a lure that she set somewhere within the tunnel in which tiny spikes of the Talent emerged from the floor that were just long enough and sharp enough to puncture the clawed feet of the Ghoules. To the beasts, it would feel as if they stepped on a sharp stone, no more than that, so they would continue walking down the path not realizing what had happened. That one touch was all that was needed to release a bolt of energy that would slowly set the Ghoule afire from the inside out without the beast even realizing it. Apparently, it would take several minutes before the energy began its work so that a great many of the beasts would be caught in the snare."

"Ingenious and gruesome," said Tarin, "and I admire her thoroughness."

"As you should," continued Rafia, "yet there was one that I read about that seemed to be particularly nasty and a uniquely horrible way to die that was worse than Mikayla's."

"What was it?" asked Bryen, his eyes sparking with interest.

"Why are young men so excited by things such as the most grisly ways to kill?" Rafia asked almost to herself.

"Because they don't know any better yet, though I must admit that our young friend here has demonstrated a unique ability to make the world a better place by removing any Ghoules and Elders who cross his path. So I would assume that in addition to being young and somewhat immature about such matters, he has an immediate need for such knowledge so that he can put it to use himself."

Bryen was about to protest Tarin's description of him as callow. Instead, he held his tongue. Tarin spoke with a smile that suggested that he was simply teasing him and trying to get under his skin, a skill that the Captain of the Battersea Guard had perfected while Bryen resided against his will in the Southern Marches. So he didn't want to give Tarin the satisfaction of knowing his barb had hit home. Besides, he really couldn't disagree with his friend's explanation. It was quite accurate.

"Perhaps so, Captain," replied Rafia with a grin of her own. "From what I could decipher, because it was not a complete text that I reviewed, rather just a few pages with handwritten notes that had been torn from a personal journal and were difficult to read because much of the writing had begun to fade, one of the Ten Magii had discovered a way to use the Talent to make rock amorphous at the touch of the Curse. If a Ghoule got too close, the Talent sensed the Dark Magic in the beast and then activated, tendrils of energy reaching out from the stone to pull the beast into the rock."

"Almost as if you were walking through the invisible barrier in the Aeyrie," offered Bryen, remembering how he had located the Seventh Stone when he was a child.

"Just so," agreed Rafia. "Although in this case, the Ghoule would never make it through because after getting dragged in a few feet, the Talent released the beast and the rock solidified. I imagine that for the Ghoule, it would be much like drowning, only in stone rather than water. A truly ghastly way to go, though I admit to feeling little sympathy for any Ghoule that might be caught in such a trap."

"I agree, that sounds like a particularly awful way to die," commented Tarin.

"Yes, though quite effective," said Bryen, who appreciated the ingenuity of whichever Magus had come up with that particular tool, his mind already working through how he could construct each of the three traps that Rafia had described for them.

"I can't dispute that," agreed Rafia. "Nevertheless, as I said, it's nothing for us to fear, only the Ghoules. You can put your worry to rest, Captain."

"As you command, Magus Rafia," Tarin replied with a sharp nod.

"I wouldn't put your worry to rest just yet, Tarin," said Bryen, who had walked slightly ahead of the other two and come to a stop at what from the side appeared to be a fissure in the wall just like the many others they had passed upon making their way through the tunnel.

Yet this cleft was different from the others, and that's why it had caught Bryen's eye. Closer inspection revealed a large hole in the center of the breach that was at least ten feet wide. The sides, which would have been rough if the crater had occurred naturally, instead were almost perfectly round and polished smooth.

With Rafia maintaining control over the sphere that lit the way for the front of the long column of soldiers, Bryen reached for the Talent, creating his own ball of light that he directed into the opening, wanting to get a better look at what appeared to be a separate tunnel that connected to theirs that had been dug through the earth by what Bryen could only assume was an animal that he had no desire to meet again. The sphere moved into the shaft for several dozen feet before it reached a bend in the burrow that curved upward.

"Is that what I think it is?" asked Tarin.

Bryen motioned with his hand, the ball of light drifting back down the shaft to hover just a few feet in front of them, illuminating the opening with a bright glare. He stepped up to the hole and reached in, pulling free from a rough stone knocked loose near the beginnings of the tunnel a long piece of dry skin that sparked blood red in the light.

"Do you know why bloodsnakes are called bloodsnakes?" asked Bryen.

"No," said Rafia, who stared at the skin with a great deal of interest, "though I'm hoping that you'll tell us."

"Declan explained it to me before I had to fight one in the Pit. Supposedly, the bloodsnake gets its color from the blood of its victims. The darker the snake, the more kills it's made. I don't know if that's true. It's likely just a story. Still, it does catch your attention, doesn't it?"

"It certainly does," agreed Tarin.

"I can tell you one thing that's true," continued Bryen.

"Somehow more than one bloodsnake has entered the tunnel," said Rafia.

"Yes," said Bryen. "Definitely more than one bloodsnake. I think Declan's concerns about a nest are legitimate."

"That's just wonderful to hear," said Rafia, her sarcasm plain.

"Here's some more good news. Unlike the specimen that you found when you were scouting the tunnel, this skin is fresh, no more than a day old if I'm right."

"I hope you're not right, Protector," murmured Tarin.

"Me too," said Bryen, "but hoping ..."

"Hoping doesn't make it real," finished the Magus. "Whether you're right or wrong, Bryen, we need to assume that you're right. And we need to be ready."

Bryen nodded. They couldn't ignore the potential threat of more than one bloodsnake hunting along the path that was their only chance of escaping the Ghoules.

"Tarin, could you please spread the word down the line?" asked Bryen. "Eyes to the front, eyes to the back. More important, eyes to the side and above. We don't want to be taken by surprise by one of these monsters."

~

THE GHOULE OVERLORD couldn't get the Protector out of his thoughts. As he looked across the water at the dim smudge of the island, it was as if the figure of the boy stood before him, that arrogant grin of his infuriating him.

Having destroyed the first span of Dark Magic that connected the beach to the island, the Protector probably thought that he was more than a match for him. The human probably savored that moment when he destroyed his creation, enjoying the rush as the Dark Magic flooded into him, filled him with a sense of his own power. Teased him with the knowledge of what he could attain if he allowed the Curse to become one with him, of how he could become a rival, a real threat, if he learned to master the Curse.

But the human was wrong, mused the Ghoule Overlord as he stared at the spirit standing in front of him, the spirit that didn't fade until he forced the image of the Protector from his mind.

So very wrong.

The Protector would never be a match for him no matter how much of the Curse he made his own. He would never be able to challenge him, even with the Seventh Stone at his beck and call.

The Ghoule Overlord was the source of all Dark Magic in the Lost Land. He was the Master of the Curse. Him. No one else.

Not the Protector. Never the Protector.

The Protector would never be anything more than a slave to the Curse. The human, if he was foolish enough to try to conquer the Curse, would learn that at the worst possible moment.

The practitioner gifted with the Curse obeyed the Curse. That meant that the practitioner of the Curse obeyed him. Obeyed the Ghoule Overlord. Because he was the Curse and the Curse was him.

With his anger intensifying as he thought incessantly about what the Protector had done, an achievement that should have been impossible, the black mist of the Curse began to surge out of the black diamond set in the top of his twisted black staff like a tidal wave, blasting across the water that separated the rocky beach from the island. Just as it did before, the black ice made of Dark Magic took shape, solidifying as it streaked across the waves.

It only took the Ghoule Overlord a few minutes to complete the task, calling forth more and more of the Curse until a span that was three times wider than the first one stretched out across the lake and connected to the Magii's bastion. But he wasn't done, broadening the reach of the black ice so that it encircled the island.

Now his Ghoules could attack the humans from any direction they chose. The humans could not herd his Ghoules and Elders as they had done during the last, failed attack.

Satisfied with his work, the Ghoule Overlord released his hold on the Curse. His black eyes flashed dangerously, catching the last rays of light as the moon descended below the mountains to the west. The dozen packs that he had been waiting for had arrived just minutes before.

His Ghoules were hungry from the long trip. They were eager. And there was no reason to delay even though the sun would not rise for a few more hours.

He needed the Seventh Stone to destroy the Weir, to conquer Caledonia, and this time he would take it. He would claim what belonged to him.

"Gurzen," said the Ghoule Overlord, his maw twisting into an angry scowl, his eyes blazing with rage, never leaving the island that rose out of the water less than a mile away.

"Yes, Master."

"You will not fail me, will you, Gurzen? Too much depends on what we do now."

"No, Master. I will not fail you. We will take the island, and we will slaughter the humans."

"That's good to hear, Gurzen," rumbled the Ghoule Overlord. "Because you have failed twice already. To fail a third time ..."

Gurzen swallowed, fully understanding the precipice that he was now balanced upon and what would happen if he and his packs failed to claim the island quickly and then butcher the humans.

"You have nothing to fear, Master. We will do as you command. You will have the artifact as you require."

"Good," the Ghoule Overlord said, nodding. "I have faith in you, Gurzen. I know that you will do as I command. Now get to it. I want the humans dead within the hour, and I want you to bring the Seventh Stone to me. Alive. I have a special fate in store for the Protector."

"Yes, Master." Gurzen nodded, the Ghoule scout trotting down to the edge of the black ice where the dozen Ghoule packs had gathered, ready to begin the next assault.

With a sharp bark, Gurzen sprinted off across the span of Dark Magic, clawed feet digging into the glassy surface, the Ghoule packs following. The Elders were right behind the beasts, already touching the Curse, ready to meet the perils they expected the Magii to throw at them.

The Ghoule Overlord ran with them as well. There was no need for him to join this fight, yet still he did. Too much had gone wrong during the first two attacks.

The Ghoule Overlord would make sure that didn't happen again. He would make sure that his Ghoules did as he commanded.

The Ghoules raced silently across the span, not howling as was their habit, not feeling the need to announce their arrival. No, in that moment the Ghoules were fixed solely on their purpose.

To kill.

The only sound that could be heard came from the rapid strikes of their clawed feet into the black ice, little chips of the surface kicked up into the air as the beasts approached the island's coast.

The Ghoule Overlord kept pace with his Ghoules. He expected as fierce a resistance from the humans as they had given him before. He assumed that the Magii accompanying the humans would try to eliminate his Elders or the Protector would attempt to do as he had done previously, using the Seventh Stone to kill his Elders and then destroy the larger span that he had created.

That's why the Ghoule Overlord was there. To stop that from happening. Yet all was disconcertingly quiet except for the click of his Ghoules' claws on the black ice as they crossed the bridge.

When his Ghoules were only a few hundred yards from the island, that silence was shattered when the Magii's defenses came into play.

Stripes of energy blazed through the sky, arcing down from the top of the gleaming turret and ripping through a handful of Ghoules who couldn't get out of the way fast enough. The utility of that attack didn't last long. The Elders formed shields of Dark Magic that they placed in front of and above the Ghoules to protect against those blazing javelins that streaked down toward them for several seconds more.

Next walls of white-hot flames sprouted randomly across the shiny surface. A few of those blasts of energy unfortunately took place within the radius of the Elders' shields. When that occurred, there were devastating consequences for the handful of Ghoules caught within the enclosure. The Dark Magic contained the blasts of fire and heat, protecting the beasts beyond the barrier. It also intensified the energy in that very tight space, the Ghoules trapped within burned to a crisp by the contained inferno.

Despite their mounting losses, the Ghoules continued their assault, ignoring the Magii's many attempts to hold them back. Through it all, Gurzen urged his fighters to advance, the beasts leaping from the black ice onto the rocky coast of the island and racing up toward the tower from every point on the compass.

Shrieks of pain and suffering echoed across the island, always accompanied by flashes of light. Some of the more aggressive Ghoules ignored the Elders' repeated warnings, charging forward before the servants of the Ghoule Overlord could clear the way for them. These Ghoules paid the ultimate price for their lack of caution, becoming victims to the many traps the Magii had set for them.

In some places, surges of energy shot up from the ground whenever a creature tainted by the Curse came near. In other locations, paper thin webs constructed of the Talent that couldn't be seen unless touched by the light in a certain way sliced through Ghoule flesh, many of the beasts losing arms and legs before they realized they had even been wounded.

Several more Ghoules stepped where they shouldn't, a blast of white light functioning much like an animal trap and cutting off a clawed foot. Although these beasts didn't lose their lives from the first strike, their injury removed them from the battle-field as combatants, those beasts unlucky enough to lose both clawed feet forced to pull themselves through a rocky patch of ground that in actuality was a minefield constructed of the Talent. They never lasted long.

During the first few minutes of the attack, the Ghoule Overlord left clearing the island of its many snares to his Elders. It was a task that they should have had little difficulty accomplishing.

Yet as the flashes of light and screeches of torment and anguish increased, his patience, never good to begin with, vanished. He had already lost too many Ghoules in his pursuit of the Seventh Stone, and he couldn't afford to lose many more. He and his Ghoules still needed to kill almost one hundred humans as well as several Magii in order to reclaim the Seventh Stone.

So having little choice, the Ghoule Overlord drew on the Curse, a thick mist pouring out from the black diamond and sweeping across the island in billowing waves, only the Library of the Magii resistant to the effects of his Dark Magic.

Dozens of flashes of light occurred in only a few seconds as the Magii's traps reacted to the Curse. This time they were not accompanied by the screams of his Ghoules, the Ghoule Overlord using the Curse to set off all the remaining snares the Magii had left for them.

The Ghoule Overlord allowed his Dark Magic to continue its work for a few more minutes just to make sure that the way was clear. When he was certain of his success, he pulled the Curse back into his staff, the island now free of the Magii's infuriating traps.

His Elders would eliminate the Magii while his Ghoules killed the humans.

He would take the Protector.

Finally he would regain the Seventh Stone and demonstrate to the Protector what true power really was.

5

COMING OUT OF THE DARKNESS

The Blood Company continued to make good progress, none of the obstacles that appeared in this segment of the tunnel impeding them for very long. They remained wary, however, weapons at the ready, eyes peeled for any hint of movement to their sides or above them whenever they came across one of the many large faults marring the path.

Many of the gladiators remembered the Volkun's difficult combat against the bloodsnake, the struggle inciting the Colosseum crowd that day to a new level of barbarity. They had no desire to experience a similar fight themselves in this confined space.

The primary adjustment that Declan made after Bryen discovered the skin of the bloodsnake was to require the gladiators to walk with greater space between them. It made sense to all of them. If they were caught within falling rock and debris or attacked by a bloodsnake, greater separation would limit the threat presented to just a few rather than to all.

That shift in approach proved to be particularly prescient just a few hours later when Jenus, who was walking in the middle of the column, felt what he thought was a small stone beneath his boot slide into a small hole in the floor, a loud click echoing through the tunnel. Hearing that noise, which seemed out of place in the passageway because they had been walking in silence for so long, everyone behind Jenus stopped for a moment, looking all around them, their concern evident in their expressions.

Frozen in place, Jenus looked back over his shoulder and shared a glance with Jerad, knowing in his gut that something bad was about to happen.

As a few more seconds passed, the fear that flashed behind his eyes dulled. Maybe he was mistaken, Jenus thought. Maybe he had nothing to worry about. Maybe it was just a loose stone.

As a few more seconds passed and nothing happened, both Jenus and Jerad began to breathe a little bit easier, Jenus actually offering the Sergeant of the Battersea Guard a small smile. A false alarm, it seemed.

Then in a flash, Jenus was gone, Jerad watching in horror as the gladiator disappeared through the floor.

The gladiators who had been walking in front of Jenus had continued to advance swiftly down the tunnel at Rafia's urging upon hearing the click. She didn't have any idea what could have caused the noise, but she thought the farther away they all were from the unlucky Jenus the better their chances of not getting caught up in whatever was going to happen next.

That's what saved more than a dozen of the Blood Company when the floor beneath the gladiator crumbled away for more than fifty feet to his front, a dark, burgeoning maw opening to consume the veteran of the white sand. The soldiers closest to Jenus scrambled to safety, reaching solid ground just beyond the edge of the new crevice, which spanned the entire width of the corridor.

"You could stand to miss a few meals, Jenus," grunted Jared. "You're heavier than you need to be."

The Sergeant of the Battersea Guard had splayed himself

across the rim of the crevice, his hand grasping tightly to the back of Jenus' leather armor. His other hand searched for purchase on anything that might keep him from sliding into the darkness with the man he was trying to save.

Much to his annoyance and then growing fear, Jerad realized that there was nothing useful within reach. While his chest slowly but inexorably slid toward and then over the lip, Jenus' weight dragging him deeper into the crevice, Jerad kicked out with his feet, trying to find something to dig his boots into to avoid both of them falling into the abyss.

Because there was no way that he was going to let go. If Jenus was going to fall, so was he.

"It's all muscle, Sergeant," grumbled Jenus, irritated by the comment even though he was hanging in the air, his death all but certain although thankfully delayed by the man holding onto one of his shoulder straps. "And it was all that muscle that helped to keep me alive in the Pit."

Jerad was right, Jenus had to admit, although only to himself. He had gotten a bit heavier than he had been in the Colosseum. After being freed from the Pit, he hadn't missed many meals, one of his many new freedoms that he had come to enjoy. Ironically, now he was about to pay with his life for that indulgence.

The gladiator felt himself slowly dropping deeper into the darkness. Although the Sergeant had a good hold of him, Jenus knew that Jerad had no way to stop himself from sliding into the hole with him.

"Let me go, Sergeant. I don't want you to die just because I stepped in the wrong place."

"We're not going to die, Jenus," replied Jerad, the strain of holding onto the gladiator forcing his voice out in a whisper.

"Jerad, let me go," Jenus said with greater urgency, his voice pleading. "You've done what you can. No one could ask any more of you. And I have a feeling that if you die because of me, that Corporal of yours will come find me in the afterlife and make my existence even more miserable than I expect that it will likely already be."

While Jenus didn't want to die, he wasn't afraid to die. After all, he had fought in the Pit for several years. But, he really didn't want to be the cause of someone else's needless death.

Jerad grunted in response, amused by Jenus' comment, finding the breath to respond. "You're probably right about that. Dani isn't one to forgive easily."

Jenus felt himself dropping slowly even farther down into the darkness, Jerad's chest now almost completely over the yawning crevasse in the floor. He understood that the end was near. It wouldn't be long before the Sergeant tipped over the edge.

"Jerad, let me ..."

Jenus never had the chance to finish what he was going to say as he was pulled out of the chasm, his head, shoulders, and then legs coming back over the crest, several of the gladiators behind Jerad rushing to his aid and dragging them both back across the floor.

"You should have let me go," said Jenus, who took a deep, shuddering breath, glad that he was still alive. After laying on the floor for a few seconds to get his bearings, he pushed himself up and offered his hand to Jerad, helping the Sergeant back to his feet.

"You should start skipping dessert," countered Jerad.

Rather than getting angry, Jenus broke out into a laugh, then clapped Jerad on the back. "As you command, Sergeant."

With Jenus and Jerad now out of danger, Rafia and Bryen stepped to the edge of the jagged cut in the floor that extended now for more than seventy feet, the stone floor on the other side that the gladiators in front of Jenus had reached just in time crumbling further, forcing the men and women to scramble farther away for safety.

Both were thinking of several choice curses that they could offer as they sought a solution to their dilemma. They were stuck in place, the distance too great for anyone to jump. It was the worst possible thing that could have happened to the Company.

Time was passing faster than any of them would have liked. If they didn't solve this problem quickly, they would be sitting ducks for the Ghoules once the beasts caught up to them in the tunnel.

"This is one of the other dangers that I forgot to mention," said Rafia. "Jenus stepped where he shouldn't have."

"How was he supposed to know?" challenged Bryen.

"He wasn't," Rafia replied calmly. "Most of the traps such as this are too well hidden. Even I can't find them without setting them off. I would expect nothing less of the Ten Magii."

"Why didn't you warn us of this hazard?"

"I didn't think that after all this time the trap could still work. We should consider ourselves lucky."

"Lucky. How so? Jenus almost died, and Jerad too."

"Yes, but that trap was designed to eliminate more than one person. Declan's decision to spread out the column saved many lives. That and the fact that the mechanism the Magii used to construct it must have locked up over time, slowing its application when Jenus unknowingly pushed down on the lever. If not for those two factors, a good many more gladiators would have died."

"Then all credit to Declan," agreed Bryen.

"Indeed," said Rafia. "Nevertheless, we still have a challenge before us."

"How to get across."

"Anything come to mind?"

"Can we use the Talent to create a bridge like the Ghoule Overlord did to attack Haven? That would be the easiest and fastest approach."

"We could …" began Rafia, hesitating.

"I sense a but."

"But doing that might draw the attention of the blood-snakes. Although we don't know if there's a connection between the two, if any of those animals are close, better to get across without the Talent if we can. Just to be safe. No reason to make our passage through the tunnel any more perilous than it already is."

"I have an idea, Magus Rafia," said Jerad, who had come to stand next to them, his arms still burning from the effort he expended to keep Jenus from slipping into the crevice.

The Sergeant looked down into the darkness into which he and Jenus had almost fallen. The thought of losing himself in a hole that might never end made him feel sick to his stomach and a bit unsteady on his feet, so he quickly turned his thoughts back to the challenge in front of him.

"What did you have in mind, Jerad?" asked Bryen.

"When I was rooting through the storeroom in the tower, I took some supplies that might be useful in a situation such as this, not really knowing if they would come in handy during our journey. The implements are very similar to what I used when I was younger and I climbed in the Northern Spine with my father."

The Sergeant of the Battersea Guard took a few minutes to explain what he had in mind, Rafia and Bryen listening intently. It was a sound plan. Besides, it was their only option for getting across the chasm if they wanted to avoid using the Talent, and time was not slowing down for them.

"Let's get to it, then," said Bryen after sharing a look with Rafia, who nodded her support. "What do you need?"

"Just a little bit of help. Give me an hour and we should be back on our way."

With that, Jerad turned back toward the column, calling for Dorlan and his squad to come forward while he started digging out the supplies that he needed from the large rucksacks that several of the gladiators were carrying, thankfully all of them on this side of the crevice. Dorlan and the others quickly went to work under Jerad's careful instruction.

After tying ropes around their waists, those ropes held by the gladiators behind them, Jerad took the lead, Dorlan right behind him. The two began working their way out over the crevice, building the framework of a rope bridge along the wall that would allow them to pass above the chasm.

Using heavy mallets, Jerad and Dorlan hammered spikes with large eyeholes into the stone. It was slow work. It had to be. Caution was necessary. They had to avoid any cracks or crevices in the rock that might give way when any weight was put on them.

Because of that, Dorlan often served as the test for the placement of a particular spike in the stone, since only Jenus and Majdi were bigger than he was. Following behind him came Kollea and the other gladiators in Dorlan's squad, running a thick rope through the eyelets in the stakes.

Despite the careful and meticulous nature of their work, Jerad and the gladiators completed their construction in less than an hour, the squad crafting a bridge along the wall, the spikes placed at chest height and then along the base of the hole so that the other soldiers of the Blood Company could climb across using the rope so long as they were careful as to where they placed their hands and feet.

"Very impressive, Jerad," said Rafia when she and Bryen inspected his work. "Clearly you are much more than just a nice smile and a pretty face."

"That's kind of you to say, Magus," replied Jerad, doing his best to ignore the snickering going on behind him among the gladiators. He then motioned toward the bridge. "No more than two at a time and make sure there's a space between you as you go. If one falls, we don't want the other one to go as well."

Rafia was the first to cross, Bryen following her once she was almost to the far side of the gap. Bryen had to give Jerad credit. Quick thinking on his part would help them stay in front of the Ghoules, because he was certain that it wouldn't take long for the Ghoule Overlord to find a way to come after them, not with Bryen serving as a beacon for the Master of the Curse thanks to the Dark Magic of the Seventh Stone.

He still wished that there was some way that he could go off on his own and lead the Ghoules away from the Company. Unfortunately, it was a wish only. He knew that was not possible -- he had to go to the Sanctuary, he had no choice -- and that it was also a bad and selfish decision.

The gladiators who had chosen to risk their lives for him would take a decision like that as an insult, to say nothing of how Aislinn would react. So he pushed that idea, which came to him all too frequently, out of his mind.

Preoccupied by his thoughts, Bryen was about halfway across the chasm when a prickling along the back of his neck made him stop. It was a sensation that he never ignored, the feeling having proved its utility time and time again in the past.

His first instinct was to reach for the Spear of the Magii strapped to his back, but he needed both hands on the rope so that he could maintain his balance.

"Bryen, what's the matter?"

Aislinn stood at the edge of the chasm, Declan and Tarin right next to her, the soldiers waiting to cross lined up behind them.

Bryen gave Aislinn a look, then lifted the fingers of one hand from the rope and motioned for her to stay quiet. Aislinn nodded her understanding. Then he looked down into the crevice. He saw nothing but darkness, his eyes unable to penetrate the pitch black.

Although he couldn't penetrate the murk beneath him, the silence that had fallen within the tunnel from the lack of boots scuffing against the stone floor did allow him to hear what he might not have heard otherwise. Not too far below his feet, maybe a dozen yards, no more, Bryen caught a very faint whisper, like a gentle wind playing through the long grass.

Normally he would assume that a sound like that was no more than the air moving through the tunnel. He didn't now.

There was no wind in the tunnel. The musty and stale air meant that the sound that he was hearing could only be one thing. A sound that he hadn't heard in quite some time. A sound that he recalled from the Pit.

Bryen looked back across to the side of the chasm where Declan stood, giving him a hard look and a nod toward the darkness below him. Declan understood immediately.

With a quick hand signal, three gladiators stepped forward to stand in front of Declan. The soldiers knelt, pulling arrows from the quivers on their hips and affixing them to their bowstrings. The three then drew back their longbows, giving Bryen a nod to let him know that they were ready. He nodded in return, then looked back down into the gloom, once again trying and failing to pierce the pitch black.

The sound that he had heard had stopped. All was still in the tunnel.

That could mean only one thing, and it didn't bode well for him. Reaching for the Talent, understanding that it wouldn't matter now, Bryen remained firmly in place on the rope bridge as he extended his senses down into the dark of the chasm.

He had barely started his search when without even thinking about what he was doing, Bryen pushed off a metal spike with his left foot and released his hold on the rope, flinging himself as far to his right along the horizontal ladder as he could.

His timing was impeccable. At that exact same moment a massive, blood-red shape, mouth agape to reveal two sword-length fangs that glittered in the light provided by Rafia's glowing sphere, shot through the space in which he had been hanging.

He only caught the sudden movement to his side out of the corner of his eye, his focus on the rope farther along the wall. He needed to grab the cable, otherwise he was going to find out just how deep the chasm really was.

As he reached for the only thing that could save him from a gruesome death, he realized that in this instance his timing was a little bit off. Perhaps even fatally so.

His left hand missed the top rope by the width of a hair, the tips of his fingers scraping across the bottom of the thick cable and then sliding across the stone, scrabbling futilely for something, anything, to grab hold of.

Just before he fell into the dark fissure, his right hand found the grip that he sought so desperately, grasping onto the lower rope just in time. The jolt of coming to such an abrupt stop shot a bolt of pain through his shoulder.

He ignored it, happy to still be alive. At least for a few seconds longer. Probably no more than that, he thought.

When he shifted his gaze back to his left, Bryen needed to take a deep breath to settle his nerves, attempting to push down his rising fear. As he hung from the rope by one hand, only a few feet away and towering above him was a bloodsnake larger than he ever thought possible.

Based on its massive girth, barely any of its body was thrusting up out of the crevice. The animal had to be at least one hundred feet long, and when the bloodsnake opened its massive gullet and hissed, its long forked tongue flickering out, the animal displayed its fangs, beads of poison dripping from the sharp points.

Bryen realized that without a doubt if the bloodsnake didn't snatch him with its fangs, it could still swallow him whole if given the chance.

That was a fate that he wanted to avoid at all costs.

The massive bloodsnake reared up even higher, its head scraping against the top of the tunnel and placing Bryen in flickering shadow as he hung precariously from the rope. When he stared into the animal's glittering eyes, those rubylike orbs almost mesmerizing, Bryen realized that the bloodsnake was about to strike. Worse, he had nowhere to go.

He watched as the bloodsnake's long body curled around itself so that its triangular head could shoot forward. Right before the animal lunged toward him, the bloodsnake swung around and hissed in anger, finding three long arrows sticking out of its flesh, the steel-tipped shafts having punched through the narrow spaces between its scales.

The bloodsnake tried to rise up even higher, but it couldn't, the ceiling preventing it. So as more of its massive body emerged from the chasm, its long, muscled length curled around itself in the tight space of the tunnel.

The wounds inflicted upon it were just an irritation to the massive creature, doing nothing more than fueling the beast's rage. With an incredible agility, the bloodsnake lunged at the archers, the gladiators scrambling back to safety as fast as they could, shield bearers stepping forward to block the blood-snake's path, Majdi, Jenus, Dorlan, and the others all getting knocked backward off their feet because of the force of the blow.

Declan and Aislinn, who had nowhere to go, the snake's whiplike attack too fast for them to escape, dodged out of the way, pressing themselves against the walls of the tunnel and watching the blood-red scales slide past them with just inches to spare.

That was all the diversion that Bryen needed. Reaching up with his left hand, he grasped the lower spike set in the wall that was closest to him. In a more stable position now, he placed his boots up against the stone of the tunnel so that he was perched there, ready to leap.

He was about to launch himself upward and try to snag the top rope when he sensed the rush of air coming up from beneath him. Without thinking, simply heeding the insistent urge to get out of the way, Bryen pushed himself off the wall just as a second bloodsnake bigger than the first shot right past where he had been clinging to the rope, its sharp fangs closing on air rather than his flesh.

The massive snake came through the space so rapidly that it slammed its head against the top of the tunnel. It didn't affect the snake in the least, though it did open a crack that spider-webbed across the ceiling, knocking several large stones free that fell into the abyss, one missing Bryen by just a foot.

As Bryen hung in the air for a split second, he deftly pulled the Spear of the Magii from his back and pushed in on the small indentation in the haft, the weapon separating into two swords, the Talent already infusing the steel. Before he began his fall into the darkness, Bryen drove one of the blades in between the scales of the second bloodsnake, gripping the hilt tightly so that he didn't drop backward into the crevice.

The bloodsnake shrieked in rage. The agony of the steel cutting into its body caused the beast to lash about wildly as it sought desperately to dislodge the cause of its pain.

Bryen held on to the grip of his sword for dear life, the bloodsnake whipping from side to side, the animal crashing against the walls and the ceiling, causing even more stones to fall free and expanding the web of cracks that extended along the ceiling. Bryen understood that he had to do something quickly before the enraged animal caused the tunnel to collapse, yet not one good idea came to mind. There was little that he could do other than try to hold on as the snake slammed him against the wall several times, attempting to dislodge him, Bryen refusing to let go of the sword's hilt despite the battering he took.

He needed a better hold, otherwise it was only a matter of

time before he fell to his death. Yet the bloodsnake's wild movements made that all but impossible.

"Behind you, lad!" shouted Declan, his friend's stentorian voice echoing in the passageway.

Catching a flash of movement at his back thanks to Declan's warning, Bryen, still grasping the hilt of the sword lodged in the bloodsnake's neck, lifted himself up a few feet, pulling his knees tight to his chest. Not a moment too soon. The first bloodsnake, now with more than a dozen arrows piercing its flesh, mouth wide, fangs dripping poison, bit into the long neck of its brethren, missing Bryen by only a few inches.

The snake had sought to pluck Bryen from his perch while he was distracted. Hissing in anger at having missed its target, the bloodsnake peppered with arrows pulled back.

In an instant, the bloodsnake that Bryen was riding twisted around to confront its unexpected attacker, enraged by the strike, forgetting its hanger-on.

Before the badly wounded bloodsnake could release its rage and launch an attack of its own upon its ilk, a bolt of white light shot from Aislinn's palm and sliced through the first bloodsnake's neck just below the head. The blazing energy burned through the scales and then flesh, filling the tunnel with the sickening stench of charred meat.

For just a moment, the bloodsnake that had attacked Bryen first remained in place, the creature's eyes widening in shock at what had just occurred. Then, with a hiss reminiscent of air being let out of a bladder, the bloodsnake dropped into the chasm, the severed head following the long body down into the darkness.

With the first bloodsnake dispatched, silence reigned in the tunnel, even the second bloodsnake not anticipating that its brethren would meet such an end. That's when Bryen saw his opportunity, and he took it.

With a hard strike, Bryen drove the sword in his left hand

into the snake's neck just a few feet above the other blade that had remained in place despite the animal's desperate maneuvers to shake it loose.

The bloodsnake reared back in fury, unable to turn its head at the angle needed to bite at the pest still on its back, another jolt of sizzling pain surging through its long body.

Bryen tore free the sword that had kept him in place for so long and plunged it back into the beast a few feet above the sword he held in his left hand. He repeated the movement again, and again, his blazing steel slicing through the animal's scales and into its flesh with impunity.

In seconds, Bryen climbed up the bloodsnake, leaving a bloody trail of more than a dozen wounds along the way, finally reaching a spot just below the snake's head.

Holding tightly to the hilts of his swords, he braced his feet against the snake's scales as if he were managing the creature much like he would a horse. Even as the snake writhed to and fro. Trying desperately to dislodge its attacker, driven mad with rage as one painful wound immediately followed the next, it proved to be wasted effort. Bryen's blades allowed him to stay in place.

Focusing on not getting thrown by his mount, Bryen almost missed Rafia, only catching the Magus out of the corner of his eye. She stood just on the other side of the chasm, a sphere of energy dancing across her palm, ready for use at the right time.

He knew that based on where he was now, she couldn't do as Aislinn had done, fearful that if she tried to kill the bloodsnake, the energy would strike him as well and knock him into the crevice. Still, despite the precarious nature of his position, he liked what the Magus was thinking.

"Lower!" shouted Bryen, and he saw with another quick glimpse that Rafia understood, her eyes narrowing as she adjusted her aim.

As soon as Rafia threw the orb at the bloodsnake's body near where it rose up out of the chasm, Bryen was on the move, pulling free both blades and scrambling to the top of the bloodsnake's head. Exactly when the sphere of energy ripped into the bloodsnake's scales and soft flesh beneath, the wound eliciting a hiss of fury, pain, and surprise from the massive creature, Bryen called on even more of the Talent so that when he drove the blazing steel of both blades through the bloodsnake's thick skull and into its brain, it was like sliding a knife through butter.

The effect of his simultaneous blows was immediate, the bloodsnake collapsing toward the side of the chasm where Rafia stood. When the beast's massive jaw slammed against the edge of the crevice, Bryen used that opportunity to escape his predicament.

Pulling his bloody blades free, he leaped back onto the tunnel floor at the far side of the gap, rolling away from the crevice. Returning to his feet quickly, he turned to watch as the massive bloodsnake's head remained in place for just a second longer, then slid into the darkness, pulled down by the weight of its massive body.

Silence fell once again in the tunnel, the soldiers of the Blood Company stunned by the fight that they had just witnessed. They had a difficult time comprehending how the Volkun had extricated himself without coming to harm from what many of them viewed as an impossible position.

Then again, this was the Volkun. It was just another incredible story to add to his growing legend.

"Stop staring into space and get moving!" shouted Declan. "There might be more of those beasts about and I, for one, have no desire to meet them!"

Declan's words jolted the soldiers yet to cross the rope bridge into action, the men and women of the Blood Company moving as quickly as they could as they navigated their way across the crevice, no one wanting to experience for themselves what the Volkun somehow had survived.

Not surprisingly, Declan was the last to come across, following Sirius, the Magus keeping a wary eye on the chasm the entire time that he used the ropes to cross the yawning hole in the tunnel floor.

"Well done, lad," said Declan, who clapped Bryen on the shoulder once his feet touched the stone again. He almost pulled Bryen into a hug, but his natural reserve, strengthened by twenty years in the Colosseum, got in the way. "You didn't lose your head."

Bryen snorted at Declan's dry humor. "How long did it take you to think that one up?"

"Came to me as soon as Lady Winborne decapitated the first bloodsnake."

"I'm glad your mind was in the right place while I was fighting for my life," Bryen said sarcastically.

"You all right?" asked Tarin, the Captain of the Battersea Guard coming toward them from the far end of the tunnel. "Leaping off a horse to attack an Elder. Riding the back of a giant bloodsnake. I'm beginning to worry about you and some of the decisions that you make. What trick will you perform next?"

"I'm fine," Bryen replied, recognizing the glint of humor in Tarin's eyes. "I only did what I had to do."

"If you say so," replied Tarin, his expression suggesting that he didn't quite believe the Protector. "Still, I'd suggest taking fewer risks. It should help prolong your life as well as mine. I don't know if my heart can take it if I have to continue to watch some of your escapades."

"I'll keep that in mind, though I never really considered that being eaten by a very large snake was within the realm of possibility when I thought of all the possible ways that I could die on this journey."

"It can't be any worse than being eaten by a Ghoule," Declan offered.

"Why would you say that?" asked Tarin, not knowing if the Master of the Gladiators was trying to be helpful or making a joke.

"Well, with the Ghoules, you'll probably be dead before they start carving you up. Unless they're desperately hungry, of course. With a bloodsnake there's a better chance that you'll still be alive, probably just seriously wounded, before it begins to swallow you. Like if that second bloodsnake had gotten Bryen. That monster would have taken him whole, and that certainly would not have been a pleasant way to go. He'd have had to cut himself out of the beast."

"Maybe so," replied Tarin, realizing that this was a serious conversation, and not sure what to make of that. "Although that would have been quite a sight, I'm glad I didn't have to watch it." Tarin then turned back to one of Declan's original comments. "So from what you're saying, when the Ghoules are hungry, they don't wait for you to die. They just dig in?"

"Does it really matter?" asked Bryen. "Neither option really appeals to me. Besides, is this really the time and place to have this discussion?"

"Then perhaps a bit more thought before you decide to play the hero," challenged Tarin, as always having a point hidden within the depths of what he and Declan were discussing.

"A word of advice, lad," said Declan. Bryen didn't respond, knowing that Declan was going to give him advice whether he wanted it or not. "When it comes to Lady Winborne, I'd do my best not to make her angry. She seems to have quite the temper, and she didn't look too pleased with how you killed the second bloodsnake with Magus Rafia's assistance."

Declan clapped him on the shoulder one more time as he walked away, Tarin going with the Sergeant, both intent on getting the Company of Blood back in order so that they could continue their journey as swiftly as possible beneath the Shattered Peaks. If the Ghoule Overlord hadn't found the tunnel yet, they assumed that he would soon.

"Who has quite the temper?" asked Aislinn, who now stood right behind Bryen, the Protector turning slowly to face the Lady of the Southern Marches.

Bryen thought that Declan's comment was remarkably prophetic. The tightness of her mouth and her crinkled eyebrows implied that she was less than pleased with him, though smartly he chose to keep that thought to himself. And a good thing too.

Because even more worrisome, Lycia stood right next to Aislinn, which was a rare occurrence as the two women tended to spend the least amount of time in each other's presence as possible. Not unexpectedly, Davin, whose spiky hair was in more disarray than usual, was right behind them with a smirk splitting his lips. He wasn't the target of their attention, so he was looking forward to the drama about to unfold.

"Rafia," Bryen responded hastily, trying to cover for Declan's comment, knowing that revealing the truth wasn't the best way to start this dialogue.

Davin nodded to him with a knowing grin, suggesting with his expression that Bryen's response was a good one, although not quite entirely believable.

"Really? I thought Declan might be speaking about someone else since he was looking directly at me when he said it."

Aislinn stood there expectantly, waiting for Bryen to respond. He chose not to, not feeling the need to dig the hole that he had stepped into any deeper than it already was. Instead, he gave her a smile, hoping that it might divert her thoughts from his actions of the last few minutes.

Clearly, it didn't. Aislinn simply smiled thinly back at him. She was content to wait him out, knowing from experience that time and silence were often two of the best weapons for getting to the truth. Most people became uncomfortable when they were the center of attention and nothing was said.

So she kept her gaze fixed on him, curious as to how long it would take before Bryen broke. Unfortunately, the woman standing next to her didn't give her the chance to find out.

"Why do you always have to take so many risks?" demanded Lycia. "Ever since we were in the Pit, you do things that most sane people know not to even try."

Aislinn sighed in frustration. So much for a well-thought-out strategy that she was certain would have borne fruit.

"What do you mean?" asked Bryen, his tone one of innocence, his grin never wavering, though it appeared to be forced now.

"Leaping onto the back of a bloodsnake? How are we supposed to keep you safe if you won't let us?" Lycia took a step closer to him, her eyes flashing dangerously, her anger radiating off her in waves. "Why did you jump on the back of a bloodsnake? That was beyond foolhardy. One of the Magii could have killed the bloodsnake, just as Aislinn demonstrated, but you were in the way."

"I didn't have a choice, Lycia," countered Bryen, his voice calm, composed. "I was hanging by my fingers, and I didn't have any other good options when that second monster appeared."

"Lycia is right, you know. You take too many risks," agreed Aislinn.

"I was just trying to get out of the way before I became that snake's latest meal."

"And climbing up a bloodsnake's neck with your swords?" asked Aislinn, who crossed her arms to match Lycia's current posture. "You thought that was a good idea? Really?"

Bryen stared at both Aislinn and Lycia, the two women bearing expressions that could wither paint. A dozen different responses came to mind. None would help him in this situation. So he settled for the truth, knowing that selecting any other answer would mean that he would simply continue to drop deeper into the hole that he was already standing in that seemed to be getting bigger all on its own.

"I was just trying to get away from the bloodsnake and do what I needed to do," said Bryen with a slight touch of exasperation. He appreciated their concern, but they needed to remember that he wasn't a child, and he did make good decisions, even when all the options available to him were poor. So rather than wilting under their gaze, his posture straightened and his gaze hardened, much as had happened before he walked out onto the white sand. He was never one to back down from a challenge, even from such two formidable adversaries as he faced now. "That's all. I just happened to be on the rope bridge when the first snake appeared. It could have been any one of us. If you'd like to continue to discuss this, we can, though I'd suggest that we do it at another time."

Before either Aislinn or Lycia could reply, Davin cut in, his eyes drawn to the edge of the crevice. When he looked down the darkness appeared to be moving in a hypnotic, undulating motion.

"Bryen, down below," said Davin, motioning to the chasm.

Bryen stepped to the edge, his sharp eyes trying to penetrate the darkness. The pitch black hid what was beneath, though Bryen could pick out enough to confirm that Davin was right to be concerned. That darkness shouldn't resemble ripples on the surface of a lake.

Reaching for the Talent, Bryen crafted several small spheres of light that he sent floating down into the murk.

The movement in the crevice stopped as soon as the light began to descend, the darkness becoming flat once again. Not a sound emerged from the chasm.

It didn't matter.

The tiny bursts of light told Bryen everything that he

needed to know when he glimpsed two pinpricks of red about fifty feet below him, tracking him, fixed on him.

The look sent a shiver of cold down Bryen's spine. After the challenge of getting across the chasm, he had grown tired of bloodsnakes, deservedly so in his opinion.

"Davin, could you please tell Rafia, Declan, and Tarin that we need to get moving right now."

"It's another bloodsnake, isn't it? I really don't care for bloodsnakes. Not at all."

"You and me both, and this one is even bigger than the other two."

"It's probably the mother of the other two. You never want an angry mother coming after you. I'll get them going."

Davin nodded, then trotted off, telling every gladiator that he came across to be ready to march in one minute while having Jenus and his squad form a shield wall to serve as a rear guard for the Company. Just in case.

"Are you going to try to kill it?" asked Aislinn, who stepped right next to him, peering down into the gloom and seeing the hungry eyes of the bloodsnake staring right back at her.

Bryen remained standing at the edge of the chasm for quite a long time, those blood-red eyes locked onto his own now. Lycia had to fight the urge to pull him back from the brink.

He could use the Talent to kill the massive animal just as Aislinn did the first bloodsnake that crossed their paths, eliminating all his concerns. After giving it some more thought, however, he decided against that course of action, another idea coming to mind.

"No, I'm going to leave that monster be so long as it leaves us alone."

"Why?" Aislinn asked, her fingers flexing as she prepared to reach for the Talent.

"The Ghoules can deal with it when they come after us."

Aislinn nodded, her eyes sparking with malice, liking the idea more than she should.

"I guess you're not reckless all the time," offered Lycia, a broad smile brightening the tight expression that had greeted him after he had survived his combat with the bloodsnakes.

"Thank you," Bryen said with a nod, understanding that their disagreement about his methods had been resolved, at least for now. "Now let's get going. If the Ghoules haven't entered the tunnel by now, they will soon, and we need as much of a head start as we can get."

6

FINDING THE WAY

"Have you found any of the humans, Gurzen? Your fighters are hungry, are they not?"

Once his overeager Ghoules had reined in their natural impulse to brave any danger, giving the Ghoule Overlord the time he needed to trigger the dozens of snares the Magii had set for them across the island, the beasts had swarmed across the rocky and sparsely forested skerry in search of the humans seeking refuge on this island.

The Ghoule Overlord knew that he was right. The Ghoules' zealousness, their lack of concern for the threats that had killed several of them before the Elders went to work, was driven by their craving, which had yet to be satiated.

"No, Master. And yes, Master." The Ghoule scout motioned toward the shimmering stone of the Library of the Magii. "My Ghoules have searched everywhere on this tiny islet, and we haven't found any. The humans must all be in the tower, perhaps hoping that they will be safe behind its stone walls. The last skirmish must have weakened them more than we thought."

That wasn't the information that Gurzen wanted to provide

to the Ghoule Overlord. The scout knew from experience what could happen when his Master lost his very short temper, a very frequent occurrence when the results that he demanded were not achieved in a timely fashion.

Yet Gurzen also knew that in the end it would cost him even more to hedge or avoid the truth. Better just to say what needed to be said and hope that the Ghoule Overlord's anger found another target instead of him.

Gurzen breathed a bit easier when the Ghoule Overlord grumbled his displeasure, but his Master did not lash out as Gurzen feared that he would.

The Ghoule Overlord, although he was loath to admit it, had been impressed by how the humans had stopped his first attack on the black ice and then funneled his Ghoules' second attack into two killing spaces. Clever. Dangerously so. That strategy had proven more effective than he had anticipated.

He could not fault Gurzen and his Ghoules. These humans were more worthy adversaries than he had ever imagined possible. They were a frustrating prey. That he couldn't deny. Of course, the challenges of the hunt did have one benefit. He had no doubt that when his Ghoules finally took the humans, it would make their soft flesh taste that much sweeter.

Still, the delay was infuriating. It was taking much too long to recapture the Seventh Stone. He could sense the artifact, though only faintly now after feeling its immense power only hours before, and because of that he assumed that Gurzen was correct. The Seventh Stone and the humans assigned to protect him had made the Magii's tower their final refuge, shielded from his Dark Magic by the defenses that they had incorporated within the redoubt.

The Ghoule Overlord picked up his head, thinking. Would that really be why his sense of the Seventh Stone had faded, becoming ever fainter as each hour slipped away?

The Talent employed by the Magii could protect the

Seventh Stone for a time, but it would not shield its power from discovery.

Without warning, the Ghoule Overlord's growl transitioned into a roar of anger. Gurzen stepped back from his Master, hoping to avoid any repercussions from his terrifying rage.

Gurzen followed, though not too closely, as his Master stalked around the Library of the Magii, the translucent stone of the tower gleaming dimly despite the cloudy early morning, the taste of the rain to come in the air.

The Ghoule Overlord spent the next hour walking around the tower, completing several circuits before finally stopping. He was certain that he could, in fact, break through. The power that he controlled would be too much for anything the Magii might have put in place to guard against such an assault.

But how long that would take him, he didn't know. Worse, he would have to be the one to do it. None of his Elders had the knowledge or the strength required to do something so complex with the Curse.

Of course, if his suspicions were correct, perhaps he didn't need to waste his time breaking into the Library of the Magii.

With his mind drifting as he thought of the fading trace of the Seventh Stone, the Ghoule Overlord came to an abrupt halt, a malevolent look sneaking onto his already frightening visage.

As strands of the Curse began to spin across the top of the black diamond, he realized that there was no doubt. He was right.

The Ghoule Overlord roared again in anger.

Gurzen and the Ghoules with him jumped back a few feet, worried that their Master was going to turn his rage on them. The Ghoule Overlord looked at his beasts with contempt. They had nothing to fear. He would save his rage for the Seventh Stone.

The Protector or one of the Magii had played him for a fool.

Again. That realization incensed him, but he would need to let that go for now.

Because now he needed to concentrate on what was truly important.

His fury at spending more time than was necessary on this isolated isle had prevented him from noticing how his link to the Curse in the Seventh Stone had changed ever so subtly. His initial belief that the Protector was safely ensconced within the tower was false.

The Seventh Stone wasn't here. The Protector had left the island and was moving farther away from him with each passing second.

He pushed down his anger, this time at himself, which threatened to cloud his thinking. How was that possible? There was no way, even with the Talent, that the Protector could have slipped past his Ghoules, past him, without being caught.

That left only one other possibility.

The Ghoule Overlord reached for more of the Curse, Gurzen watching as the thin black mist spinning atop the black diamond set in the Overlord's staff billowed and then swirled as the Dark Magic mimicked its Master's anger. The towering beast then walked around the tower once again, this time at a much slower pace. As he did so, he sent a stream of Dark Magic into the ground in front of him as he searched for what he knew would be there. He just needed to find it.

When the sun finally began to clear the horizon to the east, he located what he had been looking for beneath a jumbled rock formation that was on the opposite end of the island from the dilapidated pier that jutted out into the water.

"Gurzen, bring the Elders and the Ghoules here immediately."

"All of them?" the Ghoule scout asked, not understanding why.

"Yes, all of them. Hurry. We have little time to waste. The hunt begins again."

After Gurzen ran off, the Ghoule Overlord took in more of his Dark Magic, the black mist becoming denser as it rotated more rapidly now. Satisfied that he had pulled in enough of the Curse to accomplish the task that he had in mind, the Ghoule Overlord directed the stream of Dark Magic down into the ground beneath the rock formation.

Ten feet. Twenty feet. Nothing but dirt and stone. Another twenty feet. Fifty feet more. Still nothing but massive stones buried within the earth.

He kept going. It had to be there. It was the only explanation that made sense. He pushed the Curse even farther underground. Seventy feet more. Then another ninety feet. Finally! He had found it more than two hundred feet down.

Ignoring Gurzen and the other Ghoules who formed up behind him, the Ghoule Overlord pulled on more of his Dark Magic and pointed the black diamond toward the rock formation, releasing the immense amount of the Curse that had been building up within him.

A single blast shot forth, sending tons of dirt and rock flying into the air to fall into the lake with a series of splashes that caused the usually calm water to surge up the rocky beach again and again as the Ghoule Overlord sent blast after blast of the Curse into the ground, digging deeper and deeper into the earth, a massive cloud of soil and shattered stone hiding his work from the beasts looking over his shoulder.

The ground shook every time the Curse slammed into it, the noise resembling the rush of a tidal wave and echoing off the surrounding mountains to create a never-ending cacophony that deafened the Ghoules standing at his back.

And then he was done. He smiled evilly as he stared at the hole that he had created, waiting. The ear-splitting crescendo that reverberated off the peaks finally dissipated. With the silence came a growing confidence within the Ghoule Overlord that he would have the Seventh Stone within his grasp shortly.

Harnessing the Dark Magic still surging within him, he redirected the Curse, using his tainted power to clear the swirling, gritty cloud of choking dreck and crushed rock that blocked his view.

Several of the Ghoules standing behind him gasped in amazement as they stared down into the huge hole. It was exactly as the Ghoule Overlord had expected. A hidden tunnel that led from the tower beneath the lake to some point deeper within the Shattered Peaks, the roof of the passageway destroyed by the Ghoule Overlord's last strike.

Gurzen didn't bother to wait for his Master to give the order that he knew was coming. Instead, he slid more than scrambled down the side of the massive pit, the Ghoules and Elders massed behind him quickly following.

Clever, the Ghoule Overlord thought as he watched his Ghoules slide and crawl down the dirt and stone, their claws giving them the ability to move nimbly across the loose shale that lined the sides. Gurzen was the first through the hole, the other beasts right behind him as they poured through the smashed stone of the tunnel, his Elders already calling on their Dark Magic to light the way. Clever, indeed, though not clever enough.

The Ten Magii should have protected the tunnel with the Talent as they did the Library of the Magii. For whatever reason they failed to do so. That mistake was going to cost them. That mistake was going to make it easier for him to catch up to his prey.

Once all his Ghoules had made their way down into the tunnel, the Ghoule Overlord leapt after them. The humans could run, yet only so far now.

Yes, they had escaped, but there was only one way for them

to go, and his Ghoules would ensnare them before they saw the light of day again.

Yet as soon as he set foot on the stone floor, he heard the screeches farther down the hidden passageway.

Growling again in frustration, the Ghoule Overlord broke into a sprint, shouldering past the Ghoules and Elders who stood in his way. They had lost enough time as it was. They couldn't afford to lose anymore. He would take the lead now and clear the path of any of the traps the Magii had set in their way.

He didn't care that so many of his Ghoules had fallen victim to the ingenious snares the Magii had constructed. No, those beasts foolish enough to step into those traps deserved what they got.

The only thing that concerned him now was that every Ghoule caught in a snare meant more time lost, and that he could no longer abide.

The Seventh Stone was only a few hours down the passageway. If all went well, he would take the Protector and this chase finally would come to an end.

7

PROTECTOR OF THE PASSAGE

"Eyes sharp," advised Tarin, his words traveling easily up and down the length of the Blood Company's line as the gladiators marched at a steady clip through the passageway that led away from Haven. Although his words were just as much for himself as they were for the men and women of the Pit. "We don't want any more surprises if we can avoid them."

The gladiators couldn't agree more. They had no desire to repeat the experience of a collapsing floor that revealed a nest of monstrous bloodsnakes, so the Captain of the Battersea Guard's reminder wasn't really needed.

If the experience with the bloodsnakes wasn't bad enough, as they neared the exit to the Trench they all had been feeling distinctly uncomfortable. It was as if they were journeying in a place where they didn't belong. Where those with warm blood circulating in their veins weren't welcome. Yet there was nothing to be seen that suggested why that was the case.

With every step they took, the musty air in the tunnel became just a tad colder. Many of these men and women who thought nothing of fighting some strange creature on the white sand were beginning to notice an emotion that they hadn't sensed within themselves for quite some time.

Fear.

It could be the fact that for the last several hours the tunnel had tilted steadily downward, taking them ever deeper beneath the Shattered Peaks, how far no one could say for certain. The thought of all that stone above their heads weighed down upon them, making each step harder than it needed to be.

Bryen felt it too, a malaise brought on by the thought that thousands of tons of rock could come crashing down upon them in an instant. But he believed as well that there was more to the spreading sense of unease and peril that increased with every step they took toward the west and their ultimate destination.

"I feel like we're walking across an old battlefield where those who fell were never cared for properly," whispered Jerad, who walked right behind Bryen. "It's almost as if the spirits of the dead are about to rise from their graves."

"I doubt that's going to happen," said Tarin. "Not down here."

"Probably not," admitted Jerad. "Then again, who can say for sure? I have this really weird feeling that there's someone right behind me, looking over my shoulder, whispering in my ear, but there's nothing there. It's putting me on edge."

"That's me," grumbled Tarin, wondering if his Sergeant was starting to feel the strain of their current endeavor.

"Not you, Captain. Have no fear. My mind is still my own. Rather, it's a strange sensation. It's as if the World of Flesh has touched the World of Spirit."

"You mean a ghost?" scoffed Tarin. "There is no such thing as a ghost."

"We didn't think that the Ghoules were real until we fought them on the coastal road," countered Jerad. "So who knows how deeply the Spirit World can touch our own?"

"You might have a point," admitted Tarin. He was not one to believe in spectral beings, as he needed to see something for it to be real for him. Nevertheless, the cold shiver that ran down his spine unbidden was making him rethink that perspective, at least when it came to phantoms.

"I can't disagree with you," said Davin, who was walking right behind Tarin, no more than a foot separating them as every member of the Blood Company gave in to the unconscious need to be near their comrades, the oppressiveness of the tunnel and the strange mood that made many of them think of an open grave playing upon their burgeoning fears. "I saw a lot of strange creatures in the Pit. None of them made me feel so frightened or out of place as I do now. It's almost as if we're trespassing."

That feeling of being watched, of no longer being alone in the leagues-long tunnel, began to affect the gladiators' discipline. Ignoring Declan's earlier orders to maintain a good distance between themselves for fear of bloodsnakes and cave ins, the Blood Company instead bunched up, the unnerving sensations that all of them were experiencing driving them together. Even Declan was feeling it, not having the heart to order his gladiators to spread out once again.

Light touches on their backs and shoulders softer than a breeze. The feeling of being grasped on the arm. A cool breath at their ears, maybe even a faint, unintelligible whisper. Images of family members who had passed to the other side flashing just at the edge of their vision.

Yet whenever they tried to identify the cause, there was nothing there. Just the unsettled faces of the gladiators walking behind them or to their front, gripping their weapons tightly as if doing so would allow them to hold onto their dwindling confidence.

"It's like we're walking through a tomb," murmured Lycia. "I can almost smell the musty dirt and rotting flesh."

"Don't you think you're all being a bit dramatic?" asked Aislinn, who had worked her way up the column to join them.

She was doing her best to ignore the strange sensations that all of them were experiencing, trying to adopt Bryen's fortitude. Her irritation didn't help her. Her Protector was walking at the head of the column with Rafia, neither of them apparently bothered by the aura that permeated the tunnel.

A sensation that someone was standing right behind her, blade in hand, ready to thrust it right between her shoulder blades, sent another shiver of fear down her spine. She stepped closer to Lycia so that they were walking side by side, abandoning her attempt at stoicism and obeying the demand to be near those of her own kind. The words she offered next came out in a slight stutter.

"Even if you're right, even if there are spirits down here, they can do nothing to harm us."

"Are you certain of that, Lady Winborne?" asked Jerad, his voice faltering just a little bit as well. "You could be right. Then again, you could be wrong. Regardless, I'd much prefer it if we were facing off against a pack of Ghoules right now rather than continuing on this path. I know that desire has no real substance behind it, but there it is."

Davin and Lycia nodded their heads in agreement, Bryen ignoring them, his focus farther down the tunnel as he and Rafia led the Company from Haven. There was something waiting for them in the middle of the tunnel just a few hundred feet further down the path, something with a power that he didn't quite understand.

He couldn't make out what it might be, though he knew his rising concern was legitimate. The energy of the Seventh Stone was buzzing, making him tense, as it reacted to whatever the disturbance might be.

As he drew closer, a cold wind gusted through the tunnel, as if a storm was rolling in, the temperature dropping precipitously. It was the first touch of disturbed air that any of them had felt since they had begun their journey through the fusty passageway, and none of the gladiators enjoyed it. Rather than refreshing them, the blast of frigid air froze many of the Company to their very core. For some, it seemed that they had walked right into the afterworld.

"Hold!" Rafia commanded sharply, the Magus staring at the faint white mist that floated right above the tunnel floor, just one hundred paces to their front. The Magus' unease was made clear by the small sphere of the Talent blazing above the palm of her hand, ready for her use, in addition to the ball of light that hovered near the ceiling that lit their way.

But that light did very little to illuminate the passageway beyond the white mist. It was as if that milky haze functioned as a marker of separation, the Natural World, the world of flesh, life, and dreams where the Blood Company stood, and beyond that the Spirit World, a place of shadows and haze, of fears, nightmares, and the insubstantial.

No one said a word as they gazed down the tunnel, thoughts of bloodsnakes and Ghoules forgotten as they watched the wispy threads twist and turn, seemingly rising out of the ground as the frigid wind blew with greater strength through the passageway, the white mist unaffected by these gusts and continuing to expand until it blocked the entire tunnel.

"Do we dare walk through it?" whispered Aislinn, who like many of the others was entranced by how the light fog played across the passageway while also being terrified of it at the same time.

"No," Rafia replied hastily. "To do so would mean our deaths. Against what waits in front of us I have no defense."

"What is it?" asked Jerad.

"I didn't think this could still exist," Rafia murmured, the Magus studying the milky haze intently, both impressed and concerned at the same time. If she squinted and looked closely enough at the swirling strands, she could just make out a shape beginning to form in the murk. She was astounded as she watched the mist begin to coalesce, never having believed that this application of the Talent was still even possible. "That he could still be here after so long. Not after so many years had passed since the creation of the Weir."

"What do you mean?" asked Tarin, who had pushed his way forward to stand right next to Bryen. "Does this mist come from one of the Ten Magii's creations?"

"This is one of the obstacles that I read about in the few texts there are in the Library of the Magii about the construction of the tunnel," explained Rafia. "Well, not really a text, rather just some loose sheets of paper with a few handwritten notes provided by Oraan Kvo, the Magus given the responsibility for building the link between Haven and the Trench. In addition to explaining how the Talent was applied to build this path beneath the Shattered Peaks, he listed some of the protections that he had inserted within the expanse that would allow only those who were supposed to use the tunnel to actually do so without being harmed."

"Rafia, we can discuss the details of what this Magus did after we're out of the tunnel," said Bryen. "What is it that we face now? You said we can't get through the mist without risking our lives. If we can't, what do we do next? The Ghoule Overlord has entered the tunnel. I can sense him getting closer."

"I never thought that the magic to do this could still be in place after all this time," said Rafia. "It shouldn't be in place. It should have faded long ago."

"Rafia," urged Bryen in a stronger voice, needing to push her thoughts back on track. A sadness had crept into the Magus' voice that was heartbreaking, and he didn't understand why.

"Right, sorry," she replied, shaking herself free from whatever had dismayed her. "To your question, Bryen, I don't know. I really don't know what to do next. This is a power that's beyond me. It's beyond Sirius as well. Only one of the Ten Magii could do this. I have no solutions for you."

It was then that Declan finally made it to the front of the column, Sirius remaining at the back to protect their rear, asking the Sergeant of the Blood Company to go forward and find out why everyone had stopped.

"What's the hold up?" grumbled Declan. "We need to keep moving. Sirius says that the Ghoules have entered the tunnel. They're ten leagues behind us now, and they're gaining quickly."

"We have a more immediate problem," said Bryen.

"What are you talking about?" Declan asked, but then Tarin pointed.

When Declan turned his irritated gaze toward the white mist, the gentle swirl of its gossamer strands began to gyrate more violently, making Declan think back to the storm that had struck when they were seeking to escape the Ghoules on the Breakwater Plateau. The fog twisted into a vortex that blasted powerful gusts of wind in every direction, forcing the gladiators to crouch down and lean in to avoid being blown back down the corridor.

Through slitted eyes Rafia, Bryen, and the others at the front of the column watched in astonishment as a rough shape that gained greater clarity with every spin of the fog emerged out of the whirlwind, that figure slowly gaining greater substance. After almost a minute had passed, the gusts of wind came to an end, the transformation complete.

The white mist dissipated, replaced by a head-shaven, stout warrior wearing an antiquated leather armor that none of the soldiers of the Blood Company could identify. The hilts of twin swords stuck up over his shoulders, a flail gripped comfortably in his hands. He appeared to be a formidable adversary, but what drew Bryen's eyes most of all to this new arrival was the silver chain that circled his neck.

"What is that?" asked Jerad. "It's as if it took shape right from the mist. Is that a ghost?"

"He did," Rafia said, never believing that she would ever see with her own eyes such an application of the Talent. "And he's not really a ghost, though I guess that's as good a description as any." She understood just how much power was required to perform such a feat, a skill that no one had mastered since the time of the Ten Magii. "This was the last defense that Oraan Kvo put in place when he completed the tunnel. No one has traveled this far beneath the Shattered Peaks since the path was last used when building the Weir. The good news is that we're coming to the end of the passage. The Trench is no more than a few leagues to our west."

"What's the bad news?" asked Jerad and regretting his question as soon as he did.

"This defense that Oraan Kvo created is the most dangerous of them all."

"You had to ask," grumbled Tarin, shaking his head in disappointment at his friend.

"This is the guardian of the tunnel," said Rafia. "No creature of the Curse can pass without facing him. Neither can we."

"The guardian?" asked Aislinn.

"Yes, Oraan Kvo placed a Protector in the tunnel as a guardian. I can only assume that when the Ten Magii died, the magic holding the Protector here remained intact rather than fading away. How I simply don't know. Even in death, the Protector was chained here, still required to meet the charge given to him by the Ten Magii."

"A slave for more than a millennium," murmured Bryen, his disgust plain in his voice. Aislinn placed a comforting hand on his forearm when she saw how his face dropped as the realization at what had befallen the man struck him.

"Yes, that seems to be the case," Rafia admitted. "I assume that the Protector's spirit has been chained to this place ever since the poor man died. When the Ten Magii passed to the other side, there was no one left who could release him from his bond."

Rafia and the others had little time to contemplate that terrible twist of fate as the Protector burst into motion, sprinting toward them at an incredible pace, preparing to strike, his flail raised above his head.

Before anyone else could move, Bryen launched himself forward, the Spear of the Magii spinning in his hands, catching the spiky head of the Protector's flail with one of the weapon's glowing blades, the clang of metal hitting metal echoing loudly in the contained space of the tunnel. Despite Bryen blocking his first attack, the Protector was not dissuaded from continuing his assault.

In a storm of swift, calculated motion, the enslaved warrior tried time after time to break through Bryen's defenses. The spirit was never able to do so, the haft or the blades of the Spear of the Magii always turning away the barbed head of the flail.

Strangely, not once did Bryen push forward, doing nothing more than defending himself, exercising a remarkable level of self-control even as his training demanded that he attack his adversary.

As the combat stretched out over the next several minutes, sparks flew every time Bryen deflected the never-ending strikes by the guardian of the tunnel. The two Protectors put on a display that was the envy of all those who watched.

Feeling the press of time, the Ghoules pursuing them preying on his mind, Declan was about to step forward, Tarin with him, to help Bryen. Rafia's strong grip on his arm and a shake of her head told them to stay where they were. That this was Bryen's combat, a test that only he could pass.

The two Protectors were a blur of motion, neither man giving an inch, neither man tiring, the enslaved Protector swinging his flail with an economy and accuracy that impressed the gladiators who pressed forward to watch the combat, Bryen barely needing to move anything other than his wrists and shoulders to defend against his opponent's persistent attacks.

The ghostly Protector used a weapon that had fallen into disuse during the last few centuries, the barbed head of steel that was attached to a steel handle by a flexible chain lashing out toward Bryen with a mesmerizing precision. The weapon allowed the Protector to remain a good distance from Bryen as he attacked, making it difficult for Bryen to counter.

But he wasn't worried. Bryen had dealt with fighters who preferred to use such a weapon in the Pit, though they had been few and far between. Bryen did now as he did then, adjusting his fighting style because he understood just how dangerous the flail could be.

Traditionally, in the hands of a skilled fighter, and this Protector clearly was just that, the barbed head could reach around the edge of a shield and dig into the soldier's flesh.

Bryen's primary concern was that the Protector could wrap the chain around the haft of the Spear of the Magii and attempt to yank it from his hands. Thus, Bryen's focus on always blocking the head of the weapon, knowing that if he failed to do so the spiked metal slicing into his flesh or breaking a bone would be the least of his concerns.

The combat continued for several more minutes, neither Bryen nor the Protector giving a fingernail of ground. Through it all Bryen stayed on the defensive, holding back the aggression that yearned to break free, not striking out even when he identified more than a dozen opportunities to do so.

Then much to everyone's surprise, the ghostly Protector took a few steps back, ending his assault and opening a space between them. He touched the silver collar around his neck and motioned to the one encircling Bryen's.

"We are the same, Protector," said the spectral fighter who blocked the Company's way, a genuine smile breaking his grim countenance.

"We are," Bryen agreed.

"It is for that reason that I will allow you and your party to return unharmed from whence you came," said the Protector. "You can go no further. I cannot permit it, even though I have no desire to meet the demands of the Ten Magii and kill you if you try to go beyond me."

"I appreciate your offer, Protector," replied Bryen, one of the blades of the Spear of the Magii digging into the stone floor as he leaned against it. "But we must advance. We have no choice. We are here to complete an important task. Caledonia depends on us."

Bryen took a few minutes to explain why they were in the passage, who was coming after them, and what the Blood Company needed to do with respect to rebuilding the Weir.

"I sympathize with your cause, Protector. Still, I cannot allow you to pass. The magic the Ten Magii employed to chain me here is quite restricting. I cannot allow you to pass unless you can tell me the phrase given to me by the Magus Oraan Kvo that would ensure your safety in the tunnel. With that, I will let you by, and gladly."

Bryen looked back to Rafia, hoping that through her research she might know the answer so that they could get past this imposing obstacle. Unfortunately, the Magus didn't have an answer. She shrugged her shoulders, offering her apologies. The information she had found had been sparse at best.

"You've been in this tunnel for more than a thousand years," said Bryen, trying one last appeal to see if he could gain passage without having to continue the combat. "The Ten Magii are dead, killing themselves right after they constructed the Weir to avoid being taken by the Curse. There is no way for us to know the phrase that you require. Is there no other way we can convince you to allow us to pass? You don't deserve to be here, and I have no desire to fight you. Our mission is too important, and time is running out. Ghoules pursue us like I said."

"I am sorry, Protector," the spirit fighter replied, shaking his head sadly. "I would like to allow it. In fact, I would if I could. You seem an honorable warrior. However, the terms of my enslavement are clear. The magic of the Ten Magii will permit me nothing else. If you want to pass, and you cannot tell me the phrase, then you must defeat me."

"I am sorry, too," replied Bryen. With no other way to gain permission to pass, one of Declan's more common strictures came to mind: "You must do what you must do."

In a flash, Bryen swept one of the blades of the Spear of the Magii down toward the Protector's shoulder. When the man dodged out of the way of the lightning fast slash, Bryen's steel barely missing him, he continued his attack, all thoughts of defending clearly driven from Bryen's mind.

He knew from experience that the best way to defeat a warrior with a flail was to press him. The flail was an excellent offensive weapon, but it was not designed for defending, as Bryen had learned based on his experience in the Pit.

So Bryen attacked with a speed and ferocity that brought to mind for the soldiers of the Blood Company exactly why the crowd of the Colosseum had given their Captain the name of the Volkun. The Protector chained to the tunnel clearly was an accomplished warrior, demonstrating the skills and technique of a man well versed in the use of weapons. An opponent that none of the gladiators wanted to fight themselves. Even so, he was no match for Bryen, whose speed and intensity were night-marishly daunting.

The conclusion came faster than anyone expected, the enslaved Protector trying desperately to catch the double blades of the Spear of the Magii as they flashed toward him at an incredible speed and failing to do so after only three quick slashes. Yet rather than cutting across his opponent's neck and ending the combat with a gruesome finality, Bryen instead held one of the blades up against the Protector's throat after he allowed the chain on the flail to wrap around the haft of the Spear so that he could turn the tables and rip the weapon from the ghostly Protector's grasp.

"Do it, Protector," said the spectral warrior, helpless without his weapon. "Finish this. Give me peace. The touch of your blade will send me on my way just as it will send you on yours. I have waited centuries for this."

Bryen looked into the Protector's eyes, believing every word that the man said. He could certainly understand why. The Protector's eyes pleaded for Bryen to release him from his imprisonment. Still, knowing what was needed in that moment with regard to the mission the Blood Company had taken on, knowing as well what the Protector wanted, Bryen hesitated.

"Perhaps there is another way," suggested Rafia, the Magus stepping forward when she recognized that Bryen was reluc-tant to do as the spirit warrior asked. To destroy someone just like him. Someone burdened with the same fate and forced to endure it for a much longer period of time than he did. "As the victor, Bryen, in a situation such as this you can give the ensor-celled Protector leave to pass on without a final blow. You just need to apply a pinch of the Talent and cut the thread the Ten Magii crafted to hold this unfortunate, honorable warrior here."

Bryen thought about that option for just a few heartbeats, then seized upon the solution that wouldn't require him to slice the man's throat. Reaching for the Talent, he applied a thin thread of energy that was as sharp as a stiletto to the task, heeding Rafia's instructions as she took him through the process.

The whole procedure took no more than a few seconds, and when Bryen was done, the Protector's eyes widened. The magic that had kept him in place for so long had vanished. The Protector closed his eyes in thanks, never believing after so many years that this moment would finally come. That now he could pass on to the other side on his own. When he chose.

"Rise, Protector," said Bryen, pulling back the Spear of the Magii and offering his hand to assist him.

"Why did you free me?"

"As you know, I have been in the same place as you have," Bryen replied, tapping his fingers on his own silver collar. "Besides, it was the right thing to do."

"Most people don't do the right thing," the Protector countered.

"True, but Bryen always does the right thing," interrupted Aislinn. "Even if doing the right thing causes problems for him later."

The Lady of the Southern Marches stood right behind Bryen, still wary of the Protector, Lycia standing right next to her, twin swords in hand. The gladiator nodded her agreement reluctantly, Lycia believing that she and Aislinn were demonstrating a similar perspective on the world much too often lately, yet there was little that she could do to correct that at the moment.

"Be that as it may," replied Bryen, shifting his gaze to the two women at his back and asking with his eyes that they allow him to finish what he had started, "I would ask a favor of you, Protector, before you find your peace and pass on."

"I have been waiting for a thousand years, Protector. You ask a great deal even with the mercy you have demonstrated and the help that you have provided."

"I know," Bryen replied. "And I'm sorry that I must ask this of you. But we need your assistance if we're to have any chance of stopping the Ghoule Overlord and his Legions from conquering Caledonia."

"What do you require Protector? I will make no promises until I hear you."

Bryen took just a few minutes to explain what he needed.

"I will do as you request," the Protector agreed. "Then I will pass on. To use your own words, it is the right thing to do."

"Thank you, Protector," Bryen replied, offering his hand to seal the agreement. "May I ask your name?"

"Jediah Carlomin."

"My thanks, Jediah Carlomin," said Bryen, bringing the Spear of the Magii to his forehead and nodding to the Protector in respect. "I will see you on the other side."

"I will see you on the other side," repeated the spirit warrior, bringing his own weapon to his forehead and offering a nod of respect, the two Protectors seeing something of themselves in one another. "Just not too soon I hope."

THE GHOULE OVERLORD stood at the very beginning of the crevice that extended a good distance down the floor of the tunnel, his clawed feet curling just over the edge. His Ghoules were already making their way across, using the rope bridge that the humans had so foolishly left in place.

It only took the first pack of Ghoules a few seconds to scale the gap, pulling themselves across the ropes with a remarkable agility, then sprinting farther down the tunnel, yearning to catch their quarry. Several packs followed the first, an Elder going with each one to light the way and deal with any other traps crafted by the Magii that were waiting for them.

That flurry of activity ceased abruptly, bringing a scowl to the Ghoule Overlord's already severe countenance. The Ghoule leading the next pack, who had made it halfway across the crevice, had stopped, a strange look of concern flashing across his face. The beast then looked down into the crevice that fell away beneath him, his eyes trying and failing to pierce the darkness.

An unnatural quiet descended in the tunnel, even the Ghoule Overlord holding his breath as he sensed some other presence having joined them in the tunnel. What it could be he wasn't certain, but his primordial sense of approaching danger told him all that he needed to know.

The Ghoule hanging from the rope ladder heard a very faint noise that was no more than a few dozen feet beneath his clawed feet, what sounded like a very large body scraping across the stone ledge. The beast was about to shout a warning. Instead, the Ghoule Overlord did.

"Move, you fools!" roared the Ghoule Overlord, breaking the charged quiet. "We have no time to waste!"

Before the Ghoule Overlord's cry could spur on the Ghoules clinging to the rope bridge, a massive bloodsnake thrust up out of the darkness, freezing the beasts in place with the mesmerizing glow of its blood-red eyes. The bloodsnake bit into the lead Ghoule with a sickening crunch, its massive fangs punching all the way through the beast, the monster then dropping back down into the darkness with its meal. For a moment, the Ghoules who were still on the rope bridge were too stunned to do anything other than stare, never having seen an animal like this before, never expecting one of their comrades to die so hideously.

The Ghoules' hesitancy worked to the benefit of the even larger bloodsnake that emerged next out of the darkness, its thick scales glittering in the light crafted by the Elders and flashing specks of red across the ceiling and the walls. The animal's monstrous body filled the tunnel completely, and then its fully extended fangs shot forward faster than the eye could see, clamping around the waist of another Ghoule still hanging from the rope ladder, the snake's fangs also puncturing the beast's armored flesh from both the front and the back.

Yet this snake apparently had no desire to return from whence it came, whipping its head around violently to dislodge the Ghoule from its fangs, in the same motion catching the beast's body in its gaping maw and then using the muscles in its throat to take the dying Ghoule deeper into its incredibly long and thick body. The massive animal turned back toward the Ghoules still clinging to the rope, seeking out more prey.

The monstrous bloodsnake paid for its greediness.

A shard of Dark Magic shot from the Ghoule Overlord's staff and sliced across its massive head, opening a bloody wound, the huge animal's scales and flesh burning with an indescribable pain thanks to the cold heat of the Curse.

The bloodsnake whipped around toward its attacker, its flashing eyes fixing on the Ghoule Overlord, its hiss of anger reverberating off the walls and ceiling of the tunnel. Another blast of the Curse cutting across its flesh just beneath its jaws dissuaded the animal from attacking. Realizing the danger that it faced, and not wanting to take the risk, the bloodsnake reluctantly slithered back into the crevice before it could take another tasty morsel.

Only then did the Ghoules trapped on the rope ladder start clambering across again, moving as fast as they possibly could, having no desire to meet the same fate as their brethren.

As the Ghoules pulled themselves across the rope ladder to the other side of the crevice, the Ghoule Overlord turned to Gurzen, the scout's eyes still wide with shock at seeing the two bloodsnakes snatch his warriors from the rope with a practiced and deadly ease.

"Get them across as fast as you can," ordered the Ghoule Overlord, "before another of those animals comes up out of the dark. I do not want to waste my strength on them. I must save it for our real adversary."

"Yes, Master," replied Gurzen, the Ghoule Overlord's blazing eyes jolting him into action, the scout knowing that standing there safely away from the bloodsnakes was more dangerous in that moment than attempting to cross the crevice.

With a few choice curses from Gurzen urging them on, the remaining packs scrambled across the rope ladder with a blind abandon, the Elders on both sides of the gap prepared to use their Dark Magic to keep the bloodsnakes from interfering with their crossing if the animals dared to come out from their lair once again.

The Ghoule Overlord was the last to cross the crevice, the bloodsnakes nowhere to be found, having moved away from the tunnel and the frigid bite of the Curse. It didn't take him long to retake the lead as his Ghoules increased the pace of their pursuit.

The Seventh Stone was so close now that the Dark Magic it contained was calling to the Ghoule Overlord. Begging him to come and take it, so that it could join with him. So that he could reclaim what had been stolen from him so long ago.

That insistent demand sent a wave of pleasure through him.

His Ghoules were overtaking the humans. They might even catch the humans before they exited the tunnel, which would be to his advantage.

With that desire pushing him forward, the Ghoule Overlord sprinted even faster, his Ghoules having no choice but to match him, almost all of the beasts flagging after just a mile because of his ground-eating pace.

The Ghoule Overlord didn't care about the traps that might

await them farther down the tunnel. He didn't care if there were any more of the blood-red snakes lurking to their front. He didn't care about any of the other dangers that this cursed construction of the Magii might hold for him.

Losing all the Ghoules with him was of no concern.

The only thing that mattered now was that he reclaim the Seventh Stone.

8

———

IN THE GAP

Jurgen Klines peered to the north, searching for any signs of movement, knowing from experience that if the Ghoules were coming his way he would see nothing more than a brief flash of movement.

Nothing yet. Not even a breeze drifted down from the Shattered Peaks.

But the beasts were coming. Of that he was certain.

One of the advance scouts had returned just a few hours before. The deep gash across his sternum told Klines all that he needed to know regarding what the man had come up against.

The claw had ripped through his leather armor like it was no better than paper, the talons digging deep into his flesh and breaking several of his ribs. The scout was lucky to be alive, not only because of the severity of his wound, but also because the three other soldiers who had gone out with him on this assignment had not returned.

Klines knew that the three women who were missing would remain so.

Before the wounded soldier had passed out, he had reported that the Ghoules had surrounded his comrades. He was the only one able to break free from the trap, and that solely because of pure luck, the beast that had clawed him slipping on the soft earth of the canyon floor before the Ghoule could finish what he had started.

Klines had listened to the soldier in silence, all the while hoping that the three doomed women had died before the beasts took them. He didn't want to think of the terror and pain they would have experienced if the Ghoules had made a meal of them while they were still alive.

The Blademaster looked over his shoulder quickly, knowing exactly what he was going to see. Still, after hearing what the soldier had to say, he felt the need to check one more time just to make sure. As he liked to explain to his soldiers probably more often than they would like, details mattered. Especially when you fought beasts that held the upper hand right from the start, making a fair combat against the Ghoules anything but.

That was why ever since the soldiers of Caledonia had advanced into the Winter Pass, he had focused on one crucial objective. He wanted to make sure that they never had to fight a fair combat.

The three companies of the Royal Guard that he was leading sat on their war horses in the formation they had trained in for weeks. Klines was a stickler because he wanted his soldiers to survive. So he did all that he could to make that happen, beginning with ensuring that everyone knew exactly what they were supposed to do without having to think about it.

And now his soldiers did whatever they needed to do to keep themselves and their mounts calm yet at the same time primed for the skirmish that no doubt would begin within the hour. Based on the surviving scout's report of what was coming toward them, he was confident that the troops with him would be enough for what they would face that morning.

Klines and his soldiers were stationed halfway up the Winter Pass, the farthest that any of the forces that made up the Caledonian Army had pushed into the gorge so far. Duchess Stelekel had two objectives in mind when she had tasked Klines with taking this advance party so close to the Weir.

First, she wanted to get a better lay of the land. With her skill with the Talent, she could extend her senses for hundreds of leagues to all points of the compass, and she did that regularly to scout the gorge and its surroundings as the soldiers who fought for the Kingdom worked their way deeper among the Shattered Peaks. Even so, she believed that there was no better way to get a feel for a future battlefield than to walk it with her own two feet, or at least the feet of those she trusted.

Klines agreed with her. So he was glad he was where he was. If they were to have any chance against the Ghoules, they needed to know the territory they would be fighting in better than they knew the backs of their own hands.

Second, her reason for pushing so far forward was based on a combination of practicality and hope. The practical portion relied on the fact that engaging with the Ghoules who were continuing to cross the Weir was an inevitability. So the farther to the north that the battle began, the better, because it would mean that the beasts would have that much farther to push back the Caledonian Army before they reached the southern tip of the Winter Pass, which emptied out onto the Breakwater Plateau.

Once the Ghoules reached that point, the beasts would have free rein to go wherever they wanted to go in Caledonia. Here, in the Winter Pass, with the soaring mountains funneling the Ghoules toward them, Klines and the soldiers of Caledonia were given their best opportunity to hold the beasts, or at least attempt to do so, for any length of time.

And that's where the concept of hope came into play. Duchess Stelekel, Duke Winborne, Klines himself, everyone in the Caledonian Army hoped that they could confine the Ghoules to the Winter Pass. Of course, Klines understood the folly of placing too much faith in that desire.

Before leaving Tintagel for the Shattered Peaks and the Winter Pass, he had renewed his acquaintance with Sirius for a few hours, the old Magus having visited Tintagel many times before he was called to service in the Southern Marches. Among other matters, they had spoken of what would be required with the Ghoule Overlord and his Legions stirring. One of the many sayings that Sirius spouted so frequently during that brief conversation had stuck with him.

"Hoping doesn't make it real," said the wild-haired Magus, his dark eyes gleaming brightly. "If we base our decisions on hope, then we're dead before the fight even begins. Hope won't save us. Steel, a strong arm, and the Talent will."

Klines agreed with Sirius' sentiment, and he believed that maxim certainly applied to their current situation. The Caledonian Army might be twenty thousand strong and growing larger every day, but if the Ghoules forced ten or more Legions through the Weir, each Legion containing a thousand of the beasts along with a dozen or more Elders, then they didn't stand a chance. The massive Ghoules were too fast, too strong, and too vicious for the Caledonians to have any chance of victory if they couldn't bring to bear three, preferably four or even five, times the number of fighters that the Ghoules could.

So Klines had no choice but to temper his hope with the harsh reality that the best they could do now, assuming enough Magii appeared to combat the Elders and their Dark Magic, was to try to give the Protector the time that he needed to reach the Sanctuary and rebuild the Weir. If he could do that, the Protector could limit the number of Legions that invaded the Kingdom to a manageable number and, as a result, the Caledonians might have a real chance.

Because of that, Klines felt as if most of his reality was still built on hope. Try as he might, there was no guarantee that the Protector could do what was being demanded of him. Klines had no doubt that the young man would do everything he possibly could to repair the magical barrier that had kept the Ghoules from the Kingdom for a millennium, sacrificing himself if need be. Yet there was little to guarantee his success, so the Blademaster had no illusions about the severe challenge that young man faced.

Still, there was nothing for it. There were few guarantees in life, other than perhaps death. So just as the Protector would do what was required of him, he and his soldiers would do what was required of them.

Sirius was right. Hoping doesn't make it real. But you can't live without at least a little bit of hope, and the Protector had given them that.

If the Volkun could topple a dynasty three hundred years in the making in just a few days, who was to say what kind of chaos he could create for a monster that was more than a thousand years old and who thought of nothing else but turning Caledonia into a hunting ground for his Ghoules.

Klines pulled at the collar of his leather armor, needing to get a little air around his neck as sweat trickled down his chest and his back. Despite the cool almost cold temperature, the end of summer finally making its presence known so far north within the Shattered Peaks, he was feeling the stress of the challenge that he and his soldiers faced.

The Winter Pass would remain open for at least the next few weeks until the fall weather brought the blizzards these rugged peaks were known for. Thus the Ghoule Overlord's decision to push his beasts toward the south now.

It had snowed the night before, the temperature dipping severely once the sun dropped below the western horizon. Unfortunately, it only had been a light covering that had melted as soon as the sun reappeared the next morning. The only reminder of the extreme shift in weather was the muddy ground, something that the scout who had survived the Ghoule ambush likely appreciated now.

Of course, that was the rule in this rugged, treacherous land. Where the sun shone in the Winter Pass, the massive snowdrifts, all of them a hundred feet or more deep, melted, at least for a few months until the winter weather returned. So the ground in the center of the Pass, upon which the sun blazed for most of the day, had transitioned into a landscape of mud, slush, melting ice, and large, shallow pools of water, even a few fast-moving streams as the snowmelt flowed to the south toward the Breakwater Plateau. Where the sun failed to break through the gloom of the pass, the enormous piles of hard-packed snow remained, surviving within the shadows created by the soaring peaks.

In fact, that's where Klines was now, lying on top of one of those snowdrifts that had formed beneath a towering mountain that put the western side of the Winter Pass into dusk year round, the sun never touching this ground regardless of the time of day. Benin, his most trusted Sergeant, lay right next to him, his reddish-brown beard that, if it ran free, would flow beneath his belt, now plaited into the design of the Volkun's double-bladed spear.

The two men had known each other for decades, so they interpreted each other's moods with ease. They were both concerned, and they were both doing their best to keep that emotion hidden. Their soldiers were nervous enough as it was, having pushed several leagues ahead of the protection offered by the main army, acknowledging that doing so meant that a skirmish with the Ghoules was a given.

Even more unsettling, because none of the Caledonians had seen it before, the Weir was visible off in the distance, probably no more than five leagues away. The Ghoules coming through the magical barrier could cover that distance in a matter of hours.

At the moment the Weir itself, which extended from the ground into the sky to a height that no one could discern, and from the Burnt Ocean in the west to the Silent Sea in the east, was a major concern as it flickered from black to white and then back again with an increasing regularity, the constancy of the grey haze for which the Weir had been known since the end of the First Ghoule War more of a rarity with the passing of each day.

"Do you think that he can do it, Blademaster?" asked Benin. The veteran Sergeant had fought in dozens of clashes while serving in the Royal Guard, yet still he found that a conversation before a fight always helped to calm his nerves.

Klines didn't need to ask who his Sergeant was referring to. Only one person had been on the minds of all the soldiers who made up the Caledonian Army that had marched into the Winter Pass, the increasingly erratic behavior of the Weir and the need to correct it seeming to have taken precedence over the more immediate threat presented by the advancing Ghoules.

And rightly so, Klines believed. If the Weir collapsed, the Ghoule Overlord would flood all of Caledonia with his Legions, ensuring the Kingdom's doom. At least with the Protector still in play, they had a chance of winning what some of the soldiers were already calling the Second Ghoule War.

Klines hesitated before answering. He believed in the Protector's abilities, but no one had ever been asked to do what was being asked of the one real hope that the Kingdom had for stopping this Ghoule invasion.

"The Protector will do all that he can, or he will die trying. Of that, I have no doubt," replied Klines, his thin grey hair pulled back and tied with a black leather strap at the nape of his neck so that the strong gusts of wind that ran north to south through the Winter Pass didn't fling his long locks in front of his eyes at the worst possible moment.

"That's all we can ask of him," Benin replied with a nod. "That's all we can ask of anyone in times like these."

"I couldn't agree with you more, Benin." Klines gave his Sergeant a tap on the shoulder with his hand, then nodded toward the north and the center of the Pass, focusing on a point that was no more than a quarter mile to their front. "Did you see it?"

"Yes, just along the edge of the snowdrifts. Flashes of green and brown."

"One hundred or so?"

"Give or take," replied Benin, the blurry shapes gaining greater clarity as they approached at a breathtaking speed. "We should be able to manage them if we do this the way that we discussed."

"They're moving fast. Do you see any Elders?"

"Three."

"Be wary. There might be more. Target them first. If we take them out of the fight right at the start, then you're correct. We should be able to manage the remaining Ghoules."

"With pleasure, Blademaster. The soldiers know what to do. Besides, it looks like the beasts are going to help us out. They either don't know that we're here or they don't care." Benin slid back down the snowdrift, offering a final comment as he pulled himself up into his saddle. "I'll see you on the other side, Blademaster."

"I'll see you on the other side," Klines replied, smiling as he said it.

The saying was a common one for the gladiators who used to fight in the Colosseum, offering the words to one another right before they stepped out onto the white sand, because they never knew whether they would walk back out or were going to be dragged from the Pit, no more than a bloody corpse. The soldiers of the Royal Guard and many of the Duchy Guards had adopted the saying as well as several other aphorisms from those brave men and women.

It only made sense. All of them were captivated by the Protector who had once been a gladiator who had freed the Kingdom from the rule of an incompetent fool who, either knowingly or not, had aided the Ghoule Overlord in his efforts to weaken Caledonia and prepare the way for his Legions, thus placing every person living within the Kingdom in an incredibly precarious potentially catastrophic situation.

Klines looked back toward the north, tracking the swift movement of the Ghoules as they glided south through the pass, the beasts staying more toward the wet and mucky center so that they could avoid the large snowdrifts that extended out from each side of the tightening gorge. It appeared that Benin was correct.

Three Elders.

This would have been so much easier if he had Magii with him who could negate the Elders' Dark Magic. But he didn't. Trying to make the best of it, he thought of a question that one of the Protector's friends, the gladiator known as the Crimson Giant, asked quite frequently.

"Where was the fun in life without the challenge?"

Without Magii, Klines and his soldiers had no defense against the beasts carrying their twisted staffs of black ash that allowed them to manipulate the Curse. These were the creatures he feared the most because they could cause the greatest harm to his troops.

Under most circumstances, the Blademaster would have joined the fight right from the start, wanting to be on the ground with his soldiers. Not this time, though.

A feeling that he had learned to heed during his years of service in the Royal Guard held him back. Why this sense of unease had settled within him right now, with so much at stake, he didn't know. But he would wait.

Still, even with the wrinkle offered by the Elders, he was confident with respect to their numbers and the training and experience of the soldiers with him. All of them had fought the Ghoules before. All of them knew what to expect and what they needed to do.

So Klines would watch the clash from atop the snowdrift, at least the very beginning. Doing so would give him the chance to evaluate the tactics that Benin and his soldiers would be employing.

At the same time he would keep one eye to the north. The uncomfortable feeling he was experiencing, what he translated as a warning, now suggested to him that he was missing an important variable, and that feeling had never been wrong before.

Klines didn't have long to wait before the action began. Just below him, Benin led the three companies of Royal Guard as they swept out from behind the snowdrift and arranged themselves into their formation -- two rows, ten yards between each one -- that extended across the open ground of the Winter Pass. With a deafening cry that echoed off the bordering mountains of the Shattered Peaks, the men of the Royal Guard lowered their spears and urged their horses to a gallop. Kicking up a shower of mud behind them, their massive horses charged toward the Ghoules, the creatures' mottled green skin and brown leather armor making the beasts excellent targets against the stark greys and whites of the Winter Pass.

The Ghoules skidded to a stop in the wet muck upon seeing the mounted humans, knowing what the soldiers could do with their horses. They didn't seem the least bit worried, however, as the Ghoules raised their saw-toothed maws to the sky and howled with pleasure, relishing the chance to kill.

Perhaps it was their unabating hunger, their desire to bite

into their prey's soft flesh and gnaw on the bones of the humans, which led the beasts to spit out unintelligible gibberish at the riders bearing down on them, urging the soldiers on with their screeches and gestures. Urging the humans to ride to their doom.

Or perhaps it was primarily because of the three Elders who pushed their way to the front of the Ghoule packs, the beasts who had given themselves to the Curse preparing to disrupt the charge, long threads of Dark Magic already spinning across the tops of their staffs.

Klines watched it all unfold from his perch. It was a simple plan on the part of the Ghoules, and simple plans often proved to be the best in the Blademaster's opinion. The Elders believed that they could end the charge before it even began by releasing the Curse, allowing the Dark Magic to rip through his defenseless soldiers.

The Blademaster's strategy, although slightly more complicated than that of the Elders, was better. And though the beasts were prepared to fight cavalry, knowing exactly how to pull the humans from their mounts, the Elders were not prepared for what came next.

The first arrow that streaked through the air was no more than a blur until it appeared in the neck of the Elder standing closest to the snowdrift. The beast collapsed as soon as the steel tip pierced his flesh, becoming no more than a sack of bones, unable to paw at the projectile that had sliced through his airway and his spine.

The second Elder fell less than a second later, two arrows protruding from his chest, the third penetrating his right eye and into his brain when he turned to see what had happened to the Ghoule to his right.

The last Elder, about to send shards of the Curse toward the mounted soldiers who were bearing down on him, now no more than a few dozen yards away, sensed the threat from above. The beast ducked just in time, several arrows shooting through the air where he had been standing and slamming harmlessly point first into the mud.

The Elder growled and hissed his annoyance as he rose out of the muck. He immediately turned toward the archers, the cavalry that was almost upon him apparently forgotten as he focused his Dark Magic on the soldiers who attacked him from atop the snowdrift.

But the Elder was too slow and too distracted. A few of the industrious, more experienced archers had assumed that their first wave of arrows wouldn't take all the Elders out of the fight, so they had waited to release their steel-tipped shafts. Now they struck.

As soon as the last Elder stood to his full height of more than seven feet, five arrows sprouted from his chest, the barbed shafts burrowing deeply into his flesh, and at least two finding his heart. The Dark Magic that had been spinning wildly atop his staff winked out as the Elder fell on his back into the mire.

Benin and the rest of the Royal Guard didn't even bother to watch as the archers did their work, trusting in the skill of their comrades. The mounted soldiers remained intent on their targets, screaming in rage as they crashed into the cursing and howling Ghoules, the beasts realizing too late that they were in for a much more difficult fight, never expecting their Elders to die before their eyes.

The first row of cavalry didn't worry about whether they skewered any of the Ghoules with their spears, instead applying the lessons that had worked so well in the past when fighting these beasts, using their mounts as their primary weapons. The Ghoules couldn't stand against the weight and the force brought to bear as the war horses shouldered into them, several dozen beasts trampled within seconds, their bones broken and skulls crushed beneath the multitude of steel-shod hooves.

Yet just as the soldiers had learned to fight the Ghoules, the Ghoules also had grasped some key lessons from their previous encounters with the humans. Although a good number of their brethren were caught by the initial charge, many of the beasts timed their leaps perfectly and hurdled over the mounted soldiers, landing just behind them with little difficulty and escaping the attack. That's why the second line of soldiers, riding the exact distance that Klines had prescribed behind the first, was so essential.

The Ghoules were blazingly fast and incredibly agile. Even so, many of the Ghoules who avoided the first row of cavalry didn't have the time or the ability to leap over the second line of soldiers, those who tried usually flipped through the air or caught before they could gain the height that they needed to escape the charge, the war horses too close, plowing into the beasts with their withers, the soldiers plunging their spears into the broken and dying beasts as they rode over them.

Klines nodded his head in satisfaction. His soldiers had done excellent work. Yet even with the success of that first attack, more than half the Ghoules were still on their clawed feet or were about to be as they pushed themselves out of the muck, their focus on gaining vengeance on the prey that had the gall to play at being a hunter.

It wasn't an unexpected result as the Ghoules were notoriously difficult to kill. He wasn't worried, though. With the Elders eliminated from the fight and the Ghoules greatly reduced in number, Klines believed that once his companies wheeled back around and charged again, the skirmish would reach its inevitable conclusion. A victory for his troops.

A flash of movement brought Klines' gaze back to the north. He pushed himself to his feet, the nervousness that he had been feeling transitioning into a sense of dread that seeped into his bones as he stared farther down the Winter Pass. More streaks of green sprinted toward him. A lot more. Several hundred more, in fact, and they were coming fast.

These Ghoules knew where he and his soldiers were. They had waited to join the fight until after his troops were engaged with the Ghoule skirmishers. Worse, the Blademaster picked out at least a half dozen Elders with this larger group, the servants of the Ghoule Overlord likely using their Dark Magic to scout the way and confirm exactly what waited for them ahead.

Klines cursed himself for his overconfidence. He should have heeded right from the start the feeling that had plagued him upon seeing the Ghoules for the first time. These beasts who were now enmeshed once more with his soldiers weren't just the advanced scouts. They were also the bait, and they were meant to keep his troops in place so that the hundreds of Ghoules following behind them could close the trap.

He could have ordered a single charge and then pulled back. He should have done that. Instead, he had gotten greedy, wanting to eliminate the Ghoules in one fell swoop. Now, after their second charge, his companies were mixed in with the Ghoules, the larger battle denigrating into a series of smaller skirmishes, and his soldiers were about to be swept under by a second wave of the beasts.

Whether he could pull his soldiers free in time, he didn't know. But he had to try.

Klines slid down the snowdrift, then pulled himself into his saddle, his horse at a gallop in seconds. He needed to get his soldiers out of the fight and to the south before the oncoming Ghoules, who were now no more than a quarter mile away, overran them. Otherwise, he and all his soldiers were going to be slaughtered.

Yet strangely, even as he raced to rescue his soldiers, the primary issue facing everyone in the Kingdom continued to play through the back of Klines' mind as he worked through several strategies for pulling his soldiers free and attempting to form a rear guard so that they could move down the narrowing gorge with all possible speed.

The Ghoule Overlord was taking advantage of the weakening Weir, sending as many of his Legions through the magical barrier as he could manage while the Winter Pass remained open. Klines didn't even want to think about how many of the Ghoules had already made it through the Weir. But still, he had to wonder.

Would any of this matter in the end?

Because as Benin had noted before this fight began, the fate of Caledonia rested with a young man with little love for the Kingdom that now was depending so heavily upon him.

9

A NEW WORLD

"Some of what Magus Rafia described when I asked her what to expect I found almost too much to believe," said Jerad as he gaped at what he saw before him, the strange land illuminated by the steel-colored light of midday. He, Tarin, and the Blood Company finally had emerged from the tunnel that led from Haven all the way to the eastern side of the Trench, no other challenges placed before them along the way once Bryen bested the Protector. "She didn't do this place justice. It's incredible in a disquieting, almost chilling kind of way."

The Sergeant of the Battersea Guard stood with his neck bent at an extreme angle as he stared up at the sheer walls of the gorge. The cliffs rose for a mile or more, marking the boundary of the western side of the Breakwater Plateau. He couldn't tell for certain where the rock face ended because of the billowing clouds that hid the top of the gorge, the grey overcast filtering the small amount of light that managed to seep through.

"She's never been here before," said Tarin, just as astounded as Jerad by what he observed, and even more aware of his surroundings now that they had exited from beneath the

Shattered Peaks. The tunnel was bad enough, what with the bloodsnakes and the threat of collapsing floors, walls, and roofs. Here, in this grey place with its oppressive ceiling of clouds that appeared to be fixed in place, he felt completely out of place, as if he and the others with him were trespassing and shouldn't be here. He could tell by the looks that he caught on the faces of the gladiators who had gathered behind him that they felt it too. "All she could do was give us the information that she had gleaned from other sources. I must admit that though Magus Rafia's information may not have been complete, it certainly is quite close to what we were told to anticipate."

Not too far off in the distance the first stone spire soared into the air, at least a third of it lost in the thick cloud cover. The sandstone pillar must have been at least a quarter mile in circumference, a twisting path carved around the outside of the stone outcropping that wound its way up and into the grey murk. Tarin assumed that the winding trail continued through the clouds and led all the way to the summit.

The sides of the spire provided the only real color in this peculiar land. Large pockets of purple and white heather sprouted on the stone, joined in a haphazard pattern by a thick green moss.

"Quite a sight, isn't it?" asked Aislinn, coming to stand between the two soldiers from the Southern Marches. "Kind of how I imagined it would be. Then again, not entirely. You really need to see it with your own eyes to believe it, I guess."

"Indeed," replied Tarin, his eyes sweeping the expanse that stretched out before them for any sign of danger, "and all we need to do from here is find our way to the Sanctuary, which is purportedly ten or so leagues to the north. Of course, no one has a good sense as to its exact location, but once we locate it, we climb the stone monolith upon which it was constructed and then do whatever is required to give the Protector the time that he needs to repair the Weir. All that despite the fact that he's not really certain how to do that." Tarin grumbled to himself as he shook his head in mock amusement. "Remind me as to why I agreed to do this."

"Because you had nothing better to do," said Declan, who stepped out from the tunnel, taking in everything around him in a single glance, then nodding as if it was exactly as he expected it to be. "That and the fact that you're worried about the trouble Bryen can get himself into without having any adults around to keep him on the path of the straight and narrow. When he gets impatient, he does tend to leave a trail of destruction behind him."

"Right on both counts," agreed Tarin, chuckling at Declan's response that was in part true yet also a touch sardonic.

The Captain of the Battersea Guard didn't feel the need to mention that he considered Bryen a friend as well. The Protector had grown on him since he had first met him in the Colosseum. To his way of thinking, Bryen deserved a chance at a better life, and he couldn't pursue that until this larger task was complete. So Tarin wanted to do all that he could to help the Protector do what he needed to do. Then, finally, he could get him out of his hair once and for all.

"Now if everyone is done gawking, we need to be on our way," said Declan, pulling the gazes of every soldier in the Blood Company to him. "Remember, as Magus Rafia explained, there are dangers in the Trench that are worse than the Ghoules pursuing us."

A low murmur began among the gladiators, having listened intently as to what they could expect in the Trench and how they would need to act to have any chance of avoiding the many threats this unique environment presented. Yet only now were they beginning to understand the severity of their circumstances.

All of the gladiators looked up when they heard the sharp

shriek from an animal that glided in the air just a few hundred feet above them, its large wings twice as wide as a man was tall. Farther off in the distance they identified several similar shapes soaring through the sky, the animals spending most of their time circling the many stone monoliths that populated the floor of the Trench.

"Wyverns," said Rafia, who now stood next to Declan.

Her smile as she followed the animals through the air suggested a childlike wonder at observing something that she had always wanted to see but never believed she would get the chance to observe. The winged, serpentlike creatures were similar in appearance to dragons with their broad, leathery wings, long snouts with mouths filled with daggerlike teeth, and barbed tails that whipped about with amazing speed, the only difference besides their smaller size being the fact that the animals only had two legs compared to their larger cousins like the black dragons that were said to populate the Trench.

"They are fierce predators with a rapacious hunger, and they have little to fear in the Trench, so be wary of them at all times," continued Rafia. "Much like Ghoules, they will not wait for you to die before they begin to feed on you."

"That last part wasn't very helpful," murmured Declan.

"Perhaps not," admitted Rafia. "Still, they need to know. We don't want any surprises. Not here."

Declan grunted noncommittally, joining the gladiators as they watched in awe as a wyvern circling above them shrieked a warning, then tipped its right wing. The animal pulled both pinions in tight to its sinuous body and shot toward the ground. At the very last second, the wyvern flicked open its wings to stop its descent, its clawed feet latching onto the top of a large boulder that sat only a few hundred yards to their right.

The wyvern stared at them for several seconds, then shrieked a challenge. In that moment, the wyvern appeared to be the dominant predator in the Trench.

Unfortunately for the animal, which never had a chance to complete its cry, in a blur of motion an even larger shape burst from the cave in the base of the cliff, clamping its large jaws around the wyvern, cutting off its challenge and replacing the shriek with a crunch of bones.

The black streak then slipped right back into its lair, silence once again falling within the Trench, only interrupted by the several gasps that escaped from a few of the gladiators. The attack had taken no more than a few seconds, and it had left the Company of Blood stunned by its speed and ferocity.

"I guess I spoke too soon," murmured Rafia.

"What was that?" asked Aislinn in a whisper.

"Black dragon," replied Bryen with an almost infuriating calm. "That one was faster than the one I fought in the Pit."

"Could you have beaten it?" asked Davin, his eyes still locked on the cave from which the black dragon had emerged and that in his opinion was much too close to where they were standing.

"I don't think that I'd want to find out. That beast also was larger than the one I fought on the white sand. Much larger."

"You're not filling me with confidence," said Davin.

"I'm not trying to," replied Bryen. "I'm just trying to be ..."

"Honest," finished Aislinn testily, not amused by Bryen's need to tell the truth at a time like this when the confidence of Davin and many of those around them had fallen off a cliff. She was also slightly irritated by his habit, in part because of the shock of the black dragon's attack. "We know. In this moment, a little white lie wouldn't have hurt. None of us want to contemplate coming face to face with monsters we have no chance of defeating."

Before Bryen could offer his apologies for a response that some could have perceived as indifferent, maybe even cold, Declan continued with his instructions.

"As you just saw, we have threats all around us. Wyverns

above us, black dragons hiding in the caves. The only way to know if those beasts are in their lairs is to enter them, and that's something we're going to avoid like the plague." The Sergeant of the Blood Company's comment gained a chuckle from the soldiers standing in front of him, which was what he wanted. He was just as nervous as they were, although he had no intention of showing it. "Remember the primary rule given to us by Magus Rafia. Stay on this path."

When the Company had walked out from the tunnel, they found themselves standing on a beaten-down dirt road that was a hundred yards across. It wound its way around the spires and off to the north. Large rocks on each side marked its boundaries.

"It was created by the Ten Magii and Magus Rafia says that it is still protected by their power," Declan continued. "So long as we stay on the path, the wyverns and the black dragons and whatever else might be lurking in the Trench can't get to us. We are safe."

"There are creatures here worse than wyverns and black dragons?" interrupted Tehana.

"Possibly," replied Rafia in a calm, gentle voice. "Although I believe they've died out by now. Regardless, I only know so much about the Trench since much has been lost since Magii last set foot in this place. Just remember, you have nothing to fear so long as you stay on the path."

"That was uplifting," mumbled Sirius, Rafia's elbow to his ribs preventing him from adding anything else to the discussion.

"Understood?" Declan asked, ignoring the old Magus, his unyielding gaze sweeping over his gladiators. They were a hard and stoic lot, having seen more blood and death on the white sand than likely any other soldier in Caledonia. Fighting Ghoules and Elders didn't bother them. Coming up against a nest of bloodsnakes didn't faze them. This, though, with the black dragons and wyverns and who knew what else might be hiding in this strange land, was a bit unsettling, in part because the level of difficulty appeared to be increasing the closer they got to their final destination. He understood that, just as they did, and he could see the stress in their expressions and their stances. Still, he had no doubt that they would do all that was asked of them. "Any questions?"

"Is it too late to go home?" asked Asaia, the barbed whip that she preferred held loosely in her right hand. Her question brought a welcome laugh from all of the gladiators.

"We are a free company, Asaia," replied Declan. "You may leave any time you like. Just remember, you'll have to go back the way you came, so if you see the Ghoule Overlord as you make your way back through the tunnel, give him my regards and let him know that the next time we meet he can expect a gift from me."

That gained another, louder laugh from the assembled gladiators.

"What would that be?" asked Jenus.

"A foot of steel in his chest."

Declan's bravado brought a roar of approval and even a few cheers from the Company, giving the gladiators a much-needed burst of confidence, some of their anxiety and worry at their strange surroundings slipping away from them as they finally began to relax.

"No more questions?" asked Declan, who glanced around perfunctorily. "Good. Stick to the path. Do not wander. If you stray, you're dead, simple as that. Eyes to the side, eyes to the front and back, eyes to the sky. This is not Caledonia. This is another world. We shouldn't be here, but we are, and we will do what needs to be done."

Declan's gaze traveled over his gladiators one more time, the Sergeant even breaking out into a small smile. He was proud of these fighters for so many reasons. Perhaps the one that stood out now was the fact that no matter the circumstances they faced, they were never rattled. Any new challenge placed before them was simply another obstacle to be overcome.

"You're here because you chose to be here, but you're also here because no one else can do what you can do. Now let's get moving," Declan ordered. "Column of four. Scouts a hundred yards ahead and behind. And stay on the path!"

10

— — — — —

UNMOVABLE OBSTACLE

U pon escaping the bloodsnakes, the Ghoules' renewed pursuit of the humans had gained a uniquely frantic urgency, even after several of their number fell victim to the traps the Magii had set farther down the tunnel.

In their haste to catch their quarry, their ravenous hunger combined with their fear of their Master driving them forward, two Ghoules unknowingly ran through an almost invisible barrier made of thin, razor-sharp strands of energy that connected the ceiling to the floor and sliced through flesh and bone with equal ease. A few more of the beasts were impaled by streams of energy that shot out from the walls when they tried to pass by, leaving behind nothing but smoking corpses.

Frustrated by his Ghoules' pace, even though they were proceeding through the tunnel faster than they had been when they first entered, the Ghoule Overlord took the lead, his use of the Curse too much for the snares still hidden along the corridor. Once their Master swept the path clear of the deadly traps that remained, the Ghoules sprinted down the tunnel with an almost wild abandon, sensing that they were gaining on their prey.

Nevertheless, the Ghoules' chase was disjointed at best. Even with their Master removing the threat presented by the Talent, the beasts had to slow down much too frequently because of the many natural obstacles created by the passage of time.

The Ghoules had enjoyed a free run through the tunnel for several leagues, the Ghoule Overlord letting them go, knowing the way was clear. Yet that came to an abrupt end, the beasts massing in the tunnel, uncertain of what to do next. A freezing cold had swept down the tunnel from the west, chilling their blood and frosting their harsh breaths.

"Why have you stopped, you fools?" demanded Gurzen. "The more time we waste, the more time the humans have to escape us."

The Elder Ghoule standing at the front of the gathering beasts didn't bother to respond to the scout's admonition, instead raising a clawed hand and pointing farther down the passageway. At the very edges of the light projected by the Dark Magic that spun off the top of the beast's twisted staff stood a lone human, twin swords grasped in his hands, a flail hanging from his belt.

A primal warning flashed through the back of Gurzen's brain. He wanted to turn and run from this man. To escape, understanding that to attack this human meant his death.

But he didn't understand why he was so afraid, and he couldn't flee, not with his Master following so closely behind him. Though this man terrified him, he was more frightened of the Ghoule Overlord.

"You stopped for this?" demanded Gurzen. He wanted his words to be strong, commanding. They weren't. They came out in a shaky voice, every other syllable catching in his throat. "For one human?" The Ghoule scout tried to grunt in disbelief at the timidness of his brethren. Instead, the fear that surged through him escaped in a strangled gasp. The man blocking the path radiated the promise of a horrible death. "Not only are you fools, you are also cowards." But he knew in his heart that he was no different than the Ghoules who milled about behind him, just as afraid as they were.

Realizing that if he wanted to remain within the Ghoule Overlord's good graces, despite the feeling of dread that washed over him, Gurzen took a few tentative steps toward the human who blocked their path. He held his spear tightly in his clawed hands, the point of the weapon shaking ever so slightly in response to his jittery nerves. He breathed a silent wheeze of relief when a strong, raspy voice stopped him in his tracks.

"I appreciate your bravery, Gurzen," said the Ghoule Overlord, the Ghoules blocking the tunnel stepping out of the way so that their Master could pass unimpeded. "But I will speak with this human first. He is not what he seems."

After all the remonstrations that he and his Ghoules needed to move faster, that they needed to ignore all the dangers thrown in their way by the Magii and focus on catching the Seventh Stone no matter the number of lives lost, Gurzen didn't understand why the Ghoule Overlord spoke so patiently and seemed so curious about the man who stood calmly before them.

Even so, he knew better than to question his Master's decisions, and secretly he was thankful. Because he didn't think that he had it in him to take one more step. Bowing his head, Gurzen drew his spear to the side and backed against the wall, the Ghoule Overlord striding toward the human, his head tilting to the right as he studied the clearly unafraid somewhat amused obstacle blocking his path.

"You used to be human, but you are not human anymore," said the Ghoule Overlord, struggling to get out some of the words as he spoke the common tongue. "You are not what you appear to be."

"Neither are you," the human replied with a knowing grin.

The man's comment stopped the Ghoule Overlord short. Intrigued, he studied the man with greater intensity, his eyes widening as he caught the faint aura of white that framed his shape.

"You should be dead, Protector," said the Ghoule Overlord, having taken note of the silver collar around his neck. "That explains much."

"I should be dead," agreed the man who appeared to be completely at peace with the fact that he stood in front of the most powerful practitioner of Dark Magic on the continent, more than a hundred Ghoules standing at his back. "Circumstances rarely turn out as you would expect."

"I can help you with that," said the Ghoule Overlord. "I can help you on your way."

"That's kind of you to offer," said the Protector with a small smile that never reached his cold, piercing eyes. "But I'll wait a while longer. I made a promise that I intend to keep." Then the Protector's smile grew bigger, the man chuckling softly.

"Why are you laughing?"

"Because I can sense your frustration," replied the Protector. "It's rolling off you in waves."

"My frustrations will come to an end shortly. I promise you that."

"Once you take the Protector who is the Seventh Stone."

"Yes."

"You're making a mistake," said the Protector, shaking his head almost in disappointment. "You think that you know what you're doing, but you don't. You think that you're all powerful, but you're not. Your greed and desire are blinding you."

"I doubt that, human. You are in no position to judge me." The Ghoule Overlord gestured with his staff of black ash toward the Protector. "Now you only seek to delay. You are trying to help the thief who stole what belongs to me."

The Protector ignored the Ghoule Overlord's accusations.

He had fought the Master of the Curse and his beasts a thousand years before, and now he had come full circle. It was only appropriate that his time in the Natural World was to come to an end in this way. In a manner that he preferred, performing one more service for an honorable young man forced to the same path as he was.

"You are making a mistake. The Protector you pursue is stronger than you think. You believe that you'll be able to take the Seventh Stone from him with ease. But he is not an easy kill. You know this. You know what it will take to kill him, and you wonder if you can actually do it." The spectral Protector shook his head, his merriment clear in his eyes, which sparkled with delight. "You can't kill him. You know that but are unwilling to admit it to yourself. You are lacking. You are weak."

The Ghoule Overlord stared at the Protector, his black eyes blazing with rage. Then he growled in anger. "You can try to sow doubt. It will not work. You misinterpret the situation. I am the source of Dark Magic in the Lost Land. I am the Curse. The Seventh Stone cannot challenge me."

"In Dark Magic, no, the Protector cannot challenge you. But he can kill you, and he will. Of that you can be certain. The Protector will make use of the Seventh Stone, and he will destroy you."

The Ghoule Overlord roared in anger, not used to being challenged in this way. "You dare to threaten me! You know nothing of what you speak!"

"I know the truth," replied the Protector, relishing how easily he had infuriated the Ghoule Overlord. "The Protector who has become the Seventh Stone will kill you. I promise you that."

"And I will kill you!" roared the Ghoule Overlord.

The Master of the Lost Land issued a series of harsh guttural commands that jolted a handful of Ghoules into action, the terror that had held the beasts in place nothing compared to their fear of their Master, the beasts sprinting past him intent on eliminating the human.

Within seconds, two of the Ghoules lay dead, their midsections sliced open and their guts spilling out onto the path. Then another of the Ghoules was down, stabbed through the neck before he even had a chance to lunge at the man. Only two of the Ghoules who had rushed forward remained, and the Ghoule Overlord realized that they stood little chance against this Protector.

He understood with a cold and unnerving certainty that he could send as many of his Ghoules at the Protector as he cared to, but he would only be sending them to their deaths. The Ghoule Overlord could not overwhelm this Protector with his greater numbers. This Protector had become something else during his time defending this passageway, something more, something that only he could manage on his own.

The man was too good with a blade, and the power of the Ten Magii that had kept the Protector on task for so long aided the man in this fight, giving him a sharpness, speed, and strength against which his Ghoules stood no chance. When another of his Ghoules fell with his throat neatly cut, just one Ghoule now opposing the Protector, the Ghoule Overlord concluded that he had no choice but to take a direct role in this fight.

Even so, he needed to do so carefully, because he realized that with the magic of the Ten Magii running through the veins of this Protector, hard though it may be for him to believe, he could meet the same fate as his Ghoules. This Protector had the capacity to kill him. So as the last Ghoule fought desperately to avoid the twin blades that wove a web of steel in front of the Protector and still sliced into the beast more than a dozen times before the creature fell to the floor, the Ghoule Overlord struck with the Curse.

Wispy threads of black shot from the black diamond and

gently wrapped themselves around the Protector, the man not noticing as he focused his attention on the Ghoule he fought. When the Ghoule collapsed, his life bleeding out onto the stone, those barely perceptible threads of evil roughly tightened their grip.

The Protector tried to resist but he did not have the power to fight the Dark Magic if he couldn't bring his weapons to bear. In just seconds, it was done. The Protector remained standing in the middle of the tunnel, swords still in his grasp but his arms pressed to his sides, strands of Dark Magic preventing him from raising his blades. The only part of his body that the Protector could move was his head, and with that he gave the Ghoule Overlord a sarcastic nod.

"This proves it," said the man who had defied the Ghoule Overlord. "You can't kill me, and you don't have what it takes to defeat the Protector. He will kill you."

The Ghoule Overlord growled in fury. Rather than release the rage that immediately shot through him because of the taunt, instead he walked by the bound Protector and urged Gurzen and the other Ghoules to follow, none of the beasts bothering with the human as they ran past him on both sides.

Patience and restraint. The Protector hadn't expected either from the Ghoule Overlord.

Once the Ghoules were gone, the Protector took a deep breath and smiled. He had done his duty, and he had kept his promise to the young man who had bested him. He could pass on now and do so with honor.

"Good speed, Protector," murmured the spectral warrior who had served the Ten Magii for more than a thousand years. Bowing his head, the man began to fade away, the bonds of Dark Magic slipping from him as his flesh turned into a white mist that hung in the air for just a few seconds before it was lost in the dark of the tunnel.

11

STRAYING FROM THE PATH

"Stay on the path," reminded Rafia as she walked next to Declan in the center of the formation. "Do not stray!"

The Magus' constant refrain was the only sound to be heard in the Trench but for the shrieks of the wyverns that tracked them from above. The animals stayed well clear of the protected lane upon which the gladiators strode. Still, the natural curiosity of the creatures won out as to the trespassers below. More of the flying beasts launched themselves from their nests to examine, though from a distance, the Company of Blood as the gladiators wove their way around the stone monoliths, the towering stacks placed more closely together, some no more than a few hundred yards distant from the next, the farther they advanced toward the north and their ultimate goal.

All of the monoliths looked the same, shooting into the air to be lost in the clouds that blanketed the Trench, the haze barely moving at the infrequent touch of the wind, never dissipating, the monotony of the landscape making it hard to judge the distance traveled. That's why Sirius' use of the Talent to calculate their position in relation to the Sanctuary was so important. Despite many of the gladiators losing track of time, the Master of the Magii confirmed that they were making good progress and were halfway to their objective.

Davin and Lycia walked at the point of the formation, a few dozen yards ahead of the column, the Protector not too far behind them. Although Bryen appeared relaxed as he rested the haft of the Spear of the Magii on his shoulder, his gaze roved from side to side, up into the air, and then back down, never staying on one spot for more than a second. Inevitably, the caves peppering the base of the cliffs that formed the Trench as well as the rocky monoliths drew his eyes the longest.

Even though Rafia promised that they would be safe on the path constructed by the Ten Magii, Bryen couldn't ignore his natural instincts and the warnings of danger that continually tingled the stem of his brain whenever he stared into the murk of the black dragons' lairs. Because the spires were more tightly packed in this part of the Trench, the trail unavoidably brought them very close to some of the menacing almost sinister hollows. He didn't like that in the least, but it couldn't be avoided.

Each time they passed one of the jagged gashes in the stone, he tried to penetrate the pitch-black with his sharp eyes. It was a hopeless task. The interminable cloud covering lent everything in this forbidding land a grey cast, the shadows blending into the natural gloom of the caverns so that there was no way to discern what might lie in wait for them were they to wander off the path.

Nothing issued forth from the caves, neither sound nor movement. Nothing to suggest that any of the beasts were there or ever had been, not even the bleached bones of any prey scattered about the entrance. There was nothing but an impenetrable darkness.

Still, Bryen didn't doubt that the animals were there, not after observing the display put on by the first black dragon they had seen as soon as they had entered the Trench. The grotto from which that beast emerged in the blink of an eye was just like all the ones he stared at now.

He couldn't see the animals, but he could sense them with the Talent. Watching. Waiting. Ready to attack if there was an opportunity to do so.

Lycia's words brought Bryen back from his dark thoughts, and though her question registered in his mind, his eyes never shifted toward her, instead continuing to scan around them for anything that might be a threat beyond the wyverns that were more than happy to make their presence known and the black dragons that preferred not to.

"Tell me more of what it was like in the Southern Marches. What it was like serving as a Protector."

"We had this discussion before, Lycia," replied Bryen, clearly not in the mood for this conversation, his focus on more dangerous and immediate concerns.

"You told us some of what you had to deal with, but not all."

"Why do you need to know everything?" asked Bryen. "Maybe I didn't tell you all that happened for a reason."

"I'm just curious," replied Lycia, ignoring the testiness in her friend's voice, unwilling to share what was really on her mind. What she really wanted to talk about with him. At least not yet. "Besides, it will help to pass the time."

"Just one question," Bryen grunted, only willing to humor her for so long.

"What was the worst part of being in the Southern March-es?" asked Lycia, taking almost a minute to consider what to ask and angry with herself for not picking the issue she really wanted to raise, her courage escaping her at the last second. "Other than not spending time with me, of course."

Lycia's remark at the end actually made Bryen smile despite his mounting concerns. Still, that didn't prevent him from trying to turn the focus toward her.

"It couldn't have been worse than what you, Davin, and the others were dealing with in the Pit. You were fighting for your lives every few days, your conditions worsening. Little time to prepare. No time to heal. What was that like?"

"Stop trying to change the subject and answer the question," commanded Lycia.

"The worst part," mused Bryen, disappointed that he hadn't been able to divert her, although not surprised. When Lycia wanted something, she rarely let go until she obtained it. So his mind worked on the question while his eyes fixed on a cave in the base of the spire that they were fast approaching. He noticed that the curl of the trail would bring them less than one hundred feet from the shadowy entrance, the closest yet to one of the black dragon's nests. Even more concerning, this grotto was larger than any of the others that they had passed. He hoped that Rafia's confidence in the power of the Ten Magii was justified, because he'd hate to come up against what might emerge from this cave. "Not seeing you and Davin. Not seeing Declan. Not knowing if you and the others were alive or dead. Not knowing if I would see my friends again."

Bryen glanced at Lycia briefly when he said the last, giving her a nod and a smile before his eyes returned to the cave that grew larger with every step they took, the wyverns constant, often irritating shrieks pushed to the back of his mind. A quick search with the Talent confirmed it for him. He was right. The black dragon lurking in that cave was a monster.

"So you thought of me while you were away," Lycia said, slowing down so that she was walking next to him, giving him a gentle punch in his arm.

"Every day."

His confirmation brought a rare smile to Lycia's face. Pleased with her initial success, she decided to push a bit more and see what other pieces of information she could extract from her usually reticent friend. "So tell me about the Talent. How does it work?"

"More questions, Lycia? I said just one."

"Come on, Bryen. We can talk and stay vigilant at the same time. You don't have to be so single-minded."

"It's who I am," Bryen murmured in his defense. "You know that."

"It's who you are because you allow it to be who you are," challenged Lycia. "We talked about this in the Colosseum. Remember?"

"It's something I won't forget," said Bryen with a faint smile, though his eyes continued to sweep to both sides and then above them before starting the pattern once again. "You made quite a forceful argument."

"And wasn't I right?" demanded Lycia. "Focusing so much on one thing at the expense of everything else can be a detriment."

"Yes, you were right. I can't deny it." His thoughts drifted briefly to some of the happier moments between him and Lycia that had made their servitude in the Colosseum more bearable.

"Then you can spare a few minutes to tell me how the Talent works. Rafia and Sirius have told us how it can be used, we've seen it with our own eyes, but they've never explained how the power you control really functions."

"I don't really know how it works," said Bryen. "I just know that the power is there."

He didn't think that offering specific details would help Lycia understand. Rather, he expected that any attempt to touch on the particulars of the Talent might only complicate the explanation he offered, as only someone who could use the Talent would have any chance of understanding the intricacies of its application. So he settled for giving her a more general description instead.

"The best way to describe it is that since I'm a Magus, I can sense the natural magic of the world. It's an energy. It's all around us, always within reach. Everyone in the world can touch it to a greater or lesser degree and does, although most usually don't know when they're doing it and even when they do they can do nothing about it. For whatever reason I and a few others have the capacity to connect with and use this power in a way that most others can't. Think of the Talent as a huge river of power that I can sense. It's always there, always visible out of the corner of my eye. My ability to use the Talent allows me to tap into that river and do things that most other people can't."

"Sirius and Rafia have been teaching you how to do this, Lady Winborne as well," said Lycia, although mentioning the Lady of the Southern Marches left a sour taste in her mouth. She no longer hated the woman for what her father had done to Bryen, though she couldn't say that she liked her. She doubted that she ever would after all that had happened between her and Bryen.

"Yes, they were, although not as much lately. There hasn't been much time since we left Tintagel."

"Why do those two Magii look as though they're afraid of you? As if they don't trust you?"

Bryen took a moment to collect his thoughts before responding, not wanting Lycia to confront the two Magii if he told her the truth. Because there were some things that Lycia was better off not knowing. Better for him as well.

"Actually they're just afraid for me," Bryen said with a tight laugh. "In short, they're concerned about what I might do."

"How so?"

"Because the Seventh Stone allows me to harness even more of the Talent than I could otherwise."

"And that's a problem because ..."

"That, in itself, is not a problem. As you know, they seem to think that my becoming the Seventh Stone will give me a better chance of rebuilding the Weir. The problem lies in the fact that the Seventh Stone contains both the Talent and the Curse, and it gives the person who can use the Seventh Stone the ability to manipulate both of those distinct energies."

Lycia nodded as her mind worked through what her friend had just said, her expression suggesting that it hadn't taken her long to conclude what that really meant.

"They're afraid of what might happen if you're touched by the Curse."

"That's it exactly." Bryen nodded sadly. "Based on the expressions they give me from time to time, and from what happened to the Ten Magii when they built the Weir, it seems that Sirius and Rafia believe that my touching the Curse is essentially a foregone conclusion. That's what they're worried about."

The Spear of the Magii gave him the ability to protect himself more effectively from the Dark Magic that was locked away within him courtesy of the Seventh Stone. Still, just like Sirius and Rafia, he worried about what might occur if he made a mistake. He didn't have the benefit of centuries of training like they did, having less than a year under his belt in working with the Talent. So the possibility of doing something that could prove fatal, for him and those around him, was always in the forefront of his thoughts.

He had done his best to learn how to never allow the Curse to corrupt him, yet who was to say what might happen when he reached the Sanctuary and tried to repair the Weir. Considering the tremendous magnitude of power that went into the construction of that magical barrier, it was only logical that his chances of becoming tainted by the Curse were exponentially greater when he attempted to do what was required of him. If the Ten Magii couldn't do what they did without falling victim to the Dark Magic of the Ghoules, why should he assume that he could somehow escape the same fate?

It was then that the whispers that were always in the back of his mind pushed to the fore. He understood the two Magii's concern. It only made sense based on what had happened before. But did that worry really apply to him?

He was the Seventh Stone. Could he not do what was necessary with the Curse without having to fear the repercussions that had struck down the Ten Magii? After all, none of them had been the Seventh Stone. He wasn't being arrogant, just realistic. Or so he believed. The Seventh Stone had never joined with anyone before, so he was different, wasn't he? The whispers seemed to agree with his thinking.

"And if you do touch the Curse ..."

"They'll kill me," Bryen replied, needing to lock away the whispers that were growing in strength before he could reply. His voice was calm, dispassionate. He was simply stating a fact, showing no emotion as Lycia pulled him back from the path his mind had been following. "They've said as much multiple times, wanting to make sure that I don't forget."

"I won't let them kill you," glowered Lycia, her voice hard, quiet.

"You might not have a choice. They believe that if I touch the Curse and I'm allowed to roam free, I could become a greater threat than the Ghoule Overlord."

"That's not what I mean," clarified Lycia, although the words that came next were painful for her to utter. "If you need to die, I'll do it myself. Quick. Painless."

"Thank you," Bryen replied softly, reaching out with a hand and grasping her forearm in gratitude. He understood just how significant what Lycia had just promised him was. "Let's just hope it doesn't come to that."

"Death doesn't choose us," began Lycia.

"We choose our death," Bryen said.

A curse mixed with fear and irritation from the western side of the formation ended the conversation between Bryen and Lycia and brought them running toward the sound. What they saw turned their blood cold.

The Blood Company was directly opposite the entrance to the cave that Bryen had been staring at so intently. Kollea, walking on the far edge of the track, had tripped on a rock that had sent her stumbling across and then sprawling to the rough ground of the canyon just beyond the protection of the path. Before she had even thought to push herself back up, a monstrous black dragon erupted from the grotto, tooth-filled jaws gaping, its clawed feet digging deeply into the stone and dirt as it propelled its sinuous body toward its prey at a blinding speed, its ear-splitting shriek sending all the wyverns perched on the sandstone pillar up into the air in confusion and fear.

With barely a thought, Bryen stepped off the trail and sprinted directly toward the black dragon, hoping to distract the beast. Lycia followed Bryen, both her swords drawn from their sheaths. She placed herself in front of Kollea as a last defense, the gladiator badly twisting her ankle when she fell and struggling to drag herself back to the trail.

"Bryen!" shouted Lycia.

He ignored her, continuing his charge. He needed to get the animal to focus on him instead of Kollea.

Dorlan and several other gladiators were about to step off the trail and assist the Volkun. Sirius' powerful voice kept them in place.

"Hold!" he roared. "Do not leave this trail! You will only bring more of the beasts down upon us."

Then the old Magus ignored his own instructions, trotting up to Kollea. "Can you walk?"

"I don't think so," she replied, pain etched across her face, her fingers and palms scratched as she scrabbled across the floor of the gorge.

"Lycia," called Sirius.

"If you can help Kollea, I can try to help Bryen," said the Crimson Devil, ready to charge off after the Volkun once the injured gladiator was safe.

"You can't help Bryen," Sirius said sharply.

"I have to at least try." She knew that if she went after Bryen, it likely meant her own death. Even so that realization didn't faze her. She couldn't allow Bryen to battle the monster on his own.

"I will help Bryen," replied Sirius sternly. "To do that, I need you to get Kollea back on the path."

Cursing under her breath for not being able to do what she wanted to do, which seemed to be a regular occurrence that morning, Lycia sheathed her swords and ran back to where Sirius kneeled next to Kollea. Reaching down, she lifted the injured gladiator off the ground and helped her to hobble back toward the path, which thankfully was only a dozen feet distant.

That problem solved, Sirius turned back toward the trail. "Stay there," he ordered, sensing that more gladiators from the Blood Company chafed at his command and wanted to rush off and aid their Captain. Both Rafia and Declan nodded that he had nothing to fear in that regard.

The old Magus then focused his full attention on the much larger issue, in this case the massive dragon bearing down on Bryen. He watched in admiration as Bryen slid feet first through the dirt and loose rock, the Spear of the Magii alight with the Talent. Ducking under the snap of the black dragon's jaws, he dragged the sharp steel across the soft belly of the beast.

The towering animal reared up in rage, the spread of its huge wings putting the Blood Company in an unnatural darkness as the monstrous beast roared and hissed, twisting around as fast as it could, trying to impale Bryen with its sharp claws.

The black dragon screamed in fury again, missing its prey.

Bryen was too fast. More important, he implemented what he had learned when fighting the black dragon in the Pit. Constant movement was essential. If you stood still, you were dead.

So he spun and wove around the black dragon's claws and spiked tail, staying as much as possible to the beast's sides or even beneath its belly and in among its legs, wanting to avoid the animal's tooth-filled maw. Dodging this way and that, wherever he moved the Spear of the Magii followed as he used his double-bladed weapon to slice with a practiced efficiency across the dragon's belly, chest, legs, and wings, opening more than a dozen painful wounds in just as many seconds.

Sirius could only shake his head in awe as Bryen danced away from the black dragon's rapid-fire and fruitless attacks with an unmatched grace that the old Magus had never thought was humanly possible. This was what the Volkun must have looked like when he fought on the white sand, so fast and so focused that he defeated his opponents with an almost soulless precision.

The Magus was certain that Bryen could defeat this black dragon. Instead, he was worried more about the half dozen other monsters that burst from their lairs beneath the towering stone monolith, drawn by the black dragon's cries.

"Bryen, behind you!" shouted Sirius.

It took a moment for Bryen to glance at the caves at his back as he worked to avoid the black dragon's many attempts to skewer him with its three-foot-long claws. When he finally did, he realized that he needed to move. Right that instant.

One black dragon he could manage. Six were another matter altogether.

With a final slash of the Spear of the Magii across the back of one of the black dragon's rear legs that cut through muscle and tendon to the bone, Bryen spun around and sprinted back toward the trail. Sirius urged him on, throwing up a gleaming white barrier of the Talent right behind him that prevented the fastest of the pursuing black dragons from running the Protector down, the beast slamming into the shimmering wall with a teeth-shattering smack that left the animal dazed and even angrier.

Bryen didn't bother to look behind him until he and Sirius were safely back on the path and they could both breathe a little easier.

Bryen's last strike had maimed the massive black dragon, the huge beast falling to the rocky ground, its injured leg useless, the many other wounds scattered across its body sapping its strength. The half dozen other black dragons had, at first, thought to go after the smaller, easier prey, as demonstrated by the one beast that had almost caught up to Bryen.

Seeing their primary quarry escape back to the trail, the black dragons turned toward the prey that was now available to them. The scent of their wounded brethren's blood touching their nostrils incited a hunger and bloodlust that would have shamed the Ghoules.

The black dragons fell on the badly injured animal with a stomach-churning savagery, their powerful jaws biting into its warm belly, the beast shrieking in pain, unable to defend itself. What happened next resembled the feeding frenzy of sharks finding the carcass of a dead whale in the ocean, the black dragons tearing into the dying animal's flesh, snapping bones with their frighteningly long and sharp teeth, fighting over every last scrap of meat. In only a few minutes it was over, most of the black dragon's carcass gone but for a few long strings of flesh that were left hanging from its blood-smeared bones, many of those bones cracked or broken in multiple places.

Yet even then the black dragons weren't satiated. They stared hungrily at the gladiators who stood unmoving on the trail, both from an immobilizing terror and Declan's sharp commands for them to remain in place. Many of the gladiators didn't breathe again until the black dragons finally turned away, the beasts knowing that they had no chance of taking this smaller prey so long as they remained where they were.

"I think that's enough excitement for one day," said Rafia sternly, jolting the soldiers of the Blood Company from their dark and frightening thoughts. "Aislinn, please see to Kollea's injury. Bryen, we will talk later."

Bryen grimaced as he caught the Magus' harsh look, already knowing the substance of that conversation and how it was going to play out.

"Now stay on the path," Rafia repeated sternly. "We must keep moving. The Ghoules have entered the Trench."

12

NEW ALLIES

"**B**lood Company, form square on me!"

Declan's order echoed off the sides of the Trench, the gladiators responding to his command without even thinking, their intensive training pushing them into motion. Shield bearers took their positions at the front of the formation and locked their scuta together. Spears were right behind, ready to extend their weapons over the shoulders of their comrades. Behind them were soldiers with their swords drawn, charged with closing any gaps that appeared, and then finally the dozen archers who could rain down death on their enemies from a distance.

"How much farther do we have to go to reach the Sanctuary?" Declan asked Rafia, the Magus standing right next to him, having been at his side ever since they entered the Trench, a fact that didn't bother him in the least.

The Blood Company had made good time since they had left the tunnel, and the Master of the Gladiators knew that they were close to their objective. But his gladiators were tired, the escape across the Breakwater Plateau, their defense of Haven, and now their race through the underground passageway that had taken them from the island to the Trench wearing them down.

Despite the dire nature of their circumstances, he believed that they needed to rest, if only for a short time. With that in mind, Declan had called a halt upon learning from Aislinn that the Ghoules were only two leagues behind them. The Ghoules were too fast for them to think that they could continue to make a run for it. Now they'd have to fight their way to the Sanctuary.

Declan cursed softly, disappointed though not surprised that they didn't reach their objective before the Ghoules caught them. Just a little farther to the north, he could see the shimmering energy of the Weir shooting up into the sky, the expected grey of the barrier intermittently flashing white and black for a few seconds before returning to its primary color. Still, it was difficult to get an exact sense of how far they had to go to reach the Sanctuary because of the twisting nature of their path, which continued to weave around the sandstone pillars that soared above them.

"A league," Rafia replied in frustration, just as irritated as he was that they were coming up just short of their goal. "Maybe a little bit more than that. No more."

"So close," murmured Declan, "I thought that we would make it."

"So did I," replied Rafia with a disappointed shake of her head, "and perhaps we will. To do that, though, we'll need to deal with these beasts first."

Racing toward the Blood Company while sticking to the path came more than one hundred Ghoules, the creatures howling and snarling as they rushed toward the prey that had escaped them for much too long. Spears leveled. Eyes intent. Hungry for the soft flesh and delicious blood of the humans.

"With pleasure," Declan replied in a growl, his eyes blazing ferociously. "I'm tired of running. It's time to fight."

"Jenus, close that gap!" shouted Declan, yelling at the top of his lungs so that the gladiator heard his command over the din of the battle.

The gladiator responded immediately, stepping into the hole that had opened in the shield wall and right over the unfortunate gladiator who had collapsed to the rocky ground thanks to a Ghoule's claw ripping out his throat.

Davin and Lycia rushed forward to help Jenus, giving him time to set himself next to Dorlan and Majdi, Davin's spear darting forward and Lycia's twin blades cutting and slashing, helping to push back the Ghoules at least for the few seconds Jenus needed. That potential breakthrough closed, the twins worked their way around the square, jumping in and out of the fight with a wild abandon. Their efforts lifted the spirits of their fellow gladiators, giving them all a needed boost of energy, the deadly abilities of the Crimson Devil and the Crimson Giant helping to quell the Ghoules' never-ending assaults.

But those few moments of success were shorter than the gladiators would have liked, the beasts always surging back toward the Company's square no matter their losses, the beasts knowing that all they needed to attain the victory they craved was for one Ghoule to break the shield wall and get in among the humans. That would be the beginning of the end. Soon after that, the Ghoules would finally have the chance to feast while their Master reclaimed the Seventh Stone, and then the land of the soft humans would be open to them.

"Archers, release!" shouted Tarin, he and Jerad in the thick of the fighting, doing all that they could to hold back the attacking Ghoules.

The tightness of the Blood Company's formation aided the gladiators' efforts, many of the Ghoules getting in the way of one another when they attacked because of the lack of space and the need to stay on the trail. Still, that minor inconvenience didn't stop the beasts, who advanced with a savage brutality, some of the Ghoules so hungry that if they were lucky enough to kill a gladiator and then pull the body free from the melee they began feasting on it immediately, squabbles often erupting between the beasts as they sought to bite into their victims.

It was when the Ghoules were stationary and not darting about as was their wont that the steel-tipped arrows streaking through the air above the formation caused the most damage. A moving Ghoule was a difficult target to hit. When they were distracted the well-trained archers enjoyed a great deal of success, their barbed shafts slamming through the creatures' eyes, killing the beasts instantly. Nevertheless, those precise strikes were too few and too far between to hinder for long the Ghoules' deadly efforts.

That's why Rafia, Sirius, Aislinn, and Bryen remained in the center of the square, each responsible for defending a different point on the compass. They all wanted to use the Talent against the Ghoules to aid the gladiators in their desperate fight, knowing that if they did they could destroy the beasts.

It was a useless desire, nevertheless. They had no choice but to focus their efforts on the fifteen Elders who were situated around the square and sent shard after shard of Dark Magic toward the Company. The Magii were pushed to their very limit as they protected the gladiators against the Ghoule Overlord's insidious Curse.

Several times Bryen went on the offensive, infusing the twin blades of the Spear of the Magii with the Talent and sending spikes of energy toward the Elders. He didn't want the beasts to get too confident. His effort was rewarded in a few instances, as he killed two of the beasts who hadn't anticipated his attacks, the Talent charring them to a crisp. There were too many Elders, however, and after each of his brief victories he had to turn his attention back to protecting the men and women who were dying for him.

A handful of gladiators were already down and more were likely to follow if he couldn't extricate them from this battle, which in that difficult moment felt more like a wish than anything else. He doubted that the Ghoule Overlord would allow them to escape now that the Seventh Stone was almost within his grasp. That thought playing through his mind, Bryen glanced toward the towering beast every few minutes, the malice in his adversary's eyes strengthening Bryen's resolve.

The Ghoule Overlord could have joined the melee and possibly already concluded the fight himself. Instead, he stood behind his Elders on the center of the path, staring intently at Bryen. Apparently, the Master of the Curse didn't care about the other Magii or the gladiators or how many Elders or Ghoules died as they attacked the Company. The Ghoule Overlord only had eyes for him.

Bryen searched desperately for some solution to their increasingly bleak state of affairs as he continued to focus his attention on the Elders. The Ghoules had surrounded the Blood Company, so there was little opportunity for the gladiators to break away. Not with them restricted to the path.

As that worry consumed him, he crafted a dozen different shields that he placed in rapid succession in front of the gladiators fighting along his point of the compass to protect them against the attack of a Ghoule or an Elder, while also sending a few stray bolts toward the beasts when he could in an attempt to remind their attackers that there was still plenty of fight left in him.

Finally, his mind latched on to a specific part of the training that Declan had instilled within him so that he would have the best possible chance of surviving his time fighting on the white sand.

All too frequently, Declan liked to harp on how important it was to control the space in which you had to fight. It could be the Pit or it could be the trail that led through the Trench. It didn't matter.

The environment itself was important but not overly so. You could fight in any environment. What was exceedingly relevant was doing everything that you could to control your environment. And if you couldn't do that, whether because the enemy wouldn't permit it or for some other reason, then you needed to change the parameters of the fight within that environment.

It was risky, but what choice did he have? He wasn't certain that he could control what was going to happen if he did what he had in mind, but he was certain that the Ghoules wouldn't be able to either, and that might give him an advantage that he didn't have now.

With no other ideas popping into his consciousness, Bryen shot a stream of the Talent from the tips of his blades above the heads of the Elders and into the impenetrable cavern that was situated right in front of him, the power of his strike causing the monolith to shake as if it had been hit by an earthquake, a section of the grotto's entrance collapsing, a large pile of boulders crashing down from the pillar.

Bryen held his breath for several seconds, hoping that his action disturbed the black dragon that he sensed lurked within.

Bryen closed his eyes in frustration, the fighting having come to a stop as both man and beast were distracted by the explosion. He didn't achieve the result that he wanted. Once the cloud of dust and shattered stone settled, there was nothing to be seen but for the darkness of the now partially destroyed cave.

Cursing his luck and his incompetence, Bryen turned his attention back to the fight, the Ghoules pressing forward again, sensing that a breakthrough was imminent, the Elders urging them on as they continued to engage with Bryen and the other Magii. For several minutes more the battle raged, the Blood

Company refusing to give ground, standing strong against their enemies.

The Ghoules were close. The beasts knew it. So did Bryen and the gladiators. The shield wall was going to collapse.

Right before the inevitable breach occurred, surprisingly the Ghoules halted their attack and stepped back, putting some distance between them and the gladiators, the Elders doing the same.

It was in that moment that the Ghoule Overlord stepped forward, coming to a stop no more than twenty feet from the shield bearers, a black mist spinning lazily above the black diamond set in his twisted staff of ash.

THE WISPY MIST drifting from the black diamond thickened as the Ghoule Overlord stared at Bryen with an undisguised hatred that hinted at a ferocious craving that needed to be satiated. He ignored the humans arrayed around the Protector, the bodies of the dead gladiators, Ghoules, and Elders strewn across the trail beneath his notice. His eyes locked onto the Seventh Stone, onto the prize that he had hunted for so long that he needed so desperately.

As the silence dragged on, the tension increased. The Ghoules strained to remain still, their ravenous hunger and loathing flashing behind their black eyes. The gladiators watched with emotionless eyes, the black blood of the Ghoules dripping from their weapons.

Dorlan and the other fighters from the Pit understood that the odds were stacked against them. They didn't care. The odds had been stacked against them since they had started this journey. Now, they just wanted revenge for their many friends who had died at the claws of the Ghoules.

"You have proven to be a worthy opponent, Protector, but

the hunt is over," rasped the Ghoule Overlord, his words only intelligible to Bryen. "You will not reach the Sanctuary, and you have nowhere to go. It is time to accept your fate. It is time for you to submit to me."

"We've done well so far, escaping you and your beasts time and time again," Bryen replied in the Ghoule tongue, allowing the Seventh Stone and the Dark Magic within him to guide his words. "What makes you think that we won't get out of this as well? We've killed how many of your Ghoules and Elders since this chase began? Dozens? More than a hundred? I've lost track. And we slaughtered three of your Slayers. You may have us trapped here, but that doesn't mean that we will give up the fight. We are gladiators. We never surrender."

"I appreciate your confidence Protector, though now it borders on foolish arrogance," scoffed the Ghoule Overlord, pointing his long black staff toward Bryen. "Give yourself to me so this can finally come to an end. You have wasted more of my time than is necessary. My Legions are ready. It is time for them to conquer Caledonia as they did once before."

"And if I do surrender," asked Bryen, "what of my friends?"

The Ghoule Overlord chuckled, the sound coming out as a gravelly cough, the beast not surprised that the Protector would ask the question. The Protector was not a fool, so he already knew the answer. But the Ghoule Overlord appreciated his attempt to delay. He snorted at the humor of it all and broke out into a wicked laugh.

"Bryen, what are you saying?" asked Sirius in a whisper, his eyes never leaving the Ghoule Overlord and the beasts standing behind the Master of the Lost Land. "None of us can understand."

"He says that we have no hope of escaping," Bryen replied quickly. "He wants me to surrender."

"You can't."

"I won't," replied Bryen.

"How did you learn to speak the Ghoule language?" asked Sirius, his curiosity getting the better of him despite the grim nature of their situation. His thoughts traveled in a worrisome direction, wondering if the Dark Magic Bryen had locked within himself might have something to do with this strange ability.

"Later," whispered Bryen. "Now's not the time. Make sure everyone is ready."

"Ready for what?"

"Just pass the word. They'll know."

"My Ghoules will kill your friends quickly before they feed, because you have amused me, Protector," said the Ghoule Overlord, "and I will take the Magii myself. I will do it fast. There will be little pain. They will not suffer."

"That's quite an offer," Bryen replied.

"I can be merciful when it suits me, Protector."

"Thank you for that, but I think not."

"Are you certain, Protector? You have made my life more difficult than need be. If you do so now, I will inflict the greatest suffering I possibly can on you and your friends before I allow you to die. My Ghoules will feast on your friends before they pass on, and my Ghoules will feed slowly, so that the men and women foolish enough to stand with you now will come to understand the meaning of true terror. I will keep you alive so that you can watch. You will see all your friends killed and eaten by my Ghoules before I take the Seventh Stone from you."

"Declan," whispered Bryen.

"I can see from the glint in your eyes that you have something in mind," said the Master of the Gladiators, who had been issuing a series of commands to the Blood Company with hand signals. "What are you going to do, lad?"

"Destroy the path."

"Why are you going to destroy ..." Sirius began, but then he caught the movement behind the Ghoule Overlord near the base of the monolith after Declan gave him a nudge and a nod, redirecting the old Magus' focus.

"That's not wise," said Rafia, who had missed the exchange between Declan and Sirius. "We will be vulnerable to the creatures of the Trench."

"Do you have a better idea?" demanded Sirius. "Because I'm all out."

Before the two Magii could get into another argument, Declan interrupted. "He knows what he's doing. Make sure that you two and Aislinn are ready. Shield us as best as you can."

Before Rafia could reply, Bryen used the Spear of the Magii to latch onto the power the Ten Magii had used to create the path, the blades flaring brightly.

"We will die," said Bryen, directing his comment to the Ghoule Overlord. "But not by your hand. We will choose our own end."

In that same instant, Bryen opened himself to the energy of the Seventh Stone. There was a slight resistance to start, a reluctance to be employed in a new way. That opposition faded quickly, the Seventh Stone too insistent, too demanding, refusing to be denied, as it pulled on the power of the Ten Magii.

And then in just the blink of an eye it was done. With one final tug the Seventh Stone untied the knot, the magical construction crafted by the Ten Magii gone.

The power streamed into Bryen, causing him to stagger. He took a few seconds to adjust to the immense amount of natural magic that had just surged into him, reclaiming the balance between the Talent and the Dark Magic so essential to keeping him free from the Curse.

The power that was now added to his own was intoxicating, addicting, even frightening. And it was exactly what he needed.

His eyes now completely white, flashing brightly, he shifted his focus back to the Ghoule Overlord.

The Master of the Lost Land sensed that something had changed, both with the Protector and the world around him. Still, he wasn't certain what it was. He found out much to his horror just half a second later.

Bryen lifted his double-bladed spear toward the Ghoule Overlord and released a bolt of energy that shot just above the beast's head and slammed into the base of the monolith rising just behind them, the large cavern, already damaged by Bryen's previous effort to wake what waited within, becoming twice as wide as it had been. The immense power of the strike pulverized the massive boulders that had fallen from the entrance to the grotto and sent an explosion of rocks raining down on the Ghoules closest to the sandstone pillar.

Bryen didn't wait for the Ghoules to recover from the shock of the explosion, sending forth a second strike that erupted right in front of the Ghoule Overlord, showering him and his beasts with a tidal wave of splintered stone and dirt.

To make matters worse for the Ghoule Overlord, an ear-splitting roar reverberated throughout the Trench. A monstrous black dragon erupted from the damaged grotto in a blind rage and raced toward the creatures of the Lost Land. The Ghoules stood there, not bothering to move as the black dragon bore down on them, believing they had nothing to fear so long as they remained on the path.

The beasts didn't realize their mistake until the black dragon rushed right by the boundary stones and tore into them. The dragon crushed several of the beasts into the ground with its massive claws, catching several of the Ghoules in the chest or the midsection and flinging their broken and torn bodies several hundred yards away. The truly unlucky Ghoules were those the black dragon caught in its massive jaws, taking the beasts in a single bite.

Trying to bring order to the chaos and give the Ghoules a chance to fight back, the Elders called on their Dark Magic. They realized too late that they were too slow. The black dragon shouldered several of them aside before biting one of their number in half with its daggerlike teeth. The monstrous beast then swept clear the space around it with its spiked tail, spearing several Elders in the process and sending the rest of the Ghoules tumbling to the ground, many never to rise again.

If that wasn't enough, the situation only became worse for the Ghoules. Three more black dragons, all almost as large as the first, raced from the damaged cavern, their sharp claws digging into the rocky ground, their large tails swishing from side to side behind them and propelling them even faster toward the floundering Ghoules. Then another three of the deadly, unstoppable beasts sprinted out from the grotto, shrieking in rage, eyes fixed on the prey that had no chance of escaping them.

The Protector had forced into action not just one black dragon, but an entire nest. The Elders and the Ghoules fought for their lives, the black dragons speed and savagery frightening to behold, though something to be admired as well if you weren't the target. Because in that moment, the Blood Company was an afterthought.

"Blood Company!" roared Declan, only taking a quick glimpse at the carnage unfolding in front of him before shifting his focus back to their mission. "Form on the Volkun! Four columns. We head north! Double time!"

The gladiators instantly obeyed, positioning themselves around Bryen. Within seconds they had begun marching away from the fight, maneuvering around the monoliths as they made their way toward the Sanctuary at a fast clip, pleased to be leaving the Ghoules to the enraged and very hungry black dragons.

Although they had escaped the Ghoules, the gladiators had

no illusions regarding the massive challenge they now faced, the safety of the trail eliminated.

The wyverns that had tracked their passage sensed the change, the crackle of power that identified the energy that formed the shield gone, and were now becoming more than curious. The creatures were flying closer and closer to the gladiators, swooping down and turning away at the last second, still uncertain if the barricade truly had disappeared. When the beasts didn't crash into an invisible barrier, the braver wyverns came so close that their broad leathery wings scraped against the gladiators' shields, screeching in triumph when they discovered that what kept them from these intruders was no longer there.

The gladiators also noticed that several large shapes had begun to move within the shadows of the caves they passed. That could mean only one thing. More black dragons preparing to make an appearance, one of the monsters actually sticking its huge head out into the grey light, its eyes fixated on the Blood Company.

Recognizing that the level of danger was increasing steadily, Bryen syphoned some of the power that he had taken from the Ten Magii's creation and shared it with Sirius, Rafia, and Aislinn so that they could create a shield around the gladiators to protect them as they traversed the Trench. With a bright flash, the barrier took shape, Bryen making it shimmer brightly as a warning to the wyverns and black dragons that were now showing such an inordinate interest in them.

Even so, several wyverns still attacked from above, diving down in silent attacks, claws outstretched and aiming for the prey that ran through their hunting ground. Inevitably, the beasts slammed into the glowing barrier with a sickening crunch, their bodies broken and shattered, sliding off the rounded magical shield and coming to rest on the loose scrabble of the gorge, a tasty treat for the other residents of the Trench.

Several black dragons emerged from their lairs to snap up the dead wyverns, an easy meal to be savored. Then, rather than pursue the gladiators, having recognized that the beasts stood no chance of getting past what protected these intruders, most turned to the south and sped back the way the Company of Blood had come, drawn by the shrieks, hisses, and roars of the combatants and the ever growing stench of blood that drifted among the sandstone pillars.

13

BASE OF THE SPIRE

"That is going to be quite a haul," said Davin as he stared up the winding path that wrapped around the towering monolith, the gladiator trying but failing to pick out the top of the spire, the ever-present clouds that pressed down on the gorge hiding it from view.

The sandstone pillar resembled all the others that shot up out of the Trench, except for one distinct difference. This monstrous stone spire appeared to be taller than all the others and to support it the pillar's base was twice as wide. Those variations and its location within the Trench were the primary reasons why the Ten Magii had decided to build the Sanctuary atop its summit.

"Made even worse by the fact that the Ghoules will be pushing us up the ramp backwards while trying to kill us," said Lycia, his sister standing right next to him as she followed his gaze up into the grey murk.

"That just makes it all the more exciting," said Davin. "The last few weeks haven't given me enough of a challenge to sink my teeth into."

"You mean the fight against the Slayers on the Breakwater Plateau wasn't enough for you?" she asked.

"No, it was no different than a combat in the Pit."

"Nor our battle on Haven?"

"No. It didn't excite me. Almost mundane, in fact."

"Our escape through the tunnel?"

"No, not really."

"Even with the bloodsnakes?"

"I have to admit the bloodsnakes offered a bit of excitement," replied Davin with a grin. "But no, that was more Bryen's escapade than mine."

"You're either a fool or you have a death wish," Lycia said with a sad shake of her head.

"I don't have a death wish," Davin replied, finally turning his gaze back to his sister. "From what Magus Rafia says, Bryen has the death wish."

"You're probably right about that," agreed Lycia. "Then definitely a fool."

"I take issue with that statement," said Davin with a wry grin, "even though I may resemble a fool from time to time, the evidence is completely circumstantial."

The sparkle in his eye and Davin's self-deprecating humor made Lycia and the other gladiators standing around him laugh. Just as he wanted them to. The Crimson Giant had a very strange way of looking at the world. And after the last few hours fighting their way across the Trench, the Blood Company could do with a touch of humor to relieve the building stress. Something that the Crimson Giant tried to help with. Unfortunately, that moment of relief didn't last long as the Captain of the Battersea Guard grabbed their attention.

"This is the best place to begin our delaying action," said Tarin as he surveyed the ground where the winding ramp led all the way up the spire. The path was only twenty-five feet wide with a chest-high stone wall running along the outside of the trail. Those features would allow the Blood Company to make the most of the tight space in their defense of the Sanctuary.

"Agreed," said Jerad. "Archers forty yards up the ramp should help. They'll have good angles for their shots even with how the path spirals."

None of the gladiators were foolish enough to think that the black dragons and wyverns would prevent the Ghoule Overlord from continuing his pursuit. The animals of the Trench would delay the Ghoules, they were certain of that, though for only so long.

Then the Ghoules would come after the Blood Company with a vengeance, driven forward not only by hunger, but also by the implacable hatred of their Master. So the gladiators would make their stand here, using the natural advantages of the curling trail as they attempted to slow the Ghoules' progress up the spire, trying to give the Volkun as much time as they could while he attempted to repair the Weir.

That's all that mattered now. Not whether they lived or died, because they were all fairly certain that it would be the latter. All that mattered was that the Weir remain in place and prevent the Ghoules from ravaging Caledonia.

It was a strange position for the gladiators to be in, since they were fighting for a Kingdom that had put them in the Pit for their transgressions, some real, some imagined. Yet at the moment they could think of no better place to be. The fate of the Kingdom rested on their steel, and that was a burden they accepted.

The Volkun had fought for them. They would fight for him. It was as simple as that.

"Then let's get started," said Declan, motioning for all the gladiators to gather around him.

He explained quickly and succinctly the formation that they were going to use to hinder the Ghoules' advance up the curling ramp. There would be three rows of fighters, as always shield bearers to the front, spears over their shoulders, swords right behind. Then thirty feet behind the first formation would be the next, again three rows deep, and finally the last group of gladiators, again three rows in depth, thirty feet behind the second. The three units would rotate up and back as needed, supporting one another, because they all knew from their recent, bloody experience just how much pressure the Ghoules would be applying.

Several of the gladiators sensed that the final act of the drama had begun. There was no escape now. There was nowhere for them to go.

There was only the Sanctuary for Bryen. And for the Ghoule Overlord, there was only the Seventh Stone. A meeting between the two was inevitable. The only question now was how long the Blood Company could delay that encounter.

Declan's instructions complete, the gladiators swiftly moved into position thanks to the leadership of Dorlan and the other squad leaders, Tarin and Jerad assisting them.

"I should be here with you and the others, fighting by your side," said Bryen, a deep sadness resonating in his voice.

"You have a bigger challenge to face," replied Declan, trying to smile and finding it difficult, knowing that with the battle to come he might not see the young man he viewed as his son ever again. "We'll give you as much time as we can."

"I should at least be with you to start," said Bryen, hating the fact that once again Declan and all the other gladiators would be fighting and dying for him and that there was nothing that he could do to help them. "I know that you'll have no trouble with the Ghoules, but you can't do much about the Elders."

When they reached the base of the monolith, Bryen had released his hold on the Talent, the shield protecting the Blood Company fading away.

He wasn't concerned. As they drew closer to the Weir, the black dragons and wyverns held back, and there was no evidence of nests in the immediate area. It appeared that the animals didn't care to be too close to the electric charge of the Weir. That was a welcome surprise. It meant that the gladiators could focus their attention on a single enemy.

"That's why I'll be here," said Rafia, stepping up next to Declan and giving Bryen a nod that she hoped he took as confirmation that she would do all that she could to help the Blood Company. "Declan can worry about the Ghoules. I'll take care of the Elders."

"Don't worry about us," added Davin. "Worry about yourself. We'll manage things down here. Like I said, I need a new challenge, and this might finally be it."

"Actually, this might be more than you bargained for," replied Bryen as the two gladiators clasped forearms and then clapped each other on the back.

"If that proves to be the case, then so be it," replied Davin with a feigned nonchalance. He then stepped away toward where he would be standing in the center of the first group of gladiators, spear in hand, his goal simple. Don't allow the Ghoules to break through the shield wall. "I'll see you on the other side."

"I'll see you on the other side," said Bryen, forcing a smile onto his face as his friend walked away.

When Bryen turned back, Lycia stood right in front of him. She didn't say a word, instead reaching out and pulling him into a hug before she gave him a long kiss on his cheek. Then she turned toward Aislinn, who was waiting just a few feet away with Sirius.

"Keep him safe." Her voice was soft but her eyes were hard and filled with warning.

"With my life," Aislinn replied, giving the gladiator a nod to show that she understood her full meaning.

Lycia nodded in return, even giving Aislinn a small smile, expecting nothing less from the Lady of the Southern Marches. She still didn't like her, but Lycia couldn't find fault with Aislinn's grit.

"Now get moving," Lycia finally said to Bryen. "Do what you need to do so we can do what we need to do."

14

———

DEFENDING THE CURL

"Stand strong, gladiators of the Pit!" roared Declan. "We are the Company of Blood! And we are making them bleed!"

The gladiators maintained their three formations and strict distance from one another with a staunch discipline as the Ghoules slowly but steadily pushed them back up the winding ramp. Davin, Lycia, and all the other fighters gave ground reluctantly, having no choice but to do so, the strength of the Ghoules and the constant attacks by the Elders almost asking too much of them. Still, they made the beasts pay for each step they took in blood and pain.

The battle had started almost an hour before. Although the gladiators slowly retreated, the Ghoules had not yet forced them up the spire more than two rotations. The shield bearers did the dirty and necessary work to prevent the beasts from getting in between the separate fighting squads, allowing the spears and swords to seek the flesh of the beasts, their efforts aided by Magus Rafia, who infused their steel with the Talent so that they could cut through the Ghoules' natural armor as if it wasn't even there.

Frustrated by their slow advance, the beasts made the

mistake of allowing their emotions to get the better of their reason, their rage and appetite no match for the sharp steel and well-coordinated efforts of the soldiers. Yet even though their numbers paled in comparison to the Ghoules who littered the path, the price for the gladiators' masterful defense was costly, a handful of men and women becoming victims of the Ghoules' blackened steel or claws and falling on the dirt trail.

Several times Declan employed the same tactic to great effect to slow down the Ghoules' advance. When the first three rows of defenders began to struggle, the Ghoules pressing hard, a breakthrough imminent, on his command he ordered them to sprint back along the sides of the curling path, allowing the next three lines that waited above them to charge the beasts and then reform the shield wall. The retreating gladiators assumed their places behind what had been the third formation farthest up the trail, taking a much-needed break before they were called upon to rejoin the fight.

The rotation of fresh gladiators to face the Ghoules was the key. Declan believed that was the reason the Ghoules were finding it so difficult to advance. Strong arms, strong steel, and a cool but angry Magus.

At the beginning of the battle, the archers did all that they could from their perch farther up the trail. Yet with their depleted store of arrows, it wasn't long before they ran out, so they picked up their spears or drew their swords and joined the ranks of their fellow fighters, filling the gaps where their comrades fell.

Declan remained in his position right behind the first formation. The Crimson Giant and the Crimson Devil led the Blood Company's initial defense, never retreating up the slope when Declan called for the formation just above to sprint down and give the winded and battered fighters a chance to recover. The twins refused Declan's frequent calls to rest, instead always stepping into a breach before it could widen, skewering a

Ghoule or slicing across a beast's neck to relieve the pressure for just a few moments before the exercise began once again.

Through it all, Declan's pride in the men and women fighting with him knew no bounds, the supposed dregs of Caledonian society making him think of the warriors of legend.

Declan knew that the utility of his current defensive strategy would soon begin to show a diminishing return, so he would relish the fight while he could. The Ghoules were not fools, and it was only a matter of time before the Ghoule Overlord adjusted his strategy accordingly.

The Blood Company had no chance of stopping them. They could only hope to slow them down -- the beasts never stopping, always striving to break through the shield wall, never seeming to run out of the energy and desire to kill -- and that effort would only become more difficult with each step the gladiators took backward up the twisting path.

The Blood Company was down to seventy able-bodied fighters from their original one hundred seven, that number dropping even more every time the Ghoules attacked. And the beasts' slow push forward would accelerate as more of his gladiators fell.

Just then, Declan feared that the tide was about to turn against them for good. Two shield bearers stumbled, breaking the shield wall for only a few seconds, though that was all the time that two industrious Ghoules needed to take advantage of the opportunity, the beasts working their way into the gap and leaping over the remaining rows of gladiators, finally getting in between the two formations. If any more of the beasts joined them, the gladiators farthest down the trail would be lost.

One of the Ghoules stumbled when he landed because of a punctured thigh thanks to Kollea's quick thinking and even quicker reflexes, the gladiator stabbing into the beast's flesh with her sword while the creature leaped above her. Thankfully Tarin and Jerad reacted quickly, rushing down from where the second formation waited just a little farther up the trail to engage the beasts.

Declan thought about releasing the gladiators just above the two soldiers from the Southern Marches to aid them. He didn't. The fighting was so intense that he worried adding the gladiators to the separate combats might distract Tarin and Jerad in a way that could give the Ghoules the advantage. Instead he waited impatiently to see if he needed to respond, watching intently as Tarin, a master of the sword, wove a web of grey steel around himself and prevented the Ghoule he faced from backing him against the wall that marked the edge of the trail.

Declan smiled grimly as he watched the maneuver, realizing that Tarin was simply playing for time, before shifting his focus to the Battersea Sergeant. With each passing second, the injured Ghoule struggled even more to stay erect. Jerad faced off against that beast, using the Ghoule's limited mobility against him, scoring the Ghoule's flesh in several places.

The beast tried time and time again to turn quickly enough to defend himself from Jerad's assault, but found it impossible to do as thick black blood pulsed from the wound in his leg.

Jerad's combat ended only seconds later. When the Sergeant of the Battersea Guard feigned a lunge for the Ghoule's wounded thigh, the beast stepped back abruptly, or at least tried to, the weakening limb giving out beneath him. The Ghoule never had a chance to push himself up from the ground, Jerad thrusting the point of his sword through the beast's neck, then turning quickly to join Tarin's duel that was playing out behind him.

The other Ghoule, whose back was turned, didn't know just how dire the situation had become as he focused his full attention on his opponent. When Jerad finished the other beast, Tarin launched into a blinding attack, his sword slicing and slashing for the Ghoule's flesh, the beast using the haft of his spear to block the multiple strikes whenever possible. When he couldn't, he turned his body into the assault, catching the blazing steel with his armored shoulder or forearm and turning the blade away before it bit too deeply into his flesh.

That's why the Ghoule found it so very perplexing when he looked down and saw the sharp tip of a sword appear through his chest. But then it was gone an instant later, making the beast think that he had been mistaken, only for the steel to appear once again just a second later. And then a third time, the blade now staying in place.

The Ghoule stared down at the steel, still not understanding where the blade had come from since his opponent stood before him. He never had the chance to find the answer as the light left his eyes to the beat of the blood that pulsed down his chest and back. The beast became a dead weight, so Jerad tilted his sword toward the ground, the Ghoule slipping off the blade to fall face first onto the dirt trail.

Tarin nodded his thanks to Jerad. Then the two soldiers trotted back up the path to the gladiators who were preparing to rush down the slope and take their comrades' places.

Declan would have to thank the two soldiers from the Southern Marches for their efforts. But it would have to wait. Though the gladiators continued to keep the Ghoules from penetrating their shield wall, they couldn't prevent the beasts from slowly but surely pushing them back up and around the spire. Because of that, Declan was beginning to realize that now was the time to give the Ghoules something else to think about so that they didn't become too confident of their success.

"Do you remember that other strategy we discussed?" Declan called to Rafia, turning his sharp gaze toward the Magus.

As she had said would be the case when she spoke to Bryen, she had left the Ghoules to the Blood Company, focusing her efforts on the Elders who were tracking right behind the attacking beasts.

The Elders had thought that they would have an easy task when they discovered that they were only fighting one Magus. They learned quickly how wrong they were as they watched Rafia kill two of their number with bars of light that spun through the air and cut right through the shields of Dark Magic they tried to form a fraction of a second too late.

After that, the surviving Elders had taken her seriously. Pleased by her early success, Rafia stayed on the defensive, doing all that she could to shield the Company from the Elders' attacks with the Curse. Not unexpectedly, however, she was tiring, her continual use of the Talent and in such a large quantity wearing on her. She would continue to fight for as long as she could, of course. She would battle until her dying breath. Even so, she feared that as the Elders increased the intensity of their attacks, eventually her efforts would falter.

She was simply thankful that the Ghoule Overlord hadn't bothered to attack her himself, leaving that task to his underlings. She knew that if he had done so she stood little chance of staying in that combat for very long.

Still, she almost wished that he did join the fight now. She assumed that the monster held back because he wanted to save his strength for when he got to the Sanctuary. He couldn't afford to demonstrate any weakness when he came up against Bryen and the Seventh Stone. So she wouldn't have minded the chance to make the beast's life more difficult before he engaged in that inevitable combat. She might have been able to weaken him, giving Bryen a small advantage, but it appeared that it wasn't to be.

Hearing Declan's question, she agreed that what he had in mind was a good idea with a quick nod, never taking her eyes from the Elders who continued to attack her and the Blood Company.

"We'll do it around the next curl," she replied, adding more of the Talent to the shield that she had placed in front of the gladiators, several more Elders appearing to lend their strength to their brethren.

"Agreed," said Declan, who was already moving to put his new plan into motion.

In response to their Sergeant's commands, the Blood Company currently engaged with the beasts pulled back from the Ghoules faster than they had before.

To the surprised beasts, the retreat appeared to be a mad scramble on the part of the humans, a large space opening between the gladiators farthest down the trail and the front rank of Ghoules.

The Ghoule Overlord smiled when he saw the opportunity. He began to order his Ghoules to close the gap with their prey, thinking that he might finally have the breakthrough that he so desperately craved. If his Ghoules were fast enough, they could turn the attempted escape into a rout. Then he shook his head in frustration at what he saw happen next.

As soon as the space appeared between the Ghoules and the first rank of gladiators, Rafia struck with the Talent, a cascade of the lightning bolts she preferred to use when killing Elders directed toward this new task.

The destruction of the trail.

The streaks of energy hit with incredible precision, destroying a large segment of the winding path, the shattered stone and tons of dirt that sheared off from the side of the monolith and crashed far below at the bottom of the Trench taking several Ghoules with it.

After that, the fighting stopped for several minutes, even the Elders ending their attacks, as all the combatants waited for the swirling cloud of dirt and splintered rock to clear. When it finally did, Declan and Rafia grinned in triumph. A gap in the trail that was fifty feet wide separated the gladiators from the

Ghoules, a distance that even the Ghoules couldn't jump without a great deal of difficulty.

The Ghoules could try to pull themselves up the heather that covered the sheer sides of the monolith, but the heavy beasts had a better chance of falling to their deaths than climbing around the break in the trail. And even if the beasts succeeded in scaling the walls of the spire, they wouldn't be able to climb very fast. That would allow the gladiators to get ahead of them and continue their strong defense, perhaps even clear them from the stone with little effort with the Ghoules' focus on mastering the cliff face.

A good result for just a few seconds' work, Declan and Rafia both thought, although their grins were the only visible signs of accomplishment that either of them allowed themselves.

Because the fight wasn't over.

It was only delayed.

The gladiators had gained some valuable time, and they could use it to reset their defense, because they knew that the Ghoules would be coming for them again.

THE GHOULE OVERLORD watched the lightning bolts strike the trail in rapid succession, then closed his eyes and growled in frustration. He knew what he would be gazing upon before the cloud of grit and stone dissipated.

"Gurzen!"

The Ghoule scout appeared in front of him immediately. "Yes, Master."

"We need to move faster, Gurzen. The Seventh Stone escapes us. We need to get to the Sanctuary before he can try to repair the Weir."

"Yes, Master. I understand, Master. We are pushing as hard

as we can," Gurzen said apologetically, "but with the break in the path ..."

"You are not pushing as hard as you must!" shouted the Ghoule Overlord, his anger breaking its bonds. "You need to push harder!" The Ghoule Overlord cursed for several seconds when he finally took in the damage that the Magus had wrought on the trail. "Remember our last discussion, Gurzen? Remember the price that you will pay for failure?"

"Yes, Master," replied the Ghoule scout, his head bowed, realizing that he was closer to death now than he ever had been while fighting the humans the last few weeks. "I remember."

"I will give you one more chance, Gurzen," grated the Ghoule Overlord as he struggled to control the rage building up inside him. "One more chance. Do you understand?"

"Yes, Master."

"Do not fail me."

"Yes, Master."

"Send a pack of your best climbers up the side of the monolith. They are to come at the humans from behind."

Gurzen couldn't stop himself from questioning his Master's decision, the words spilling out, the Ghoule scout realizing that he may have just made his life forfeit. "The humans will expect that, Master. They will shift their forces and be ready for such an attack. Our Ghoules will be vulnerable, unable to defend themselves."

"That's the idea, Gurzen," replied the Ghoule Overlord, so focused on his goal that he let Gurzen's transgression pass unpunished. "The Ghoules climbing the monolith will distract the humans. Divide their attention. That will give me the time I need so that we can resume the real attack."

Gurzen was about to protest again, then quickly thought better of it when he saw that doing anything other than following his Master's orders in that moment would mean his death, the black mist that had been twisting lazily above the black diamond set atop the Ghoule Overlord's staff now rotating at the speed of a whirlwind.

"Yes, Master," the scout replied, running off to pick a dozen Ghoules he thought most able to dare the climb that the Ghoule Overlord demanded.

The Ghoule Overlord watched the scout go, seething at how easily the humans continued to delay his efforts.

He didn't care how many Ghoules died in service to him. He didn't care how many Elders died in service to him.

Legions had died for him in the past. Legions would die for him now.

The lives of his Ghoules didn't matter.

The only thing that mattered was that he take the Seventh Stone and then destroy the Weir.

15

REAL CHALLENGE BEGINS

The first faint touches of the clouds that wreathed the monolith caressed Bryen's skin, offering a promise of cooler air and a touch of moisture, tiny dew drops beginning to appear on his leather armor and clothes, as he, Aislinn, and Sirius made their way up the twisting path, the three now a dozen or more rotations above the Blood Company. They had lost count, all three lost in their own thoughts, all three wondering if they could play the role assigned to them, the role that was absolutely essential to stopping the Ghoule advance in the Winter Pass.

Bryen wanted to go faster as the haze wrapped itself around him and his companions, preventing them from seeing more than a few feet in any direction, each of them nothing more than a dim shape as they continued to climb. The only thing that remained visible was the packed dirt beneath their boots. But he ignored as best as he could the urgency that felt like a beating drum in his head, although the rhythm grew louder, more insistent, with every step that he took.

"I warned you that you would need to get into better shape,

Sirius," said Bryen. "This is worse than climbing in the Northern Spine or the Shattered Peaks."

Bryen's comment made Sirius scowl in disgust as he sucked in the wet air, trying to catch his breath after the exertion of the last hour. He wanted to offer a few choice words in response.

Instead, he held them back, knowing that the Protector was only teasing him. Besides, he didn't want to waste what little air he was taking into his lungs. Bryen's dig brought to mind the conversation they had when he, Bryen, and Rafia had escaped from Haven the first time the Ghoules had come for them and Sirius had struggled to reach the summit of one of the mountains that surrounded the glacial lake.

What irritated the old Magus wasn't what Bryen had said, but rather that the Protector was right. He should have been in better shape. He should have spent more time during the last few years outside of the Broken Tower in Battersea.

He had known it then just as he knew it now. But he hadn't, rationalizing over the years that he needed to devote most of his time to researching the books and other resources that would allow them to prepare for the return of the Ghoule Overlord and mount an effective defense, a moment that he believed approached rapidly. That event, which would determine whether Caledonia escaped a second Ghoule onslaught, took precedence over his fitness.

Sirius growled in irritation. He should have taken more time to think things through. Taking a few more hikes wouldn't have killed him.

In fact, they probably would have helped him not only physically, but also mentally, allowing his mind to drift and make the connections between the disparate pieces of information that he had dug up that were so important to his task.

Sirius growled again. It was too late now for regret. Events were coming to a head, one way or another. All he needed to do was make it to the top of this cursed spire, and he would do that even if he needed to drag himself across the ground on his hands and knees into the Sanctuary.

"I am not a gladiator so I don't spend most of my day staying in shape so that I can fight to the death," he protested. Then he softened his tone as he realized what he said sounded quite hard-hearted and might be taken as an insult. "I am more than one thousand years old, so this is the best that you're going to get from me."

"If Rafia was walking ahead of you, you would probably be climbing a bit faster," joked Bryen.

Biting back a sharp retort, in part because the Protector was correct, a small smile even cracking his grim visage, the old Magus picked up his pace at least for the next few rotations as they worked their way through the billowing mist, their hair now wet from the moisture of the clouds.

They were at least a mile above the floor of the Trench. How much farther they needed to go none of them could say with any certainty.

Yet even with the wispy streams of white cocooning them from the outside world, they could still hear the muted sounds of steel clashing with steel and the screams of pain and anguish, excitement and fright, that carried up the spire as the gladiators struggled against the Ghoules far below.

"I know what you want to do," said Aislinn.

"How do you know what I want to do?" asked Bryen, who kept a wary eye on Sirius, ready to provide any assistance if he needed it. Sirius was beginning to tire again, Bryen's comment only giving the old Magus a brief burst of energy.

"Because I know you," said Aislinn, who walked right next to Bryen, the two just a few feet behind Sirius as he wheezed his way closer to the crest. She could see Bryen's thoughts playing across his face. "You can't. If you want to help them, you need to stop the Ghoule Overlord. To do that, you need to rebuild the Weir. That's the only way. Rushing back down the spire won't help anyone but the Ghoules."

"I know, you're right. It's just that this is a hard thing to do," said Bryen. "I left my friends below so that they could die for me."

"They know that it was hard for you to do, and that's why they care about you so much. Because they know you care about them. Remember, they all wanted to play a role in this. Theirs is to buy you time. Your role is to fix the Weir. My role and Sirius' role is to help you do that."

"You're assuming that I even know how to rebuild the Weir," quipped Bryen.

His dread at the possibility of failing in his task continued to plague him, though not as much as it had when he first learned what was expected of him. His fear at being in this position, of having so much rest on his shoulders alone, even though he wasn't certain that he knew what he was doing, had diminished to a certain extent. The Seventh Stone had gifted him a memory of watching the Ten Magii construct the Weir, giving him a guide that he could follow. Providing a small glimmer of hope and confidence.

If all continued to go well, Bryen assumed that within the hour he would soon learn if he could improve on their work ... or destroy it entirely. Hopefully the former, though Bryen was a realist thanks to Declan. So he preferred to consider all the possible conclusions rather than just the one that he wanted.

"You'll figure it out," Aislinn said, her confident smile broadening. She reached up and ran her fingers gently across the scars marring his cheek and neck. "You're not just a pretty face after all."

Aislinn's remark made them both laugh, helping to eliminate just a bit of the anxiety that infested both of them. Bryen because of what he was expected to do. Aislinn because of her fear for him and what she might be required to do if he failed and the Curse touched him.

That fear for her Protector, present since they had begun this journey, had increased with each step that they had taken as they made their way to the Sanctuary. She had fought back savagely against the paralyzing terror that threatened to consume her when she allowed her mind to wander too much, primarily by focusing on what she needed to do and not thinking about what might happen.

Despite her best efforts those scenarios of how what was to come could end played through her mind with greater frequency. Only one scenario, the most unlikely to come to pass, provided her with any solace.

She glanced to the side, taking a quick look at Bryen before returning her gaze to the path that stretched out before them, needing to watch her step because of the smothering clouds. Her greatest fear wasn't that Bryen could die, although that possibility frightened her. No, her greatest fear was that she would be called upon to kill him.

If that proved necessary, could she do it?

She didn't know. When Rafia had raised the issue with her, she didn't have an answer, just as she didn't have one now.

"Children," huffed Sirius as he continued to climb with them, not missing the conversation between Bryen and Aislinn even as he concentrated on putting one foot in front of the other. "You'd think you'd have other things on your mind at a time like this."

The old Magus' gasp broke Aislinn from her depressing thoughts, making her and Bryen laugh just a little bit more.

After just a few more rotations around the spire that they completed in silence, the clouds began to fade away and the path finally evened out, the dirt giving way to the glimmering stone set in the top of the monolith. They had reached their objective.

For just a few seconds, the three Magii spun around slowly, taking in the incredible view. All around them the crests of the many other monoliths that rose out of the Trench poked through the oppressive clouds, which gleamed red and orange thanks to the fading sunlight of late afternoon.

The sounds of the battle below them drawing closer cut through their brief reverie and pushed them on to the next step, Bryen leading the way as he walked across the summit and then between two granite columns, disappearing from sight when he stepped down into the depression the Ten Magii had dug out of the top of the sandstone pillar.

Aislinn and Sirius followed him through at a slower pace, trying to take in everything that they saw around them. Sirius hadn't been here since the Ten Magii died in service to Caledonia, and even with the urgency of what needed to be done, he took a few seconds to get reacclimated to this place that crackled with the power of the Weir.

He had been away for far too long. He had promised himself that he would return here regularly to honor the brother who had given his life to ensure that the Weir was built, yet as was so often the case, he had allowed other priorities to get in the way. He regretted that now, although there was nothing for it. He could manage his regrets if he survived what he suspected would be the greatest combat in the history of the Kingdom.

Aislinn eyes widened as she took in the gleaming, translucent stone, so similar to that of the Aeyrie and the Library of the Magii, that covered every inch of the monolith's crest, only at the very edge the purple and white heather encroaching upon the Magii's construction. As she walked between two of the columns in pursuit of Bryen, she trailed her fingers across the stone, reading the names carved into the top and recognizing only one.

Keldragan.

She felt a burst of energy when she stepped off the staircase and into the excavated depression. She was in the Sanctuary, a place of legend, a place that she never thought that she would be, a place that she never thought she would need to be.

For Bryen, walking down into the bowl-shaped hollow brought with it an almost unwelcome familiarity. He had been here twice before, neither time of his own choosing.

He glanced quickly around the Sanctuary, six of the Seven Stones -- emerald, ruby, black opal, white pearl, sapphire, jade -- held in place on their pedestals by three strands of razor-thin gold. Each Stone pulsed brightly with the Talent and the Curse, black and white, black and white, always alternating into a grey cast of energy that shot up into the air to maintain the Weir even after all the centuries that had passed. The last pedestal, set in the middle of the depression, sat empty, just as he knew that it would be.

Though the Sanctuary looked the same to him, it felt quite different than the first two times he had been there. The power contained within the Weir buzzed harshly now, almost as if the two distinct energies fought against one another, every few seconds the energy blasting up into the sky flickering erratically between black and white rather than maintaining a more solid grey color.

Bryen knew that this could be the result of the Weir decaying over the centuries, and it likely was, at least in part. But he understood as well that it was more than that.

He acknowledged that the cause was him, or rather the Seventh Stone within him, the artifact upsetting the weakening balance between the Talent and the Curse that had kept the barrier in place for more than a thousand years.

Leaning against the open pedestal, Bryen closed his eyes. He took a deep breath and tried to push out all the distractions, all his fears, his worries, his concerns, just as Declan had taught him, trying to attain the calm that he required, because he needed to get started. He couldn't wait any longer. Not only because he knew that the Ghoules were pushing the Blood Company back up the monolith toward the summit, but also because his presence here was a threat to the overall integrity of the Ten Magii's magical construction.

The longer that he, and through him the Seventh Stone, remained within the Sanctuary, the more unstable the Weir would become. And though he didn't know what might happen as a result of that, based on what he was experiencing now he certainly didn't want to find out.

Still, he hesitated, his emotions fighting to break through the calm that he so desperately needed. As the Weir flashed angrily, Bryen felt an increasing urgency that filled him with anxiety.

He was here. Finally. After so much struggle. After so many lives lost.

Could he do what was required? Or would it be too much for him? Would all of his efforts and all the sacrifices made for him by others to reach this point be for naught? Did any of this even matter?

Doubt froze him when he opened his eyes and looked down at the empty pedestal. He couldn't concentrate, the flashing of the Weir almost mesmerizing, distracting him. Then a gruff voice ran through Bryen's mind, carrying with it the words that he had heard so often while growing up in the Colosseum.

"You must do what you must do."

Bryen smiled, the calm that he had sought finally settling over him. With a nod to Sirius and a sad smile for Aislinn, Bryen reached for the Talent and opened himself to the power of the Seventh Stone.

16

UP THE SLOPE

The Ghoule Overlord watched as the first pack of scouts selected by Gurzen began to climb the sheer cliff face of the sandstone pillar. The Magus had done the unexpected. She had taken a major risk, and it had worked out in her favor.

Brave. It would be of little matter in the end.

The Magus hadn't stopped them. She had only delayed them.

She would be the first to die, he decided. Her insolence would come to an end. Painfully. She would come to understand the meaning of real power. And then he would feed on her flesh first.

Those delicious thoughts fled his mind in an instant.

He could feel it.

Looking up, he tried to pierce the clouds that hovered above them, but to no avail. The mist was too thick.

His efforts to take the Protector had been for naught.

He could sense the power. He could sense the Seventh Stone.

So be it.

It would end where it had begun so long ago.

In the Sanctuary.

"ASAIA, ON THE CLIFF SIDE!" shouted Jerad.

The Sergeant of the Battersea Guard almost recognized the danger that was coming toward them from above too late. He hoped that the gladiator just a few feet to his left could address this latest threat, because he couldn't. He still had his hands full.

He had just prevented a Ghoule who had tried to sneak up the other side of the monolith from stabbing his Captain in the back, slicing across the beast's throat with his blood-drenched sword in the nick of time, the beast falling where he stood, reaching futilely toward the long gash across his neck, the gush of blood spurting through his clawed fingers. But he wasn't done, not by a long shot. There seemed to be no end to the Ghoules coming for them.

When the odds were against you, there was only one thing that you could do, Jerad thought. Change the odds. He meant to do that now.

Jerad stood there calmly, ready, waiting, his gaze implacable as a Ghoule pulled himself up the sheer rock of the monolith at an incredible pace, undeterred by the perilous handholds, snarling with undisguised hatred. The Ghoule's black eyes, never leaving Jerad's, flashed with a ravenous hunger. He ignored the beast's sneer, which revealed the creature's serrated teeth and the fate that would befall him if he lost this combat.

The Ghoule assumed that the soldier standing above him would swing down for his head with his sword. If he was fast enough, and the Ghoule knew that he would be, he would keep to the side, avoiding the blow, and then slice into the human's soft flesh with his claws.

That mistaken assumption cost the beast his life. Rather

than making the obvious play, Jerad instead aimed for the Ghoule's claw, and not where the claw was, but rather where he assumed that it would be, because he had observed how the Ghoule had tensed, preparing to make his move. The sharp steel severed the beast's daggerlike fingers in a single swipe.

The Ghoule howled in pain as thick black blood streamed from the stumps of his digits, the beast now hanging from the white and purple heather that grew in the cracks and crevices of the sandstone pillar by just one claw as his wounded claw swung away from the cliff face. Yet even though he was in pain, even though his risk of falling had increased exponentially, the Ghoule didn't panic.

The beast kicked with a clawed foot once, twice, and then a third time, finally finding purchase in the small notch that he had just created, and then he did the same thing with his other clawed foot. Balanced once again and ignoring the severity of his injury, the Ghoule looked back up at the soldier who blocked his path, cursing at the human in his harsh, guttural language.

Jerad stared down at the wounded beast without compassion, then smiled maliciously. He was impressed that the Ghoule had succeeded in stabilizing himself. Still, it wasn't going to be enough to prevent his death. Jerad swung his blade, the steel sparking against the rock.

The Ghoule's eyes widened at what he took to be a poor stroke, a harsh laugh escaping the beast because of the soldier's ineptitude. With a miss like that, this human taking his clawed fingers had to have been luck.

Jerad didn't say word, just giving the beast a nod and a wink. Then in a flash the thick stalks of heather that the Ghoule was holding onto with his claw gave way, the steel cutting through easily, the beast falling backward and away from the sandstone pillar with a howl of rage that lasted until he smashed into the ground far below.

Jerad was impressed. The Ghoule had expressed his fury until his inevitable end. That took commitment. That was something he understood as he turned away from the edge with a determined look and jumped back into the fight.

Asaia didn't bother to respond to Jerad's hurried shout, identifying the Ghoule scrabbling toward her out of the corner of her eye. The beast had decided to climb even higher up the monolith so that he could launch himself at her and the other gladiators from above. Thanks to the Sergeant, she was ready.

The Ghoule thought that he was being clever. He was about to find out that he was functioning under what would prove to be a painful and soon fatal misconception. The beast launched himself through the air, coming at the woman from what he believed was her blind spot, claws extended so that he could rip into the soldier's flesh from behind.

Asaia spun quickly and, with a flick of her wrist, her barbed whip shot out, slicing across one of the Ghoule's eyebrows, eliciting a shocked grunt of pain, his vision clouding with blood. Asaia calmly stepped out of the way as the Ghoule tumbled across the dirt path and slammed against the stone wall that circled the outside edge of the spire.

The beast jumped back up to his clawed feet and roared in anger, ignoring the fiery sizzle of his wound and the embarrassment of his fall, swiping at the blood that was pouring down his brow and blinding him in one eye. Realizing that there was little that he could do to stop the flow in that moment, with another roar the Ghoule lunged at Asaia with his bone knife gripped tightly in his other claw.

Much to the Ghoule's misfortune, Asaia wasn't where the Ghoule expected her to be, having already rolled away from him and ending up behind the beast. She snapped her whip out again with a resounding crack, the sharp steel tip scoring the beast's back. And then again, Asaia leaving a second streak across the Ghoule's broad shoulders before he could even register the pain of the first strike.

The Ghoule spun around, enraged that he had missed the human who seemed to be playing with him, his muscled back on fire. His anger exploded into an inferno when he realized that once again his prey wasn't there.

Asaia had already moved to the other side of the trail, whip lashing out again, the steel tip and cord screaming through the air. This time the spiked point dug deeply into the Ghoule's side, Asaia pulling it free just as quickly as it dug in between the beast's ribs. The Ghoule arched his back as this new agony burned through him, a large chunk of his flesh torn out along with part of his lower rib when the barb ripped free.

The pain of his multiple injuries drove all rational thought from the Ghoule, his fury pushing him forward, his desire to kill the human who was mocking him trouncing his reason. The Ghoule lunged wildly for Asaia with his bone knife. He misjudged a third time.

The blood streaking down his eye disoriented the beast, and the uncontrolled power of his strike pushed him off balance. Before he could recover, the Ghoule felt the sharp puncture of a spear being driven through his back and then his heart, the steel point appearing through his chest. He remained in place for just a moment, stuck like a pig, then sagged, all his strength draining out of him in just seconds.

"Well done," said Tarin, tilting the dead Ghoule down toward the rock-strewn trail and then ripping his weapon free with a nasty twist.

"I have a great deal of experience in killing," Asaia replied, the gladiator responding so matter of factly that Tarin didn't know how to respond. "This combat was no different than any of the others. Ghoules die just like anything else, they just tend to take a bit more work because they don't die easily."

"I'm glad you do," Tarin replied. "Now let's get back to it.

Two more Ghoules are coming up on the other side. We can't let them get above us."

Asaia nodded then ran farther up the trail, already looking forward to the next combat. Every Ghoule she killed increased the chances that the Volkun would gain the time he needed to fix the Weir. That's all that mattered to her, meeting her responsibility to the man who gave her the chance to free herself from the Pit.

Tarin and Jerad led the fight above the Blood Company, having taken the squads commanded by Dorlan, Asaia, and Jenus farther up the incline so that they could prevent the Ghoules, who were pulling themselves up the pockmarked cliff face with greater prowess than the gladiators thought possible, from attacking the Blood Company from behind. If they failed in their assignment, the gladiators would be caught in a vise from which they'd have no hope of escape.

Much to Tarin's pleasure, the Ghoules charged with scaling the sheer monolith still spent just as much time trying not to fall as they did trying to climb. They were large beasts and, even with their remarkable agility and speed, quite heavy. As a result, more often than not their weight was too much for the roots of the heather that sprouted from the cracks on the sandstone pillar if they hung in one place for too long, forcing the beasts to scramble to find a better hold, then often having to halt their ascent altogether so that they could attempt to locate a safer route up the stone.

That was when the gladiators usually struck, tracking the disjointed rhythm to the Ghoules' movement on the stone. The very focused and angry soldiers of the Blood Company were more than happy to help the beasts fall to their deaths with a few well-placed pokes with their spears or, in Asaia's case, her barbed whip. Many of the gladiators did as Jerad had done, seeing little need to attack the beasts directly when they could simply cut through the roots of the heather to aid their efforts.

Even so, just as many Ghoules succeeded in their climbs as met their ends on the rough terrain below, and that led to some vicious fighting. Dorlan, Jenus, and the men and women of their squads engaged the Ghoules with a controlled fury, recognizing for the first time since the beasts had begun to push them up the spire that here, above the main fight, they finally enjoyed the advantage.

The Ghoules were dangerous creatures, yes, but the gladiators knew how to fight them. The three squads tasked with protecting the Blood Company's rear put that knowledge to good use as they brought their greater numbers to bear on the handful of beasts who made it up the cliff face.

Both Tarin and Jerad understood that this separate attack by the Ghoules was just a distraction. It still needed to be dealt with, though. And despite the risk and the rapidly diminishing odds that the Ghoules could take the Blood Company from the rear, the Ghoules kept coming. Just like their brethren below them they were hungry for the taste of human flesh.

Even more important, the Ghoule Overlord required it of them, and the beasts had no choice other than to comply. So despite the fact that the Ghoules didn't achieve the breakthrough desired, the Ghoule Overlord was still pleased, because even though the Ghoules who were swept off the cliff face by the gladiators failed to eliminate their adversaries, they were serving their Master's purpose, nonetheless.

"FORWARD!" roared Davin, the gladiator rushing toward the Ghoules, his wild grin and blazing eyes giving him a maniacal expression.

The beasts were sprinting across the black ice that now spanned the gap in the trail, their clawed feet digging into the hardened Dark Magic, giving them the traction that they needed to make it up the curling slope and charge toward the Blood Company, shields and spears waiting for them.

Lycia and the three other gladiators lined up next to her joined Davin in his charge, using the outside wall of the ramp on their right side to protect one flank, safe in the knowledge that another squad of gladiators would be covering their other flank. With an unrestrained but disciplined fury they slammed into the handful of Ghoules with their shields, knocking two to the ground.

Davin and Lycia dispatched those beasts quickly and efficiently with a sharp punch of his spear through one of the Ghoule's eyes and a slash of her sword across the other's throat.

Not unexpectedly, the remaining Ghoules recovered swiftly, pushing back ferociously against the gladiators, the beasts undeterred by how quickly two of their number had been eliminated from the clash.

The fighting devolved into a blur of motion, the battle so fast, Davin, Lycia, and the other gladiators didn't have the time to make conscious decisions. Instead, they obeyed their instincts as they cut, slashed, and lunged, dancing with the Ghoules just as they would any of the other many combatants they faced in the Pit, allowing their hard-earned experience to guide them, to keep them alive.

"Back!" roared Davin.

Lycia and the other gladiators with him responded immediately to the command, pulling free from the Ghoules and dashing back up the slope.

The Ghoules stared in confusion for just a second, not anticipating such a maneuver when the humans outnumbered them. Before they could take advantage of what the beasts perceived as the humans fleeing, another squad of gladiators charged down the trail and slammed into them, knocking one of the Ghoules over the side of the wall during the rush to fall to his death while using their shields to push the other beasts back down the slope toward the arced bridge crafted of the Curse.

Just as he had done when attacking Haven, the Ghoule Overlord had used his Dark Magic to reconnect the two sides of the winding trail, ordering his Elders to keep the Magus who was such an irritant busy so that she couldn't interfere with his work. Once the Ghoule Overlord's bridge was complete, the beasts charged across the now covered space with a fierceness that intensified with every step their clawed feet took up the slope.

The Ghoules had broken through the shield wall several times upon reaching the rocky trail once again. They sensed that their prey was weakening as they pushed back the gladiators step by step, the humans having no choice but to retreat up the slope because of the pressure applied and their steadily decreasing numbers.

Declan hated this new reality, but he wasn't surprised, knowing as well that there was little that he could do about it. He was working with fewer fighters, Tarin and Jared taking three squads to eliminate the Ghoules above them and the Ghoules killing a handful of gladiators when they gained a foothold at the top of the span thanks to the Elders sending several shards of the Curse into their midst before Rafia could put the necessary shield in place. Now the Ghoules were trying to continue their advance up the twisting slope as more of their brethren followed them up and over the bridge.

In response to the Ghoule's latest gains, Declan had shifted his strategy for a third time, forming the Blood Company into wedges of five that he staggered across the trail, ten wedges in all. Some wedges attacked while others dropped back, and if there was a rhythm to it, the Ghoules so far had failed to decipher it, which was exactly the way Declan wanted it.

The Corporals in charge of each squad made their own decisions as to when they attacked or retreated, and so far it was working. The new approach had caught the Ghoules off guard, making the beasts hesitate, slowing down the advance, although Declan doubted that they would be able to make use of their advantage for much longer as he gazed down toward that cursed black ice.

He needed to speak with Rafia.

Immediately.

THE GHOULE OVERLORD stalked up the span that he had crafted, surveying the clash taking place farther up the slope. He grinned with an evil intent, pleased that his strategy was working so well.

The Ghoules selected by Gurzen to scale the sheer face of the monolith, most of them dying for their efforts, nevertheless were succeeding in their larger task. Dividing the humans' attention, thereby weakening their efforts to hold back his Ghoules who pushed up the trail, forcing the humans back toward the clouds that were now no more than one more rotation up the spire.

That meant that they were almost to the Sanctuary.

Now was the time. He knew it. The end was coming.

He had stretched the humans to the point of breaking. Now he could crack their defense and slaughter them.

He savored the thought of his victory, which was so close that he could almost taste it.

With that desire driving him, he was about to order his Ghoules to charge straight up the middle of the ramp, ignoring the fighters on their flanks, so that they could split the humans into two groups. Breaking the rhythm of the humans' attack would break them.

Before he could order the change in tactics, two bolts of

lightning streaked out of the smothering clouds and slammed down right where the black ice met the fractured trail.

The bursts of energy killed two Elders, turning their bodies to ash. The blasts almost struck the Ghoule Overlord as well, but he had sensed the power coming toward him, forming a shield of Dark Magic around himself just in time.

He tried to demonstrate his disdain for the attack by staring daggers at the wild-haired Magus opposing him. He realized immediately that it was wasted effort. The glare from the after-effects of the lightning prevented him from seeing anything but a dim shape, and he doubted that this Magus, who seemed to not care that she was challenging the Master of the Curse, would be anything but amused and pleased by his mounting irritation.

When the blinding flash finally dissipated, the Ghoule Overlord shifted to a deeper emotion. The beast howled in anger as he watched the humans run around the curve in the trail in a much too orderly fashion. Clearly, the humans were battered, but they were not broken, and that discovery infuriated him.

He struggled not to give in to his rage.

The Dark Magic in the Seventh Stone was calling to him. The Curse wanted him. And he needed the Curse.

His eyes blazing brightly, he turned to the handful of Elders who still remained alive after the Magus' surprise attack.

"Two of you will concentrate your attention on the Magus," he hissed. "She is weak and growing weaker. She cannot continue this for much longer. You will keep her busy. The rest of you will attack the other humans. You will destroy them. You will clear a path to the summit. Is that clear?"

The Elders nodded quickly, not wanting to fall victim to their Master's volatile temper.

The Ghoule Overlord nodded, then turned his focus toward Gurzen.

"Form the Ghoules into a single wedge that stretches across the trail. As soon as the Elders attack the humans, you are to charge the center of their line and break their formation once and for all. Once through, keep moving. Don't worry if you leave any humans alive behind you."

"Yes, Master," Gurzen replied weakly, having reservations about the plan but knowing that now was not the time to voice them. Now was the time to obey, no matter the potential cost.

"End this now," continued the Ghoule Overlord in a deadly whisper. "This foolishness has continued for far too long. If you don't, then I will feast on you instead of the humans."

"AN EXCELLENT TRY," said Declan. "A pity that it didn't work."

He had watched with both interest and anticipation as Rafia called down once again the lightning with which she had proven to be so effective in the past. He had hoped that a lucky strike might eliminate the Ghoule Overlord, though he called himself a fool for thinking such a creature could be killed so easily. The beast was too wily, too aware, and too strong to be caught out in such a way.

"It was worth a shot," she replied, bolts of light streaking from her palms as she struggled to keep back the Ghoules who had crossed the black ice so that the gladiators would have a bit more time to escape around the bend and set their defense once more before the beasts were upon them, the clouds that drifted down the trail hopefully something that could aid them in that effort.

"At least you got rid of a few more of those bastards with the staffs."

"That was certainly enjoyable," admitted Rafia, who stepped backward with Declan as they continued up the trail, always keeping her eyes on the Ghoules, assuming that they would begin advancing once again.

Declan heard the exhaustion in the Magus' voice and studied Rafia closely. He took in her strained features, understanding that she had reached the limit of her strength. They had asked quite a lot of her, more than they had a right to, in fact. Yet still she had given all that they had required and more. That realization and the fact that the Blood Company was now being attacked by the Ghoules from both directions on the ramp made his next decision quite easy.

"Can you call down two or three more bolts of lightning just in front of the advancing Ghoules?"

"I don't know if those strikes will do much. I don't have enough strength to destroy the trail again. And the Elders will be expecting it. They'll be able to protect themselves."

"You don't need to worry about that. Just enough power to startle them. That's all. With that we can pull back."

"But if we pull back ..."

"We don't have a choice," cut in Declan. "If we don't, we die here on the trail. And if I'm going to die on this day, I want to at least see the Sanctuary first."

Rafia nodded grimly, knowing that Declan was right, that his fatalistic perspective was justified in their current circumstances. So she began pulling in more of the Talent. She was bone-tired, but she could do this at least.

She wanted to see the Sanctuary as well before she died.

17

FALTERING DEFENSE

Aislinn stared down the steps, looking into the heart of the Sanctuary. Her Protector stood motionless in front of the empty pedestal. She could sense the power that he had just connected to. Not just the Talent, but also the almost unfathomable power of the Seventh Stone. It coursed through him, pulsing, much like the waves of the Silent Sea smashing against the Battersea coast.

She was proud of him. Proud of all of them. They had achieved their objective.

They had gotten Bryen to the Sanctuary.

Now it was up to him.

"Can he do it?" asked Sirius. She was so focused on the man she loved that the old Magus stepped right next to her without her even knowing.

She didn't hesitate at all when responding, her voice strong, certain. "He can and he will."

Sirius nodded, watching the young man who was the only connection that remained for him to all the people he had lost over the centuries. The young man who was both a possible savior and a potential threat, the answer to that mystery about to be revealed.

Sirius wasn't one to hope, because you could build nothing on hope. But now he did. He hoped that Bryen achieved the impossible.

No. That wasn't good enough. He believed that he would.

"He will," Sirius finally agreed.

Bryen had not failed them yet. He wouldn't now.

"Come on," Sirius said, turning back toward the path that led to the summit of the monolith, hearing the sounds of the battle below drawing ever closer. "Bryen will do what he needs to do. We need to do what we need to do."

"DECLAN, I NEED YOU!" shouted Rafia, her cry twisting around the spire.

She had done as Declan asked, trying to catch the Elders by surprise and slow the Ghoules, thereby giving the Blood Company the chance to break away from the beasts and gain some breathing space. But it didn't work. The Elders defended against her attack much too easily and now the beasts were realizing that the victory they craved was near.

The Blood Company continued to back its way up the curling road, each step demanding blood, sweat, toil, and tears. All the while, the Magus used the last of her waning strength to keep the Elders at bay, sending bolts of energy streaking toward the advancing Ghoules that were meant more to distract than to kill, though if the latter happened, she certainly wouldn't mind.

She had sniffed out the Ghoule Overlord's strategy, the monster ordering several of the Elders to keep her busy so that the remainder of his servants could attack the gladiators. A good approach, she had to admit. Yet she refused to allow that to happen, even as her growing weariness threatened to overwhelm her.

Rafia was too stubborn to acknowledge when the odds were stacked against her. So she had dug deeply within herself, finding a hidden reserve of strength that she didn't know that she had.

She killed one of the Elders meant to divert her with a bolt of energy that caught the beast off guard, sending the energy curling around the Ghoules standing in front of him and enjoying the protection offered to them by the barrier of Dark Magic he had constructed. The Magus had faltered for just a second when the other Elder tasked with opposing her sent a shard of Dark Magic her way right before the demise of his partner.

The beast had never expected her to recover so quickly, yet she had, and she went after him instead with very final consequences. The Elder defended against the lightning bolt that streaked out of the sky, grinning as he did so, preparing his own attack that would follow, never thinking that a Magus would apply such a mundane approach as throwing a dagger at him until he saw the hilt sticking out of his chest and Rafia's smug smile. She knew that the beast was dead before he crumpled to the trail.

Having cut the noose that the Ghoule Overlord tried to set over her neck, now she was doing all that she could with the last of her energy, crafting shield after shield and throwing it up in front of the gladiators as they maintained their brave retreat, doing everything possible to protect them from the Elders' Dark Magic.

But she had reached her limit, passed it in fact, and she knew it.

Sweat poured from her body. Her very bones ached. Her vision was blurry, the black spots dancing at the edges progressively getting bigger and suggesting that unconsciousness wasn't too far away.

All she could do was hope that she could maintain her strength long enough so that the gladiators could disappear, at least for a few minutes, in the clouds that beckoned just a hundred feet farther up the trail.

She feared, nonetheless, that it was already too late. The Ghoule Overlord had recognized the gladiators' deteriorating conditions and changed his strategy as a result. He had formed his Ghoules into a tightly formed wedge aimed at the center of the Blood Company's shield wall.

This time, after so many attacks, after being beaten back so many times, the beasts finally broke through. The Ghoules howled in triumph, then sought to come at the soldiers from multiple directions, preventing the gladiators from closing the gap in their line.

The Ghoule Overlord assumed initially that the battle was over as soon as his beasts got behind the humans. His Ghoules would slaughter their prey and then they would rush into the Sanctuary just as he had ordered. Instead, the Ghoule Overlord growled in frustration and disbelief, his Ghoules failing to take advantage of the gap.

Realizing that they had no chance to close the breach, the soldiers of the Blood Company immediately reverted to their previous lives, making use of the experience gained while fighting on the white sand of the Pit, the larger battle devolving into distinct combats spread across the trail. And though the Ghoules made progress against the gladiators here and there, dispatching a handful after several minutes of desperate and ferocious fighting, Declan and his gladiators refused to yield to the inevitable. They refused to go quietly.

They were the Company of Blood, after all. They would extract as much blood from their enemies as they could before they spilled their own on the winding path.

Rafia sent another bolt of energy toward an Elder. The black mist spinning atop the beast's staff had formed into a black spear that the beast was preparing to throw at Asaia. The gladiator's back was turned, her barbed whip scouring the flesh of the unlucky Ghoule opposing her. Yet even though she had marked the beast a dozen times with the steel tip of her favored weapon, still the Ghoule fought on.

Asaia remained patient even as her frustration mounted. The Ghoule should be dead by now. Yet the beast ignored the pain, ignored his wounds, probably believing that victory was close now that he and his brethren had shattered the shield wall and that he still had a chance to partake in the spoils. She surmised that he could probably already taste the soft flesh that would be his.

Assuming he defeated her, of course. As that thought passed through her mind, Asaia barked a laugh that drew a sneer from her opponent that she found quite amusing. This Ghoule couldn't kill her. The beast was dead. He just hadn't realized it yet.

The Elder targeting Asaia should have been paying closer attention to what was going on around him, because he didn't even realize he was under attack from another direction until Rafia's slash of light slammed into his shoulder. The powerful blast charred his flesh and knocked the beast over the waist-high wall that spiraled around the outside border of the path, the Elder falling to his death with a disquieting shriek as the Talent continued to burn deeply into his body.

Watching the beast tip over the edge, Rafia was inordinately pleased with herself. She had killed another Elder even as her energy was draining away from her. A bone-deep resignation instantly replaced that brief feeling of pleasure. She caught the movement out of the corner of her eye.

A Ghoule just to her side was about to drive his blackened spear just under her ribs, and there was nothing that she could do to stop the beast. She knew the end was coming, she had known for the last few minutes that with her flagging strength that it was assured. She just didn't think that it would be this very moment.

Right before she felt the cold steel slide into her flesh, Declan was there, fighting his way to her, heeding Rafia's call. He knocked the Ghoule's spear to the side with a rapid cut of his sword. Continuing his motion, the Sergeant of the Blood Company stepped down onto the beast's spear and forced it from the Ghoule's claws with a quick kick. The Ghoule tried to snatch up his weapon again, but he was too slow, Declan slicing across the beast's midsection with a backward swing of his steel.

The Ghoule dropped to one knee, his claws ineffectually attempting to close the deep slash, the beast trying to keep the organs that threatened to spill out in place, not realizing that his effort was wasted, that his death was already certain. Declan used the beast's distraction to drive the tip of his sword through the back of the Ghoule's neck, severing his spine at the same time.

With a sharp tug, Declan ripped his sword free, then glanced at Rafia from top to bottom, making sure that she hadn't been harmed. Satisfied that she was all right, he nodded to her, then pushed his way deeper into the fight. He sought out the combats in which his gladiators were struggling, jumping in and out, his blade a blur, sweeping, slashing, cutting, lunging as he tried to kill as many of the Ghoules as he could while the beasts were engaged with his fighters.

Still, even with Declan's heroic efforts, it wasn't enough to turn the tide of the battle. The Ghoules were too many. The handful of remaining Elders were proving to be more than a match for Rafia, and the Company of Blood was too few in number now to do anything other than fight for their lives as the odds continued to turn against them, more Ghoules sprinting up the path toward them.

Yet though the tide had turned, the Ghoule Overlord would have to wait just a while longer to claim his victory.

Sirius stalked out from the clouds farther up the trail. Sizzling strands of the Talent rippled across his robes. His hair stuck straight up. His eyes blazed with fury and purpose.

The Master of the Magii had arrived.

The old Magus didn't waste any time. Lances of energy shot from his palms. The first Ghoule struck simply disappeared, his body bursting into flames because of the Magus' fiery power.

Next an Elder felt his wrath, Sirius sending a bolt of power that was so strong that it shot right through the beast's shield and then his neck, the Ghoule's head tumbling from his shoulders as his body slumped to the ground.

That was just the beginning.

For the next few minutes, Sirius dominated the battlefield, bolts of the Talent ripping into the Ghoules with an unstoppable strength, leaving behind charred bodies and ashes, forcing the beasts back down the trail toward their Master.

"To the summit!" urged Sirius, streaks of energy hissing toward the Ghoules, the Elders attempting to use their Dark Magic to block his strikes now that the shock of the Magus' attack had worn off.

Declan repeated Sirius' cry, helping several wounded gladiators to their feet and pushing them up the slope toward the clouds. As he draped one gladiator across his shoulders and then began to walk up the trail, he promised himself that the men and women who had fallen on the path never to rise again would gain the vengeance that they deserved against the Ghoules.

Their deaths would not be in vain.

THE GHOULES WERE TOO stunned by the Magus' surprise attack to do anything other than stare once they had pulled free from the humans, astonished by the power and violence of the assault, not even caring that their prey had disappeared into the mist and toward the top of the monolith. All thoughts of pursuit left their minds as the Elders battled the old Magus. The human continued the fight for a few minutes more, keeping the servants of the Ghoule Overlord busy as he shot bolt after bolt of energy toward the beasts.

To the watching Ghoules, the Magus seemed less concerned about hitting them than keeping them in place, focusing instead on the Elders, and that was fine with them. But then the human gave the Ghoules a parting gift, sending a dozen blazing spears toward the beasts before he stepped back a few feet and vanished in the clouds.

None of the Ghoules were struck by the energy, the Elders combining their power and keeping their shields in place despite the potent onslaught, though it certainly got their attention.

Then silence fell on the trail, Ghoules and Elders alike seemingly rooted in place, the packed dirt littered with corpses, most of them servants of the Ghoule Overlord.

"Follow them, you fools!" roared the Ghoule Overlord, who had kept at the back during the fight so that he could save his strength for the Seventh Stone even though every fiber in his being had itched to take on the Magus, recognizing the man. "We have them beaten! If you want to feed, then you must kill them!"

Their Master's sharp remonstration finally got the beasts moving again, the Elders and Ghoules digging their sharp claws into the dirt of the trail and then launching themselves into the wispy haze.

"ALL WE CAN DO NOW IS fight for time," said Declan urgently. "That's the only thing that matters. Understood?"

"Yes, Declan," Lycia and Davin both replied in unison. They realized just as he did where the fight had taken them, what was required of them now.

"Good, because we're too few to do much of anything else now, even with the Magii helping us, and we have nowhere to go." Declan took one glance at the small plaza that stretched out before him, taking in the shimmering stone that formed the crest as well as the ten columns positioned in a large circle that marked the boundary of the Sanctuary and the resting place of the Seven Stones, a plan for defending the space immediately coming to mind. "Davin, you have the right flank. Lycia, the left."

"We can't hold them here," said Davin. "There's too much space. The beasts will flank us."

"I know, and we're not going to try," replied Declan. "Forget the open area here on the summit. It's a death trap. We fight right in front of the columns and use them as part of our defense. We don't want the Ghoules to break us. We will flow with them around the hollow when they try to take us from a different direction. We don't stay in a static position. We move along the columns as the situation requires. We're simply trying to buy Bryen the time to do what he needs to do. Clear?"

They both nodded.

"Then let's get to it."

What was left of the Blood Company, now no more than half of its original number since they first set out from Tintagel, took their positions just in time. Only seconds later the Ghoules burst out of the clouds by the trail and sprinted across the gleaming stone, swords and spears to their front, howls of hunger and deafening shouts of rage preceding them.

As Declan had wanted, the gladiators employed the columns effectively, using them to anchor their flanks as they formed into two rows, shields in the front, spears and swords in the back. They didn't have enough gladiators still able to fight to form a third rank.

With the heavy losses that they had suffered, that was the best that they could do. They were simply thankful that they had enough fighters still alive to fill the space between the ten columns as the Ghoules struck.

The beasts slammed against the locked scuta and the bloody fight that had taken place all the way up the winding ramp of the monolith began once again. Claws, swords, and spears shot forward, Ghoules and gladiators both seeking to pierce the flesh of the other.

The beasts fought savagely, knowing that a single rupture in the human line would spell the end of their defense.

The gladiators fought with a controlled rage, their decisions instinctual, their movements economical, just as if they were once again fighting on the white sand.

The usually quiet Dorlan roared in rage, slamming the bottom edge of his scutum straight through the clawed foot of the Ghoule who crashed into him with a force that would have knocked a smaller gladiator over the rim of the depression. The sharp metal on the bottom of the shield sliced off several of the beast's toes.

The wounded Ghoule reared back, bellowing in pain, and that's when Kollea struck. The gladiator who was never far from Dorlan drove her sword through the beast's heart, then stepped back so that Dorlan could shove the dying beast away. In the same motion, the mountain of a man raised his shield to block the spear thrust by the Ghoule right behind the one who had just met his end.

A smart move, Dorlan thought, to try to take advantage of his brethren's death. But the Ghoule wasn't fast enough, because when the beast lunged, he left his side open to a counterstroke. This Ghoule shouldn't have focused solely on

Dorlan, nor believed that he could push the gladiator out of the way with his greater bulk. Those two mistakes proved costly for the Ghoule and gifts for the gladiators.

Dorlan held his ground, keeping the beast's spear to the side, which allowed Asaia, who stood right next to Kollea, to make use of the opening that he gave her. Having looped her barbed whip around her belt because the weapon was more hindrance than help in close quarters, she drove the spear she had picked up from a fallen gladiator right into the Ghoule's side, skewering the beast like a chicken on a spit.

Jenus, fighting on the far side of the Sanctuary, held two scuta, one in each hand. He used the curved pieces of steel primarily as weapons, punching at the Ghoules with the thick, curved shields as if he were fighting in a boxing match. Two Ghoules already lay on the ground, their faces smashed in by the heavy steel, while two more tried and failed multiple times to get past the gladiator's shields. Jenus wouldn't allow the beasts to close with him, using his surprising agility for someone so large quite effectively and always keeping the pile of bodies that were the result of his efforts between him and the Ghoules.

One of the Ghoules tried to leap not only over his fallen comrades, but also Jenus, believing that getting behind the massive human would mean the end of this duel.

It only proved to be another mistake, because Jenus saw the move coming. When the Ghoule leaped into the air, at just the right moment, Jenus lifted the scutum in his left hand, catching the beast in the knee and giving him an extra push that threw the Ghoule off balance and flipped him upside down.

The beast landed hard on his back, the wind knocked out of him. When the Ghoule tried to push himself up from the ground and suck in a breath, Jenus slammed the bottom edge of his shield down onto the beast's throat, crushing his windpipe.

Tehana fought right behind Jenus, marveling at the gladiator's speed and savagery. The huge fighter appeared to be more a force of nature than a man, which was all to the good for her, because it gave her several opportunities that she wouldn't have gotten otherwise. Like the Ghoule who was frozen in place, amazed by what had just happened to his brethren.

Rather than launching himself at Jenus while the gladiator was finishing the Ghoule who thought to jump over the shield wall, this one had remained in place, still trying to comprehend his comrade's demise when Tehana struck.

She lunged with her shortened trident. The spike in the center that extended beyond the other two by more than a foot proved particularly handy as it dug deeply into the Ghoule's groin. The other two blades each pierced a thigh, the Ghoule collapsing to the ground in agony.

Tehana left the Ghoule there, not feeling the need to finish the beast, knowing that he was out of the fight for good. Instead, she turned her focus toward another Ghoule, this one pressing Jenus from the other side with a series of spear thrusts that forced the gladiator to twist from side to side, the beast's attack so fast that she could barely catch the motion with her eyes.

She was certain that in the end, Jenus would get the better of the beast. But thanks to Declan's constant training and unending stream of sayings, she knew as well that in any combat you should only expect the unexpected, and that's what happened at exactly the wrong moment for Jenus.

The gladiator had raised the shield in his right hand to block the Ghoule's thrust, yet when he tried to plant himself to deflect the powerful strike, his back foot slipped on the body of one of the Ghoules he had killed just moments before. The misstep left his gut exposed.

The Ghoule noticed the opening immediately, pulling back his spear and preparing to drive it right into Jenus' belly.

Though the Ghoule was fast, he wasn't as fast as Tehana. Recognizing what the beast planned to do, she stepped in right behind Jenus and through the slight opening between his two shields, lunging with her trident, the sharp steel punching through and shattering the creature's knee.

The Ghoule howled in agony, falling to the ground. Before he could rise, Tehana struck again, slamming her trident into his throat. She stepped back behind Jenus after that. The gladiator had pushed himself back to his feet and was preparing to meet the next wave of Ghoules charging toward them.

"Thank you, Tehana," rumbled Jenus. "Quick thinking on your part."

"You're welcome," she replied, her throat raw, desperate for a drink of water.

"Remind me never to call your trident a fork again," Jenus said.

Tehana would have offered a sharp reply in most circumstances, but she saw the smile that twisted the big man's lips, so she smiled as well. She didn't have a chance to offer the more suggestive, ribald response that immediately came to mind because she needed to turn her attention to the next pack of Ghoules that was now upon them.

Similar scenes played out across the narrow circumference of the ten columns as the Ghoules attempted to swarm the gladiators with their greater numbers, the Blood Company proving its name, taking the Ghoules' blood and spilling their own, bending repeatedly though never breaking. When one gladiator fell, another gladiator stepped up, keeping the shield wall strong, the columns serving as anchors in their defense.

Through it all, Declan stood in the entrance to the Sanctuary that led down into the hollow, watching the fight develop, ready to throw himself into the mix wherever necessary. For now, though, his gladiators were holding strong despite the viciousness of the Ghoules' assault.

Nodding to himself in satisfaction, he took a quick look over his shoulder, glimpsing Bryen, who stood in the middle of the depression, leaning against the translucent lectern upon which Declan assumed the Seventh Stone was supposed to sit. With Bryen down in the hollow, the Weir flickered wildly in response to the artifact that had joined with him.

Declan could only hope that the lad knew what he was doing, because there was nothing that Declan could do to assist him with regard to rebuilding the Weir. That fact grated on him, so he sought to aid Bryen as he could. Until his dying breath Declan would do whatever was required to give Bryen as much time as possible to at least try.

Declan turned back toward the summit with that objective in mind, then wondered how much time he could legitimately expect to buy for the young man. Because now the Elders yet to meet their demise strode out of the fog and approached the ten columns, spreading out around them. With them came the Ghoule Overlord, the monstrous beast finally emerging on the summit and shouting a stream of orders to his servants.

That's when the Magii struck. Sirius had taken responsibility for defending the north side of the rim while Rafia did the same on the south. At the same time, both released a deluge of scorching power toward the Elders that forced them back toward the trail.

The beasts raised their shields crafted from the Curse to deflect the thousands of pellets of energy that shot toward them. Although the spheres were no larger than a marble, that didn't make them any less deadly.

One Elder learned that the hard way. The beast failed to raise his shield fast enough and, as a result of his languidness, fell dead onto the translucent stone with dozens of smoking holes in his chest.

With Rafia and Sirius occupying the Elders, Aislinn jumped into the fight. She concentrated on the Ghoules, spinning in a slow arc just at the top of the hollow, sending bolts and spears of energy toward any beast who threatened to break through the shield wall.

Several Ghoules fell dead, ripped apart by the blazing energy. Several Ghoules ducked out of the way just in time, escaping her attacks. That success was only temporary, the gladiators attacking the crouching Ghoules faster than a striking cobra, wounding or killing the beasts with steel rather than the Talent.

Declan was pleased as he took it all in, noting how the momentum of the battle had shifted in just seconds. Maybe they could give Bryen the time that he needed.

And if not ... well, it had been a good fight. One he could be proud of.

18

A FORMIDABLE CHALLENGE

Bryen stood in the center of the sunken Sanctuary as still as the columns that surrounded the lip of the bowl-shaped depression, one hand tightly gripping the steel haft of the Spear of the Magii, the other pressing down hard on the translucent stone of the pedestal. Not blinking, not seeing anything other than the three razor-thin wires designed to hold the Seventh Stone, his focus so complete.

Although it took all of his willpower not to, he refused to allow himself to look up. His curiosity and concern regarding what was happening to his friends just above the rim of the hollow warred with his need to maintain his concentration.

He could hear the battle raging around the ten pillars, the screams and the howls of anger, pain, terror, and pleasure, the clash of weapons and claws, the sickening sound when steel or claw slid into flesh. It called to him. Even so, he had to ignore all that. He had to let it go.

He had to focus on the task that only he could accomplish. The task that would determine the fate of the Kingdom and all the people living in it. The task that terrified him more than fighting a black dragon in the Trench.

Because he understood that if he failed now, he wouldn't be the only one who died. It would be untold thousands upon thousands.

Hunted, killed, then eaten by the Ghoules.

On the white sand, his death meant little in the larger scheme of the Kingdom. Here, it meant everything, and that intense pressure made it difficult for him to think, to do what he needed to do.

Bryen tried to block out the flashing brilliance of the six Stones on their pedestals, black and white flaring wildly in the corner of his eye as the stream of energy shot up into the sky to form the barrier that protected the Kingdom. He tried to ignore the sharp buzzing sound that came from the Weir as the two powers that were used to build it – the Talent and the Curse – clashed, seeking to break free from one another, thereby unraveling the bond that had been forced upon them a thousand years before.

Making his task all the more difficult was the fact that although he was more than willing to do what was required despite the risk entailed, acknowledging and accepting the ultimate sacrifice that might be required of him, he wasn't sure how to do what he needed to do.

He had planned on taking an approach similar to what he had done in the Library of the Magii when he first wove the Talent and the Curse together under the watchful gaze of Rafia and Sirius. He thought that it would work, confirmation coming from the memory the Seventh Stone shared with him of when the Ten Magii constructed the Weir. And, in all honesty, it was the only idea that had come to mind, because he didn't know what else to do.

None of the Magii's research had unearthed any information that would assist him with this endeavor. Because of that lack of knowledge, he was worried. Worried to the point of not being able to take the next step.

He was frozen.

He feared that he was overthinking the whole thing. But was he? Were his concerns legitimate? Was he destined to fail before he really even began?

Bryen remembered the glimpse that the Seventh Stone gave him of the Ten Magii constructing the Weir, his thoughts trailing back to that singular moment when Viktor Keldragan for just the blink of an eye made the tiniest of mistakes. While weaving the two conflicting energies together, he had touched the Curse.

Faintly, no more than a caress. Still, it had been enough to corrupt Viktor and, because he was linked to his peers, serving as the linchpin and managing the overwhelming flow of power, the other nine Magii working with him.

So Bryen hesitated. Would he make the same mistake that his forebear had with the same devastating consequences?

Was this the only way? Did he need to contaminate himself in order to achieve his larger goal? Did he need to sacrifice himself to have any chance of success?

In just the last few minutes, Bryen had reached for the power of the Seventh Stone several times. He could feel the energy within the artifact waiting for him. He could feel that power wanting him to take it. He could feel the artifact demand that the energy that it contained be released.

Because the Seventh Stone knew where it was. The Seventh Stone knew why it was there. The artifact had been crafted for this purpose, and it wanted to be used for this purpose. Still, Bryen wavered.

What was wrong with him?

He had fought in the Pit for ten years. During that time on the white sand, he had never hesitated. It didn't matter what opponent he faced, whether man or beast. He had learned that if you hesitated, even just for a second, you died.

He thought that he had worked that weakness out of his psyche. Apparently not.

Then in a moment of enlightenment he realized what was holding him back.

It was so obvious, yet it had been such a long time since he had experienced this emotion.

He was afraid. The moment that he had been dreading for so long was finally here. Now he would find out if he had not only the power, but also the precision needed to accomplish the most fearsome and arduous task ever demanded of a Magus.

He was frightened of failing. Terrified of proving to himself and others that he wasn't the person that he thought he was.

It was as simple as that. Yet there was more to it.

He realized as well that he was frustrated. The gladiators, his friends, who were positioned around the rim of the Sanctuary, were fighting for him. Dying for him.

He wanted to join the fight. He wanted to help his friends, the men and women who had committed themselves to him.

He knew in his heart that he couldn't. He needed to trust that his friends could manage the Ghoules, because they trusted him to fix the Weir.

Nevertheless, it bothered him.

Declan's words, as they so often did in times like these, played through his mind.

"You must do what you must do."

He would do just that. Succeed or fail, he would do what he needed to do.

Employing his training as a gladiator, Bryen closed his mind to everything that was going on around him. The sights, the sounds, the smells, the distractions, his own fears and worries.

In seconds, his focus was keen. He stared at the translucent stone until there was nothing in his world except for himself and the pedestal.

Then, and only then, did Bryen reach for the Talent, the double blades of his spear glowing brightly as he pulled in the natural magic of the world and then opened himself to the power of the Seventh Stone, the energy scouring his body clean from the inside out with a welcome warmth.

DECLAN SQUEEZED himself into a small gap that had opened between Jenus and Asaia just in time, slicing with his sword across a Ghoule's leg right below the knee and almost through the bone. The wound stopped the beast from forcing his way through the shield wall.

The Ghoule hobbled backward, howling in anguish, his lower limb still attached, although by nothing more than a few shredded sinews and a splintered shard of white. Off balance, the Ghoule fell over the body of one of his brethren who had died with a spear thrust into his throat.

With that Ghoule out of the fight, the gladiators gained the second that they needed to recover, relocking their scuta so that they could reform the shield wall.

Tarin and Jerad stood just a few places away from the breach that Declan had closed, thrusting their spears over the shoulders of the shield bearers to their front. Tarin's lunge took a Ghoule in the throat, the beast stumbling away from the clash, trying to breathe and stanch the flow of blood at the same time and failing to do either. Jerad's thrust, which followed right after his Captain's, pierced the meaty bicep of another Ghoule's sword arm, the beast dropping his weapon involuntarily.

Renata had been waiting for just such an opportunity, slipping into the space between Jerad and Tarin just long enough to bring her morning stars to bear. Her two foot-long clubs struck the wounded beast more than a dozen times in only a few seconds, the sharp spikes that framed the end of each one leaving the Ghoule bleeding from his chest to his groin with a spatter of horrific gashes and a pool of blood rapidly puddling at his clawed feet.

The gladiator stepped back with a satisfied smile, certain that the Ghoule was dead even if the beast didn't know it yet himself. Although Renata appeared to be a kindly grandmother, she was anything but. Her true self came through in moments such as this, revealed by the hard glint of her eyes and her complete lack of compassion for her adversaries.

When she fought, she fought to survive. It was that simple.

And so it continued all around the ten pillars that formed the outside border of the Sanctuary. Slash following slash. Blow following blow. Lunge following lunge.

The Ghoules attacked viciously, seeking to penetrate the gladiators' line. The gladiators held their ground, attempting to give Bryen as much time as they could to repair the Weir.

Yet despite their extraordinary efforts, it was becoming harder and harder for the men and women of the Pit to maintain their position. With each gasping breath that they took, the pressure from the Ghoules increased, their Master, a menacing presence at the back of the beasts, demanding the victory that he required.

Davin led the defense on the west side of the rim. Even with his responsibilities, he could always be found in the middle of the action, spear slicing through the air, ripping apart the Ghoules' leather armor and then cutting deeply into their flesh.

Even with the gladiators' struggles, he felt good about how things were going, because they could always be worse. He had learned that the hard way on the white sand. Due in large part to several of the gladiators fighting with the Crimson Giant, the Ghoules hadn't broken the shield wall. Yet.

Majdi, a large man known for his frequent belly-shaking laughs, was difficult to anger. But he wasn't laughing now. No, he was angry, the thought of all his friends who had died at the claws of the Ghoules foremost in his mind.

He fought with a barely controlled rage. Holding his scutum in place with one hand, he absorbed every Ghoule blow on his steel shield as if it was nothing more than a knock on the door. Every so often, when he judged the time was right, he reached over the top of his shield with the blacksmith's mallet that he used with such destructive skill, shattering clawed hands, breaking bones with an incredible frequency, and smashing skulls with an almost manic glee.

Nkia, who was never far from Majdi, was just as much of a menace. Using her preferred jambiyas, the traditional curved daggers of her homeland, she engaged in her bloody work with a controlled abandon. Whenever Majdi struck with his hammer, Nkia came at the Ghoule from his unprotected side.

She aimed for the beast's throat or the side of his neck, which usually resulted in a splash of thick black blood that briefly formed a cloud in the air before staining the translucent stone of the summit. And if neither of those options was available to her, a quick jab to the kidneys usually did the trick, the strike just as effective though not as showy as her first line of attack.

The two gladiators were proving to be a murderously dangerous combination, much to Davin's delight.

Lycia was doing all that she could to hold back the Ghoules on the east side of the rim. She wove a web of steel around herself with her twin swords, slashing and cutting, reminding the gladiators fighting with her why the crowd in the Colosseum had named her the Crimson Devil. She was a whirlwind of motion, her blades a maelstrom of havoc as they whipped over the shoulders of the shield bearers to cut into any unprotected Ghoule flesh.

Knocking a Ghoule's spear to the side, Lycia slashed across the beast's arm, pivoting so that she could spin back around and continue with her attack. Before she could complete her movement, Chesin, one of the youngest gladiators freed from the Pit, was there, reaching over Caellia's other shoulder to stab the beast through his armpit, giving his sword a twist for good measure as he ripped the bloody steel free.

Caellia, who was almost as broad as Dorlan and perhaps even more dangerous, though she did tend to smile more, was smiling then in spite of the furor of the battle. The wounded Ghoule could do nothing to defend himself as she smashed the beast in the face with her scutum, then drove the metal edge of the curved steel into his midsection, doubling the Ghoule over and almost cutting him in half.

In the tighter space created by the columns that bounded the Sanctuary, the Blood Company was holding its own. For how much longer, however, no one could say. They were still outnumbered. More Ghoules continued to fill the ranks of the fallen beasts, the newest pack right at that moment trotting up the ramp and emerging out of the clouds onto the shimmering stone of the summit, the beasts sprinting across the small plaza to join the fight.

So there was nothing for the gladiators to do but fight until they couldn't fight anymore.

THE GHOULE OVERLORD shifted his weight from one clawed foot to the other as he stood on the shimmering stone of the summit, scarcely able to control himself. He was no more than a few dozen feet from the ten pillars, no more than a few dozen feet from the Seventh Stone, but his Ghoules had yet to force their way past the humans.

Needing to release the tension that was building within

him, he tapped the end of his long black staff on the stone. The pace of the wood hitting the crest kept time with his growing impatience, the tap tap tapping sounding more and more like a single, continuous beat.

This hunt should have ended long ago, and well before they reached the Sanctuary. In fact, the humans should never have escaped the Dark Forest in the first place and made it this far. The Slayers should have slaughtered them there in the wood.

Yet still the chase continued, the humans demonstrating an almost inhuman capacity to keep themselves and their defensive line intact. He didn't know if he should fault his Ghoules or credit the skill and bravery of the humans for the stalemate that had emerged atop the monolith.

He couldn't see the Protector from where he stood. He could sense the power radiating from just beyond the pillars. It was that power that he focused on now. The Curse contained within the Seventh Stone called to him, and that's really all that he cared about in that moment.

All of his plans hinged upon obtaining the Seventh Stone.

The Ghoule Overlord growled deeply, trying and failing to release some of his burgeoning aggravation, silently imploring his Ghoules to break the human line. He was distracted from his thoughts when the Weir began to flicker even more wildly than it had before, flashing black and white, even disappearing entirely every few seconds, the streams of energy blasting up into the sky faltering, before coming back into place with a seeming reluctance.

The Ghoule Overlord understood that the Weir was weakening, yet what was happening now wasn't caused by the slow degradation of the barrier. Then the rhythmic tapping of the Ghoule Overlord's staff on the stone stopped, his eyes widening, his maw breaking into an evil grin.

The tremendous power of the Seventh Stone, its utility as an amplifier, was interfering with the flow of energy between the Stones that maintained the Weir. That confirmed what he suspected. The Protector was in the Sanctuary, attempting to repair the barrier and demonstrating little skill for the task.

If the Protector failed, then the boy might destroy the Weir for him.

The Ghoule Overlord's grin at that conclusion turned into a frown as he considered a possibility that had seemed more fantasy than reality. It took ten of the most powerful Magii in the Kingdom to craft the Weir. They had needed the Seventh Stone to do it.

Even if the Protector was now the Seventh Stone, the boy couldn't do what it had taken the Ten Magii to do.

Could he?

Surely, it was a fool's errand. It had been from the start. It had to be.

The Ghoule Overlord's scowl shifted to actual concern when he sensed the Protector open himself to the power of the Seventh Stone. Desperate to master the immense energy in play in the Sanctuary, he realized that he couldn't wait any longer for his Ghoules and Elders to do what they should have done already. He couldn't take the risk that the Protector might actually be able to repair the Weir when he was so close to achieving his larger goal. He couldn't take the risk that the Protector became even more powerful than he was.

Better to take him now.

A sable mist began spinning slowly above the black diamond set in the Ghoule Overlord's staff, picking up speed as more of the Curse streamed out, until finally a massive cloud that was darker than the cells beneath the Temple of the Ghoules took shape. The Dark Magic whipped around faster and faster, the gloom slowly twisting and turning, separating and coming back together, a vague shape that stood over ten feet tall slowly forming. As the Ghoule Overlord continued his work, the Curse hardened into a thick, smooth skin that resembled the black ice that he had used to span the break in the trail.

It wasn't long before the Ghoule Overlord's creation was complete, the cloud of Dark Magic fading away to reveal what the Master of the Lost Land had crafted. The creature was so large and broad that it appeared to blot out the fading sun, its sharp claws creating frightening shadows on the stone of the summit.

In a burst of speed that was set in motion when the Ghoule Overlord flicked his staff toward the Sanctuary, the beast sprinted across the stone, knocking over three Ghoules and then two gladiators and crashing through the shield wall. At the entrance to the hollow, the creature didn't bother to stop, jumping down the steps and landing in the dirt with a ground-shaking thud that left two huge, clawed footprints in the ground.

The magical beast snarled from the very depths of its chest as it searched for its quarry.

With barely a sniff, the monster had the scent, drawn toward the power of the Seventh Stone, charging toward Bryen with a blood-curdling roar.

DAZED, his vision blurry, his head ringing, Declan still managed to push himself up to his knees, lunging wildly with his sword. He cursed himself for his poor aim, missing the Ghoule's gut that he had been targeting. Nevertheless, he succeeded in jabbing his steel into the Ghoule's knee before the beast could follow through the breach created when that monster knocked over him and two of his shield bearers and rushed into the Sanctuary.

He wanted to chase after whatever creature had ripped a hole in the shield wall, knowing exactly where the monster was headed and for what purpose. But no matter his desire, he couldn't. He needed to stay here and fill the gap.

The Ghoules were already shifting their efforts toward the breach, wanting to make use of the opening that the massive monster crafted of shadow had created. If the beasts got behind the gladiators, the Blood Company's defense would crumble.

That worry guiding his thoughts, Declan had no choice but to stand his ground against the three Ghoules who sprinted toward him.

He was a practical man. He had needed to be in order to survive in the Royal Guard and then in the Pit as a gladiator.

He already knew how this battle above the clouds was going to end. That unavoidable conclusion didn't bother him. He was a fighter. If he was going to die he wanted it to be with a sword in his hand.

His only regret was that he couldn't go to Bryen's aid. So he promised himself that he would take at least one or two of the beasts charging toward the gap with him before he was dragged across the white sand.

Buoyed by the promise he made to himself, Declan jumped onto the Ghoule who was writhing on the ground in agony, the beast unable to stand because of his mangled joint. With a quick thrust of his dagger beneath the beast's chin, the steel punching up into his brain, a thick stream of black blood gurgling out of his saw-toothed maw, Declan batted away with his sword the dying Ghoule's ineffectual swipes at his throat.

Rather than getting up after the beast took his last breath, he rolled off the corpse and kicked out with his right leg, slamming his boot into the front knee of the Ghoule who was leading the charge. The beast shrieked in surprise and pain, his leg bending at an unnatural angle, as he fell atop the dead Ghoule, the ligaments in his knee beyond repair.

Declan smiled viciously, pleased that he had forced another of the beasts out of the fight. Still, he held no illusions. He knew that his end was coming. The other two Ghoules were too close to him, one already stabbing his spear toward Declan's chest. The blackened tip would punch right through his ribs before Declan could get his sword up in time to deflect the attack.

Resigned to his circumstances, Declan screamed several curses at the onrushing beasts that would have made the most callous gladiator blush. Everything around the Master of the Gladiators faded away as his eyes contracted solely on the spearpoint of the charging Ghoule's weapon, the point growing bigger in size with each long stride the beast took toward him.

Declan wanted to see the steel slide into his flesh. He wanted to see his death as it happened. That had always been his desire, ever since he fought on the white sand.

But at the very last second, a flash of bright white light forced him to close his eyes and look away. When he turned back, black spots clouded his vision. When finally he could see clearly again, he realized that Aislinn was standing next to him, and two piles of ash, what Declan assumed used to be the two charging Ghoules, were just a few feet in front of him, the gusts of wind blasting across the summit sweeping away the last of the beasts.

Good timing on the Lady of the Southern Marches' part, Declan thought. Then he remembered the Ghoule with the injured knee, fearing an attack from behind. He was about to spin back around to finish the job, only to discover that there was no need. Aislinn beat him to it, slashing down with her glowing sword and decapitating the beast.

Relieved to still be alive, Declan finally pushed himself to his feet. Much of his leather armor was covered in blood. Of course, that didn't bother him in the least, because thanks to the frighteningly capable young woman who had decided to watch over him, none of the blood was his own, all of it belonging to the Ghoules.

"You're a menace, did you know that?" proclaimed Declan with a malicious and proud grin.

Aislinn smiled for the first time since the battle for the Sanctuary had begun. "You can thank Bryen for that. He was very thorough with his training."

"I'm glad that he was. If he hadn't been, I'd probably be dead."

"That's still a good possibility," said Aislinn as she pointed with the tip of her sword at the pack of Ghoules that had just appeared on the summit, the new arrivals now sprinting toward the gap in the gladiators' shield wall.

Declan was about to issue a series of commands, then held his tongue, realizing that there was no need. Majdi was there, shifting into place to close the hole in the wall of steel, locking his scutum with those of the gladiators on both sides just in time to bear the brunt of the next Ghoule rush.

Satisfied that the line would hold for at least a little while longer, Declan turned to pursue whatever monster had gone after Bryen. Aislinn's words stopped him in his tracks.

"It's a Golem. It's an abomination. A creature made by the Ghoule Overlord, a physical reflection of the Curse. There's nothing that you can do to fight it. Only a Magus can take it on and have any hope of surviving the encounter. Even then the Magus' chances are slim at best."

"Bryen needs our help. He can't fight that monster and repair the Weir at the same time."

"I know," replied Aislinn, her voice hard, ringing with the authority of her rank. "That's why I'm going after it."

She then leapt down into the hollow, sword and the Talent at the ready.

～

"Did you see that?" asked Rafia.

The two Magii fought back to back, one focusing on one side of the Sanctuary, one on the other, both concentrating on the same task. Killing Elders. And barring that, preventing the servants of the Ghoule Overlord from assailing the gladiators with the Curse.

"A Golem," grunted Sirius as he shot a bolt of energy at an Elder who thought that he could sneak around on his left by trying to mix in with the Ghoules attacking the Blood Company on that front. The ploy didn't work, although the Elder's crafty approach did save his life. Instead of ripping through the servant of the Ghoule Overlord, the surge of power tore through the Ghoule standing in front of him. The energy of the resulting blast sent Ghoule body parts and gore flying into the air in every direction, forcing the Elder to scurry back from the fight. "I haven't seen one of those since the First Ghoule War."

"Maybe it's a good sign," suggested Rafia. "Maybe the Ghoule Overlord is growing desperate. Maybe what Bryen is doing is making him nervous."

The Magus flicked her wrist, three small spheres of energy shrieking across the battlefield and slicing through an Elder's knee and then his black staff, the maimed beast collapsing to the ground with a terrible shriek, whether because of his injury or the fact that he could no longer employ Dark Magic because of his broken staff, Rafia didn't know, and she didn't really care. The battle had become nothing more than a numbers game to her, and the wounded Elder was simply one more combatant knocked out of the fight.

She did care about the Golem, however. That terrible invention was tied to its creator. The monster would do whatever the Ghoule Overlord ordered it to do, and it would do it effectively and efficiently because the Golem was impervious to steel and to both Dark Magic and the Talent. Consequently, there was no way to defeat it. It was virtually indestructible.

"One of us needs to go after it," said Sirius as he sent a stream of the Talent off to his right, trying to catch an Elder by surprise, cursing under his breath when he missed by no more than a whisker.

"We can't," replied Rafia. "Not at this moment. We need to focus on the Elders. If we don't ..."

"I know," mumbled Sirius.

If the Elders were given free rein in the battle, then the battle would end quickly and not in the Blood Company's favor. All that he and Rafia could do was continue the fight and hope that Bryen realized what he was up against before the monster killed him.

BRYEN FOUND the amount of power that was used to construct the Weir mindboggling. How could the Ten Magii, even if they were the most powerful practitioners of the Talent of their era, have managed such a massive flow, much less woven the two warring magics together at the same time? He found that thought almost inconceivable.

He had shifted his concentration away from the pedestal to the Weir, using the energy gifted to him by the Seventh Stone to study how the Talent and the Curse had been plaited together to form such a unique construction. Here in the Sanctuary it looked no different than it had when he had examined the weave and flow when he flew along its length while riding Banshee, the two disparate powers threaded together so precisely that there was no way to tell where the weave began and where it ended.

Yet no matter how many times he studied it, there was the one anomaly that always drew his eye. The one weakness to the entire design that worried him and made him hesitate even though he understood that time was precariously short.

When Bryen manipulated the Curse, he always did so with a thin layer of the Talent protecting him from the taint of the Dark Magic.

The Ten Magii hadn't done that when they had worked with the Dark Magic, at least not as carefully as he did. And it was that lack of protection that had led to the Ten Magii's downfall. Yet strangely it had also proven to be the key to their incredible creation.

Despite the fact that the two distinct energies naturally repelled one another, the Ten Magii had woven them together into a single whole that had lasted for almost a thousand years before the Weir had begun to weaken.

What the Ten Magii had done had ensured the integrity of the magical construction yet had doomed them at the same time. Ironic, but uniquely appropriate when he considered the conflicting yet symbiotic relationship between the two energies. It was because of that strange symmetry that he assumed that he would need to do much the same if he were to repair the Weir.

But how was he to do it without touching the Curse himself? Could he even do it without touching the Curse? Or was he doomed to follow the same path as the Ten Magii if he was to have any hope of success?

Bryen didn't have the time to continue pondering the issue, diving to the right, then rolling away when he sensed the menacing presence swipe at him from behind, the massive shape that pulled in all the surrounding light slamming a bar of what looked to be black ice down into the dirt where he had been standing.

Bryen ducked out of the way again, finally getting a good look at the creature as he dropped beneath the bar. The monster resembled a Slayer, though it was slightly larger. Its skin was smooth, glassy, not a single imperfection visible. He had read about monsters such as these when he was in the

Library of the Magii, Rafia suggesting that he devote some time to knowing what his enemy might one day send to kill him.

Bryen evaded another swing, and then one more, the large bar of black ice swishing through the air as he dodged around the pedestals. He never thought that he would ever come up against a Golem. If he remembered correctly, there was no known way to destroy one of these monsters.

Driven by the Dark Magic with which they were created, Golems never tired, as proved to be the case with this one. The monster followed Bryen at a furious pace as he danced around the pedestals, trying to keep one between him and the Golem at all times, the beast barely giving him time to breathe.

For just a moment, the Golem paused its attack, unwilling to swing its bar through the stream of energy that shot up into the sky from one of the Seven Stones. That hesitation gave Bryen the chance to really study the beast.

It was larger than any Ghoule he had ever come across, including the Ghoule Overlord, though it had the same clawed feet and hands. Besides the shiny perfection of the monster's body, perhaps the most disconcerting aspect of the creature was that it didn't have any eyes. Then again, the monster had no need for sight, since it hunted its prey based on the scent given to it by the Ghoule Overlord. Just like the Slayers.

Bryen was pleased that he remembered the basic characteristics of the Golem. He was less pleased in that in his readings on this and the other beasts the Ghoule Overlord had crafted to achieve his particular ends, there had been no mention of any weaknesses.

And right now that was the information that he needed most. His focus shifted to that specific problem as he watched the bar the Ghoule was using as a weapon transform into a new shape, the Curse shifting its structure, now appearing as a large scythe.

The Golem stared at Bryen for a few seconds, or at least

Bryen assumed that's what the monster was doing since he couldn't really tell for sure. Then with a lightning-fast burst of speed, the Golem shot around the pedestal, swinging for Bryen's neck with the scythe.

The unexpectedly swift movement caught Bryen by surprise. He pushed himself off the pedestal he had been standing behind and out of the way just in time, though because of his haste his hip caught the corner of the stone as he did so, the unforgiving rock knocking him to the ground.

The Golem continued its assault, swinging with the razor-sharp Dark Magic as Bryen scrambled backward like a crab, using his hands and feet to drag himself away, the tip of the weapon made of the Curse stabbing into the dirt instead of his flesh with every strike, though with every strike that frightening tip getting closer and closer.

Bryen felt a surge of dread run through him when his back slammed against the wall of the depression, knocking the breath from him. He had nowhere else to go. The Golem had cornered him, and he was certain that the monster wasn't going to give him an opportunity to look for a way to escape, the creature already raising the scythe above his head to drive the point through Bryen's chest. Out of options, Bryen reached for the Talent.

He knew that it would be of little use against a creature such as this and that it was already too late, the scythe cutting down toward him. Still, he had to try. He refused to be easy meat.

But before he could craft a shield to defend himself, a blinding blast of energy forced Bryen to avert his gaze. Just then the sharp black tip of the scythe froze in place, no more than a few inches from his heart. The blast of the Talent had slammed right into the monster's broad back. It had no visible effect on the creature other than to catch the Golem's attention.

The Golem turned slowly, following the scent of the power

used against it, fixing its attention on Aislinn, who stood on the other side of the depression with a blazing sphere of energy dancing atop her palm.

Bryen made use of the distraction that Aislinn provided, regaining his feet and swinging for the monster's neck with the Spear of the Magii, the double blades glowing brightly with the Talent.

The Golem spun back around, catching the blade on its scythe with a seeming indifference.

The monster and Bryen stood opposite one another, the blade of his spear holding the scythe in place, the two combatants locked in a struggle in which neither seemed able or willing to move. The most disconcerting aspect of the entire experience for Bryen was the strange reality of fighting something that displayed no emotion.

The Golem didn't care. It simply did. It was nothing more than a manifestation of the Ghoule Overlord's power and will. A tool to be used, and a deadly one at that.

And now Bryen wasn't sure what to do with their weapons locked together, worried that if he tried to break away from the monster, the Golem would cut him down from behind. The solution came to him in the form of another blazing ball of energy, Aislinn's latest attack slamming into the Golem's back once again, drawing the monster's attention just for a second and giving Bryen the time that he needed to slide away from the silent creature.

At least now he had Aislinn to help him, which meant that he might live a little bit longer. But the primary question remained. A question that he feared for which he didn't have an answer

How did you destroy a magical monster that couldn't be destroyed?

"Doing all right, Majdi?" asked Declan.

"Never better," shouted the gladiator so that he could be heard over the din of the fight. "You have nothing to worry about. The Ghoules won't be going any farther than they are now. You have my word on that."

The usually loquacious gladiator seemed to be enjoying himself, smiling brightly with a manic look in his eyes as he slammed the scutum he held into the chest of the Ghoule who had reached for Declan with his spear over the top of the gladiator's shield. That decision cost the beast dearly, Nkia slipping around Majdi's other shoulder and driving one of her jambiyas into the Ghoule's throat, the beast collapsing as a thick flow of black blood streamed down his chest.

"I never doubted you, Majdi," replied Declan.

"Thank you for your confidence, Declan. I do appreciate it."

As Majdi continued to ramble on while fighting and killing Ghoules, Declan let the gladiator's words flow over him as he took a moment to examine the battle within the battle that he could do little about.

Sirius and Rafia continued to fight the Elders, helping to maintain the Blood Company's strong defense, the gladiators having recovered from the Golem's charge, the shield wall intact. But that defense only would continue for however long the two Magii could keep the Elders at bay. Recognizing that both Sirius and Rafia had their hands full, with his gladiators in good form and not in immediate need of his assistance Declan thought that he might actually be able to make things a bit easier for the two practitioners of the Talent.

Declan picked up a couple of spears that lay on the stone next to the Ghoules he had killed with Aislinn's help. He hefted one in his right hand a few times. The weapon was longer and heavier than what he was used to, but it was still serviceable for what he had in mind.

Once he was certain of the weight, Declan twisted his body

back as he had learned to do so long ago as a soldier in the Royal Guard, throwing the first spear in a smooth motion. The lance of blackened steel flew through the air and slammed into the chest of an Elder who was sending a stream of Dark Magic toward Rafia.

That flow of the Curse ended abruptly, the Ghoule standing in place a moment longer, confused as to what had happened, having some difficulty comprehending the steel that had sprouted from his chest. The beast toppled onto his back, the barb that had pierced him punching into the stone beneath him, the haft of the weapon sticking out of his sternum.

Not bad for his first throw thought Declan. His confidence increasing, he turned his attention to an Elder on the other side of the rim who was dueling with Sirius. After hefting the spear a few times to ensure that he had a good feel for the weapon, Declan threw it in an easy motion, understanding that accuracy was more important than strength.

The Elder he targeted this time was farther away than the first, which he used as his excuse as to why he didn't kill the beast outright, the spear only taking the Ghoule in the collar-bone. Even so, the wound was enough to distract the beast, shocking the Elder and breaking his concentration, the shards of Dark Magic he had been throwing toward the Magus sputtering out.

This brief interlude was all the time that Sirius needed. He killed the Elder with a bolt of energy that ripped through his body and left nothing but a smoking husk on the glimmering stone.

Declan smiled with a feral pleasure. Two Elders down in less than a minute. That meant less pressure on the Magii, and in turn less pressure on his gladiators. Not a bad result in his opinion.

Unfortunately, he didn't have more than a few seconds to savor his success, having to step forward and join the shield wall as another group of Ghoules pounded across the summit screaming for blood.

EVERY SO OFTEN A SOLDIER OF the Blood Company glanced down into the hollow for a second or two. That's all the time they could permit themselves as they continued their resistance against the Ghoules. Still, it was enough for them marvel at the Volkun and the Vedra fighting together.

Both were incredibly fast. Both were incredibly intuitive with their movements and decisions. It was as if the two could read one another's minds, two warriors fighting as one.

They also could sense the frustration emanating from Bryen and Aislinn as they coordinated their efforts against the Golem, trying a variety of different attacks, seeking some way to destroy the monster, yet finding no solution. Blades didn't work, steel simply sliding off the smooth surface of the monster in a flash of sparks. Even their Talent-infused weapons skittered uselessly across the Dark Magic of which the Golem was made.

Employing the Talent directly didn't work either. The blasts of energy merely glanced off the monster. Distracting it, yes, slowing it down, yes, but doing nothing else of importance.

Trusting that Aislinn could keep the Golem busy, the Vedra attacking with a series of lunges and slashes that in only seconds would have ripped apart any other opponent, Bryen allowed his mind to drift, thinking back to what little he had read of the Golem.

One key fact kept playing through his mind.

The Golem was immune to Dark Magic and the Talent, true. So neither power would be of use in trying to kill it. But it was constructed with the Curse. So if it had been made with the Curse, did that not mean that it could also be unmade?

Calling once more upon the Seventh Stone, ensuring that the Dark Magic within him was safely locked away, Bryen directed the power of the artifact toward the Ghoule Overlord's creation. At first nothing happened. The Golem, with its back turned to Bryen, blocked a series of Aislinn's mind-numbingly fast blows with his scythe and didn't bother to parry others, allowing the steel to slide off his hardened shell whenever it chose knowing that those blows would have no effect.

Maybe he needed to give the artifact within him greater freedom to do what it did best.

Bryen noticed the change when he intensified the pull of the Seventh Stone. The Golem's body became rigid, freezing in place, its back arching, arms splayed to the side.

Although what happened next was invisible to the naked eye, Bryen could see it clearly with the Talent, watching as the Seventh Stone latched onto the Golem, demanding the Dark Magic from which it was made, the flow of energy into the artifact beginning as a trickle and rapidly escalating to a powerful tide. In just a few breaths, the Seventh Stone drained the monster dry, the Golem disintegrating rapidly until every speck of the Curse had been consumed, flowing through the Spear of the Magii and into the Seventh Stone.

Bryen smiled at Aislinn, giving her a nod of thanks. He couldn't have done that without her. Yet even with that combat over, he growled in resignation.

The larger battle still remained.

19

THE COMBAT BEGINS

Incensed, the Ghoule Overlord slammed the end of his staff onto the shimmering stone of the summit, tiny cracks spreading in all directions across the smooth surface, not stopping until they reached the base of the columns. He had felt the exact moment that the Protector had destroyed his Golem.

The thief!

Stealing the Curse from him with the Seventh Stone. Stealing the Dark Magic that belonged only to him, that could only be given by him, and then making it his own.

Such arrogance! Such insolence!

He had never believed that such a thing could happen. None of the Magii during the War of Expansion had been able to defend against his Golems. None of them could do anything with the Curse. None of them ever dared do anything with the Curse until the Ten Magii crafted the Weir.

But this Protector was a different entity entirely.

He realized then that this Protector who time after time had denied his attempts to regain what had been taken from him was not just an aberration. No, he was something else. Something more. Something dangerous.

The Protector was a real threat.

Because the Protector was learning how to master the Seventh Stone.

That truth gnawed at him, as it couldn't be denied. But it could be reversed.

He needed to put a stop to the Protector's education immediately. He could not allow the Protector to become a greater danger to his plans than he already was.

He would not allow the Protector to become greater than he was.

He needed to recover the Seventh Stone. Now.

It was a task that only he could complete. It was the only way to ensure that he remained the Master of the Curse.

His Ghoules and Elders had failed. As did his Slayers, his three favored assassins dead. And now his Golem destroyed, a creature that until now was infrangible.

With that one overwhelming need playing through his mind, consuming him, driving him, a massive cloud of darkness began to form above the top of his staff, the tainted energy bursting out from the black diamond, swirling around the Ghoule Overlord like a tornado, black sparks and threads of power whipping out, electrifying the air, muting the bright sunlight striking the crest to a dull grey.

His rage and his desire guiding him, with a bone-breaking force the Ghoule Overlord slammed his staff down onto the stone of the summit. His Dark Magic swept across the shimmering rock, shattering the smooth surface of the plaza, dozens of large fissures streaking toward the humans who stood against his Ghoules.

When those jagged streaks of black smashed into the pillars on the southern side of the crest, a powerful blast of energy shot up into the air, the Dark Magic repelled by the Talent that was used to build the Sanctuary, the two powers slamming into one another, the resounding roar of the clash echoing through the Trench like a never-ending thunder.

As the kinetic wave of energy exploded across the top of the monolith, the Ghoules and gladiators first were forced to turn away from one another and then break apart entirely, the power so strong that it felt as if they were going to be swept off the summit. It took several seconds for the competing magics to dissipate, the crackling energy, streaks of black and white sizzling in the air, finally fizzling out and leaving the Ghoules and Elders standing poised to resume the battle, just a dozen yards separating them from the gladiators, who remained entrenched between the columns.

Yet the clash of arms didn't resume across the sandstone pillar. Instead, a strange silence settled upon the crest, all eyes drawn to the Master of the Ghoule Legions.

That hush was finally broken when the Ghoule Overlord strode purposefully across the stone, black eyes blazing with hatred and disgust, his staff thunking sharply against the fractured stone with every step that he took.

It was time to end this. It was time to claim what was his.

"You will allow your people to continue to fight for you?" asked the Ghoule Overlord, stopping near the entrance to the Sanctuary, no more than a spear's length away from the shield wall, obviously unconcerned by the gladiators who stood before him. He spoke in the common language so that the men and women standing before him understood what he said. Although some of the words were difficult to interpret, Majdi and the other fighters who blocked his way were able to make out enough of the words to get the gist of what he said. "You will allow your people to continue to die for you? Even though they have no hope of surviving this fight?"

"They will do what is necessary to defeat you, just as I will," Bryen replied, calmly though forcefully, his voice carrying across the summit, as he walked up from the hollow and came to stand at the top of the steps so that he could look the Ghoule Overlord in the eyes. "The Blood Company is a free company. They fight when they choose. When they must. They fight because they know the darkness that you bring to Caledonia. They understand the cost of giving you what you seek. As do I."

"They fight for you, Protector. Not for a Kingdom. A Kingdom, in fact, that had no use for them other than to make them bleed. If you don't know that by now, then you are a fool. And I know that you are not a fool."

"Perhaps I am for taking on this quest," replied Bryen, his eyes cold, emotionless. "If that's the case, so be it. I have made my decision. It will not change. I will not give you the Seventh Stone. But you knew that already." He did not have the patience to engage in much of a dialogue with his nemesis. He had a single responsibility to complete, and every second that the Ghoule Overlord wasted with talk was another second lost, the Weir continuing to flicker wildly, in danger of disappearing entirely with the Seventh Stone in such close proximity. "So what is it that you want?"

"I want to finish what we started," replied the Ghoule Overlord. "I want to finish what we began the last time that we were here."

"Single combat."

"Something that you should be familiar with, Protector. You are no more than a slave from the Pit after all."

"I am that," Bryen agreed with a grin that was mirrored by every one of the gladiators standing among the ten columns of the Sanctuary, "and proudly. But I am much more than that. We who have fought on the white sand are so much more than just that."

Bryen studied the Ghoule Overlord for a moment, intrigued by the beast's intensity. His adversary was primed just like one of the black dragons living in the Trench, prepared to launch himself at him when the opportunity presented itself, the beast actually struggling to contain his rage and ... something else. The Master of the Curse was quite intimidating to begin with, made all the more so because the black of his eyes sparked with the power of the Lost Land.

Yet despite the tremendous power cascading through the Ghoule Overlord, the enmity and hunger radiating from the beast, Bryen realized that his nemesis was no different than any of the other opponents he had fought in the Colosseum.

They had all wanted the same thing.

The Ghoule Overlord was desperate to kill Bryen. That didn't surprise him. He understood that already, what he wanted. And it didn't bother him in the least, because after ten years on the white sand he was used to it.

Now there was another emotion driving this huge, ancient beast. An emotion that Bryen had never expected to see. It was this new, surreal reality that brought a faint smile to his lips.

Fear.

The Ghoule Overlord was trying not to reveal it, but Bryen could tell thanks to his long experience in the Pit. The tic at the crease of one eye, how his claws wrapped around his staff continued to squeeze the black ash every few seconds.

The Ghoule Overlord was afraid. Either of him or the power that he manipulated. Perhaps even both.

That was good to know. That fact he could use.

"Or much less if you prove to be the coward that I know you to be," challenged the Ghoule Overlord, sneering out the words, trying to provoke the Protector into a rash action, hoping that the insult would resonate with the other gladiators. "Prove me wrong, Protector. Fight me now. Fight me for the lives of your people. You can end all this right now by accepting my challenge. For you, it should be no different than a combat on the white sand."

Bryen stared at his adversary with an intuitive gaze, allowing the tension to build, the Ghoule Overlord leaning forward, his posture and look suggesting that he could barely contain himself, that he was desperate for this fight. Yes, he would use that knowledge now. Bryen smiled wolfishly, his eyes becoming sharp and frigid in just an instant.

"I accept your challenge," Bryen replied. Aislinn, who was standing just a few feet away from her Protector, shot him a look of apprehension, as did Rafia and Sirius from where they stood on the rim of the Sanctuary. He ignored them. They had nothing to fear. He knew what he was doing. His key priority had not changed. "First, though, I'm going to fix the Weir. I'm going to make sure that you and your Ghoules can never set foot in Caledonia again. Once that's done, you'll have my full attention. So enjoy what little time you have left, because at the end of our third combat the Master of the Curse will become nothing more than a memory."

Bryen didn't think that the Ghoule Overlord was going to appreciate his response, and he was right, the black mist that always spun atop the black diamond doing so with greater violence now, the Dark Magic a marker for the beast's moods, the Ghoule Overlord's current humor clearly darker than the Curse itself.

"I think not!" roared the Ghoule Overlord. "After I kill you, I will feast on your bones. The only thing that will be left of you will be the knife on my hip. The same fate waits for your friends. They will die by the claws of my Ghoules."

"Saying and doing are two different things," explained Bryen. "As you've seen during your hunt, we are not easy prey. So come at us at your own risk. We're ready for you. Have no fear of that."

The Ghoule Overlord roared again in anger, insulted by Bryen's impertinence. "I am the Master of the Lost Land! No one challenges me and lives!"

The Ghoule Overlord dug his clawed feet into the stone and bent at the knees, about to launch himself over the shield wall and at the Protector. He never got the chance to do so, instead having to raise his black staff to his front to block the sword that was slicing through the air toward his neck.

"If you want to kill Bryen, you'll need to kill me first!" screamed Lycia, who had sprinted between Majdi and Jenus, using the two gladiators' bulk to mask her attack. She hoped to make the Ghoule Overlord bleed since Bryen had the monster's complete attention. Maybe with a bit of luck even a strike that would take him out of the fight.

But it was not to be. The Crimson Devil continued her attack after the Ghoule Overlord parried her first slash, her twin blades whipping toward the beast's ribs, then chest, then thigh, then hip, and so it went. The only noise that could be heard atop the summit was Lycia's steel meeting the thick wood of the Ghoule Overlord's staff.

Lycia became more frustrated as she continued her assault. No matter what she tried, the Ghoule Overlord blocked every one of her strikes. And though she used her twin blades with magnificent skill and grace, she knew within the first few seconds of the combat that it wouldn't be enough, the Ghoule Overlord barely having to move to ward off her blows.

This was a combat that she could not win. Still, that realization didn't stop her from pressing her opponent.

The Ghoule Overlord actually seemed to enjoy the very brief fight, or perhaps he was just amused that a human had the temerity to actually attack him, though that did not last for very long.

He remained focused on his primary task, the task that had been driving him for centuries.

Before Bryen or any of the other gladiators could move, with a contemptuous glare, the Ghoule Overlord shot a bolt of Dark Magic from the black diamond, the Curse striking Lycia's chest and knocking her backward across the stone to slam into the shield wall. Her leather armor that protected her torso was in tatters, her skin charred and smoking where the corrupt energy had burned through her flesh. Worse, her breath came to her in painful gasps, her body unable to manage the parasitical Dark Magic surging through her.

Fading in and out of consciousness, Lycia realized that she was going to die.

That didn't bother her.

No, what stuck in her craw as her eyes closed was the fact that she had lost the combat before it had barely even begun.

BRYEN WATCHED in horror as Lycia flew back across the stone, crashing in a heap right in front of Majdi. The fight had taken no more than a few breaths, everyone too shocked by Lycia's brave but foolish act to do anything more than watch in astonishment as she launched herself at the Ghoule Overlord.

It was Lycia's scream of anguish when the Dark Magic struck her that finally broke the spell that had been cast upon him and the other gladiators.

A sharp, concentrated anger burned through Bryen as he sprinted toward the beast who had harmed his friend. The blades of the Spear of the Magii, glowing brightly with the Talent, whistled through the air toward the Ghoule Overlord's neck.

The Master of the Ghoules expected the blow, swinging his staff up and catching the blade in the wood, the steel digging deeply into the black ash. No more than a few inches separating them, Bryen pushed against the Ghoule Overlord's staff with his spear, wanting to force his shining blades closer to his enemy's mottled green flesh.

Muscles straining, the veins on his neck bulging, even though he put every bit of his strength into the effort, he couldn't do it. The Ghoule Overlord was too strong, the staff not budging a hair.

"That is your failing, Protector," said the Ghoule Overlord, switching back to his own language. "It is your downfall. You care. That is why you will die. And when you die, I will destroy the Weir. Then my Legions will take your Kingdom and feed on your people. There is no point in trying to resist. You are only wasting your time. You cannot stop me. You are weak. Too afraid."

If the Ghoule Overlord thought that he was going to succeed with his goading and enrage Bryen to the point where he would allow his emotions to take control, the beast was mistaken. Bryen had spent too much time on the white sand. He knew the words of desperation when he heard them.

The Ghoule Overlord was strong, powerful. But Bryen could not forget what he had seen in the beast right before Lycia attacked him.

Fear.

More important, fear of him. That gave Bryen a surge of confidence that energized him.

"Better to care than not," replied Bryen in the Ghoule language through gritted teeth.

If the Ghoule Overlord wanted to talk, that was fine with him. Because he was interested solely in fighting. Sliding his steel down the Ghoule Overlord's black staff as he dipped his shoulder and spun away, he whipped the Spear of the Magii back around, aiming a blade for the beast's shin.

The Ghoule Overlord brought his staff down just in time to keep the blade from slicing across his flesh, then had no choice but to dance back a few feet, catching the glowing blades with his staff a dozen more times as Bryen continued his attack with a dazzling display of speed, his actions so fast that he and the Ghoule Overlord appeared to be no more than hazy shapes surrounded by streaks of white and black light, sparks flashing every time the two weapons, one touched by the Talent, the other by the Curse, met.

The Ghoule Overlord grudgingly continued to give ground, moving back closer to his Ghoules, Bryen's ceaseless attack demanding more from the beast than he had been forced to give since the First Ghoule War. Several times the Spear of the Magii came within a whisker of cutting into his flesh.

Rather than be worried by that increasingly likely possibility, instead he was exhilarated. The Ghoule Overlord grinned sadistically, even laughing with pleasure, as he parried every slash and lunge, never ducking out of the way or seeking to elude a blow. Always standing tall, demonstrating his contempt for the Protector.

The Protector could fight no better than this, of that the Ghoule Overlord was certain. Now all the beast needed to do was to find the right moment to seize the momentum. Once he did, the Seventh Stone would be his.

The Ghoule Overlord's cackle stopped abruptly, the beast's eyes changing, the fear he worked so hard to hide revealed to all. Shock surged through him as he realized that every time he used his staff to block the Protector's steel, the Spear of the Magii cut off a sliver or chunk from the twisted black wood. That had never happened before. It should never happen. It wasn't possible.

His staff that contained the black diamond, the very source of the Curse in the Lost Land, was indestructible, or so he had thought.

With this unsettling discovery, the Ghoule Overlord concluded that he needed to end this combat as quickly as possible, worried about what might occur if the Protector continued to chip away at his staff. So he shifted to the attack, blasting a shard of the Curse from the black mist spinning atop the black diamond toward the Protector. And then several more.

Bryen barely had time to defend himself since he was so close to the beast. Even so, he deflected the Dark Magic hurtling toward him with his Spear, batting away each spike of darkness with his blades.

Aggravated that his attack had failed, though able to put some space between them, the Ghoule Overlord then sent a swirling cloud of the Curse toward Bryen, the billowing haze rushing toward him like a whirlwind.

Bryen understood what the Dark Magic would do if he allowed it to touch his skin. The beast sought to entrap him, then kill him slowly, the Dark Magic designed to wrap itself around him and drain away not only his power, but also his very essence, much as Bryen had done to the Elders on Haven.

Bryen smirked, pleased to see that his reaction to this latest attack irritated the Ghoule Overlord even more. The cloud of Dark Magic didn't bother Bryen in the least. He simply cut through the billowing murk with the Spear of the Magii, the Curse burning away at the touch of the Talent-infused blade.

Before the Ghoule Overlord could recover from his surprise at the ease with which the Protector had foiled his attack, Bryen sent several bolts of energy toward him, using the blades of his Spear as focal points so that he could augment the power.

The strength of his assault not only forced the Ghoule Overlord to craft a shield to defend himself, but the beast also had no choice but to step back a few more feet and add more of the Curse to his shield or risk losing control over the energy that was protecting him from the Talent, the Ghoule Overlord momentarily stunned by the ferocity of Bryen's blitz.

That surprising development sent another burst of confidence through Bryen. The Ghoule Overlord had started this fight, and Bryen promised himself that he would be the one to finish it.

∼

BRYEN CHARGING toward the Ghoule Overlord pushed Aislinn into motion, the Lady of the Southern Marches rushing to Lycia's side. The usually prickly gladiator was scarcely responsive.

Kneeling down, she tried to peel away the burnt leather from Lycia's flesh, needing to determine just how bad the wound was. What she saw made Aislinn lean back in horror.

The Dark Magic had burned through Lycia's leather armor and scorched her flesh along her lower ribs. There, Lycia's skin was burned and cracked, the muscle beneath charred. Even more terrifying, Aislinn saw the Curse worming its way deeper into her body, a web of black already sprouting from the wound and extending up to her chest and down her abdomen.

Not having a moment to lose, Aislinn reached for the Talent, attempting to draw out the Dark Magic before it could take hold within Lycia, doing as she had done with Bryen when he was teaching her how to use the Talent to heal. Nothing happened.

Anger at her failure and fear of what that meant mixing within her, she tried again. Nothing.

She couldn't latch onto the insidious Curse no matter what she tried, the Dark Magic sliding away from her grasp as if it had a mind of its own. Maybe it did.

Aislinn watched with a morbid fascination and growing trepidation as the corrupted energy spread rapidly throughout Lycia's body. The web of Dark Magic pulsed faster and in a deeper black every time Lycia took a shallow, shuddering breath, the tendrils now reaching down into her legs and up into her arms.

Once the Curse reached the gladiator's heart, Aislinn knew that the end would come. Lycia would succumb to the Dark Magic raging through her.

Aislinn's eyes watered, tears beginning to flow down her cheeks. She tried one more time, desperate to grab hold of the

Curse. And then again. And again. Time after time, refusing to give up.

Yet with each attempt the Dark Magic slipped away from her. Not knowing what else to do, she concentrated a stream of energy toward Lycia's wound just below her ribs, to the place where the Curse had first struck her, thinking that she could burn away the corruption with the clean power of the Talent.

Even that didn't work, the Dark Magic resisting her efforts, fighting back. That struggle between the two powers sent Lycia into convulsions that only served to weaken the wounded gladiator further. Fearing that she was only hastening Lycia's demise, Aislinn released her hold on the Talent.

"I'm sorry, Lycia," Aislinn whispered, her tears falling onto the gladiator's seared armor. "I'm sorry. I'm trying to help you. But nothing that I'm doing is working. I can't do anything about your wound. The Dark Magic is too strong."

Lycia, her eyes fluttering rapidly as she struggled to regain consciousness, reached up blindly, grasping Aislinn's hand. She gave the Lady of the Southern Marches a weak squeeze with her fingers, Lycia mouthing the words "Thank you." Then the wounded gladiator's body began to shiver violently, a cold fire burning through her.

Lycia knew what was coming. She knew that her body was failing, fighting against the Dark Magic that was coursing through her but unable to stop the Curse's advance. She understood that her death was near. Still, she refused to give up. No matter the pain, no matter the suffering, she would never surrender.

Aislinn watched in horror, wishing that she could do something to help, anything, hating that she had become no more than an observer. When the shivering stopped, and before Lycia lapsed back into unconsciousness, before the inevitable end came, with her grip surprisingly strong for this one final task, Lycia pulled Aislinn down toward her and whispered into her ear.

"Look after Bryen. He might not show it, but he needs someone he can trust in his life. Someone not from the Pit. Someone who can give him the balance that he needs." Tears formed in Lycia's eyes, whether from the pain wracking her body or the sense of loss or both, Aislinn didn't know. Then those same eyes hardened. The Crimson Devil appeared one final time. "Promise me!"

Aislinn nodded, her tears running freely down her cheeks. "I promise," she whispered. "I promise. You have my word."

"Thank you, sister," said Lycia softly, then her hand loosened from Aislinn's and the gladiator sagged back toward the stone, finally lapsing into unconsciousness as the web of Dark Magic reached for her heart.

Aislinn's tears flowed freely, not only because Lycia was dying, but because the gladiator, the woman who had hated her from the moment she had appeared in the Pit while she was a captive in the capital, had called her sister.

The ultimate compliment.

It was a mark of respect between gladiators who fought on the white sand. Somehow during the long journey from Tintagel she and Lycia, despite their competing desires, had become more than just wary acquaintances.

Aislinn wished that she could do more for Lycia. She was frantic to help her. But what was required, if it even was possible now, was beyond her.

Even so, there was one thing that she could do. She could hold onto her sister's hand and keep her safe until she passed, so that Lycia knew that she wasn't going to die alone.

THE GHOULES and gladiators watched intently, unable to move, unable to breathe. They were bewitched by the combat.

It was as if they had become a part of the translucent stone, no longer combatants themselves, rather just spectators to the duel between the Volkun and the Master of the Curse. The fight continued at a furious pace, their movements so fast, so measured, yet so intense, that the observers struggled to follow the action.

If it wasn't the steel of the Spear of the Magii meeting the hardened wood of the Ghoule Overlord's staff, it was the Talent and the Curse hurtling through the air. Back and forth the combat raged, the two adversaries shifting effortlessly from attack to defense to attack again.

Allowing his instincts and intuition to guide his latest assault, his spear flashing brightly as he spun a web of energy with his blades that forced the Ghoule Overlord to glide away from him, Bryen glanced behind him for the briefest of moments.

Aislinn was with Lycia. She was trying to help her, but he could tell that it wasn't going well.

He wasn't surprised, knowing firsthand how difficult it was to heal a wound caused by the Curse. The fact that he could not go to his friend and try to save her ate at him. He wanted to step away from the fight, though he knew that he couldn't.

So he permitted his fury to build, keeping it contained within him, keeping it cold, not wanting it to burst into flame at the wrong time, allowing it to strengthen his resolve. He needed to concentrate on this combat, and a focused fury could help him do that.

He also noticed how the Weir flashed more violently now, the barrier even disappearing for several seconds at a time before flaring back into place with an angry hiss. As each second passed, the magical barrier that had lasted for more than one thousand years, that had protected Caledonia from the incursions of the Ghoules, was not only weakening, but also disintegrating, in large part because he was there, disrupting the discordant union of the conflicting powers.

Bryen feared that the next time the Weir vanished, it wouldn't return, the flow of energy coming to a stop for good, never to begin again. That thought terrified him, because he didn't believe that he had the knowledge or the strength to construct the Weir from scratch.

Fix? Maybe. Craft a completely new barrier? Not likely.

The Ghoule Overlord noted the flash of concern that crossed Bryen's face, and he chose that moment to take advantage of the Protector's momentary distraction. The massive beast launched a new assault, swinging his staff at Bryen's head.

Another chunk of wood fell away from the staff as Bryen blocked the cut with the blade of his spear. The same thing happened again when the Ghoule Overlord pivoted and swung back around for Bryen's hip, the Protector's spear in place well beforehand to catch the blow and slice another long splinter off the staff that held the black diamond.

And so it continued, the Ghoule Overlord growing increasingly incandescent as the Protector parried every one of his attacks, taking another chunk or sliver of black ash from the staff every time he did so. No longer able to control his rage, the Ghoule Overlord swung his staff at Bryen's knee. As soon as he saw the Protector move to parry the strike, the Ghoule Overlord adjusted the height of his swing, redirecting his weapon midstroke toward the Protector's throat.

Bryen adapted instinctively, though only just in time, blocking the staff with the haft of the Spear of the Magii. A good result, though not good enough. Now his spear was parallel to the ground, and the Ghoule Overlord had not disengaged.

As a result, Bryen was moving back across the stone as he struggled to reset his feet and regain his balance. At the same time he tried to prevent the Ghoule Overlord from using his staff to push the haft of the Spear of the Magii back against his windpipe, the beast's strength almost too much for him.

He was desperate. He needed to get out of this position, swiftly, but he didn't know how.

He could see the wisps of the Curse dancing off the black diamond, which now was no more than a few inches from his face. As soon as that jewel touched his flesh, the Ghoule Overlord would win. The beast would take what he wanted. The Curse residing within the black diamond would make him its own in an instant, breaking the prison within him that contained the Dark Magic that he had locked away, freeing the tainted power to consume him from the inside out.

"You are mine, Protector," grunted the Ghoule Overlord harshly. "Because the Seventh Stone is mine. Better to give in. Better to surrender. Better to die now rather than extend the pain that I will inflict upon you."

Bryen ignored the Ghoule Overlord's taunts, trying not to retch because of the beast's rancid breath. His shoulders bunched, his back flexed, the muscles in his arms bulged and strained as he struggled keep the black diamond from touching him.

Yet despite calling on every ounce of his strength, the jewel, which radiated a ruinous malevolence, came closer and closer. First a finger away. Then just a knuckle. Next just a hair, the black diamond now only a whisker away from touching Bryen's skin and claiming him for its own.

Not knowing how else to extricate himself from a dire situation that was leaning toward lethal, Bryen did the only thing that came to mind, hoping that it gave him a chance, however slim it might be, at saving himself from a fate that was worse than death. He opened himself to the Seventh Stone, allowing the raging power of the artifact to flood into him. The blades on the Spear of the Magii pulsed brighter than the sun, becoming so blindingly intense that the Ghoule Overlord had no choice but to look away.

As Bryen expected, the Curse contained within him smashed itself against the barrier he had created to keep that despicable power locked away, the tainted energy desperate to connect with the Dark Magic of the black diamond. It was wasted effort. Thanks to the Spear augmenting his strength, Bryen maintained control over the Dark Magic, crushing the Curse's attempt to run rampant.

That done, Bryen focused on the Talent, using the Seventh Stone to pull in more of the power than any Magii could ever hope to manage on his or her own. It was with that immense amount of energy that he pushed back the Ghoule Overlord.

It began slowly, the Ghoule Overlord's staff moving away from his neck by just a hair, and then Bryen regained the distance of a knuckle. Pleased by his success and feeling stronger than he ever had before, Bryen continued to apply the power of the Seventh Stone until he had forced a finger between them, the black diamond now less of a threat as he nudged it farther away from his flesh.

Bryen gave his nemesis a sardonic grin. All this progress despite the Ghoule Overlord's best efforts to finish him. The beast was straining, struggling now to maintain his position.

It didn't matter what the beast attempted. The Ghoule Overlord had lost the momentum as soon as the Protector touched the Seventh Stone.

A massive burst of energy flared right in front of the Ghoule Overlord, the beast stumbling back, the blast sending a shockwave across the top of the monolith.

Not done, Bryen drove the point of one of the blades of the Spear of the Magii into the translucent stone. Another blinding flash of white energy erupted, the entire summit blazing brightly, the translucent stone sending a beam of pure white light into the sky that was followed by a thunderous boom that reverberated throughout the Trench.

When the blinding flash finally dissipated, Bryen stared coldly at the Ghoule Overlord, the beast trying to understand what had just happened.

It was the stare of the gladiator who had fought and lived for ten years on the white sand. It was the stare of the Volkun. And it promised death to anyone who chose to oppose him.

Bryen was about to advance on the Ghoule Overlord and continue the combat when he felt a hand on his shoulder. It took a moment for Bryen to pull himself from the place that he had gone in his own mind as he prepared to kill the Ghoule Overlord.

Sirius stood there. Tired. Looking older than he ever had before. But his eyes burned with purpose and threads of energy sizzled across his robes and his body.

"Do what you must do," said Sirius, the old Magus stepping in front of him and blocking him from the Ghoule Overlord. "Fix the Weir if you can. This fight is mine now."

Sirius didn't wait for Bryen to nod his agreement, instead whipping around and releasing a massive stream of energy that took the Ghoule Overlord by surprise, slamming into the beast and knocking him backward across the cracked translucent stone almost to the beginning of the trail that led up to the summit.

With that, the spell of the combat between Bryen and the Ghoule Overlord was broken, the larger battle erupting once again atop the monolith, the Ghoules charging toward the gladiators, the gladiators meeting them with their shield wall.

Nodding to Sirius, Bryen ran through a small gap between Majdi and Declan that quickly closed, patting the pillar with Viktor Keldragan's name carved into it as he passed by, taking the steps that led down into the hollow two at a time.

He wanted to help Lycia, he was desperate to help Lycia, but he knew that time was running out. The Weir was becoming dangerously erratic, the buzz of the energy contained within it frighteningly loud.

If he was going to fix the Weir, he needed to do it now.

If he succeeded, he would do all that he could to aid Lycia. And if he failed, then Lycia's death wouldn't matter. Because then they would all be dead.

20

RESTORATION

Bryen raced down the steps and skidded to a stop right in the center of the Sanctuary's hollow, the empty pedestal reserved for the Seventh Stone to his front. His left hand still grasping tightly to the haft of the Spear of the Magii, Bryen pressed his free hand onto the translucent stone.

Understanding the complexity of the challenge he faced, Bryen tried to close his mind to everything that was going on around him. It was a difficult, almost impossible, assignment that he had given himself.

To ignore the sounds of the battle raging just above him. To ignore the streams of power, both the Talent and the Curse, that blasted in and around the columns of the Sanctuary. To ignore his fears and worries for his friends. To ignore his doubts about his abilities and himself.

Declan's gravelly voice rose above the din of the clash, the Master of the Gladiators urging his soldiers to hold strong, attempting to rally the Blood Company as the Ghoules slammed against the shield wall again and again, desperate to find a crack to exploit.

"Stand! Fight! Die! We are gladiators! That's what we do! Now do it well!"

He heard Rafia let loose a long string of curses as she sent bolt after bolt of the Talent streaking toward the Elders, doing everything that she could to keep the beasts from turning the Curse on the gladiators.

Davin behind him on the rim of the depression, seemingly having a very loud, curse-filled conversation with himself that was interrupted by the sharp barks and grunts of pain that accompanied every thrust of his spear into Ghoule flesh.

Dorlan, the giant of a man usually quiet during a combat, raging against the Ghoules and seeking to spark his comrades to even greater endeavors: "Make the stone run with their blood, brothers and sisters! Make the bastards bleed!"

Kollea's screams unintelligible though just as loud as Dorlan's, the gladiator, as always, fighting side by side with the man she loved.

He heard the Ghoule Overlord pushing his beasts forward, demanding that they break the shield wall, even as the creature dueled Sirius. By the monster's surprisingly buoyant tone, Bryen sensed that his nemesis believed that victory was close at hand.

All of the noise and commotion complicated Bryen's many attempts to focus on the duty that only he could perform. The duty that was the sole reason for this treacherous journey. The duty that had cost so many of his comrades their lives.

Bryen didn't know how long the Blood Company would be able to stand against the Ghoule onslaught. He didn't know how long Sirius could hold off the Ghoule Overlord. He didn't know if he could accomplish what was required of him.

He did know that he needed to work quickly. He needed to get back into the fight. He needed to help the men and women fighting and dying for him. And he couldn't do that until he repaired the Weir ... or died trying.

But how to begin? How to attain the calm required for the work that he needed to do?

Finally, after so much struggle and doubt, he had reached the moment that he had dreaded and longed for both at the same time. Dreaded because of his fear that he would fail and curse Caledonia to the ravages of the Ghoules. Longed for so that regardless of what happened next, the anxiety attached to what was expected of him would at long last be replaced by the answer he had been searching for to the questions that had plagued him since he had accepted responsibility for restoring the Weir.

Would he have the courage and the strength to manipulate both the Talent and the Curse? Would he be able to resist the temptation of the Curse? Would he escape the corruption of the fouled Dark Magic? Would he frustrate the Ghoule Overlord and save the Kingdom? Would he even survive what he was about to attempt? Would he doom the Kingdom and all in it to a terrible fate?

Forcing down his own worries as best as he could, and not knowing what else to do, Bryen closed his eyes and seized the Talent. The blades on the Spear of the Magii shifted from a dull glow to a brilliant intensity as he filled himself with the natural power of the world.

Remembering what he did on Haven when Sirius and Rafia were teaching him how to control the Dark Magic within him, Bryen followed that same process again, ensuring that the thin barrier between the Curse and the Talent was in place before opening himself to the Seventh Stone.

As the power surged within him, filling every pore in his body, he welcomed the familiar feeling. The energy gave him greater clarity, as if the veil through which he had been looking at the world had been removed, everything else around him falling away.

The noise.

The sensations.

The emotions.

There was only the energy.

The Talent.

The Curse.

The two powers doing battle within him, but that fight muted thanks to the help of the Spear of the Magii, the Giant-crafted weapon modulating and keeping at a manageable level the demands being made upon him by the conflicting energies.

Satisfied that he had both distinct powers under control at least in that moment, Bryen, shielded with the Talent, reached tentatively toward the Weir, seeking to connect with the erratic streams of energy that pulsed off six of the Seven Stones.

The first few times he tried, he pulled back at the last second, fearful of what might happen. Anxious that the tremendous power of the Weir would be too much for him. That he would fail before he even began.

Steeling himself for whatever might happen, understanding that he couldn't continue to delay with his friends fighting for their lives, Bryen reached out again and forced himself to keep going. With just a faint touch, a spark of electricity shooting from the tips of his fingers to his toes, he was instantly pulled in, caught within the magical construction, a part of the Weir.

He felt the power surging not only within him but also all around him. The energy was more than he could have possibly imagined. More than he had ever suspected.

At the outset, the experience thrilled him, the energy scouring his body clean, sweeping away his weariness, rejuvenating him, giving him a strength that suggested that he could do anything that he wanted. That no one could challenge him. That right now he could duel the Ghoule Overlord and be safe in the knowledge that he would walk away the victor.

With that exhilaration came a dawning realization that sent a bolt of terror straight to his heart.

The power that he had connected to, the power that had connected to him, was doing what it wanted to do, not what he wanted it to do. He was trying to control the energy contained within the Weir, using the Spear of the Magii to do so, but it wasn't working.

He dreaded that he couldn't do it. The power within the Weir was more than any single Magus could ever be expected to manage effectively.

The power was intoxicating. It was electrifying. It was so tempting.

But it was too much for him.

He was losing himself. His very essence was slipping away from him. Who he was, every aspect of his vitality, was joining with the power facilitated by the Seven Stones. Once that transition was complete his greatest fear would become reality.

To make matters worse, even with the Spear of the Magii in his hand, the Dark Magic in the Weir called to the Curse locked within him, reaching for the tainted energy, seeking to join with it. Wanting to become one.

With each passing second, the Dark Magic became more insistent, pushing harder against the barrier that Bryen had constructed within himself. When that consistent, steadily increasing pressure failed to break through, the Dark Magic slammed against the papery shield, desperate to crack it, to shatter it, the Curse frantic to escape, to consume him. To gain vengeance against the one who had imprisoned it.

Because of that intensifying struggle within him, that feeling of warmth and rejuvenation that had flowed through him at the start was replaced slowly by a pain that seized every muscle in his body. The agony was so intense that he could think of nothing else, focus on nothing else. It felt like his insides were being ripped apart as the Talent and the Curse warred within him.

Bryen strove as best as he could against an energy that he could barely comprehend, much less have any chance of facilitating. He fought harder than he ever had in the Pit.

Still, the power was too much for him. Too demanding. Too insidious.

And in that instant he realized that he was dying. Either the Curse was going to corrupt him and make him its own or the huge amount of Talent surging within him was going to burn him to a crisp.

He was fighting a losing battle, a battle from which he couldn't disengage, and he didn't know what to do.

Right when Bryen felt as if he was about to tip over the edge to lose himself in the maelstrom of power that fought for dominance within him, a strong voice played through his mind.

"Focus on the Seventh Stone. Just the Seventh Stone. Not the Spear. Not the Talent. Not the Curse. Just the Seventh Stone."

Bryen had never heard that voice before, though it sounded weirdly familiar. Very familiar, in fact. Desperate for some solution, the pain he was experiencing making him feel as if he was being torn apart, he tried to do what the voice said. To concentrate just on the Seventh Stone.

He couldn't.

The powers warring within him, disabling him, ripping him apart, making his whole body burn, wouldn't allow him to do it. There was nothing but the fire. Nothing but the torment. Then a memory burst into his fading consciousness that he thought that he had forgotten.

He was standing in the Pit, the sun flashing off the white sand, Declan right in front of him. Bryen held a very large sword in his hand. He was only a child, having been in the Colosseum for just a few weeks, and he was having a difficult time keeping the tip of the heavy weapon that he was holding from touching the feathery crystals.

"Why is this happening?" asked Bryen, his voice soft, cracking from a combination of terror and confusion, still not certain as to why he had been sent to the Pit. "Why to me?"

"Why doesn't matter, lad," replied Declan gently, understanding his charge would need time to adjust to his new surroundings. "You can do nothing about the why. Forget the why. What matters is that it is happening. If you want to stay alive, you need to learn how to fight. Instead of asking why, ask how. The why can't help you. The how will."

"This isn't what I ever wanted," said Bryen, feeling sorry for himself, tears beginning to form in his eyes.

His parents had been murdered the year before and he had narrowly escaped with his life. Ever since then he had been living on the streets of Tintagel. Eventually, his luck had run out. The City Watch had arrested him for stealing a few pieces of food. For that, he was now in the Colosseum, preparing to fight for his life.

He didn't understand why this was all happening to him. He didn't want any of it to happen. Still, it had, and he had no control over anything at the moment other than deciding whether he would listen to what the Master of the Gladiators was trying to teach him.

His father had taught him to use a bow and how to handle a dagger. Not a sword. Bryen lifted his gaze from the dully gleaming steel. He stared across the sand at Declan.

The Master of the Gladiators was watching him. No, not just watching him. Studying him.

Bryen realized that Declan could read him like a book. The man could sense the pity that threatened to incapacitate Bryen. He could sense his fear and his indecision and how he hoped that this was all nothing more than a dream.

Then it hit him, and when it did, Bryen saw Declan's eyes

widen, as if he wasn't sure it would happen. The man had been waiting for him to reach this point, hoping that he would. Knowing that all his time and effort would be wasted if Bryen didn't reach this point.

Because Bryen realized that not everyone did. That everything he was feeling upon being thrown into the Pit was exactly how everyone else sent here felt.

But none of that mattered now. The only thing that mattered now was the choice he made. Would he give in without a fight? Would he allow his new circumstances to crush him and seal his fate? Or would he accept his new reality and learn to function within it?

Bryen's gaze hardened, his grip strengthening on the hilt of the sword that he could barely hold. Then Declan nodded, a motion meant to give Bryen some much-needed confidence, apparently having seen what he was looking for.

"Lad, there are few things in our lives that we can control," Declan said in his gravelly voice, Bryen realizing now how patient the grizzled veteran had been with him as a boy. "Those that we can, we cherish. But the fact is, bad things happen. All the time. And they happen to good people. They happen to bad people. Some people get what they deserve, most don't. There's no rhyme or reason to life. All we can do is manage what is given to us. Control what we can control. Navigate the tide of what we can't. Make the most of what life gives us." Declan stared at Bryen, his own eyes hardening. "Now do you want to die in the Pit?"

"No," Bryen replied quietly.

"Good. Because I don't want you to die either. Now do what I taught you to do. You don't just fight as a gladiator with a length of steel. So forget the sword for now. When you fight, you also fight with your mind. Now do as I taught you. Close your mind to everything around you. The sights. The sounds. The smells. Forget the distractions. None of that matters. Focus on what's inside you. Focus on the beating of your heart. Let the rhythm of your heart take you where you need to go."

The memory faded in a flash, though not Declan's instruction.

Bryen did exactly as his friend and mentor had taught him. He focused solely on the beating of his heart. Ignoring the pain, the fear, the worry. Ignoring all that was occurring around him. Sensing, hearing, feeling only the flow of his blood through his veins and the pounding in his chest. Then slowly, ever so slowly, he recognized that the control that he was so desperate for, the control that he had lost, had returned to him.

Bryen realized the mistake that he had been making. He understood now that he couldn't control the immense power flowing through him and around him.

He could only control himself. Finally, with that realization, he achieved the peace and the serenity that he had been seeking for so long and had been just beyond his grasp because he had been looking at the world in the wrong way.

Bryen smiled, though only briefly, pleased with his step forward, though knowing that this was only the first step in a longer process.

Concentrating just on the Seventh Stone within him, he began to understand how the artifact was more than just a tool for holding the Talent and the Curse. He realized that it also was something that could be used to regulate the Talent and the Curse, just like the Spear, although it was thousands upon thousands of times stronger.

He also concluded something else. Something that was critically important he had missed ever since the artifact merged with him. The Seventh Stone was a catalyst, and now he thought that he knew why.

When he opened his eyes again, he was standing in the middle of a small dome constructed of the Talent.

Who had done this? It wasn't his creation.

Because of the dome, everything beyond the shield was blurred. The fighting that raged around the ten pillars. The Weir itself, which continued to flash dangerously. All of it was pushed to the side. More subdued. Less concerning. Not as pressing.

Bryen turned back to the pedestal, still thinking about what he had to do next. He took a step back, startled. On the other side of the translucent stone a man framed in a shimmering white mist stood in front of him. He was hazy, there but not really there, ghostlike because of the lack of substance. The figure reminded him of the Sentinel he had dueled in the tunnel.

Bryen could sense that the figure appearing opposite him was a Magus. And then it came to him. He was a spirit, tied to the Seventh Stone. Tied to him.

He had never seen the Magus before. Even so, he looked very familiar.

As he studied the figure more closely, it all fell into place. The same build, the same facial features, the same wavy hair. The same sardonic twist to his lips.

Bryen knew who he gazed upon. It all made sense now.

Viktor Keldragan.

When the spirit saw the recognition dawn in Bryen's eyes, the man smiled warmly. Then nine more spirits took shape around the boundary of the protective dome. He didn't recall all their names though he knew who they were. They were unmistakable.

The Ten Magii.

"I've been waiting for you, nephew," said Viktor Keldragan. "Well met, Protector."

"All this time?"

"All this time," replied Viktor, still smiling broadly, nodding with a small pleasure. "We knew that you would be coming.

That you would have need of us. We just didn't know when for certain."

"How could you know that?"

"You already have the answer to that, nephew."

Bryen studied Viktor. He was beginning to see another likeness in the Magus' strong face. The eyes, the nose, the shape of the mouth. It wasn't exceedingly strong. Still, it was there. It was enough for him to make the connection that he should have made long ago yet had failed to do because of all the other issues and challenges swirling around him.

"You sound just like Sirius. Never really giving an answer."

"Yes, well, we did grow up together. So that does make sense."

Bryen's gaze sharpened, giving Viktor the stare that he was so famous for when he fought as the Volkun on the white sand.

All the disparate pieces were coming together to form a larger whole. Finally, he was beginning to understand. Finally, he made the linkage that he had been seeking since the start of all this, since he had left the Southern Marches and gone to Haven in search of a way to remove the Protector's collar and better manage the Dark Magic residing within him.

He shook his head in irritation. Bryen had been so absorbed in achieving those goals, and then trying to learn how to repair the Weir, that he had failed to notice this one key detail that had been under his nose, quite literally in fact, ever since he had arrived in Battersea to serve as Aislinn's Protector.

Bryen set those thoughts to the side. He needed to concentrate on the Weir now. On the task that only he could complete. Maybe. Hopefully.

"You and the other Magii are part of the Seventh Stone. Your essences are a part of the Seventh Stone. It happened after you constructed the Weir. You were waiting for me because you knew that your work wasn't complete."

"Right so far," agreed Viktor.

"The Weir wasn't what it needed to be. You picked me when I was a child and I touched the Seventh Stone. You recognized who I was. When my father let me wander through the Aeyrie and I found the hidden room. You knew who I was before I even found the artifact."

"In part, yes. We did select you, although it wasn't really us entirely," explained Viktor, "the Seventh Stone having the final say in the decision. And there was more to it than that. We couldn't force you to do what was needed. We couldn't force you to join with us. So you did have a role to play in the decision as well. You didn't have to take the gift that we gave you. That the Seventh Stone offered you. You could have refused."

"But I didn't," nodded Bryen, recalling the experience of meeting the Seventh Stone when he was just a child.

"But you didn't."

"How did I accept the gift?" wondered Bryen. "I was just a child. All I remember was a flash of light and then waking up in my father's arms."

"You didn't fight the Seventh Stone when its magic first worked its way into you," replied Viktor. "You accepted what the Seventh Stone offered you, the good and the bad. The balance contained within it. As soon as you touched the Seventh Stone there was, if I might call it such just for the sake of simplicity, a meeting of the minds. You both agreed on the union. So what happened to you at the Aeyrie during your Test was inevitable. It was preordained. It was just a matter of when, and the when was then. You are the Seventh Stone, and the Seventh Stone is you, because you both agreed to that bonding. As long as you live, that will not change. The Seventh Stone will always be a part of you, and you will always be a part of the Seventh Stone. Whether or not it remains within you, you can never again be separated. Two become one, and the one is stronger than the two."

Bryen thought about what Viktor was telling him, giving it a few seconds to settle as it was quite a lot to take in. It certainly made sense to him. Of course, it would have been helpful if Sirius had explained all this to him earlier rather than leaving it to his brother to explain it to him now when the fate of the Kingdom hung in the balance. Then again, he understood the old Magus' hesitation. If he had sought to educate Bryen in this area, Sirius would have had to explain several other more uncomfortable facts to him then as well that he clearly wasn't ready to discuss.

"Can you help me with what I need to do?" asked Bryen.

"Do you acknowledge the price you might be required to pay to gain what you want to achieve?" asked Viktor.

Rather than take issue with Viktor answering his question with a question, Bryen thought for a few seconds. He was more than aware of the potential cost to him. Even more so he was aware of the cost to so many others if he didn't do his duty. "I do."

"And you are willing to pay that price if it becomes necessary?"

"I am," Bryen replied without hesitation.

Viktor stared at Bryen, studying him, seemingly glimpsing his very soul, then he nodded, apparently satisfied. The spirit didn't waste any more time, beginning to explain what would be required.

"You know how to achieve what's required," said Viktor. "You already demonstrated that you know how to weave the Talent and the Curse together."

"Yes, but if I do it the way that I've done it before, the weave won't be strong enough. Of that, I have no doubt. Just as the Weir is doing now, the barrier simply will degrade over time. It's just a temporary fix, not a long-term solution."

"Correct, and that's where we," said Viktor, motioning with his hand to the spirits encircling them, "made our mistake as well. One of them, anyway. We didn't wrap the

Curse in the Talent as you did. Because of that failure, the Curse enjoyed a prominence in the construction of the Weir that it should never have attained. Our design was flawed from the very beginning as we gave the Curse a path to corrupt our creation. And the Curse didn't waste any time in doing so."

"You speak as if the Curse is alive," said Bryen, though as he said the words another truth that had been playing around the edges of his consciousness gained substance. He understood now that his words were right on point.

"It is," confirmed Viktor. "We didn't understand that either back then. It's because of that failing that the Weir has weakened over time. It wasn't the fact that we wove the Talent and the Curse together. It was that our failure to protect against the Curse allowed the Dark Magic to slowly eat away at the Weir, to grow and spread, to knock the two powers that began in balance out of balance. That's why the Weir is dying."

"So the approach that I planned to take to reconstruct the Weir is the right one?" asked Bryen.

"Yes, to reconstruct the Weir, you can do the same that you did when you wove the shield in Haven," agreed Viktor. "What you did then is no different than what we did so long ago. So long as you keep the Curse wrapped in the Talent as you do so. If you fail to do that, you will do no better than we did."

"What aren't you telling me?" asked Bryen, his eyes narrowing.

"Why do you think that I'm not telling you everything?"

"Because you look just like Sirius does when he decides not to give me the full story."

Viktor smiled at that, somewhat chagrined. The Seventh Stone certainly had picked wisely with this one. "I assume that you irritated Sirius quite a bit by not accepting what he had to explain at face value."

"That was often the goal," admitted Bryen with a smile of

his own. "And it was deserved since he has a penchant for holding things back."

Viktor shook his head in amusement. He would have enjoyed working with this young man, teaching him about the Talent, the Curse, and the Seventh Stone and how it was all supposed to work together. Unfortunately, it was not to be, because Viktor and the other Magii had identified the essential knowledge that the Protector would need now only recently.

"You're right that there is more that you need to know. A twist of sorts. But I promise you that if you make it that far in the process of restoring the Weir that you will have nothing to fear."

"Why should I trust you?" asked Bryen, his natural wariness coming back into play. He understood that he would only have one chance at this, so he wanted to do all that he could to ensure his success. "We are family, but we don't know each other."

"There you are wrong," said Viktor. "I know you better than you know yourself thanks to our connection through the stone. And you know me just as well. You need only look in your heart, in your own spirit, to know the truth. In many ways, we are cut from the same stone, if you will forgive the phrasing. We believe the same things. We look at life in the same way. And, it's because of all that, and because we are family, that you can trust me. We are Keldragans. We put others before ourselves. We take risks that no one else will. We tell the truth, no matter what that might cost us. And I tell you now that I and the other Magii will give everything we have to assist you."

Bryen stared at Viktor for almost a full minute, finally deciding that he could trust his ancestor, allowing the Seventh Stone within him to be his guide and judge in the matter. Then again, with time pressing, he really had little choice. "I won't be touched by the Curse?"

"You shouldn't be if you manage the two powers correctly

and carefully," replied Viktor. "Keep the Curse wrapped in the Talent while you are weaving. We will stay with you the entire time you are working, for there is a role for us to play as well during this exercise."

"And this twist you mentioned?"

"At the right time, when I tell you, you will use the Spear of the Magii to draw out the Talent encasing the Dark Magic. The Curse and the Talent will no longer be separated, and the two distinct energies will become one. If done correctly, the Weir will remain, never to fail, never to degrade. The balance that is missing from the Weir now will have been achieved, a balance that can never be altered."

"How likely is that twist to work?" asked Bryen.

Viktor mused about his question for longer than Bryen would have liked. "Theoretically, it should. All of the Magii agree on that. Although practically, it's never been done before. Thoughts and reality don't always join together as we might hope or like. So we will just have to see."

"Wonderful," Bryen grumbled under his breath. "You certainly do know how to fill someone with confidence."

"I try my best," replied Viktor with a grin, his expression essentially a mirror of Sirius' few and brief moments of amusement.

Bryen shook his head in mild annoyance. It was no different than he had expected, and there was nothing for it. He was probably going to die, whether he succeeded or not. So he might as well begin, because his friends were depending on him.

"Let's get to it, then."

"You're ready?" asked Viktor.

Bryen nodded, corralling the butterflies flitting about in his stomach. "I am."

"Good," replied Viktor. "Because first, we must destroy the Weir."

"I HAVE BEEN WAITING for this, Magus," growled the Ghoule Overlord, "for a very long time. But rather than making you suffer, I will kill you quickly. I have more important prey than you. A combat that truly matters."

The beast flicked his staff and sent a bolt of the Curse speeding right toward Sirius' chest. If the energy struck, the Magus would be destroyed, the power employed so potent that it would turn his flesh and bones to ash in an instant and then continue on to tear through the shield wall of gladiators who stood behind him.

"As have I," shouted Sirius, having to take a few seconds to decipher some of the words his adversary spoke in the common tongue.

Unfazed by the Dark Magic shooting toward him, with a curl of his hand, a stripe of the Talent, blazingly bright, burst from Sirius' fingertips, the energy slashing right through the Curse, the slivers of darkness negated and sent twisting away on the strong winds that gusted across the top of the monolith.

A murderous smile cracked Sirius' thin lips. He had been waiting for this opportunity. For quite some time, in fact. Ever since his much too short duel on the white sand in which Bryen thankfully had intervened. And based on that humbling experience, as he had waited, his worries about his ability to manage a combat effectively with the Ghoule Overlord had festered, seeding his mind with doubts.

He realized now, as he battled the monster who had consumed his thoughts for centuries, as he called upon the Talent on a level that he had rarely done so in the past, that there had been no cause for his concerns.

Sirius recognized that he had wasted his time and energy by giving in to his fears.

Because he was doing what he feared he wouldn't. He was protecting the Protector. For as long as he could.

He realized that it wasn't the combat that worried him. It was the anticipation of the duel. With that gone, he had adopted the fatalistic perspective so frequently demonstrated by the Protector.

Kill or be killed. And even though this was a fight to the death, even though he did not dispute that the Ghoule Overlord facilitated more power than he could ever hope to manage, Sirius felt good. He felt more alive now than he had in quite some time.

He was in his element now. There was no more contemplating. There was only doing.

What would be would be.

Wanting to keep the Ghoule Overlord off balance and put him on the defensive right from the start, Sirius continued his motion with his hand. Adding more power to the Talent, he launched a stream of crackling energy toward the beast.

The neat maneuver caught the Ghoule Overlord by surprise, forcing the Master of the Curse to hurriedly form a shield of swirling black mist that solidified just in time. The large, shadowy buckler blocked the blindingly brilliant energy, though not before a sliver of power thinner than a hair slid over the edge of the barrier and cut across the top of the Ghoule Overlord's shoulder, leaving a long, smoking slash of burnt flesh in its wake.

"You will pay for that, Magus!" spitted the Ghoule Overlord, his rage driven more by his embarrassment at being struck than from the pain of the wound. "Now I will kill you slowly because of that! You will feel a torment that you never before imagined. A pain that will make you beg for your death, and even then, I will not give it to you. I will keep you alive, no more than a plaything, and I will not let you go until I am done exacting every ounce of agony from your flesh and your spirit that I possibly can."

Sirius was about to reply, a savage grin twisting his lips -- he might die this day at the hands of this beast, but at least he got one good strike in, and he believed that he could get in a few more -- when movement to his left kept the words in his throat. His eyes widened when he saw a Ghoule rushing toward him, spear extended, about to drive the blackened steel into his hip.

Worried that stopping his assault against the Ghoule Overlord to deal with this unanticipated attack would leave him open to the beast's reply with Dark Magic, Sirius tried to twist out of the way and avoid the sharpened steel. He recognized too late that there was nothing that he could do. The Ghoule was about to skewer him like a pig on a spit.

Sirius' eyes widened, his body tensing, as he prepared to absorb the blow. His eyes widened even further when, shockingly, Declan appeared.

The Sergeant of the Blood Company, pushing himself through the shield wall and sprinting across the stone, knocked the Ghoule's steel away from Sirius right before it pierced the Magus' flesh. Not allowing the Ghoule to recover, Declan advanced toward the creature, his blade whistling through the air and slicing deeply across the beast's shoulder, cutting through muscle and tendon and leaving the Ghoule with only one arm to fight.

The Ghoule shrieked in disbelief, stepping back across the stone as he tried to keep Declan away from him. The beast found the task increasingly difficult because of the unwieldiness of employing his large spear with just one clawed hand.

Sirius nodded his thanks to Declan, breathing a welcome sigh of relief as well. The Magus assumed that the gladiator probably didn't see it, Declan still focused on the wounded Ghoule, the beast continuing to back away slowly. With every step, the beast's movements slowed, rivulets of thick black blood gushing from the wound.

The old Magus had no doubt as to how that combat was going to end. Sirius instantly turned back toward the Ghoule Overlord, a feeling of dread settling in his stomach as he saw what was waiting for him.

The Ghoule Overlord grinned at him now, his black eyes blazing with hatred and anticipation. The Master of the Ghoule Legions had kept his shield in place to prevent Sirius' stream of Talent from striking him, adding more Dark Magic to the barrier over time so that the white-hot power became no more than an annoyance. That challenge under control, now a new cloud of the Curse spun atop the black diamond, the black mist forming into several spheres of pitch-black energy.

Sirius had a choice to make, and less than a second to do so, understanding that with a flick of the beast's wrist those orbs would shoot right toward him. Continue with the stream of energy with the hope that he could break through the Ghoule Overlord's defenses, although with the ease with which his adversary had blocked his attack that didn't appear likely, or release the flow, craft a shield as quickly as he could, and hope that his defense would be strong enough to keep those menacing orbs from blasting through his barrier and then into him.

He chose the latter strategy, abruptly ending his attack and working as fast as he could to form his shield. His work was forgotten for just a heartbeat when a massive blast of energy that rocked the sandstone pillar made him duck.

A handful of lightning strikes slammed down into the cracked stone of the summit right in front of the Ghoule Over-lord. Dirt and shattered pieces of translucent rock blasted up into the air, the power of the blows, one after the other, ten in all, so strong that they forced the Ghoule Overlord to move back a dozen feet so that he could avoid the worst of the barrage.

Sirius looked behind him. Aislinn stood protectively over Lycia near the entrance to the Sanctuary, still guarding the fallen gladiator. Apparently, she was protecting him as well, because his student likely had just saved his life.

The Lady of the Southern Marches missed her tutor's nod of thanks, Aislinn already having shifted her attention toward the Elders Rafia was battling to a standstill on the far side of the hollow. She was preparing to send several lances of energy toward the beasts, hoping that even if the Elders blocked her attack, her assault would demand their full attention, thereby leaving them open to the inevitable attack that Rafia would be more than ready to initiate right after hers.

Thankful for the unexpected assistance, Sirius' grin turned feral when he spun back toward the Ghoule Overlord. He appreciated the timely support, but he knew the truth. He didn't have the strength or the skill to defeat the Ghoule Overlord in a fair combat. If he allowed this duel to continue much longer, he was in all probability going to die.

That didn't bother him as it might have centuries before. No, he had seen enough of the world to understand that his time was coming to an end, and he was at peace with that because he was finally doing what he had promised his brother that he would do. He had watched his brother die a thousand years before, right on this very spot, in fact, and in the heat of the moment, Sirius had vowed to seek revenge for Viktor. Yet that vow remained unfulfilled.

That memory fixed in the back of his head, for the first time in a very long time he felt calm, as if all his worries and fears had melted away, those anxieties replaced by a certainty that filled him with a much-needed infusion of energy. If he was going to die this day, he could think of no better way for it to happen.

He might not gain the revenge he sought, but he would give everything he had to attain it.

⁓

"You want me to destroy the Weir?" demanded Bryen, giving his uncle a look of absolute incredulity. "Are you insane?"

"Yes," replied Viktor calmly. "Well no, I'm not." Viktor leaned closer to Bryen as if he were sharing a secret. "To rebuild the Weir, you must destroy it first. Our work must be removed entirely. There is no other way. The Weir must be new. Clean. Free of the taint that slowly destroyed it over the centuries. It must be built the way it should have been a thousand years ago. You must start anew."

"But if I destroy the Weir now, there is no guarantee that I can rebuild it. Even with the Seventh Stone, I might not be strong enough. The Ghoules will be able to enter Caledonia unhindered."

"That's the risk we'll need to take," continued Viktor. "Although I doubt the Seventh Stone would have selected you if it didn't believe that you had the strength and the skill to do what would be required of you."

Bryen wasn't convinced by the logic that Viktor offered him, though it seemed that he had little choice other than to follow the path being laid out before him. Because he wouldn't be able to do what was necessary without the spirit Magus' guidance.

"Show me."

Viktor nodded, pleased, then did as Bryen requested, giving him a brief and very quick tutorial on how he could stop the flow of energy from the Stones and redirect it. Doing that would cause the Weir to disintegrate.

Having listened studiously to Viktor, with a nod of understanding and a gulp of worry, Bryen reluctantly began the process that Viktor had outlined for him, reaching for the

Talent and opening himself to the Seventh Stone. For the next step, he linked the artifact to the energy flowing through the other Stones.

That done, Bryen began the more difficult part of the operation. Shifting the flow of energy from the Stones away from the Weir and instead diverting it into himself.

A scary proposition if he thought about it, which he didn't, instead focusing solely on the task at hand rather than the consequences.

Creating this new channel allowed the Seventh Stone to absorb the immense amount of energy that made up the Weir. With the help of the Ten Magii, who had joined hands and were somehow manipulating both the Talent and the Curse, separating the weave to craft two distinct energy streams, the Seventh Stone then compressed the two competing powers so that they could be contained safely within him.

As the Seventh Stone and the Ten Magii drained the energy from the other Stones, Bryen initially feared that he was about to burst, much like before when he had come close to exceeding his boundaries for the amount of the Talent and the Curse that he could manage on his own, his body ripped apart by the warring energies. He realized that his concern was misplaced.

Thanks to Viktor and the other Magii helping him, and his own continued focus on the Seventh Stone and facilitating the transfer of power away from the Weir, the massive streams of the Talent and the Curse flowed into him without a mishap, and he finally began to understand not only the limitless capacity of the artifact within him, but also how he could regulate that capacity as needed.

He wished that he had mastered this skill earlier in his instruction. It would have made his life much easier, giving him greater confidence in his ability to work with the Seventh Stone and maintain control over the Curse. Then again, as Sirius had liked to say so many times during their training, oftentimes you only learned a lesson when you were ready. Or when you had no choice but to do so.

As the last of the magical barrier flowed into the Seventh Stone, the Stones sitting upon their pedestals drained dry, a blinding flash of light erupted from the hollow followed by a rumble of thunder that shook the monolith for almost a minute and reverberated throughout the Trench.

It was done.

The Weir was gone.

The work of the Ten Magii was no more.

21

AS YOU COMMAND

"The Weir is gone? You're certain?"

"Completely. It vanished while we were disengaging from the Ghoules. One moment it was there, the next it was gone," replied the Blademaster.

"Do you think that the Weir will return?" asked Kevan Winborne, hope in his voice, though he feared that it might be misplaced.

The Duke of the Southern Marches, commander of the vanguard of the Caledonian Army, understood just how important the magical barrier that had kept the Ghoules from the Kingdom for centuries was to their increasingly difficult efforts to hold the Winter Pass. He also understood what would happen if the Weir never came back into place, and that was a future that he really didn't want to contemplate.

"Who can say? We can hope, and I will. I have faith in the Protector. He is not one to give up without a fight. There is no reason not to believe that he will do all that he can to meet his charge."

"As do I," Kevan muttered.

"So we fight on and do our part. We must deal with the threat before us."

"You're right," Kevan agreed, turning his thoughts to the more immediate challenge they faced. "We need to focus on what is coming our way now and not on what we can't control. How far?"

"Less than half a mile" said Jurgen Klines. "No more than a minute or two with these beasts. They'll be on us swiftly."

The Blademaster had made it back to the spearhead of the Caledonian Army with what was left of his advance guard just moments before. His soldiers struggled fiercely to disengage from the Ghoule scouts, finally doing so after several minutes of hard fighting. Every soldier killed felt like a stab to his heart, visions of so many of his men taken from their saddles playing through his mind as he rode back across the mucky ground of the Winter Pass hellbent for the south, the Ghoules right on the hooves of their horses.

The entire way he cursed himself for a fool. He had lost a third of his soldiers during the skirmish, a dozen more falling to the Ghoules pursuing them, and he could have lost all of his troops if they had not broken free from the beasts when they did, the additional Ghoule packs coming toward them from the north more than enough to finish them.

He considered himself undeservedly lucky to get so many of his soldiers to safety, if only temporarily. Because he knew what was racing toward them. He knew how hard the imminent battle would be.

"Good," replied Kevan. "We will use the Ghoules' belligerence against them for as long as we can."

With that idea dominating Kevan's thoughts, he had lined his companies across the width of the Winter Pass. He believed that with the peaks rising sheer and shaping the boundaries of the canyon, the precipitous snowdrifts on each side extending from the sides of the gorge and compressing the space, combined with how the gap narrowed here naturally, the sides pushing in to reduce the width of the route to no more than a few hundred yards, he would have a better chance of stopping the Ghoules' advance.

"Dani!"

"Yes, Duke Winborne?"

The Corporal of the Battersea Guard had been waiting just a few yards behind him for the orders that she knew were coming. Her long, blond hair had been braided down her back and then tucked beneath her leather armor so that it would stay out of the way during the fight. She held her spear tightly in one hand, the other hand loosely holding the reins.

Confidence radiated from her. Yet just as she did every time she was called into action, she felt the need to justify her Duke's trust in her, the Lord of the Southern Marches having given her command of the Battersea Guard in the absence of Captain Tentillin and Sergeant Brexston. This would be another opportunity to do just that.

"You know what to do."

"Yes, Duke Winborne," replied Dani with a fierce grin, eager to begin.

She urged her horse to the front of the long column of soldiers arrayed across the Winter Pass. Although the Caledonian Army combined the Royal Guard as well as the Guards of several Duchies, Dani had little concern about their ability to work together. The soldiers were all well trained, the last few weeks spent specifically on coordinating the movement and ensuring good communication between the different companies. Because of that very intensive and painstaking work, Dani had the columns moving in less than a minute.

Kevan and the Blademaster watched from their vantage point atop a snowdrift, pleased by what they saw. The soldiers demonstrated their training and discipline, the first line of cavalry at a gallop in seconds, the second line following just twenty yards behind, a third line twenty yards behind the second, and the fourth just beginning to get their war horses up to speed as the Ghoules began to appear to the north.

At first just a few packs, then hundreds. The beasts sprinted toward the cavalry, their hunger driving them forward, eerie howls and shrieks of challenge resounding off the walls of the canyon.

The strategy was quite simple, its effectiveness having been proven in previous skirmishes with the beasts. No one in their right mind wanted to get caught in a pitched battle with the Ghoules. That outcome was to be avoided at all costs. So speed and maneuverability were the keys. Nevertheless, it had to be done the right way and with the right timing since the Ghoules were so fast and agile, and they relied on those traits. That meant employing the soldiers' most important weapon. Their mounts.

The soldiers of Caledonia put that advantage to use right at the start of the fight, the first line of cavalry slamming into the disorganized Ghoules, shouldering them out of the way, a few soldiers using their spears to full effect, although most allowed the momentum of the charge to do their bloody work for them.

Rather than ride deeper into the Ghoules, the first line of cavalry split in half and wheeled back around both sides of the Pass, skirting the snowdrifts so that the second line could charge into the beasts, who continued to sprint toward them in a haphazard rush. And so it went, one line of cavalry after another crashing into the Ghoules, preventing the beasts from forming an effective defense, each line of soldiers then breaking away and reforming at the back of the continuously moving formation so that they could charge once again in an unbroken rhythm.

During the first few rushes, everything went well for the Caledonians, the cavalry making good use of their decided edge, the Ghoules struggling to defend effectively against such a coordinated assault. But as more Ghoules sprinted onto the battlefield, it became more difficult for the mounted soldiers to extricate themselves from the beasts once they were engaged.

Smaller clashes erupted across the breadth of the Winter Pass as soldiers endeavored to break free from the Ghoules but found doing so all but impossible as they became caught within the milling mass of beasts. The wet and mucky ground, newly revealed by the blazing sun that had melted the snow in just the last few weeks, didn't help matters. Several soldiers crashed to the turf when their horses slipped and fell to the muddy peat.

"I had hoped for a better result," said Kevan, the sheer number of Ghoules joining the fight becoming a potentially unsolvable problem, bogging down the flow of attacks. Once the charges came to an end, the soldiers would cede the momentum to the Ghoules, a reality they wanted to avoid at all costs.

"We both did," replied Klines, a tinge of frustration evident in his voice. "And these are only the scouting packs that have come together. We have yet to bear the brunt of a Ghoule Legion."

"You're not filling me with confidence, Blademaster," muttered Kevan, irritated that the Ghoules were adapting so easily to the strategy he had put in place, many of the beasts now leaping over the charging soldiers, pulling them from their saddles as they did so and turning the larger battle into individual combats that were decidedly one-sided. He had no choice but to acknowledge that the beasts had broken the tempo of the fight that he had needed to maintain for a much longer period of time if they were to have any chance of success.

"I'm not trying to," said Klines, his eyes never leaving the skirmish to his front. He experienced an almost overpowering urge to go down there and fight with his soldiers. But he couldn't do that. Not yet anyway. Now, he had to concentrate on his larger responsibilities. How to keep his soldiers alive. "We need to change our tactics or we risk being overrun."

Kevan took just a few more seconds to study the battle, grimacing at what he observed. The charges had come to an end, his many companies now mixed in with the Ghoules.

The Caledonian troops maintained their discipline, knowing what they needed to do in just such a situation, yet they struggled to form into larger units. Kevan understood with an increasing desperation that if his troops failed in that endeavor, the beasts would continue to build on their momentum by cutting off small groups of soldiers from the larger force. Doing so reduced the Caledonians' ability to hold their ground, allowing the Ghoules to push his soldiers back to the south.

The Caledonians fought bravely, forming into squares whenever they could as they retreated, but retreat they did. They had no other choice. Unable to use their war horses in the fight as they would have preferred, and with a large number of Ghoules still charging through the gap from the north, Kevan's hope of containing the Ghoules within this small section of the Winter Pass faded quickly. Now he had but one goal to strive for.

Survival.

He had already lost several companies of soldiers in just a few minutes, and he could not afford to allow that to continue. That and the fact that whatever gains his cavalry had made at the beginning of the fight were now gone, his soldiers almost back to the point where they had started their initial charges, confirmed for him that the situation had taken a dire turn.

Could they hold the Ghoules here? That was the key question now running through Kevan's mind. Much to his disappointment, his quick and brutally honest analysis told him that with their current strategy the answer was no.

If the Ghoules pushed them back a few hundred yards more, the Caledonians ran the risk of being flanked as the Winter Pass broadened behind them, extending for almost a quarter mile from side to side before beginning to narrow again farther down the trail. That was more than enough space for the Ghoules to turn the battle against them.

"Agreed. I assume that you have something in mind?"

"Flying wedges," replied the Blademaster.

Kevan took a moment to consider the suggestion, a small glimmer of hope flashing behind his eyes as he thought about it. It was a good idea. With the soldiers in formations that resembled arrowheads, they could press the Ghoules caught between them, and the beasts would have a difficult time trying to crush the tip of each disposition. The challenge for his soldiers would be disengaging from the beasts and gaining the space needed to adopt the new formation.

"And every so often we send one of the wedges forward, just to keep the beasts honest."

"Exactly so," nodded the Blademaster.

"Excellent idea."

Kevan didn't waste any time implementing the change in tactics, issuing a new series of commands and sending messengers to all the company commanders. It took longer than he would have liked, but he had to take into account the difficulty his soldiers faced in trying to pull free from the Ghoules. The beasts continued to press his soldiers doggedly, refusing to allow them to pull back without exacting as heavy a price as possible.

Even so, much to Kevan's relief, after several minutes of brutal fighting the new formation was in place thanks to the determined efforts of the Sergeants and their well-disciplined troops. A dozen connected wedges pointed toward the north, resembling a long line of serrated teeth. Each wedge was two rows deep, the soldiers in the second row prepared to aid the soldiers in the first row at the first sign of trouble, a small reserve in the center of each wedge ready to be called upon if circumstances became truly grim. Or rather grimmer than they already were.

For the next hour, the Caledonians employed their training and battled the Ghoules to a standstill. The Blademaster's new approach aided their efforts tremendously, the Ghoules unable to penetrate their defenses despite a series of vicious attacks.

The soldiers added unpredictability to their maneuvering, doing all that they could to keep the Ghoules guessing, employing an inconsistent rhythm by having one of the wedges charge forward to drive into the Ghoules, then regain its position in the line before the beasts had a chance to recover. That irregularity helped to blunt the Ghoules' attacks, the beasts now demonstrating a wariness that to a certain degree tamed their usual belligerence.

And, when the opportunity presented itself, the sides of two connected wedges charged toward one another, crushing the Ghoules between them, before returning to their places in the line. Kevan also added a particularly effective and deadly twist to their efforts. Roving bands of archers who moved back and forth behind the lines, concentrating their fire wherever it appeared that the fighting was hottest.

Despite enjoying more success than they had thought possible during the last hour, both Kevan and the Blademaster understood that they were no longer seeking a victory. Rather, they were playing for time. Because the numbers weren't in their favor. For every Ghoule they eliminated, two or more of their soldiers fell, and those kinds of losses only ensured one kind of result.

So it was with a good bit of relief that Kevan and the Blademaster watched from the top of the snowdrift as the Ghoules pulled back unexpectedly, putting fifty yards between them and the Caledonians. That relief quickly turned to dismay as the first Ghoule Legion came sprinting down the Winter Pass from the north, an orderly mass of beasts one thousand strong.

What had been an exceedingly difficult tactical situation to begin with had just worsened drastically, particularly when the dozen or more Elders accompanying the Legion pushed their way through the front rank, staring intently at the soldiers lined up against them. Clearly, the beasts were not impressed. Perhaps they had expected more of a challenge.

"This doesn't bode well," said Kevan.

"No, it doesn't," replied the Blademaster, his resignation growing as the Elders gathered together, the insistent pointing toward the Caledonians suggesting that they were arguing about their plan of attack.

Kevan and the Blademaster both knew what the Elders could do with their Dark Magic. Without any Magii to support them, they would have no defense against the Curse. The Elders could choose wherever they liked to force their way past the Caledonians. The Ghoule Legion would follow, broadening the breach and then wrapping around the soldiers to ensnare them in a trap from which they wouldn't be able to escape.

"Have no fear of the Elders," came a familiar voice from below. "We'll keep them busy."

The two veteran soldiers looked down from their perch, smiles cracking their grim expressions as Noorsin Stelekel, Duchess of Murcia and General of the Caledonian Army, rode up. A dozen men and women came with her. They looked like schoolteachers and physicks, nary a blade between them, but Kevan and Klines knew that these unassuming, almost forgettable people were much more than that. The Blademaster could see the spheres of energy dancing above the palms of several of the Magii, who obviously were eager to get into the next round of the fight.

"Your timing is excellent as always, Noorsin," Kevan called down.

"I used the Talent to scout ahead of you and saw what was coming your way. I assumed that you could use some help." Just then dozens of companies of soldiers began appearing behind Noorsin, the leading units of the Caledonian Army trotting into place behind the Caledonian line to buttress the soldiers who had fought so well and so hard to prevent the Ghoules from streaming farther down the Winter Pass.

"Is the Weir still down?" asked Kevan.

He was pleased to see Noorsin, the Magii, and the soldiers who came with her. Even so, his larger worry remained. The longer the Weir was down, the more Legions the Ghoule Overlord could send into Caledonia.

The question running through his mind was what was the tipping point? Could enough Ghoule Legions make it into the Kingdom before the Weir took shape again -- assuming it ever did -- to ensure the Ghoule Overlord's victory over the Caledonian Army?

"For now, yes," replied Noorsin. "For how long is anyone's guess."

"So we focus on what we face before us," said Kevan, the Blademaster nodding his agreement.

"That we do," replied Noorsin. She then turned toward a short man with short hair who appeared distracted, his glasses perched on the very end of his nose, three balls of the Talent skipping through his always moving fingers. "Benjin, would you be so kind as to lead the Magii to the positions that we discussed? Once you're ready, let me know and we will begin. Better that we take the initiative than allow the Ghoules to do so."

"Of course, Noorsin," replied the Magus, who quickly led the practitioners of the Talent closer to the front, some of the men and women placing themselves right in the middle of the Caledonian line, others breaking off from the group, then jumping down from their horses so that they could climb the snowdrifts that towered in the shadows that stretched out from the mountains on the western and eastern sides of the gap.

"Captain Klines, I believe the Royal Guard is at the center of our lines, is it not?" asked Noorsin, shifting her attention to the Blademaster.

"It is," he confirmed, the Duchy Guards from the Southern Marches, Murcia, Roo's Nest, and the Three Rivers forming into ranks on each side.

"Would you care to lead them?" asked Noorsin. "I know that they would appreciate having you with them."

"I would indeed, General Stelekel. Thank you."

"Excellent," said Noorsin. "We will start on your command."

With a vicious grin and a grateful nod, Klines slid down the snowdrift, then pulled himself into his saddle, leading his horse through the arriving companies of fighters to the very center of the line. The soldiers of the Royal Guard moved their horses out of the way and offered him nods and often a few brief words of respect as he passed.

It wasn't long before he sat on his horse a half dozen yards out in front of the Caledonian Army in the open space that separated the soldiers from the Ghoules, the Legion of beasts staring at him.

The Ghoules appeared confused, their expressions suggesting that they were wondering why a lone human would be so foolish as to put himself in such a dangerous position. Even the Elders appeared uncertain as to his motives, stopping their conversation and instead focusing their attention on him, clearly curious as to what would happen next.

Klines turned away from the Ghoules, showing them the backside of his horse. Many of the soldiers watching him chuckled at that, appreciating his muted bravado. He allowed his gaze to scan across the Pass, locking eyes with as many of the soldiers as he could.

True, these soldiers came from the capital of the Kingdom

or its various Duchies. But on this day, here and now, their differences didn't matter. Where they came from wasn't important. What mattered was why they were there.

On this day, they were not soldiers of the various Guards. Today and so long as the Ghoules continued to threaten the Kingdom, they would fight together. They would fight as soldiers in the Caledonian Army. Because if these soldiers failed to meet their responsibilities, then Caledonia was lost. The Ghoules would rampage through the Kingdom, destroying everything and everyone they cared about.

All the soldiers knew this already. The Blademaster could see it in their eyes. They understood why they were there. They understood what they needed to do. But staring out at the monstrous Ghoules, many of the beasts gnashing their serrated teeth together -- designed so perfectly for ripping into flesh and grinding bone, a reminder of what would come to those who fell in the battle -- didn't make it any easier for them.

Klines had never been one for grand speeches, believing that one's actions spoke louder than words. Even so, he believed that something needed to be said now. Something that would give the soldiers some hope in the face of what appeared to be more than just challenging odds.

Using the stentorian voice that had become so familiar to those who trained with him on the practice ground in the Corinthian Palace, he began.

"You all know the Volkun. You know he is the reason that we have this chance to fight for our homes, for the people we love. He is the reason that we are here today rather than being taken by surprise by these beasts who want to do nothing more than feed upon us." Murmurs of agreement ran through the soldiers. Klines simply continued, knowing that these men and women were already in the right frame of mind for what they were about to be ordered to do. "When I was speaking to the Volkun after he killed Marden Beleron and fought the Ghoule

Overlord on the white sand, I asked him what it was like to fight in the Pit. He said it was a rather simple way of life. There was only one rule. Kill or be killed."

Absolute silence greeted Klines' words. Just as he had expected. For many of these soldiers, the Volkun was more than a man. More than a gladiator. He was a legend.

"That is what we will do today. Kill or be killed. We fight today for our Kingdom. For Caledonia. But more important, we fight for our families. For the ones we love. Because there is no doubt that if we don't, the Ghoules will take our land and feast upon our husbands and wives, our sons and daughters. So it is as simple as fighting in the Pit. Kill or be killed."

Absolute silence continued to reign, even the Ghoules who were no more than a few dozen yards away seemed to be listening, even though Klines assumed that only a few of the Elders could understand what he was saying.

Once again, he ran his gaze along the Caledonian line, locking eyes with as many of the soldiers as he could. He didn't know if what he had said had any effect or offered any value to the men and women who would be risking their lives in just a few moments. Nevertheless, he did catch something in their eyes that hardened his own resolve.

There was no fear in those thousands of gazes despite the dangers and the odds that they faced. There was only purpose. There was only a focus on what needed to be done. There was a belief in themselves and what they were fighting for.

Then a metallic pounding broke the silence, pulling Klines' gaze to Benin. His Sergeant, who sat on his horse in the very center of the Caledonian forces, was hitting his spear against his shield, the noise echoing through the gorge. Benin gave the Blademaster a nod, continuing to strike metal to metal in a set rhythm that grew louder as other soldiers soon mimicked him. It wasn't long before there was a pounding tempo reverberating off the surrounding mountains that quickly intensified into a deafening roar.

The Blademaster smiled viciously, nodding to his soldiers to demonstrate his respect for them, then wheeling his horse around. For just a moment, he stared at the Ghoules, the Elders still in front, apparently amused by what they had just observed, clearly unconcerned. They wouldn't be amused for long. Of that, the Blademaster would make sure.

Klines pulled his sword from its scabbard and lifted the blade into the air, the sun flashing off the steel. As if through some silent command, the clash of steel on steel behind him ended abruptly.

The Blademaster then lowered his sword and pointed it at the Ghoules, at the same time urging his mount forward, the large war horse reaching a gallop in only a few seconds.

A shout louder than he had ever assumed that he could emit blasted from his throat: "For Caledonia!"

The cry was taken up behind him, the sound sending a thrill of excitement through his body. Klines didn't bother to look behind him, instead focusing on the Ghoule that he had selected for his first target, steering his mount with his knees in that direction. Because he knew what followed after him.

The Caledonians screamed in rage, taking up the shout of the Blademaster as their own. They urged their horses forward with a cold determination, seeking the blood of the Ghoules.

22

STARTING ANEW

"The Protector has failed, Magus," the Ghoule Overlord barked out in a laugh as he and Sirius continued to oppose one another, the Curse and the Talent surging between them, flashes and streaks of black and white coloring the air. "The Weir is gone. Caledonia belongs to me."

Sirius didn't bother to turn around to confirm his fears, remaining square to his opponent as he considered his options for how else he might be able to gain the upper hand. Because he was running out of ideas quickly.

Nothing he had tried so far had worked. But for that single slice of the Talent that had cut across the Ghoule Overlord's shoulder because the beast was too slow to form his shield, none of his attacks had worried his adversary, the Master of the Curse demonstrating his contempt for Sirius time after time.

He, on the other hand, had at least eight burns smoldering across his flesh -- he had given up trying to keep track -- having failed to defend several of the Ghoule Overlord's attacks properly, and it wasn't for lack of trying. He was thankful that the Dark Magic only had charred his flesh rather than slamming into him with its full force and seeking to corrupt him from within, knowing that if that happened, he was worse than dead.

Even still, he had no desire to die from a thousand painful cuts. Yet what was he to do?

Sirius had felt the Weir falter, weakening at an incredibly fast rate. It was as if the energy used to construct the barrier was being drained away. Then, in just minutes, the only defense keeping the Ghoules from rampaging through Caledonia disappeared entirely.

The Ghoule Overlord could be right. Bryen might have failed. But the Protector wasn't one to give in easily. Sirius could only hope that Bryen was working his way through the challenge, seeking a solution. That whatever happened with respect to the Weir was only a temporary setback.

"Maybe so," Sirius replied, trying to inject a confidence that he didn't feel into his voice. "Then again, maybe not."

With a growl of anger, Sirius sent a cloud of the Talent hurtling toward the beast. The assault distracted the Ghoule Overlord, if only for a moment, as it forced him to call upon his Dark Magic, a misty shield of black surging around him and preventing the blazing energy from settling across his mottled green flesh.

Sirius couldn't worry about Bryen now. He had given him what time he could. There was nothing else that he could do for him.

Although he could do something for himself that might also help Bryen. Even if Bryen failed to raise the Weir once again, perhaps Sirius could gain a small victory, wounding the Ghoule Overlord or at least weakening him so that if the Protector faced him in a combat, he would have a better chance of killing the beast.

That thought immediately became his goal.

Still, he was concerned. Even if he gained some small measure of success, Sirius feared the worst. From what he had discovered from his current fight, killing the Ghoule Overlord was almost an impossibility.

His vow to his brother would go unfulfilled.

"WELL DONE," said Viktor, impressed by Bryen's skill and his ability to break down the complex and make it simpler and more manageable. Although he shouldn't be surprised. Sirius had always been a thorough and detail-oriented instructor, aggravatingly so as he had learned firsthand, and that nitpickiness was proving its value in this, the most crucial of moments. "Are you all right, lad?"

Viktor stared intently at Bryen, trying to discern any hint of what might be going on within him. From what he could see, the Protector appeared to be the same as he was before he had used the Seventh Stone to absorb the Talent and the Curse that had been a part of the Weir.

But appearances could be deceiving, as he believed they were now.

Sparks of white and black, signifying the two discrete energies, shot intermittently across Bryen's hands and forearms, bursting out of his skin and disappearing just as rapidly. And his eyes had changed color, the sharp, deep grey replaced by one pure orb of white and the other of pure black, both flaring brightly in a constant, alternating rhythm, providing a hint as to the tremendous amount of energy that was surging within him and seeking to be released.

"For now," Bryen nodded. "I feel a little strange, a little off, almost like I have vertigo mixed with the worst headache known to man."

"That's not unexpected," said Viktor, though he had said it more to make Bryen feel better about what he was dealing with than out of any true knowledge of what his nephew might be experiencing, since no one had ever done what Bryen was doing now, and he had no way to judge the effects of the massive amounts of disparate energy upon him. He hoped that he was speaking truly. Because if he wasn't, he feared what might happen if Bryen lost control of the power now contained within the Seventh Stone. "The Curse is under control? You're certain?"

"Yes," Bryen said with an unassuming confidence. He heard himself speaking, yet to his ears it sounded like the words were coming from a far-off distance, echoing faintly. "But we need to do this quickly. I don't know how long I can maintain the balance I have right now."

Even though he had established a form of equilibrium with the help of the Seventh Stone, the Curse and the Talent continued to grapple within him, much like the wrestlers he had watched on occasion in the Colosseum. There was no telling when the pushing and shoving would become an all-out war.

He had it under control for now. Yet that fact didn't eliminate his worry. Not only because he believed that one misstep on his part could free the Curse that he had locked away, corrupting him just as had happened to the Ten Magii, but also because he was eager to restore the Weir.

The longer the magical barrier was down, the more time the Ghoules would have to enter Caledonia unimpeded. Knowing how fast those beasts could move, he feared that even if he succeeded in his task the Ghoules could get enough Legions into the south so that the fate of the Kingdom would have already been sealed, regardless of the best efforts of the Caledonian Army.

"Agreed," said Viktor. "So let's get to it." The nine Magii stepped closer to Bryen, circling around him and then linking their hands again, Viktor now included. They stared at Bryen with hope in their eyes, and a little bit of fear, remembering how they had failed to construct the Weir as they thought they would and not wanting to make the same mistake again. "Draw from the Seventh Stone within you and begin the weave as you know how to do, protecting yourself from the Curse with the Talent. Send the flow into the Stones. Once you get started, we will help you to speed the process along."

"Pull from the Seventh Stone?" asked Bryen, his voice sounding peculiar to his own ears, the hint of fear unmistakable.

The time had come.

"Yes," confirmed Viktor. "The Seventh Stone will regulate the flow once you start the weave. Just let it do its work. It will ensure that you go only so fast as is safe."

Still a bit unsure regarding all the details of what was about to happen, particularly how the spirits of Ten Magii could still manipulate the Talent and the Curse and aid him in his task, he ignored his concerns because he had no other options other than to try to do the one thing that frightened him the most.

Rebuild the Weir.

Dying at the claws of the Ghoule Overlord was, in his mind, nothing compared to the sense of defeat that would crush his spirit if he failed at this essential endeavor, because his work now was tied not only to his fate, but also to the fates of all those living in Caledonia.

Before his escalating fears and doubts could get the better of him, Bryen began his work, reaching out to the Seventh Stone and marveling for just a second at the immense amount of energy at his beck and call. Then he began, weaving together the Talent and the Curse as he did on Haven, taking the two streams of competing energies offered to him by the artifact, plaiting them together until they were virtually indistinguishable, ensuring the whole time that the Curse was wrapped within the Talent, the layer incredibly fine but critical to his success and his own safety.

"Excellent," said Viktor, nodding his head in approval, impressed by the quality and finesse of his nephew's labor. "Keep weaving. We begin now."

At first, Bryen didn't notice any change as he worked furiously to take the rapidly accelerating streams that the Seventh Stone gave to him and weave the Talent and the Curse together, the Curse always wrapped in the Talent. It wasn't very long, however, before a very faint multicolored glow began to illuminate the Sanctuary, the natural colors of the Six Stones flashing irregularly until finally finding a cadence as Bryen continued to bind the streams.

The colors were barely perceptible, much like the embers of a fire that had burned through the night. But they grew stronger and brighter, as if those very same embers that had been about to be extinguished instead had been stoked back alive.

Smiling at his success, Bryen glanced quickly around him. He watched in wonder as the spirits of the Ten Magii worked with him now, also accepting streams from the Seventh Stone to accelerate the labor, doing exactly what Bryen was doing, their essences that had been a part of the artifact for a millennium freed specifically to assist Bryen with this task.

As the Ten Magii joined with Bryen, the glow of the Stones became even more vivid, flaring with a strength and brilliance that hadn't been seen in centuries, the power emanating from the jewels sending a kaleidoscope of colors flashing through the Sanctuary. Bryen had to pull his gaze away, unable to look at the jewels anymore, focusing instead on the translucent stone of the pedestal so that he could maintain his concentration.

Then much to Bryen's shock, without picking up his gaze so that he wouldn't be distracted, he sensed that the Seventh Stone had added a key and unexpected resource to the mix. The artifact was now pulling not only from the Talent of the

Ten Magii, but also drawing on the Curse contained within the black diamond that was set atop the Ghoule Overlord's staff.

He could feel that stream of Dark Magic curling through the air just over his shoulder, flowing reluctantly but inexorably into the weave that centered on him and then circulating back out to the Stones set around the hollow.

It was an incredible experience to be in the very middle of, the power and precision in play mindboggling. It might even have been exciting, if not for the fact that most of the time Bryen simply tried to focus on what he needed to do. To do anything other than concentrate on the weave put him at risk of getting swept away by the storm of energy roiling within him.

"Does the Ghoule Overlord know what is happening?" asked Bryen, curious as to whether his nemesis was aware that the Seventh Stone was stealing the Curse from him and that ironically the source of the beast's power was playing a major role in thwarting his larger plan.

"If that monster doesn't yet, he will soon. It won't matter, though. There is nothing that he will be able to do to stop this process from reaching completion."

"Even with all the power that he can manipulate?"

"Even with all the power he can manipulate," confirmed Viktor, who along with the other Magii continued to weave the Talent and the Curse together, offering their plaits to Bryen so that the Seventh Stone could distribute the woven energy to the other Stones. "The Ghoule Overlord has lived a long time because of that power, in fact his very existence depends upon it, but I suspect that he has forgotten that the power that he controls is also controlling him. He is not a master of the Curse as he likely believes. The Curse is the master of him. Just as you are a host for the Seventh Stone, he is a host for the Curse. And right now the Seventh Stone is the stronger master, making of the Curse what it must."

Bryen thought about what his uncle had just revealed,

believing that it was a crucially important discovery. Unfortunately, he didn't have the chance to pursue it further.

"Place your hand on the pedestal," said Viktor. "We begin the next step now."

Bryen did as his uncle requested. As soon as his palm touched the pellucid stone, a flash brighter than the sun blasted through the Sanctuary. Much like a thunderstorm, it was accompanied by a resounding clap that shook the monolith to its very base, tons of loose rock sliding off the sides of the spire and crashing far below to the bottom of the Trench.

Bryen didn't see or hear any of that. Instead, he stared down at the shimmering rock in wonder, amazed by what was occurring right in front of him. The Seventh Stone, the fist-sized diamond that had merged with him, was beginning to regain its shape, a blinding stream of white flowing out of his chest, directed toward the center of the pedestal. In seconds, the process was complete. The artifact solidified and resumed its position on the pedestal, cradled by the three razor-sharp gold wires.

Through it all, the flow of the Curse and the Talent continued, the Dark Magic from the black diamond flowing directly into the Seventh Stone, Bryen and the Ten Magii continuing to weave the two energies together, the braid surging into the now pulsing Stones.

Bryen noticed that something else was happening now as well. The Stones were beginning to shoot thin, faint streams of energy up into the air. Those first flows weren't very strong to begin, the streams pulsing into the sky and then disappearing just as fast as they had first appeared.

But Bryen didn't care. Those streams were evidence that what he and the Ten Magii were doing was working.

So it went for several minutes, Bryen and the Ten Magii heartened by what they saw happening, redoubling their efforts, until finally the power contained within the Stones had reached a critical mass. Those very fine, weak streams of power intensified and strengthened, blasting up into the air with a now undeniable power and connecting farther above the pedestal that held the Seventh Stone.

"Well done," said Viktor, the Magus clearly pleased. "Well done, indeed. Keep weaving. All is going as it should. As we hoped that it would."

Bryen didn't even need to think about what he was doing now, his entwining the Talent and the Curse together, the threat from the Dark Magic contained by a thin layer of the Talent, having become second nature to him. As the minutes passed and he and the Ten Magii accelerated the pace of their work, he watched in both pleasure and astonishment as the energy coming from the other Stones and meeting above the pedestal, just a hundred feet above his head in fact, pulsed faster and brighter, the light so strong now that he couldn't look at it directly.

But he could feel it, the electricity in the hollow making the hair on his head, his arms, and on the back of his neck stand on end. He was so captivated by what he was doing that he almost missed Viktor's next instruction.

"Beautiful work," said Viktor. "Now let it go."

Bryen hadn't even realized that he had been holding back the energy flowing through him, or rather that he and the Seventh Stone continued to restrain the surge of power coming from the other Stones. Because even though the Seventh Stone was no longer physically a part of him, there was still a connection between them, much as had been the case with the Protector's collar, just as Viktor said there would be.

Bryen realized that regulating the power of the Seventh Stone didn't require the artifact to be a part of him. So working in conjunction with the Seventh Stone he did as Viktor instructed, releasing the flow.

With an explosion of air that blasted out through the ten

columns and across the summit, the Seventh Stone managing the tide of energy the entire time, that primary stream of power that had formed just above Bryen's head shot up into the sky with an uninhibited urgency, pulsing rapidly, the black and white of the competing powers giving way to the familiar grey-ish, often transparent plait that had been the bane of the Ghoules.

The rebuilt Weir expanded at an incredible speed, stretching toward the sun until it reached some unseen point and down to the floor of the Trench, then from there spreading to the east and the west, following the same path that had been taken when the Weir was first constructed a thousand years before.

"Beautifully worked, lad," said Viktor. "Now hold onto the power for just a moment more. We are almost done."

"The Spear of the Magii," said Bryen.

"Yes. The twist I spoke of. When I command it, use the Spear to slice through the stream of power coming from the Seventh Stone."

"That will be enough?"

"It will," said Viktor, then adding quickly, "theoretically."

"You're not certain?" demanded Bryen, once again both irritated and amused at how similar Viktor and Sirius were.

"I'm as certain as I can be."

Just like Sirius, Bryen said to himself. Always sure in what he thought, even if he had yet to prove it.

"Now!"

With a quick flick of his wrists, Bryen slashed through the stream of energy just as Viktor ordered, freeing the Seventh Stone from the flow. Yet the action did more than just separate the crafted energy from the Seventh Stone.

The tip of the Spear remained connected to the Weir. The blade flared brilliantly for a few seconds as the Talent that he had used to encase the Curse surged back into his weapon, wrenching free from the Dark Magic and allowing the Curse and the Talent to merge as one within the Weir.

With a final flash that began in the Sanctuary and ran along the length of the Weir, it was done.

There was no flickering. No flashing. No warring between the two energies.

The weave was so perfect, the black and white of the competing powers merged into a light grey that was so fine that it was almost invisible. Perhaps most impressive, no matter how closely Bryen looked, he couldn't see the weave.

"Congratulations," said Viktor. "The Weir has been remade. It will never fail again."

23

CERTAIN FATE

For the first time in a very long time, Sirius felt free. It was as if from one breath to the next he had shed all of the burdens that he had taken onto his shoulders the last few centuries.

The Weir weakening. The Ghoule Overlord and his Legions stirring. Guarding the Seventh Stone.

Gone.

Because now he was only in the present. There were no thoughts of the past. There were no concerns regarding the future.

There was no more thinking. There was no more planning. There was no more worrying.

There were no more doubts or fears or worries as he questioned every decision that he had ever made, a habit that he hated yet couldn't elude.

Now, there was only doing what he did best, what thrilled him the most. Using the Talent.

Although he was no longer the most powerful Magus in Caledonia -- Bryen had claimed that accolade, Aislinn not too far behind him -- he was the most skilled, and he was putting that prowess to good use right then.

His combat with the Ghoule Overlord filling him with a purpose and energy that he hadn't experienced in centuries, Sirius used every trick, every morsel of knowledge, that he had learned during his more than one thousand years, sending streams of the Talent, spikes of sizzling heat, spears of light, webs of power, even throwing a few of Rafia's favored bolts of lightning into the mix, as he did all that he could to keep the beast from hindering Bryen's efforts in the Sanctuary.

So far everything that he had tried had worked, helping to keep him in the fight. His varied and persistent attacks kept the Ghoule Overlord guessing, the monster surprisingly off balance, unable to seize the initiative.

For how much longer that would prove to be the case, Sirius couldn't say with any certainty. Because Sirius was faced with a stark and very unforgiving reality.

He was tiring, and the Ghoule Overlord wasn't. In fact, from where Sirius stood, just twenty feet away from his opponent, it appeared as if the Ghoule Overlord was getting stronger with each passing second, the beast harnessing more and more of his Dark Magic, a seemingly endless supply flowing out of the black diamond, the monster finding that he needed to put in less effort to defend against Sirius' attacks.

Sirius had a limit with the Talent that he could not exceed. If he did, the natural power of the world would destroy him, and the Ghoule Overlord would have an open path to Bryen.

"Your brother was weak, old man," rasped the Ghoule Overlord, seeking to distract his adversary with his use of the common tongue.

"Tetric was always weak," agreed Sirius, his concentration never wavering as he threw several dozen daggers of light toward the Ghoule Overlord, the monster knocking away each one with his twisted staff.

"You will meet the same fate as he did," the beast continued, his teeth-filled maw opening into a grotesque smile of pleasure, the Ghoule Overlord sensing that the momentum was shifting in his direction. "I will make you mine just as I did with him. Tetric wanted the Curse. Craved it. So will you."

"I am not my brother," Sirius growled heatedly.

The Ghoule Overlord had been talking to him constantly ever since the combat had started. Insults. Threats. Even promises. Anything that might divert his attention at the worst possible moment.

Sirius had ignored every single attempt to break his concentration, or at least he had tried to, a few of the jibes and taunts hitting a bit too close to the truth. Nevertheless, Sirius refused to display his anger or his disgust, knowing what would happen if he gave in to his urges.

Now was not the time to falter. Now was the time to stand strong, much like a gladiator in the Pit.

Why the Ghoule Overlord felt the need to try to distract him, Sirius didn't know. The combat had begun less than a half hour before, and within minutes the Ghoule Overlord had pushed Sirius to his limit.

Sirius knew it. The Ghoule Overlord knew it.

Even so, Sirius had found a way time after time to continue the fight, grasping every opportunity to extend the duel for as long as he could. But Sirius' worries were multiplying. The beast was grinning wickedly now, preparing another series of attacks, appearing unconcerned by anything that Sirius might throw at him.

"You are no different than he was," chuckled the Ghoule Overlord, sending a flash of darkness toward Sirius that the Magus blocked with the buckler constructed of the Talent that he had affixed to his forearm. "Playing with powers you don't fully comprehend. Believing that you know and understand more than you actually do. Not understanding what true power really is."

"I do know one thing, you miserable wretch," said Sirius, his expression serious, unwavering, as he flicked orbs of energy no larger than marbles toward the beast.

The Ghoule Overlord swiped away the blazing spheres of power with a single swing of his staff. His contempt for the Magus was plain. The human was nothing more than a bug to be stepped on, nothing more than the final obstacle before he claimed the prize he craved so desperately.

"What would that be, Magus? That your death is assured on this spire? That once I'm done with you, I will kill the Protector and destroy the Sanctuary?"

"You're right, I might die here and now," Sirius admitted quietly, though his words traveled easily across the short distance that separated him from his adversary.

Before he could finish what he was about to say, for just a heartbeat he lost his train of thought. A shiver shot up Sirius' spine, not of fear, but rather of expectation. He could sense the immense amount of power that was now being applied in the hollow. He didn't need to turn around to see what was going to happen next, instead feeling it in his very bones, though the thought of it brought a cunning look to his grim countenance.

For the first time since his combat started, Sirius smiled. "But I believe that your end is destined to occur here as well. You will not escape the summit alive. That I promise you."

Before the Ghoule Overlord could reply, the beast's black eyes, which swirled with the Curse, widened. A howl of rage that swept across the summit followed as he watched helplessly as the Weir slammed back into place, the woven energy of the Talent and the Curse streaking in all directions to reconstitute the barrier hated so by the Ghoules.

The Weir of the Ten Magii had been destroyed. The Weir of the Protector had taken its place.

Now it was Sirius' turn to laugh with pleasure. Bryen had done it!

The young man's success filled Sirius with joy and a pride that he couldn't contain. The Protector had done it!

Unexpectedly memories of Bryen's parents, Alana and Loren, suddenly played through the old Magus' mind. They would have been proud of their son as well. But thinking of the two murdered Magii tempered Sirius' exultation, a deep sadness once again burdening his soul.

A sadness that he realized that he could never escape. A sadness that he never wanted to escape. Because for him, that sadness, which was never far from the edge of his emotions, was a form of penance for him. A cost that only he could bear. A cost that he had to bear.

He had failed Alana and Loren. He had failed Bryen for so long and in so many ways. Yet the Protector had not failed him or the people of Caledonia.

Despite all the obstacles placed in his way, Bryen had done it! He had rebuilt the Weir!

The primary defense against the Ghoule Overlord and his Legions was back in place.

The excitement of that achievement radiated through him, rejuvenating him. Giving him an additional vigor that he had not encountered in centuries. A vitality that he needed desperately now if he was to have any chance of surviving the next few minutes.

He could feel the energy rushing through him, begging to be released. With a malicious grin, he acceded to that demand, sending stream after stream, bolt after bolt of the Talent hurtling toward the Ghoule Overlord. Finally, the beast struggled to defend himself as he was forced to come to grips with the fact that his plans and dreams, a thousand years in the making, were crashing down around him.

Reveling in the fight, marveling at the immense quantity of

power that he was using, Sirius pressed his attack. He knew that the longer he could keep the Ghoule Overlord occupied, the better it would be for Bryen once he finished what he was doing in the Sanctuary.

But then Sirius sensed a dangerous and frightening change in their duel. It was visible in the Ghoule Overlord's eyes. In just seconds, the beast's rage transformed into cold calculation and the need for revenge.

Sirius' eyebrows shot up in worry when the Ghoule Overlord slammed his twisted black staff down onto the cracked stone of the summit, the concussion of the powerful blow sending the Curse toward him in a torrent. The old Magus sent more of the Talent into his buckler, expanding his shield so that it covered his entire body. And just in time. His magical scutum absorbed much of the blast, though not all.

The force of the shock wave was so strong that Sirius was flung backward, head over heels. He landed heavily on his back, barely able to breathe as a terrible pain ripped through his chest. He assumed that the explosion of power had broken several of his ribs. It probably did even worse damage to his insides that he didn't want to think about because there was little that he could do for his injuries. Besides, he didn't have the time to check how badly he had been hurt.

His adversary loomed over him, placing Sirius in shadow. Hate radiated off the beast in shimmering waves.

The Ghoule Overlord stared at the old Magus with rage-filled eyes and a lethal intent, the beast preparing what Sirius assumed would be the final strike of their combat, the Curse spinning fiercely across the top of the black diamond. Not yet ready to give up despite the severity of his injuries, Sirius rolled to his side with a scream of agony. The pain was almost too much for him, the Magus fearing that he would pass out.

Still, through sheer stubbornness, he managed to push

himself to his knees. If he was going to die, it was going to be on his own terms.

At that exact moment, he watched as the Ghoule Overlord released his Dark Magic from the black diamond, the shard of energy streaking right toward him. Sirius knew in an instant that he didn't have the strength or the ability to defend himself. He was too tired. Too weak. His injuries were only accelerating his decline.

The end had finally come.

Then in a brief flash of lucidity he recalled something that he had learned when he had fought the Ghoule Overlord in the Pit when the beast still wore his brother Tetric's shell.

At the time Bryen had teased him about how the Ghoule Overlord had escaped him, wondering if the old Magus could do the same. Sirius had been shocked by what the Ghoule Overlord had done with the Curse, but he had been paying attention. Because he believed that you could do the same thing with the Talent. If you were strong enough and had the necessary skill.

The rest of his life now counted in seconds, Sirius tried with the last of his Talent what he had seen the Ghoule Overlord accomplish on the white sand of the Pit. A portal of shimmering white formed right in front of him, the mist beckoning to him. It was no more than a few feet in height and width, but that's all he needed.

Although the gateway wasn't exactly what Sirius had in mind with the Curse screaming toward him he didn't care. He was simply happy that it worked.

Sirius scrambled as best as he could through the gateway, falling more than crawling, but it was enough. Just barely. As soon as he made it into the darkness, the portal closed, the Dark Magic streaking through the space where he had been kneeling just a moment before.

24

POWER TO HEAL

Bryen stared in wonder at the Seventh Stone, the diamond as large as his fist raised just above the pedestal by the three razor-sharp gold wires, the last time he had seen it when he was a child. The jewel flashed a brilliant white, not only because of the power contained within it, but also as a result of the sunlight that filtered down into the hollow, the faintest touch setting the artifact ablaze.

Even though he and the Seventh Stone were no longer one physically, they still were one and the same. They were connected and always would be. The power of the Seventh Stone would always be Bryen's to call upon, to use as he needed.

He understood now how the Seventh Stone truly functioned and how its sentience connected with his own. That, in itself, wasn't surprising. What was surprising was that at the very farthest reaches of his consciousness, Bryen also could sense the Ten Magii.

They, too, were a part of the Seventh Stone. And now they were also a part of him. As soon as the artifact had joined with him, the Magii had connected with him as well, their skill and knowledge, their power and experience, becoming his own.

He was thankful for that. He doubted that he could have crafted the Weir without them. Although it was a bit disconcerting when he really thought about it.

Pulling his gaze away from the Seventh Stone, he used the Talent to study the power soaring into the sky from the Stones, the beams of energy strong and untainted. The Weir shimmered a faint greyish white that often appeared clear to the eye. To Bryen's way of thinking, the barrier resembled a cloudy glass that gained greater clarity depending on how you looked at the magical construction when the sunlight hit it.

The Weir was solid, yet it also gave an appearance of flexibility, which didn't make sense to Bryen. Nevertheless, it was the only way that he could describe what he was seeing when he examined the barrier.

Most important, the Weir no longer flickered. The weave held strong, reflecting the creation of something new, something previously not thought possible, his and the Ten Magii's work a creation for the ages.

The barrier was much like the translucent stone used to construct the Aeyrie, the Library of the Magii, and the small plaza surrounding the Sanctuary. Solid as a rock, yet almost perfectly clear as well. Not stone, but a substance stronger than that. More enduring. Similar to the first Weir in many respects, though completely different in others.

"Thank you," said Bryen, turning toward Viktor, the spirits of the other nine Magii lined up behind him now, all of them with smiles of contentment, their failure finally erased after the passage of a millennium. "I couldn't have done this without you. Without all of you."

"And we couldn't have done it without you," replied Viktor, the other Magii nodding toward him in respect and silent thanks for his acknowledgement of their contribution and for helping them lift a crushing burden from their shoulders.

"Will you pass on now?" asked Bryen, remembering what had happened with the Sentinel in the tunnel that led from Haven to the Trench. "Will you and the others now be free from the Seventh Stone?"

Bryen assumed that the Ten Magii wanted to break their link to the Seventh Stone, to gain the rest that had been denied them for centuries, and he couldn't blame them for that desire.

Although a part of Bryen hoped that Viktor and the other Magii might remain. He barely knew them, yet still he felt a bond with the Ten Magii that suggested the ties between them went beyond the blood that he and Viktor shared.

His working with the Magii to reconstruct the Weir had affected him in an almost unfathomable way that he hadn't anticipated and greatly appreciated. It was as if their working together forced them to reveal their inner selves to one another, sharing their very essences, and that relationship continued even though the task they had partnered on now was complete.

Viktor paused for a moment before replying, thinking, then smiling. "No, I don't believe that we will. We will stay. We are a part of the Seventh Stone. And we are now a part of you. Those two truths will never change. Besides, I have no doubt that there is more that you will need from us."

Before Bryen could ask what his uncle might mean by that, Viktor urged him to shift his focus to what he needed to do next, because though the work of the Ten Magii was finished, his own wasn't. "We will talk more another time. This battle is over. The Weir is rebuilt. But the war with the Ghoules has just begun, and the only way to guarantee the safety of Caledonia is to kill the Ghoule Overlord and destroy the Curse. To ensure our work here remains strong, you must cleanse the Lost Land of the Curse."

"What do you mean cleanse the Lost Land?"

"That is a question for another time. Go. Your friends need you now."

Bryen nodded, then turned and ran swiftly toward the stairs, not stopping even when Viktor called to him over his shoulder as his uncle and the other Magii faded away, their work, at least on this day, done. "And remember, if there is need, use the Seventh Stone. You and the Seventh Stone are one. You will always be one. The power of the Seventh Stone belongs to you and you alone."

Bryen listened to what Viktor had just said, but he didn't give it much thought, pushing it to the side for later, assuming, of course, that he survived the confrontation that he was rushing toward. The confrontation that had frightened him when he had first realized that it was inevitable, that he couldn't escape if he was to meet the charge he had accepted.

But now, he wanted that confrontation. He hungered for it.

To be free of the white sand, he needed to free himself. No one else could do it for him. The same logic applied now. If he wanted to be free of the Ghoule Overlord, he needed to free himself. There was only one way to do that. But first, he needed to help a friend.

Racing up the stairs two at a time, Bryen skidded to a stop and knelt down next to Lycia. Aislinn still stood above the wounded gladiator, keeping the promise that she had made to her sister, protecting her with the Talent and steel, whichever proved necessary.

Bryen glanced quickly around him just to get the lay of the land. Sirius stood in front of the entrance to the Sanctuary, no more than twenty feet away, a maelstrom of energy surging around him as he continued his duel with the Ghoule Over-lord. The Master of the Lost Land had given himself to a rage that Bryen was certain would only help to extend the combat, Sirius wisely using the beast's unrestrained fury against him.

The old Magus was demonstrating just as he had so many

times during their lessons together that a clear mind and clarity of purpose could overcome an almost overwhelming strength, at least for a time. Power and precision were both essential to a Magus' success. At the moment, Sirius' precision blunted time and again the Ghoule Overlord's power.

The primary cause of the Ghoule Overlord's anger was quite obvious, glaringly so, in fact. The reconstruction of the Weir destroyed the beast's carefully laid plans, leaving him only with those Ghoules who already had crossed into Caledonia before the barrier slammed back down to help him in his attempt to conquer the Kingdom.

Whether the Ghoule Overlord had pushed through enough Legions to achieve his objective, Bryen didn't know. He could only hope that he had worked fast enough to limit the number of beasts who made it into the Winter Pass to a number that the Caledonian Army had a chance of defeating.

He wondered as well whether the Overlord's anger was inflamed by the beast's realization that the black diamond, the jewel that was the source of his power, that served as the reservoir for the Dark Magic of the Ghoules, had been appropriated by the Seventh Stone, the Ghoule Overlord's own power used against him. Whether the beast knew it or not, Bryen planned to make use of that piece of information when the time for their combat came.

But that combat would have to wait. At present, it appeared that Sirius had everything well in hand. The Talent sparked off his robes. His hair stood on end in response to the electricity circulating around him. His grim countenance mixed with an unbridled joy as he fired bursts of energy from the palms of his hands, forcing the Ghoule Overlord to dance to his tune for a time as the beast's rage hindered his efforts to mount an effective defense. For the time being, the old Magus seemed to be in control of the combat.

Bryen shifted his gaze to the Ghoules. The beasts still

attacked the Blood Company, which was firmly entrenched between the ten columns, although it was not a concerted effort. Rather just one or two of the beasts exhibited any initiative as they charged the shield wall. The Ghoules were less committed to the task now that the Weir was back in place, paying more attention to their Master and the duel that had enmeshed him.

That lack of drive could have also resulted because of the determination and resolve of their opponents. Even with their greatly reduced numbers, the Blood Company continued to demonstrate a martial skill and tenacity that was having a clear and decisive impact on the beasts.

The gladiators had reduced the ranks of the Ghoules by more than half their original number in the time it took Bryen to recreate the Weir. Declan, Tarin, Jerad, and Davin continued to lead the fight, the two soldiers and the two gladiators urging the Blood Company to even greater heights through word and example, pushing the Ghoules back from the verge that marked the heart of the Sanctuary.

Believing that everything was well in hand at least for the time being, Bryen shifted his attention to Lycia. Her sweat-streaked face was pale, and her color had taken on a greyish cast. Bryen placed his right hand gently on her sternum, avoiding the burnt, smoldering flesh just below.

Lycia's breathing was shallow and fading, and he realized that she was losing rapidly what little strength she had left. The web of Dark Magic was spreading within her, the tendrils of black reaching out from the wound beneath her ribs, moving quickly in all directions, now only a few inches away from her heart.

"Can you help her?" asked Aislinn, the desperation in her voice sending a surge of fear through Bryen.

The Lady of the Southern Marches shot several bolts of energy toward the few Elders who remained alive on the monolith's summit, she and Rafia working together to kill the handful who had yet to succumb to their predations, doing everything that they could to ensure that they didn't turn their attention toward the Ghoule Overlord's combat with Sirius.

"I can try."

"You need to do better than that," demanded Aislinn more harshly than she meant to, her eyes narrowing for just a second in annoyance. She had struck one of the Elders a glancing blow, slicing across his thigh with the Talent. She should have finished the beast. Even so, it had been enough to distract him, his shield of misty Dark Magic slipping. Rafia took full advantage, throwing a spear of energy right through the beast's chest, the creature dead before his body hit the stone. "You can't let her die. She doesn't deserve to die."

Bryen didn't respond. Aislinn was right. He couldn't let Lycia die. But to keep that from happening, he needed to focus. The wound was the worst that he had ever seen caused by the Curse, the putrescence corrupting Lycia with an alarming alacrity.

Reaching for the Talent, he locked away his doubts and scanned Lycia's wound. It was much like he remembered with Aislinn's father, although much worse, the Dark Magic working its way through Lycia at an almost unstoppable rate. The Curse should have killed her by now, but she continued to fight, holding on with her fingernails, too stubborn to die. Yet he feared that no matter what he did, she was too far gone. Still, he refused to let her go to the other side. Not without a fight.

To save the Duke, Bryen had found the infection's weakest point. Unfortunately, he couldn't take that approach now. He didn't have the time. So he had no choice but to work faster than he would have preferred and hope that his combination of power and precision didn't kill his friend in the process.

Using the Spear of the Magii as his focal point, he opened himself to the energy of the Seventh Stone. Bryen breathed a sigh of relief when it worked. The energy of the artifact filled him, surging through his body, even though the jewel was not physically a part of him anymore.

He then applied that energy to Lycia's wound, approaching it differently than he had in the past, understanding that time was short. He employed the Talent as if he were cauterizing a wound, sending the cleansing energy streaming into Lycia, the white-hot power burning through the Dark Magic.

Lycia responded immediately to the battle that Bryen forced upon her, her body shaking uncontrollably, her back arcing, her eyes as wide as saucers. The entire time Bryen kept his hand pressed against her chest to hold her in place and ensure that the power of the Seventh Stone flowed into her.

"Bryen, what's going on?" asked Aislinn, concern in her voice as she caught what was occurring out of the corner of her eye, her worry for Lycia increasing.

"It has to happen," Bryen replied with a cold certainty. "It's the only way that I can help her. Otherwise, she dies."

Lycia's shivering increased in intensity, her eyes closed but her mouth opening in a silent scream that threatened to break Bryen's concentration. He ignored his friend's torment, staying on task even though it pained him to watch what Lycia was experiencing.

"But can't you ..."

"It has to happen," Bryen repeated firmly. "Don't worry. I know what I'm doing."

And he did. He felt firmly in control of the tremendous amount of power that he could facilitate through the Seventh Stone. Finally, he felt comfortable in who he was and what was expected of him.

He put that confidence to use, guiding the Talent as it scoured Lycia clean, finding and destroying every last speck of the Curse. The Dark Magic having no defense against the power that he brought to bear.

Then he was done. He had expunged the Curse. Releasing his hold on the Talent, Bryen offered a quiet murmur of thanks to the Seventh Stone for aiding him. A strong color had returned to Lycia's face, and she was breathing more evenly now.

For just a few seconds, Lycia opened her eyes, then reached up, her fingers lightly touching the scars on Bryen's cheek and neck. Her hand dropped back down to her chest and she smiled, closing her eyes, exhausted but alive, the Talent continuing to heal her as she fell into a deep sleep.

After he was certain that Lycia would be all right, Bryen looked up and to his horror saw Sirius knocked head over heels onto his back as the Ghoule Overlord sent a shard of the Curse from the black diamond directly toward his chest, Sirius crafting a portal of swirling white that he somehow scrambled through on his hands and knees. The gateway disappeared as soon as he fell through, the Curse missing him by no more than a hair as it passed right through the space an instant after the old Magus escaped.

The Ghoule Overlord's scream of rage at his prey eluding him brought a smile to Bryen's lips. He had to give Sirius credit for that maneuver.

But he was worried. Watching Sirius for just a few seconds, he could tell that the old Magus was weakening. That he didn't have what was needed to continue the combat.

Whatever injuries Sirius had suffered just moments before only confirmed the conclusion that Bryen had reached. It was time for someone else to take his place in the combat.

Staring with a cold resolve at the Ghoule Overlord, Bryen pushed himself to his feet and began walking through the melee, the glowing Spear of the Magii spinning slowly in front of him from his left hand to his right and then back again.

The Blood Company would finish the Ghoules. Rafia and Aislinn would kill the Elders.

Critical results, yes, but one combat now took precedence over all the others.

Bryen had rebuilt the Weir. He had healed Lycia. Now there was only one thing left for him to do.

Kill the Ghoule Overlord.

25
____

THE END

Sirius laughed softly upon realizing that he was still alive. Then he forced himself to stop. It hurt too much to laugh as he could barely breathe, the pain of his broken ribs worsening with each second, making it hard for him to think. And he needed to think, because he still had a combat to finish.

He gritted his teeth as he pushed himself to his feet, his hand going to his side. He was hurt worse than he had believed, his lungs barely working. He was probably bleeding internally in several places. He was finding it difficult to stay on his feet. His balance was poor. His ears rang as if he had been hit in the head with a hammer multiple times. And there were black specks at the edge of his vision that were growing bigger with every worrisome wheezing breath that he took.

Sirius tried to push all that away from him. It was hard, the agony beginning to pulse through his body. Still, he did it, at least enough to dull the pain so that he could regain some much-needed clarity.

There wasn't much that he could do about his current condition. However, he could try to help Bryen one more time, and perhaps in doing so pay the debt that he owed the young man and his parents.

Having decided on his next course of action, Sirius tried and failed to stand up straight. That slight effort was too much for him. So he stayed hunched over instead as he worked to calm himself before he took his next step.

One hand on his shattered ribs, he took in everything around him with his blurring vision. There wasn't much to see.

He didn't know where he was. The fog swirling around him prevented him from seeing anything at all, not even his hand when he held it more than a foot in front of his face. Whatever this place was, it reminded him in some ways of being atop the stone balanced on the mountain peak when taking the Test to become a Magus.

Nothing to be heard. Nothing to be seen.

He would have liked to have gotten a better sense of what this place was, but satisfying his curiosity didn't matter now. Because although he didn't know where he was, he did know where he needed to go and what he wanted to do.

And much to his relief, he knew exactly how to get there.

Reaching for the small stream of the Talent that he could still facilitate, a portal of spinning white mist reappeared right in front of him. Sirius took a slow step toward the gateway, and then one more, each shuffle sending a jolt of fiery torment up and down his spine, his many injuries protesting even this small action. Still, he refused to allow his failing body to keep him from the task he had given himself.

Step by slow step he forced himself to the other side of the portal. With a final burst of strength, Sirius stumbled through the gateway.

A smile broke through his agonizing grimace. He was right where he wanted to be. Right behind the Ghoule Overlord, who was cursing up a storm after having seen his prey avoid his last attack and disappear within the swirling mist.

His energy fading quickly, Sirius latched onto the last of his Talent, forming a small dagger of blazing energy. Then he thrust forward as quickly as he could, his injuries slowing him as he aimed for the Ghoule Overlord's lower back and spine. Even the Master of the Curse wouldn't be able to survive such a blow if his aim was true.

Yet even in a rage, the Ghoule Overlord had noticed the movement behind him, the white mist that the Magus had used to escape him having hinted at what the old man had done and what he could do. So the beast, sensing the threat, did the same, leaping through a portal of black that he crafted with the Curse right before Sirius' dagger plunged into his mottled green flesh, the blazing energy instead punching out uselessly into the thin air of the summit.

Before Sirius could even spit out the curse that came to mind at having lost his best opportunity for killing the Ghoule Overlord, a shiver of fear ran down his spine. In that moment, he realized that the time of his death had come. His opponent had gotten the better of him.

"Clever, old man," hissed the Ghoule Overlord from right behind him, "but not clever enough."

With a roar of fury the beast stabbed the sharpened end of his black staff into Sirius' back, the blow so powerful that the tip ripped through the old Magus' belly. At the same time, the Curse surged out from the twisted wood and began coursing through the Master of the Magii.

"And I am not done with you yet," whispered the massive beast, his serrated teeth right at Sirius' ear. The Ghoule Overlord smiled in pleasure as his adversary's face twisted into a horrifying mask caused by his excruciating pain, the Magus unable to scream because he couldn't pull a breath of air into his lungs while he was impaled on the staff. "I will feed on you right before you die."

With a sickening squelch, the Ghoule Overlord tore his staff free, Sirius falling to his knees, then slumping down onto his back, his legs drawn up beneath him, the bright sunlight shimmering off of the cracked stone upon which he lay.

"You are no different than your brother," murmured the Ghoule Overlord. "You both died at my hand."

Sirius knew that his end was near, not having the strength to reply, even though he was desperate to do so. Even though he failed to kill the Ghoule Overlord, he didn't believe that he actually failed. He had achieved his objective, admittedly at a terrible cost, though a cost that he was more than willing to pay.

He could go to the other side in the belief that he had done all that was humanly possible to aid Bryen.

The Ghoule Overlord, his feral grin highlighting his sharpened teeth, lifted his staff above his head with both claws, then drove the cursed stave down toward the dying Magus' heart with all his might.

Instead of feeling the satisfying punch of his twisted crook sliding through the Magus' chest, the Ghoule Overlord floundered as his stave was knocked away from its target at the very last second, the beast needing to take several stumbling steps to regain his balance. The Ghoule Overlord growled in anger as he stared down at his staff, the sharpened tip hanging by a thin splinter thanks to the keen, Talent-infused steel of the Spear of the Magii.

When the Ghoule Overlord finally turned back around, needing a few more seconds to gain control over his boiling rage, the Protector stood just in front of the wounded Magus, his double-bladed spear spinning slowly, almost contemptuously, right in front of him.

"Finally," the Ghoule Overlord hissed. "I have waited too long for this. You will not evade me this time."

Before the beast could leap at his long-sought prey, Bryen seized the initiative, his spear a blur of glowing steel as he swung for the Ghoule Overlord's neck. The beast blocked the blade with his twisted black staff, then he shifted his grip and turned the staff parallel to the ground to parry the slash that was directed toward his hip. And so it went for the next several seconds, the Protector cutting, slashing, and slicing, never letting up during his assault, the Ghoule Overlord gliding across the crest, getting his staff in place just in time to parry each blow.

The Ghoule Overlord grinned in delight, believing that he was managing the Protector's attack with ease and not realizing that at that moment Bryen wasn't interested in killing the beast. At least not yet.

Rather, his intention was to drive the Ghoule Overlord farther away from Sirius so that he wouldn't have to worry about the old Magus. With every strike of his steel on the Ghoule Overlord's blackened stave, he was able to do exactly that, forcing the beast closer to the trail that led onto the summit.

Once he gained the space that he desired, Bryen reached for the Talent, the two blades on the Spear of the Magii blazing even more brilliantly as the power of the natural world filled him. His eyes crinkling with determination, Bryen sped up his attack. His blades slashed through the air so swiftly that they appeared to be nothing more than streaks of light, the glowing steel meeting the Ghoule Overlord's twisted staff of Dark Magic time after time, sparks flashing when the two weapons met.

There was no give in either fighter. Both held their ground, neither willing to step back. The combat raging with a ferocity that reminded those gladiators who could spare a glance what it was like when the Volkun fought on the white sand.

Speed. Constant motion. Decisions based more on instinct than thought. An unfathomable aggression and determination.

The shadows reaching across the summit of the sandstone pillar stretched almost to the edge of the crest before the two combatants finally stepped away from one another. Neither had scored a mark, although Bryen had succeeded at chipping several more long slivers of wood from the Ghoule Overlord's staff.

Unfortunately for the Protector, the Ghoule Overlord appeared refreshed, as if the combat of the last hour had little effect upon him. The beast seemed energized … and hungry.

Bryen, on the other hand, was beginning to feel the effects of all that had happened during the last few days. The fight on Haven. The escape through the tunnel and then across the bottom of the Trench. The climb up the spiral path that wound around the monolith. The tremendous amount of energy required to use the Seventh Stone and work with the Ten Magii to recreate the Weir. All of that and much more had exerted quite a heavy cost on him, and that cost was coming due at the worst possible time.

"This is how it should be, Protector," rasped the Ghoule Overlord. "This is how it ends. I will kill you and take the Seventh Stone. Then I will feast on your flesh and bones."

"You say that quite a lot," replied Bryen with a raised eyebrow, "almost like you need to convince yourself that you'll actually do it."

"You appear confident now," countered the Ghoule Overlord. "But I know the truth. You are weak and growing weaker. You cannot destroy me."

"Maybe," Bryen replied with a shrug, "but that doesn't mean I won't keep trying. To get what you want you're going to have to earn it."

"As you wish, Protector," acknowledged the Ghoule Overlord, having expected no less from his adversary. Foolish and wasted effort, he believed, but there was no questioning the Protector's courage. "It is your death. How you meet it is up to you."

Tired of the conversation, the Ghoule Overlord began what

he believed would be his final attack, swinging his staff for Bryen's legs, forcing him to leap over the swipe. Bryen had barely gotten his feet back beneath him when the Ghoule Overlord's next attack came. The black staff, a trail of the Curse drifting from the black diamond, slashed toward his head.

Bryen caught the strike with the haft of his weapon, but this time the Ghoule Overlord didn't back away. Instead, he continued to push forward and down, doing as he had once tried before. Attempting to press the black diamond into Bryen's flesh.

If the beast succeeded the combat would be his. The Curse would consume the Protector in seconds.

Bryen strove to hold back the beast, gritting his teeth from the effort as every muscle in his body quivered. The Ghoule Overlord was too strong. Having no other choice, fearful of the black diamond's touch, Bryen ducked to his right, sliding his left leg behind him as he rolled away, catching the back of the Ghoule Overlord's right leg. He used the beast's lurching effort to stay on his feet to avoid the Ghoule Overlord's clumsy swing with his staff that was aimed for his chest.

Although the Ghoule Overlord missed Bryen with his latest attack, he recovered quickly. Rather than attack with his staff this time, the Ghoule Overlord remained where he was, sending a shard of the Curse streaking toward Bryen.

With an incredibly fast, compact swing, Bryen knocked away the Dark Magic. That was just the beginning of this latest assault. The Ghoule Overlord laughed with pleasure as he threw dozens of fragments of the Curse at Bryen. The Protector held his ground, batting away each one with the blazing blades of the Spear of the Magii.

Through it all, Bryen was thankful that the weapon aided him in maintaining control over the Dark Magic within him, the Curse that was locked away barely stirring despite Bryen fighting its Master. Yet though that concern was tempered, another raised its ugly head.

As the combat intensified, the Ghoule Overlord apparently in no rush to finish him, Bryen could feel his strength continue to wane. Not only because of the demands of the combat, but also because of the huge amount of the Talent that he was using to defend against the Ghoule Overlord and his Curse.

Bryen could understand why he would tire in a combat such as this. But why not the Ghoule Overlord? His adversary was expending just as much effort as he was. If anything, the beast only seemed to be getting stronger.

Then Bryen began to understand why the combat was shifting in the Ghoule Overlord's favor. With the Weir back in place, the Seventh Stone was no longer pulling on the black diamond and stealing the beast's energy.

The Ghoule Overlord had access to the immense amount of corrupted power contained within the black diamond without restriction while Bryen was fighting solely with the power that he had within himself. Foolishly, he had not reached out to the Seventh Stone, the artifact resting on the pedestal in the center of the hollow.

The Ghoule Overlord knew that as well, his smile broadening when he saw the comprehension dawn within the back of the Protector's eyes.

"You are not what you were, Protector. You no longer have the Seventh Stone."

"That doesn't mean that I'll stop fighting you," Bryen replied as he swatted away another streak of the Curse, already prepared for the next one.

"No, I suspect not. You are too stubborn. You have spent too much time on the white sand." For just a moment, the Ghoule Overlord halted his attacks, instead appraising the Protector with his emotionless eyes, running his long tongue across his lips and serrated teeth. "But it does mean that you will die."

"Not if I kill you first," countered Bryen.

"Believe what you must, Protector. You cannot destroy me now. I am too powerful. I am the Curse!"

With that, the Ghoule Overlord began his attack once again, sending a dozen shards of the Dark Magic at Bryen all at one time. With an incredible skill and speed, Bryen dodged or batted away each one.

Watching the Protector's display with a mounting frustration, the Ghoule Overlord determined that a new approach was necessary. Just as the Protector knocked away the last shard of the Curse that the Ghoule Overlord had flung his way, a thin mist shot from the beast's black diamond.

The darkening haze enveloped Bryen in seconds, pressing down on him, seeking to pierce the thin layer of the Talent that he had placed around himself at the very last second. Crouching down as the mesh of black grew heavier, the weight forcing him toward the ground, millions of tiny pinpricks shooting out from the Dark Magic every second in an attempt to shatter his barrier, Bryen sent a steady stream of the Talent into his defense to keep it strong and in place.

Bryen realized quickly that his current position wasn't sustainable for much longer. The Ghoule Overlord's Dark Magic eventually would find a way through his shield, and then the Curse would smother him.

He needed to do something. Fast.

But what? He had no good idea for dealing with this latest threat.

The blanket of Dark Magic continued to push down on him, forcing him to his knees, the overwhelming power of the Curse requiring him to pull on more and more of the Talent, that constantly increasing demand draining him of his energy, of his ability to defend himself. Then, as happened frequently when Bryen faced a challenge that he wasn't certain how to address, one of Declan's many sayings ran through his mind.

"If you can't win the combat, make certain that your opponent can't win the combat either."

It had taken Bryen quite a while to figure out what Declan had meant by that. Now, he put that instruction to good use, in large part because he didn't know what else to do.

Using the Talent, remembering what Sirius had done to make his escape, Bryen crafted a portal of spinning white mist right beneath him, the gateway resting on the ground since the Ghoule Overlord's blanket of Dark Magic continued to weigh on him. Then he dove through the mist, taking the Spear of the Magii with him and allowing the portal to vanish as soon as he was free of the Curse.

Pushing himself back to his feet, Bryen closed his eyes and took in several deep breaths before he stared out into the fog that surrounded him, the haze thick and billowing, making it difficult for him to see more than a few feet to his front.

He had eluded the Ghoule Overlord's trap. Now, he hoped that he would have a few moments to think and recover, but it wasn't to be. A prickle down the back of his spine sent him rolling to the side, a bolt of Dark Magic shooting through the air right where he had been standing.

The Ghoule Overlord stepped out of the portal that he had created, following Bryen, allowing the gateway to disappear once he had entered the foggy realm.

"You can't escape me so easily, Protector. I won't allow it."

Bryen watched for just a few seconds as the Curse began to spin once again across the top of the black diamond. Afraid that the Ghoule Overlord was about to employ the same covering of Dark Magic that had forced him to this strange, misty world, Bryen rushed forward and slashed with one of his glowing blades, slicing off a chunk of wood from the Ghoule Overlord's staff when the beast raised it to defend himself, disrupting the beast's concentration. Then he stepped back into the fog and disappeared from sight.

Remembering another of Declan's lessons, Bryen decided that it was time to play a game of cat and mouse and use his current environment to his advantage. He sent a bolt of the Talent from the tip of the Spear of the Magii toward the Ghoule Overlord, then immediately moved on silent feet to a different location within the fog.

Hearing a growl of irritation, Bryen did the same thing again, using the Ghoule Overlord's curses to determine where he should aim the streaks of light that he shot with increasing regularity. Each attack elicited a shriek of anger as the Ghoule Overlord either was forced to defend himself or leap out of the way at the very last moment, the beast struggling to track Bryen's movement within the thick, billowing mist.

Bryen didn't care so much about hitting the Ghoule Overlord, though he certainly wouldn't have minded if he did. Rather, he was just trying to buy himself some time to think. He needed to find some way to continue the fight, some way to take advantage of the Ghoule Overlord's weaknesses.

Now it was Bryen's turn to growl in irritation.

He had yet to discover those weaknesses. Nothing he had tried so far had worked. Except for one tactic. A tactic that brought to mind his first combat with an Elder Ghoule on the coastal road of the Southern Marches.

He was having little success against the Ghoule Overlord himself, but he was chipping away at the beast's stave.

Yet even that could only take him so far if he only succeeded in slicing off a few dozen splinters from the twisted staff. That effort wouldn't do him much good in the end if he couldn't break the staff entirely.

"This is what you must do," laughed the Ghoule Overlord. "Hide in the fog? You are too much of a coward to face me?"

"I'm still alive," replied Bryen, who drifted silently around the Ghoule Overlord, no more than ten feet away though concealed from the beast. "I'm still a problem for you. I view that as a victory in and of itself."

"Your victory will be short-lived," grumbled the Ghoule Overlord, who sent a streak of black through the fog toward where the beast thought his adversary was hiding.

The Curse shot through the mist well away from Bryen. As soon as he had spoken, he had moved, knowing that the Ghoule Overlord would track his voice to press his attack.

"We'll see," Bryen whispered, using the Ghoule Overlord's latest assault to pinpoint the beast's location and lunge forward, lightning fast, slicing across his adversary's calf with a shining blade then withdrawing just as swiftly back into the fog.

The Ghoule Overlord's howl of pain drifted away with the haze, bringing a smile to Bryen's lips.

"So you do bleed," Bryen said in a taunting voice, still moving as quietly as possible within the fog, unwilling to reveal his location to his nemesis. "If you can bleed, you can die."

"Enough of this!" roared the Ghoule Overlord. "You can make me bleed, but you can't destroy me. You are an irritant. A fly. Nothing more. You don't have the power of the Seventh Stone anymore. You can do nothing of consequence to me without the artifact."

Slamming the shattered tip of his staff onto the stone floor, the forceful blow finally breaking off the end, a wave of the Curse burst forward, sweeping away the fog for more than a hundred feet around and finally revealing the Protector.

Bryen stood calmly no more than twenty feet away from the Ghoule Overlord. His confidence had returned. His enemy's last words had helped him solve the puzzle that had plagued him since the combat began.

The Protector finally revealed, with a look that could have melted steel, the Ghoule Overlord flung a streak of the Curse at him.

But Bryen was already gone, having crafted another portal with the Talent and stepping through the spinning white mist.

WHEN HE EMERGED from the gateway, Bryen took a deep breath to settle his nerves. It wasn't an easy task.

His heart was racing and his mind was working just as fast, reviewing various scenarios and how they could play out as he considered the incredibly difficult task set before him. What he hoped would give him what he needed to defeat the Ghoule Overlord.

He was back in the hollow standing right in front of the Seventh Stone, staring down at the dazzling artifact. He knew that he only had so much time, that his nemesis would figure out where he had gone, so he needed to make the few seconds that he had count.

The Ghoule Overlord was too strong for him now. The essentially limitless Dark Magic of the black diamond gave the beast an advantage against which Bryen had no good response. Even with the unique qualities and abilities given to him by the Spear of the Magii, he couldn't compete with the Master of the Lost Land for very long.

So if he continued the combat as it had begun, his death was certain. That was a reality that he couldn't ignore.

None of the many scenarios for combating the Ghoule Overlord that played through his mind really appealed to him. None but one that he kept coming back to, what the Ghoule Overlord had said in the fog jogging his memory.

"When there is need, use the Seventh Stone."

He didn't comprehend the value of Viktor Keldragan's comment until just now.

He had been a fool not to understand what his uncle was explaining to him. Even though the Seventh Stone was no longer physically a part of him, he was still bonded to the artifact.

The Seventh Stone had picked him. The Seventh Stone had merged with him. He and the Seventh Stone had become one. He and the Seventh Stone were one. They always would be. That could never be undone.

With Bryen's mind set on his next step, he felt more confident. Sensing the change taking place in front of him, the spinning black of a gateway appearing just on the other side of the pedestal, he lifted his eyes from the Seventh Stone.

The Ghoule Overlord cackled with an undisguised glee when he emerged from the portal, the spinning mist dissipating as soon as the beast walked out into the Sanctuary.

"Quite the hunt, but it stops here," rumbled the Ghoule Overlord. "You have tried my patience one too many times. You die now, Protector. You will not evade me again."

Bryen stared at the Ghoule Overlord, his cold grey eyes without emotion, hard, unyielding. The eyes of the Volkun. Then without a word Bryen opened himself to the Seventh Stone, reaching out to the artifact, seeking what he needed, seeking what was required if he was to have any chance of killing the Ghoule Overlord. The Seventh Stone responded with a brilliant flash of light, the fist-sized diamond rapidly dissolving into a sparkling white mist that swirled above the pedestal.

"No!" roared the Ghoule Overlord. "No! You cannot do this." The beast's expression was one of shock, never thinking that this could happen a second time. "This is not possible."

Bryen ignored the beast, unconcerned by the angry mist that began to spin atop the black diamond, a shard of Dark Magic forming, the Ghoule Overlord desperate to stop what he was doing, understanding the danger of allowing the transformation to proceed to its inevitable conclusion.

But it was already too late. The deed was done. The Seventh

Stone had responded to Bryen's need with an unsurprising alacrity.

The essence of the Seventh Stone surged into him, violently jolting him as if he had been struck by lightning. The joining sent an almost paralyzing electricity up his spine that made him stand on the tips of his toes, his back arching, his arms spread wide, the force of the union so great that he almost dropped his spear because of the immense amount of power, both the Talent and the Curse, that took their places within him once again, the energy of the Seventh Stone working its way through every pore in his body to complete the merger for a second time.

AISLINN LOOKED ALL around the summit, searching for any new threats. The Weir was intact once again. A tremendous achievement, and one for which Bryen should be proud and the rest of them were extremely thankful. But even with that victory, several large challenges remained.

As she stood above Lycia, protecting the gladiator who shifted regularly between lucidity and unconsciousness, she couldn't locate her Protector. She had glimpsed a few scenes of the combat between him and the Ghoule Overlord, but saw no more than that.

She could only spare a few seconds of her time as the Ghoules and Elders remained constant and more immediate dangers. From what she observed, Bryen seemed to be holding his own against the Master of the Lost Land at least for the moment.

Still, she was worried about him. Blade and staff had been replaced by the Talent and the Curse when last she caught sight of the duel, and now she couldn't locate Bryen or the Ghoule Overlord anywhere on the crest. The last she had seen of Bryen, he had slipped through a portal, the Ghoule Overlord disappearing in the same way immediately afterward. As far as she could tell, neither had returned.

She could do little for him even as she struggled to contain her worry. All she could do, which was worth very little in her opinion, was hope that her Protector was all right.

Aislinn could still feel him. Bryen was alive wherever he had gone. But how he was faring against the Ghoule Overlord now she had no way to tell. And as Noorsin liked to say, "She didn't like not knowing what she didn't know."

Aislinn finally succeeded in pushing her worry to the very back of her mind, needing to focus on what was going on around her. With the Weir back in place, the fight atop the monolith had shifted, presenting her and the Blood Company with some unexpected though very welcome opportunities.

Since the Ghoule Overlord's disappearance, the battle in front of the Sanctuary raged with a renewed energy. Now the Blood Company slowly but surely was advancing from between the ten pillars, extending their line, pushing back the demoralized Ghoules, no more than a few dozen of the deadly beasts still alive.

On the other side of the Sanctuary, she watched with savage pleasure as Rafia released a cathartic scream when she killed the last Elder on the crest with a streak of light that she sent curling around the beast's shield of Dark Magic, the spike slicing right through the side of his ribcage and into his heart.

Aislinn would need to talk to the Magus about how she had done that with the Talent. Curling the power around a barrier was a useful skill that she wanted to acquire, one that she wished she had learned at the very start of her training because it would have proven particularly useful during the fight to defend the Sanctuary.

With the last Elder no longer a threat, she was about to turn her attention to the few remaining Ghoules, wanting to help the Blood Company finish the creatures. She didn't get the chance.

A blast of white energy shot out from the hollow of the Sanctuary, blinding anyone who might have been looking at it and setting the stone monolith shaking for several seconds. Then, over the din of the fight, she heard a howl of rage that reverberated off the Weir and brought a savage smile to her lips.

Aislinn and her Protector might not be connected by the collar anymore. Nevertheless, she didn't need the artifact to know what was happening. She could sense that her Protector had returned, and feeling the immense power that pulsed within the depression, she could guess at what he had just done. One thing, though, she knew for certain.

Bryen was angry. Very, very angry. Yet true to his character, he was also focused and under control, his rage condensed into a cold purpose. She could sense an even stronger emotion radiating from him as well. Driving him forward.

Vengeance.

Aislinn smiled even more grimly as she launched several daggers of light toward the Ghoules trying to defend themselves against the advancing gladiators on the western side of the Sanctuary. With her latest attack, she killed one Ghoule and wounded another, allowing Asaia and Jenus to push forward and through the Ghoule line, getting behind the beasts.

It wouldn't be long now. The battle would end soon. Of that she had no doubt.

The Master of the Lost Land was about to get what he deserved.

~

"It's more than possible," replied Bryen in the harsh, guttural language of the Ghoules. "It is inevitable. And there is nothing that you can do to stop it."

Bryen glowered at his adversary as he stood across from the Ghoule Overlord, the three gold wires on the pedestal that had held the Seventh Stone empty.

The change within him upon merging again with the Seventh Stone filled what Bryen could only describe as a void. When the artifact left him while he and the Ten Magii were rebuilding the Weir, it had felt as if he had lost a part of himself. Now that missing part had returned.

Bryen understood the Seventh Stone now, just as the Seventh Stone understood him.

The Ghoule Overlord roared in fury. The Master of the Lost Land's black orbs blazed with an almost uncontrollable ire, his rage knowing no bounds as his claws dug into his twisted black staff.

He had failed to destroy the Weir. He had failed to release the full might of his Legions on Caledonia. He had worked for this for more than a thousand years, but he had failed. Time and time again.

Thanks in large part to the Protector who stood before him now, who did not fear to challenge him. Who had no respect for the Curse.

With a flick of his wrist, the Ghoule Overlord released the power surging through him, the shard of darkness that had formed above the black diamond shooting straight toward the Protector's heart.

Bryen had no time to defend himself, the Curse streaking toward him across the pedestal, the Ghoule Overlord so close that he could smell the beast's rancid breath every time he roared. So rather than form a shield with the Talent that would never take shape in time, he raised his palm in front of his chest, hoping that his assumption was correct.

Time seemed to slow down as he watched the Dark Magic speed toward him. Yet with the new understanding that he had gained thanks to the Seventh Stone, Bryen was calm, composed. He was more curious than worried. Right before the Curse slammed into his sternum, the shard of darkness froze in place, suspended in the air, no more than a hair away from touching Bryen's hand.

The Ghoule Overlord stared in amazement. He had never suspected that something like this could happen. That the Protector could exercise such control over the power that belonged to him.

He was the Master of the Curse. Him! No one else!

The surge of confidence that he had felt upon releasing the bolt of corrupted energy, what he thought would be the final strike that would ensure his victory, and the certainty that he would kill the Protector, faded away, leaving him confused and unsure. All that he believed, all that he knew with respect to the Talent and the Curse, had changed drastically in just seconds.

The Ghoule Overlord leaned back from the pedestal, his massive head rising, his eyes widening, as an inescapable truth wormed its way into his brain.

The Protector was something more now. Something that shouldn't be, couldn't be, but was.

The Protector was something exceedingly dangerous.

Worse, the Ghoule Overlord wasn't certain that he had the power to defeat him. That realization coincided with the beast's mouth opening in shock, the implications of what he had just determined almost too much for the Master of the Ghoules to contemplate.

He had never known weakness. He had never known fear.

Until now.

While the Ghoule Overlord's expression slowly shifted from one of supreme confidence to one of concern mixed with the slight tinge of alarm, Bryen used that brief respite to recall his conversation with Rafia when they were both on Haven and she was helping him learn about what it would mean to have the Dark Magic within him. His immediate, and admittedly natural, reaction was to be afraid of what it meant to have the Curse be a part of him, knowing what would happen if he made even the slightest misstep in how he managed the Dark Magic.

Recognizing Bryen's consternation, Rafia had suggested that he adopt a different perspective than the one that was most obvious. Rather than viewing his situation as a death sentence, she had implied that it could also be an opportunity, so long as he learned not only how to shield himself from the Dark Magic, but also how to apply it effectively in conjunction with the Talent.

He had taken her advice, using the Seventh Stone and the Curse wrapped in the Talent on the Haven pier to stop the Elders' attack. He had just done it while fighting the Golem. He would do it again now.

The Ghoule Overlord believed that he couldn't be destroyed. That he was the source of the Curse. However, the beast wasn't entirely correct.

He was the Curse, yes. But only because the Curse had made him. And what was made could also be unmade.

With that realization, Bryen sharpened his gaze, his eyes locking onto those of the Ghoule Overlord. He wanted the beast to understand what was about to happen to him. He wanted this monster responsible for the deaths of so many of his friends to understand that the rules of the game had changed, and not in his favor.

Bryen's smile turned almost feral as the shard crafted of the Curse that hung in the air between them slowly dissolved, the thin stream of Dark Magic flowing meekly into Bryen through his open palm.

"No, you can't do that!" protested the Ghoule Overlord, realizing the implication of what the Protector had just done. What it meant for him. "You can't. I won't allow it!"

Bryen ignored the Ghoule Overlord. With a flicker of his fingers the Seventh Stone answered his call, a hollow cord crafted of the Talent shooting out and latching onto the Ghoule Overlord before the beast even knew what was going on. The Ghoule Overlord's eyes widened in terror, his shrieks filling the hollow and drifting out across the summit, first reflecting his rage, then rapidly shifting to reveal his rising, uncontrollable fear.

The Master of the Ghoules could do nothing but watch in growing horror as the Curse began to seep slowly out of him through the cord and into the Protector. The Master of the Lost Land tried to fight it, to hold his power within him, to not let it be stolen, but all to no avail. The pace increased swiftly, the Dark Magic trickling then gushing into Bryen, rushing into the Seventh Stone, the Ghoule Overlord powerless to stop it.

The black diamond pulsed furiously, mirroring the Ghoule Overlord's fury and fear. However, just like its creation, the Curse was impotent against the power of the Seventh Stone. As the transfer of Dark Magic progressed, the flashing darkness of the black diamond slowed gradually and then came to a stop entirely, the usual threads of Dark Magic that spun off the jewel nowhere to be seen.

With the Curse being ripped loose from the Ghoule Overlord, the beast's vitality suffered as well. The monster was frantic to stop what was happening to him, he tried to resist, but he could not stand against the energy being brought to bear against him. And then the pain struck him, the sensation that every cell in his body was being torn apart overwhelming him, the feeling that the Seventh Stone was shredding every fiber of his being becoming all consuming, driving him mad.

Just a few heartbeats later, it was done, the transfer ending just as quickly as it had begun. The Seventh Stone had drained every last speck of the Curse from the Ghoule Overlord.

The transformation of the Master of the Lost Land was stunning. In the place of the vigorous, terrifying beast who had stood eight feet tall, his shoulders broad, his back straight, his black eyes promising death and destruction, stood a shell of his former self.

His back was bent, his sickly green skin was covered by brownish spots that seeped a putrid reddish liquid, his body nothing more than withered flesh, his muscles barely hanging onto his bones. The creature that now stood in front of Bryen could barely hold onto his twisted black staff, which now rose more than two feet above the shriveled figure.

Bryen wasn't surprised by the metamorphosis, because he realized now that was all that the Ghoule Overlord was and had ever been. A shell for the Curse. A host. Nothing more.

Yet despite what had happened, despite the loss of his Dark Magic, a tiny bit of the fire and defiance that was so much a part of the Ghoule Overlord's character remained. The beast swung his staff for Bryen's head with what little strength he could muster.

Bryen blocked the blow easily with the Spear of the Magii, which when it struck splintered the staff into a dozen pieces of smoldering wood, the black diamond wriggling loose from its enclosure and falling from its perch, shattering on the pedestal upon which the Seventh Stone used to rest.

Although somewhat taken aback by what had just happened to the Ghoule Overlord's jewel, Bryen didn't hesitate. He allowed Declan's training to guide his hand.

Kill or be killed.

That had been the rule on the white sand. That was the rule here in the Sanctuary.

With a lunge faster than a scorpion's striking tail, Bryen drove one of the blazing blades of the Spear of the Magii through the Ghoule Overlord's crumpled and sagging chest. He held the beast there for several seconds, allowing his nemesis to reach the conclusion on his own that the end had come. The combat was over. Bryen didn't permit the beast to slide off the blade until after he had watched the flickering black of his eyes wink out for good.

A sense of relief filled Bryen as he stared down at what remained of the Ghoule Overlord, the terror of Caledonia slumped on the ground, dead, no longer a threat to the Kingdom.

It was over. Finally. He had eliminated the greatest enemy Caledonia had ever encountered.

Bryen thought that he should feel more satisfaction with the result that he had just achieved. After all, no one had ever defeated the Ghoule Overlord, and he was not supposed to survive this encounter to begin with. But he had.

Maybe it was because of the voice in the back of his brain that had served him so well on the white sand. The voice that had issued warnings at just the right time to keep him alive when he had no right to remain so was now offering another warning.

A premonition, perhaps. He had won this combat. But the fight was not yet done. More was still required.

The Ghoule Overlord was the Curse and the Curse was the Ghoule Overlord. He had destroyed the Ghoule Overlord.

But had he destroyed the Curse?

He thought about that for a few seconds as he stared at the remains of the black diamond, remembering what else he had learned from Viktor Keldragan regarding the relationship between the Ghoule Overlord and the power the monster wielded. Those thoughts were confirmed when he watched the pieces of the black diamond that littered the top of the pedestal transform into a black mist that lifted several feet into the air, spun a few times around the shimmering stone, then shot right through the Weir and back into the Lost Land.

For a moment, all Bryen could do was stare as the Curse fled. Then he shook his head in resignation. He should have assumed as much. Nothing was ever straightforward when it came to the Talent or the Curse. Nothing was ever easy.

The voice in the back of his head had been right.

Thanks to Viktor, he knew where the Curse that had once formed the black diamond was going. He knew what it would try to do next.

The physical manifestation of the Ghoule Overlord was dead. Not the spirit. The spirit of the Ghoule Overlord still lived. The Curse still lived.

He and the Blood Company had won the battle, but for them to win the war, Bryen needed to destroy the Curse. Otherwise, the Ghoule Overlord would return once the Dark Magic of the Lost Land had taken a new shell.

"You old fool," muttered Rafia. "You shouldn't have done this. You had no cause to challenge the Ghoule Overlord on your own."

Kneeling next to Sirius, tears streamed down the Magus' face, dropping every so often onto his cheeks. He could barely feel them. He could barely feel anything at all, even the horrendous pain wracking his broken body beginning to subside into nothing more than a dull ache as his organs began to shut down. He was barely breathing now, his blood pumping out onto the shattered stone of the summit from both his chest and his back, the Curse continuing to work its way through him, the Dark Magic unstoppable.

"I had to do it," he replied in a whisper. "It was the only way.

It was the only way to help Bryen. To give him the time that he needed."

"You must do what you must do," murmured Declan, who stood just above Rafia, Aislinn right next to him.

"Rightly so, Master of the Gladiators," agreed Sirius as a rough cough sent him into a series of painful spasms that interrupted his train of thought. Once the pain had subsided, he finished what he was going to say. "We all must do what we must."

The wounded Magus felt more than saw a tall shadow drape itself over him. He smiled, though it hurt him to do so.

Bryen had survived. He had won. If Sirius' life was the price of victory, then he was more than willing to pay it.

"I will miss you, Rafia," Sirius said.

"Don't say that, Sirius," protested Rafia, the flow of her tears increasing. "This isn't the end."

"It needs to be said," Sirius replied, reaching up and clasping her hand with what little strength he had left. "I will miss you."

"I will miss you too," Rafia replied, nodding, hating that it had come to this.

"I know you will," Sirius said with a barely perceptible grin. "Just don't miss me too much."

"Even now," said Rafia, shaking her head in wonder, her lips quirking into a small smile even as her tears continued to fall. "Even now your arrogance cannot be denied."

"Thinking about it now, you were right. There needs to be more to a relationship than just comfort. Passion, love, trust ... it all needs to be there. You were right."

"Save your breath, Sirius," pleaded Rafia, not knowing why Sirius' mind had turned to the argument that they had been having for more than a decade.

"Find that," continued Sirius, ignoring her, his dull eyes

sharpening for just a moment. "Find that, Rafia. We didn't have that, but you still can. You deserve it."

"Sirius, please stop talking," said Rafia, her hand still holding his. "Save your strength. Once we heal you, we can discuss all that. I look forward to it."

"You can't heal me," said Sirius softly. "My wounds are too severe. The Dark Magic running through me is too strong. It's already taken hold. My fate is sealed."

"But Bryen ..."

"Even the Protector can't help me now," said Sirius calmly. "Besides, I did what I set out to do. There is nothing left for me now. I can pass to the other side in peace."

"Sirius ..." Rafia began, her tears becoming a steady stream, blinding her.

She didn't know what to do. The tendrils of black were peeking out above the collar of his robes, the threads of the Curse now streaking across his hands. She didn't want to admit it, but he was right. She knew that. And she hated that Sirius was right.

Even Bryen with his skill in healing and his connection to the Seventh Stone could do nothing for Sirius now. It was asking too much. Just attempting to heal him would simply hasten his death, the old Magus too weak.

"Let me go, Rafia," said Sirius quietly. "Please let me go. It is my time now. All I ask is that you remember our better days."

Unable to say anything else, Rafia nodded in reluctant acquiescence. Then she felt the presence standing behind her. She gripped Sirius' hand tightly one more time before she leaned down and kissed him softly on the cheek. Then she allowed Declan to help her to her feet, Aislinn holding her other hand in support. They led her to the other side of the Sanctuary where several gladiators of the Blood Company would benefit from her skill as a healer.

"I'm glad you're here, lad," said Sirius.

Bryen knelt down next to Sirius. After scanning the old Magus while he was saying good-bye to Rafia, he realized with just a touch of anger that Sirius was correct. Even with his abilities to heal, magnified by the power of the Seventh Stone, nothing that he tried could save Sirius.

Sirius probably had known it as soon as the Ghoule Overlord had struck him with the Curse, the shock and pain of that realization still fixed in the old Magus' eyes.

"I'm sorry, Sirius," Bryen began. "I know you like to be right, and unfortunately in this instance you are. There is nothing I can do."

"It is done?" asked Sirius, disregarding Bryen's comment.

"Yes," replied Bryen, though he couldn't bring himself to clarify his response with the words "for now." He held back. He didn't want to upset Sirius. Not in his last moments.

"Good." Sirius smiled, though doing even that now sent a new wave of pain screaming through his rapidly failing body. "Good."

Not knowing what else to say, Bryen reached down for Sirius' hand, the old Magus demonstrating his appreciation for all that Bryen did with a weak squeeze. For almost a minute, they stayed there in silence, the seconds between Sirius' ragged breaths lengthening.

"You were really quite impressive," offered Bryen, finding the dragging silence oppressive.

"You mean my attempts at killing the Ghoule Overlord?" asked Sirius in a rapidly weakening voice that required Bryen to bend closer so that he could hear him.

"No," Bryen replied with a slight chuckle. "I was quite impressed that you learned something new. I never thought that I'd see an old dog learn a new trick. You proved me wrong with that portal of yours."

Sirius didn't have the energy to be insulted even if he wanted to be. Still, he couldn't stop the small laugh that erupted from him, even as it sent more waves of pain through his body, a thin stream of tainted black fluid beginning to flow from his lips.

"Even now you seek to irritate me," said Sirius in mock annoyance.

"Actually I was offering you a compliment. You almost beat the Ghoule Overlord."

"You're being too kind," muttered Sirius. "I never had a chance against him."

"I beg to differ," replied Bryen.

"Always being difficult," muttered Sirius softly, though clearly the Magus appreciated the comment.

That last remark brought a smile to Bryen's lips. Even with all that had happened, things hadn't changed between them.

"I wanted to thank you for what you did," said Bryen. "I couldn't have done this without you. Any of it."

Sirius ignored Bryen, never comfortable when someone offered him thanks or a compliment. Instead, the Magus turned his head to the side, allowing his eyes to take in what was around him. From what he could see, the summit was littered with the bodies of dead Elders and Ghoules and unfortunately too many gladiators.

The battle was done. Finally.

"You've done well, lad. Better than anyone had a right to expect."

"I couldn't have done it without you," corrected Bryen.

"I just helped when I could. Don't give me more credit than I deserve."

"Thank you nevertheless." Bryen squeezed Sirius' hand a bit harder, catching how Sirius' eyes had begun to glaze over, realizing that the end was approaching and hoping for just a few more seconds with him. "I'm sorry, grandfather. You've given too much. I wish this could have all concluded differently."

"I know, lad," replied Sirius, his words barely audible, his eyes no longer seeing anything but a cool, welcoming darkness. "I know. I gave what I could willingly. It was the least that I could do." Sirius brought his other hand up, covering Bryen's hand with his. "So you've spoken with Viktor?"

"Yes," Bryen admitted. "He and the other Magii helped me build the Weir."

"He told you?"

"Not directly, but he said enough."

"I wasn't going to keep it from you forever," murmured Sirius. "It's just that …" The old Magus needed to take a moment to gather his thoughts, knowing that he was expelling his last few breaths. "Every time I thought of Alana and Loren and what happened, how I failed to help them, to help you, all that pain and sorrow … I just wasn't ready to deal with it. I'm sorry."

"I know," Bryen replied, trying to relay through his tone and his expression that he understood what Sirius had done and why.

"I'm sorry that I failed to protect your parents. But I was able to protect you. At least for a little while. I was able to protect you." Sirius' words grew softer, the pain leaving the Magus' body as his head tilted back onto the stone, Bryen realizing that the Curse had reached his heart. "I protected the Protector."

Then Sirius' hands slipped from Bryen's as the Magus' last breath left him.

For several minutes, Bryen stared down at Sirius Keldragan, not knowing what he should feel, his emotions conflicted. All he could do was whisper a silent, final thank you before he placed Sirius' arms across his chest and then pushed himself up off the stone.

"You must do what you must do."

Declan's words played through his mind, his thoughts automatically shifting toward what came next. He had done what needed to be done with the Weir. He had done what needed to be done with respect to the Ghoule Overlord. But he was not yet done.

He was certain that Sirius would agree with him on that, and he was not about to let his grandfather's death be for nothing.

The Blood Company had survived the journey from Tintagel, though not without great loss of life. Half the number of gladiators who started out on this mission had gone to the other side.

He didn't know how many Ghoule Legions had made it into Caledonia before the new Weir took shape, but he would find out shortly. And he was certain that Duchess Stelekel and the Caledonian Army would be hard-pressed in the Winter Pass if they weren't already.

No, their work was not yet done.

They couldn't stay here. He needed to get to the Winter Pass.

Just then a powerful shriek shattered the silence that had fallen across the Sanctuary. The noise brought a sad but hopeful smile to his face.

So many of his friends and comrades had died. More likely would. Yet there was nothing he could do about that.

This battle had been won, but the war had just begun.

A war that he meant to win. That he had to win.

26

HELP FROM ABOVE

"The odds were against us from the beginning," said Noorsin, "and they're not improving."

"That's one way to put it," replied Irelda, standing next to the General of the Caledonian Army, her expression calm, determined. "That doesn't matter now. What matters is what we do. The odds won't stop us from putting up a good fight."

"No, they won't. The more important question is how long we can stay in the fight."

"As long as necessary," replied Irelda with as confident a voice as she could muster, because even she was finding it difficult to have faith in her own words. She understood how difficult what they were trying to do would be. She just never guessed that their situation would become so dire so quickly.

Noorsin and Irelda stood on one of the snowdrifts on the eastern side of the Winter Pass. The ninety foot pile of ice and snow, which had taken several minutes to climb, gave them a very good and exceedingly frightening view of what was sprinting toward the Caledonians.

Noorsin had positioned the dozen Magii who were the first of the Order to make it this far north into the Shattered Peaks along the width of the Winter Pass, each one responsible for securing a particular section of the Caledonian line. She understood that the number of Magii with her was far below what would be required if they were to mount an effective defense against the steadily increasing number of Elders who were arriving on the battlefield.

More Magii were coming. She knew that for a fact. She also knew that they wouldn't even enter the Winter Pass at its southern tip for several more days, and from there it was another few days more north up the gap to where she and the bulk of the Caledonian Army now battled against the Ghoules.

The morbid thought that popped into her mind was whether the arrival of the other Magii would even matter. With the pressure currently being applied by the Ghoule Legions -- that pressure likely to intensify as more Ghoules came down from the north -- would the Caledonian Army still exist by the time the Magii reinforcements joined the fight?

She feared that she already knew the answer, and she chose to keep that to herself. It would only get in the way of what they needed to do.

Noorsin cursed herself for a coward, shutting away the useless concerns that plagued her. She needed to focus on the here and now, not on what could be. So she turned her mind back to the dilemma facing them, looking for some way, any way, to improve her soldiers' chances of surviving the coming attack.

Yet nothing came to mind.

Having shifted her forces a league farther north after the first skirmish with the Ghoules, wanting to make use of this even narrower slice of the Winter Pass, she believed that they might stand a chance. The battlefield she had selected functioned as a funnel of sorts, limiting the number of Ghoules who could attack at one time.

She had ranged the Caledonian Army across the breadth of

the canyon, which, including the massive snowdrifts that endured beneath the shade provided by the mountains on each side, was only a few thousand yards across.

The strategy really was quite simple. Hold. At all costs.

Kevan and the Blademaster both had agreed that they should be able to repel the Ghoules at this location in the Pass. At least for a time.

Of course, neither was willing to commit to how long that time might extend, and she could understand their hesitation.

Worse, they had based their assumption on the belief that they would be facing one Ghoule Legion at a time.

That assumption had been proven wrong, and they were already beginning to pay the price for that miscalculation.

The Ghoules were moving down the Winter Pass faster than any of them had assumed that they would, the still melting snow not enough of an obstacle to slow down the beasts for very long. Although the Caledonians had not budged an inch when the first Ghoule Legion slammed into their shield wall, Noorsin worried about what was going to happen when the second Ghoule Legion joined the first.

Those thousand more beasts were less than a mile away, and they were coming fast. Once they joined the fight, the Ghoules would be able to ratchet up the pressure to a possibly unbearable level.

Nevertheless, she continued to have faith that they could hold. She had confidence in Irelda and the other Magii who had joined them. She trusted Kevan and the Blademaster, Kevan leading the eastern wing of the army and Klines the western wing. Those two had already demonstrated their skill, knowledge, and, perhaps even more important, their adaptability. Several of the adjustments the two soldiers had made as soon as the battle had begun were exacting a heavier toll than they could have hoped for from the Ghoules.

That was all to the good. In consequence, she hoped that

even when the second Ghoule Legion arrived, her Caledonians would hold strong, Kevan and the Blademaster adjusting as needed, the narrow breadth of the canyon aiding their efforts.

But would they be able to do so when the third Ghoule Legion, this one no more than an hour behind the second, arrived on the battlefield? She didn't know. And what of the fourth that was no more than an hour behind the third?

Noorsin cursed herself for a coward a second time in just the last few minutes. There was nothing that she could do about those concerns. Better to stop thinking. Better just to do.

She might be the General of the Caledonian Army, but as soon as the fight began, their success and survival against the Ghoules rested less with her and more with the individual actions and decisions of not only Kevan and the Blademaster, but also the Sergeants and the Corporals and every single soldier in the fight.

It was a somewhat frightening conclusion, that one or two soldiers, whether because of their bravery or their cowardice or a good decision or a bad decision or a touch of good luck or bad could sway one way or the other the outcome of the Caledonians' desperate attempt to keep their homeland free of the Ghoules. Even so, it was the truth, and she preferred to deal in the truth rather than fantasy, no matter how harsh that truth might be. All she could do now was present herself as a confident and strong leader and be prepared to change strategy if any new threats or unexpected opportunities emerged. With that thought in mind, Noorsin used the Talent to search to the north to confirm the location of the third Legion. Her initial estimate was correct. An hour at most. Even so, Noorsin felt a brief surge of unexpected confidence. Assuming that the Magii could keep the Elder Ghoules at bay, so long as they remained in this section of the Winter Pass, they should be able to hold the Ghoules in place. Only so many of the beasts could come at them here at one time.

Their odds of doing that would steadily decrease if the Ghoules succeeded in pushing them back a few hundred yards, because not too far to their rear the Winter Pass broadened to a breadth of almost a quarter mile, which was much too long a front for them to have any hope of standing against three Ghoule Legions.

For now, though, all was well. The Caledonian Army was fully committed, and a quick inspection showed no immediate areas of concern in their defenses.

Yes, the second Ghoule Legion was pushing toward the front, the beasts hungry to join the fight, and that could make things more difficult for her soldiers. But at the moment, the thousand-more Ghoules desperate to get into the battle were making circumstances more difficult for their already engaged brethren than for the Caledonians.

Noorsin smirked in delight if only for a second. The two Ghoule Legions were getting in each other's way, too many Ghoules trying to fight in too small a space. That development confirmed for her some of her earlier decisions, the terrain that they had selected for this battle already proving its worth.

It was also working to the Magii's advantage. With little room to maneuver, the Elder Ghoules were finding it difficult to exploit their larger numbers even against so few practitioners of the Talent. So, at the moment, the dozen Magii were more than a match for the servants of the Ghoule Overlord.

"Can we hold against three Legions?" asked Irelda, who, like Noorsin, had just used the Talent to confirm what was coming toward them from farther down the gorge.

"For a time, yes. So long as we remain here. If the Ghoules push us farther south, we'll have no choice but to retreat for several leagues before we'll be able to mount a successful defense again."

Irelda nodded, not feeling the need to reply. Always looking to see as much of the bigger picture as possible, the Magus expanded her search with the Talent, this time checking the flanks of the Caledonian Army. She hissed in surprise at what she discovered. Their circumstances, difficult to begin with but manageable for now, had just become more harrowing. Dangerously so, in fact.

"Noorsin, look to the west among the mountains flanking us," said Irelda, her tone more an order than a request, her time as a teacher coming to the forefront in a situation such as this when time was short.

Noorsin did as Irelda suggested. Her eyes widened in shock as she turned to her left, peering at the sheer sides of the mountains, hoping to see with her own eyes what had caught her attention but still was too far away to get a good look without the aid of the Talent.

They had been wrong. They had believed that there was no way that the Ghoules could do anything in this section of the Winter Pass other than a frontal assault. Clearly, they should have spent more time scouting this terrain. All she could do now was hope that they could address this new danger swiftly, because if they didn't the entire army would be at risk.

Realizing that she'd never be able to get a messenger to the Blademaster in time, she used the Talent instead, reaching out with a stream of magic to connect to the Captain of the Royal Guard, who had just reformed the lines to her left after leading a cavalry charge that had surprised the Ghoules and pushed the beasts back several hundred yards, giving the soldiers on the western flank a brief respite until the milling beasts sorted themselves out and attacked again.

"Blademaster!"

"You can talk in my mind? That's quite impressive, General Stelekel."

"Later, Blademaster. Look to the cliffs to your west. Ghoules!"

"Silence!" hissed Kerik. The Elder Ghoule stared at the Ghoules lined up behind him, several of them barking and hissing at one another, noises that might drift down to the humans beneath them. "Do not give us away. If you do, I'll kill you myself!"

The beasts quieted quickly. Satisfied, Kerik jerked his head in the direction they had been going, and once again they began to scramble along the hidden trail that curled around the mountainside.

Cursing silently, Kerik allowed several packs to pass him before he continued on his way. This wasn't a trail. It was no more than a series of landslides that had left a tiny ledge that even a mountain goat likely would avoid. The Ghoules had managed so far only because their clawed hands and feet made them quite adept at climbing, which was what they were doing now. They weren't walking a path. They were scaling a cliff face.

Kerik and the several hundred Ghoules with him had begun their climb two hours before, needing to go slowly and carefully because of the danger involved.

He had opposed the decision to brave the sheer side of the mountain. He had kept that thought to himself, however.

Nibli had ordered the attack, and Nibli was the Ghoule Overlord's voice in the human lands. When Nibli spoke, he spoke for the Ghoule Overlord. So there was no point in offering any dissent if he wanted to stay alive. Better just to obey and hope for the best.

So far, he had lost a dozen Ghoules, the beasts falling to their deaths, whether because of their own stupidity, such as moving too fast or missing a handhold, the steepness and the difficulty of the barely existent trail, the loose rock sliding out from beneath them without warning, or some combination, he really didn't care.

He had no patience for excuses. The only thing that mattered to him was that the Ghoules who died did so without making a sound. He didn't want to alert the humans to their position. If that happened, whatever advantage they hoped to gain would be lost.

Just a few places behind him, Kerik heard a desperate scrabble in the loose rock, then a curse, followed by a surprised grunt, and then silence. He waited for several seconds, counting to seven just so that he could judge the distance. Then, just as he had guessed, there was a quiet thump. No scream. No shriek or moan.

Another Ghoule had just fallen to his death. Even so, he was pleased. Not by the loss of another fighter, instead by the fact that the Ghoule had obeyed his command. If you were going to die, you were expected to die quietly so as not to arouse the suspicions of the humans that he could see just off to his left and beneath him, the fools having no idea that he and his Ghoules had almost completed their risky maneuver.

It wasn't long before Kerik had to push himself to the front of the trail. His Ghoules had halted, having come to the end of the path, the narrow cut along the scarp simply coming to a stop one hundred feet above the ground.

His Ghoules were agile and powerful warriors, their physical attributes incomparable to their prey, but even they would balk at such a jump, if not for the large snowbank that halved the distance that they would need to drop to reach the canyon floor. With a nod, the Ghoules began moving again, leaping from the trail into the snow far below, then digging their way out and sliding down onto the rocky ground of the Winter Pass.

Kerik followed once a good number of his Ghoules had leapt off the trail. As he pushed himself free, having come to a stop when the snow reached to his chest, he smiled.

They were behind the humans' lines and their prey had no idea. It was time for the slaughter to begin.

∼

WITH HIS SOLDIERS so close to the western wall of the Winter Pass, Klines had no choice but to adjust his strategy to this new and unexpected threat. In the tight space, his cavalry would be more hindrance than help, so the three Royal Guard companies had dismounted and formed into testudos, the formation that the gladiators had used with such great success during their fight in the tunnel against Marden Beleron. In three large squares, shield bearers with their scuta locked together formed the outside edge, spears were right behind them to lunge over their shoulders, and swords were in the center to close any potential breaches in the formation.

The fighting was intense, the Ghoules charging toward the Royal Guard with an abandon Klines put down to the beasts' almost insatiable hunger. So far, even with the beasts pressing them hard, his decision to leave their mounts behind appeared to be the right one.

The Ghoules had driven deeply into the flank of the Caledonian line, pushing toward the center. He and the soldiers with him had succeeded not only in stemming the advance, but also forcing the beasts back toward the scarp and the snowbank from which they emerged.

As Klines and his soldiers advanced toward the west, they stepped over the remains of the Ghoules' initial attack, the beasts leaping down from the hidden trail just above and killing several hundred soldiers before he and his companies were able to bring their might to bear. The horrific toll of that surprise attack, mixed with an unquenchable hate for the Ghoules -- the beasts already having eaten the remains of several of their fallen comrades, many likely when they were still alive -- filled the Caledonians with an added and needed burst of determination.

Whether that would be enough, Klines didn't know. The momentum that the Royal Guard had gained upon first engaging with the beasts had dissipated. Although he and his companies had halted the Ghoules' progress, the beasts were holding their ground now, maintaining a small and potentially devastating foothold that dug into the Caledonians' western flank, and for the last several minutes, that hadn't changed.

Klines knew that he and his soldiers needed to keep moving forward. If they didn't, the Ghoules who were still leaping down from the trail that looked to be no more than a few inches wide at best would eventually turn the tide against them. That realization coincided with the formation of a cold knot of fear in his belly.

He understood that he couldn't let that happen, but it wasn't going to be an easy task. In fact, with no reinforcements available, it might even be impossible.

Standing in the center of one of the three testudos, the Blademaster set his concerns to the side as he glanced quickly to his right and then his left. His formations appeared to be in good shape. No gaps or breaches in the ranks. No pressure from the Ghoules that was worrying his soldiers any more than was expected. He was about to order his troops to advance once again when his words caught in his throat.

Rising above his testudo just a few hundred feet away was a massive snowdrift that kept getting bigger every few minutes. That was a good sign. It meant that he and his soldiers were getting closer to the canyon wall. What was worrisome was the Elder Ghoule who stood knee deep in the snow, shrieking orders in the guttural, indecipherable language of the invaders.

For just a second, their eyes met. While Klines' widened, the Elder Ghoule's narrowed. Then with a flick of his wrist a shard of Dark Magic shot from the top of the beast's staff, straight for Klines.

The Blademaster raised his sword, realizing immediately that it was a foolish gesture yet not knowing what else to do other than stand there like a fool. There was nothing that his steel could do to defend against the Curse.

He was going to die. He was certain of it. His brief hesitation was going to cost him his life, because it was too late for him to move out of the way, the Dark Magic shooting right toward him.

Klines tumbled to the ground, struck in the chest, though not by the Curse, the Dark Magic smashing into the muck where he had been standing. The Blademaster found himself in a tangle of arms and legs, his Sergeant pushing himself up from the mud and then hauling Klines to his feet.

"That was a foolish thing to do, Benin," castigated Klines, his voice sharp.

"It was, Blademaster," the Sergeant agreed amiably.

Then Klines smiled in gratitude. "My thanks, Benin. Your foolishness saved my life. I owe you a debt."

"Consider it a debt already paid, Blademaster. I owe you more than one life."

Klines nodded and smiled again, but it quickly turned to a look of horror. "No!" yelled the Blademaster, who lunged for Benin even though he knew in his heart that he was already too late.

While Benin was helping him to his feet, the Elder Ghoule sent another streak of the Curse toward them, this one flying straight and true for his Sergeant's back.

Klines slammed into Benin, knocking him to the ground now and fearing that he had just landed on top of the smoking corpse of his Sergeant.

"I didn't know you cared so much about me, Blademaster," said Benin with a sly smile, the Sergeant nodding to what had formed behind them.

Klines grinned as he rolled off Benin and then helped his Sergeant to his feet. The shard of Dark Magic was nowhere to be seen, destroyed when it slammed into the large shield of white energy that had appeared unexpectedly in front of the two soldiers of the Royal Guard.

"I just couldn't bear the thought of not seeing what you would come up with next for your beard," replied Klines.

"A good thought," said Benin. "I'll have to think on the next design. Not until after this fight, of course."

With that, Benin turned back to the battle, urging the shield bearers to push forward with a mix of curses and encouragement.

Klines looked back over his shoulder, nodding his thanks to the Magus who sat on a horse behind the testudo. If he wasn't mistaken, the man's name was Cinjin. His hair was almost as intricately braided down his back as Benin's beard was, and though he appeared to have an amused expression on his face, his eyes never smiled.

Cinjin nodded in return, then released his hold on the shield that he had crafted just in time to save the Blademaster's life. The Magus stared at the Elder Ghoule, the beast standing atop the snowbank, having been thwarted twice now, likely cursing up a storm as strands of the Curse began to flow once again around the top of his staff.

Cinjin hated Ghoules. He hated Elder Ghoules even more, because it was an Elder Ghoule who had murdered his family.

That thought filling him with an irrepressible urge to kill the beast, the Magus sent a stream of blazing spears toward the Elder Ghoule who was leading this attack. The beast blocked the first few lances, but there were too many in the end, three of the spears slamming into his body, the first into his clawed foot.

Cinjin had learned through experience that when fighting Elder Ghoules, they often forgot to extend their shields of Dark Magic below their shins. This one had made that mistake, and it had cost the beast, losing one leg and his control over the Curse at the same time. The final two spears pierced the beast's chest and gut, leaving behind nothing but a charred husk of burnt flesh on top of the snowdrift.

Nodding with satisfaction, Cinjin wanted to turn his attention to the Ghoules, thereby aiding the soldiers who were trying to drive the beasts against the huge pile of snow. It was proving to be a difficult task as more of the Ghoules kept jumping down from the hidden trail.

But he couldn't. Another Elder had just leapt down from the narrow path and taken the place of the beast Cinjin had just dispatched. The Magus had no choice but to focus his full attention on his latest challenger.

Klines watched it all with a jaundiced eye. Even with Cinjin keeping the Elder occupied, he could see what was happening. More Ghoules were joining the fight than his soldiers were killing. It wouldn't be long now before he'd have to make another decision. Either continue to push for the canyon wall and hope to crush the beasts against the rock or retreat.

As more and more of the Ghoules joined the fight, he feared that he already knew the answer. And it didn't bode well for his chances of holding the Caledonian Army's left flank.

"Come on, you bastards! We're soldiers of the Royal Guard! If these beasts are going to kill us, then they're going to have to fight a lot harder than this!"

A roar erupted from the three companies of soldiers who stood strong against the Ghoules, energized by Benin's exhortation. The Ghoules had pushed them hard, more of the beasts leaping down from the trail and into the snowbank in what at times resembled a waterfall of mottled green. Once they dug themselves out, the beasts rushed to join the fight.

They were aided in their efforts to pierce the shield wall by the next Elder Ghoule who appeared in their midst, the servant of the Ghoule Overlord drawing Cinjin's attention and preventing the Magus from helping to keep the beasts from swarming them. With that Elder now otherwise engaged, the soldiers stopped retreating and stood their ground instead with a stubborn desperation that impressed the Blademaster.

How long that would remain the case, Jurgen Klines couldn't say. Even with the Magus, so long as an increasing number of Ghoules pushed their way into the fight, the conclusion of this skirmish was fairly obvious in his opinion. He had no additional resources to draw on, no other companies to call to his aid.

The bulk of the Caledonian Army was in the thick of combating the two Ghoule Legions that finally had achieved a rough coordination and were now working together rather than against one another.

Klines silently cursed himself for the hundredth time in the past hour for failing to identify the cut in the slope that allowed the Ghoules to get into their rear. Yet there was nothing for it now. They couldn't cut off the flow of Ghoules leaping behind the Caledonian line.

All they could do was match steel against claw, something that Benin clearly relished. He was not a man of nuance. He preferred to do rather than think. And right now he was doing quite well.

The Sergeant of the Royal Guard was a whirlwind of motion, appearing to be everywhere at once, joining the shield wall wherever the fighting was hottest. The large man with the intricately carved beard had become the savior of the soldiers of the Royal Guard and the scourge of the Ghoules.

"That's it, lads!" shouted Benin, having pushed his way right behind two soldiers so that he could stab across their shoulders with his sword. Through a quirk of fate, he took a Ghoule through the eye rather than harmlessly across his armored shoulder when the beast slipped in the mud. But he was never one to question his luck on the battlefield. He simply accepted it and moved on, because you never knew when that luck was going to turn on you. "We fight for the Blademaster! We fight for Caledonia!"

His sword slashed down once again, his luck holding, the steel blade missing the Ghoule's neck and instead slicing off his clawed hand, which held the beast's sword. The spears right next to him finished the wounded Ghoule with a few quick, well-placed thrusts.

"Make these beasts pay with their blood for every step they want to take into our Kingdom!"

Another roar erupted from the throats of the several hundred soldiers seeking to protect the Caledonian Army's left flank, the Sergeant urging them forward, slippery step by slippery step through the sucking mud and slush. The three testudos continued their slow advance, their interlocked scuta forming a wall of steel, the spears just behind preventing the Ghoules from leaping into their squares, their goal the snowbank that was now less than a hundred feet away.

But the shift in momentum in favor of the Caledonians ended just as abruptly as it began. Two more Elders appeared at the end of the trail on the rock face, their twisted staffs of black ash unmistakable.

THE BATTLE against the single Elder had continued for longer than Cinjin would have liked. The two found themselves evenly matched and neither had yet discovered a way to break through the other's swiftly crafted shields.

The only benefit of the combat was that it kept the Elder from aiding his Ghoules, although Cinjin didn't think that boon would be of much relevance for much longer. With this many Ghoules trying to sneak around the Caledonian flank, he assumed that more Elders would be joining the fight soon enough.

So he needed to kill this Elder. Not only to help the soldiers he was fighting with, but also for himself. In his mind, killing Elders was the best way to honor his murdered family. Yet his frustration continued to grow, the duel dragging on.

Obviously, the beast was quite skilled and experienced with the Curse, yet he wasn't really bothering to attack, instead simply doing his best to deflect Cinjin's attacks. The Elder was playing for time, and the Magus could guess why, so if he was going to end this fight any time soon, he needed to try something different.

He was just about to do so when the tenor of the combat changed abruptly. Just as Cinjin had expected that it would. He grumbled about his bad luck, although he knew that this swift turn in his fortunes resulted primarily because he had failed to kill quickly the Elder standing above him on the snowbank.

Cinjin had no choice but to halt his attack and nudge his horse with his knees, the destrier spinning away from where it was standing, allowing the Curse thrown at Cinjin by one of the two other Elders who had jumped down into the massive pile of snow and joined the fight to slam harmlessly behind him. The Magus then raised his shield made of the Talent, protecting himself and the soldiers around him against the spears of tainted power that streaked down from the top of the snowdrift.

With Cinjin now occupied by two of the Elders, the third focused on easier prey, sending several lances of Dark Magic smashing down into the soldiers' shield wall. The power of the strikes shattered the Caledonian line, turning the soldiers who were hit directly by the Curse into ash and knocking back those on the periphery of the blast several dozen feet. The Ghoules took advantage of the breach in a flash, sprinting through the gap.

For several seconds, it appeared as if the beasts were about to break through the testudo in the center of the formation, no one in a position to prevent the screaming beasts from running rampant behind the Caledonian lines except for the Blademaster and Benin, who raced into the space.

The Blademaster demonstrated an economy of movement and deadly precision that was second to none, gliding through the melee in silence as he sliced at the Ghoules as if he were a skilled butcher and they were no more than pieces of meat. Benin, on the other hand, was a maelstrom of wild movement and sound, yelling louder than the Ghoules as he swung his sword with a controlled ferocity, his wide sweeps of steel designed less to kill, leaving that handiwork to his Captain, and more to keep the Ghoules back so that only a few could come at them at one time.

The two soldiers stemmed the tide for the moment, but they both knew the truth. They could hold for only so long against so many Ghoules.

Cinjin was desperate to help the Blademaster and the Sergeant battling just to his front, the two men no more than a dozen feet away, fighting like devils as they attempted to beat back a half dozen of the Ghoules on their own.

A valiant effort, though likely doomed. The Magus knew that it was only a matter of time. Some of the soldiers who had been knocked backward by the blast had pushed themselves up from the muck and were slowly shaking the cobwebs from their heads, thinking to rejoin the fight once they got their feet under them again. But too many lay still, never to rise again.

Even worse, there was nothing that Cinjin could do until he eliminated the Elder Ghoules, two of whom continued to attack him, keeping him focused on them rather than the other Elder who now was coordinating the Ghoules' efforts to split the shield wall even wider.

Cinjin grunted in disgust, less than pleased with the current circumstances. Still, that didn't mean that he couldn't try to change them. Desperate times required desperate measures, so he turned to a trick that he had picked up from Noorsin.

While maintaining his shield, he crafted hundreds of small pellets with the Talent, then flung them around the edge of his barrier toward the two Elders who stood above him.

The beasts had no choice but to defend themselves, both crafting shields just in time to block the attack. The tiny spheres that had the power to pass through flesh and bone flashed ineffectually against the barriers of Dark Magic when they struck.

Cinjin had no illusion that he would harm the beasts with his latest attack. That was all right with him, because the assault did distract the Elders, giving him the few seconds that he needed to accomplish what he really wanted to do, using another trick that he hadn't employed in centuries that he hoped would prove useful.

In the small amount of time that he had to work with, Cinjin spun a web of the Talent, the strands so thin that they couldn't be seen unless caught in the flash of the sunlight. With a flick of his wrist, he nudged his creation through the gap in the Caledonian line.

Cinjin could do nothing directly to help the Blademaster in that moment. Even so, he wasn't too concerned, as the Blademaster and the Sergeant appeared to have everything well in hand at least for the time being. He could, however, slow down the Ghoule rush so that the beasts didn't overwhelm the two soldiers.

Satisfied that the Caledonians would hold at least for a few minutes more, Cinjin shifted his attention back to the two Elders who stared down at him with a malicious glint in their black eyes from atop the pile of snow. The beasts had released their shields and were preparing to launch another attack, the Curse spinning swiftly around the tops of their staffs, the two beasts apparently having decided to combine their efforts.

Having no desire to allow the Elders to continue to enjoy their advantage in numbers, Cinjin decided on a new approach for these beasts as well, turning his focus away from the Elders above him, concentrating instead on what they were standing on. Two bolts of blazing white light shot from his palms, the energy burning into the base of the snowbank.

The effect was immediate. The heat of the power employed by Cinjin melted the hard-packed snow, a small river of steaming water crashing down onto the canyon floor, taking the two Elders with it.

Cinjin never allowed the two floundering beasts to rise again, sending two bolts of the Talent right through their chests. Grunting again, this time in satisfaction, he watched for a few seconds as dozens of Ghoules tried to dig themselves out of the slush that had cascaded down onto them.

The Magus even allowed himself a small smile. The Ghoules would continue their attack, of that he had no doubt, but he had gained the Caledonians a bit more time, and that was what they were playing for. That was why they were in the Winter Pass to begin with.

A high-pitched shriek of agony caught Cinjin's attention and pulled his gaze back to the gap in the Caledonian line. The Blademaster and the Sergeant continued to hold their ground against a half dozen of the beasts. Beyond them, closer to the gap in the shield wall, a pack of Ghoules lay dead, their bodies sliced apart with a mechanical precision.

The scream came from the remaining Elder Ghoule, the beast having collapsed to the ground, his head connected to his neck by just a few loose strands of flesh and sinew, the creature also having lost a leg, arm, and claw. Cinjin's smile broadened as he studied his handiwork with the detached curiosity of a scientist.

He had taken what Irelda had taught him to do and then put his own twist to it. The web made of the Talent was designed initially as a defensive tool, as a way to prevent creatures of Dark Magic from attacking from or going in a certain direction. The web would latch onto and then smother any creature of the Curse, burning through their flesh to the bone.

But rather than keep his creation in one place, he had sent it hunting instead. For the Elder Ghoule. The web had worked perfectly, drifting toward its quarry, barely visible, barely acknowledged except for the dead Ghoules it left in its wake, only harming those touched by the Curse, until the energy finally found its prey, wrapping itself around the Elder Ghoule before the beast even knew what was happening.

Cinjin decided that he would have to use this weapon again. It had proven more effective than he thought it would.

With the Elders removed from this section of the battlefield at least for the present, Cinjin was about to focus once again on the Ghoules, who even with the loss of their leaders were preparing to attack again, many of the waterlogged beasts back on their clawed feet, their hunger and anger still burning within them.

A shout from the Blademaster kept him from doing that just a little while longer. Instead, he urged his horse away from the center of the Caledonian line.

"Companies, separate! Ten yards!"

Klines maintained the calm focus that had served him so well when he charged into the gap with Benin in a valiant and likely doomed attempt to keep the beasts from getting behind the main Caledonian Army. He and Benin had succeeded for a period of time, though Klines understood that their efforts couldn't last. Eventually, the Ghoules would widen the gap, what with the beasts continuing to jump down from the trail. So he resigned himself to the inevitable.

That was until Klines heard the sound that brought a smile to his forbidding countenance, and then he felt the earth begin to shake, drops of water and splatters of mud dancing off the ground and into the air all around him.

His soldiers responded immediately to his command, the timing perfect as the Ghoules were still trying to organize themselves after Cinjin converted half the snowdrift into slush and ice. The two companies on the flanks shifted ten yards to the left and right respectively, which allowed the center company to split in half, the gap in their line created by the now dead Elder the breakpoint, one side moving to the left five yards, the other five yards to the right.

Some of the Ghoules began to charge toward the much larger gap that the soldiers offered them, believing that they could speed through the breach and then sweep around the soldiers from behind. Their recklessness proved to be their downfall.

Before the ambitious Ghoules had gotten more than a few yards into the breach, Kevan was there with several companies of cavalry, the soldiers using their war horses to great effect, the animals' shoulders crashing into the Ghoules, knocking them to the ground, the steel-shod hooves of the destriers following behind finishing the lethal and quite effective work those in the lead had begun.

At the same time, another troop of soldiers swept around the Caledonians' left flank just as another company did the same on the right, the cavalry coming at the Ghoules from three directions at once and forcing them against what was left of the snowbank and the canyon wall.

"Excellent timing," said Klines. "My thanks."

"It was the least that we could do," replied Kevan, having brought his horse to a halt in front of the Blademaster. The Duke of the Southern Marches took a moment to survey the Blademaster and his Sergeant's work, a half dozen Ghoules lying dead in the mud thanks to their efforts. Very impressive, and likely on a scale similar to that of the Volkun. "I saw what the Magus did to the snowbank."

"Yes, Cinjin certainly knows what he's doing."

"That he does. Once we're done with the beasts here, let's have him finish what he started. If he can reduce the size of the snowdrift with the Talent, maybe even eliminate it entirely, then we can stop worrying about the Ghoules using that goat trail to get at us from behind."

"A good thought," agreed Klines. "I'll speak with him about it."

As the Blademaster trotted toward the Magus, Kevan turned back toward the battle playing out beneath the cliff face. His deadly charge had done its work, and now his cavalry and the Blademaster's soldiers were finishing the beasts who had tried to sneak up on them from behind.

Yet despite their success at countering the Ghoules' surprise attack, the larger problem still remained. Two Ghoule Legions were advancing all across their line. The Caledonians were holding, but with the advantage the Ghoules had in terms of the number of Elders fighting for them, their already poor odds of surviving this fight were rapidly diminishing.

The Elders already had killed three Magii, increasing the stress on the few who remained. And once the third Ghoule Legion took the field, that event just moments away, Kevan was certain that despite their best efforts, eventually the Ghoules would push them back to where the Pass widened. Then, the beasts would swoop around their flanks as he and his riders had just done.

When that happened, the Caledonian Army would experience the same results as the Ghoules just did.

They'd be slaughtered.

⁓

"*Are you ready?*" asked Bryen.

The tone that he had used to ask the question revealed his desire to get started. He had used the Talent to link to the leader of the other flight of Griffons so that they could speak to one another in their minds, the success of what they were about to attempt depending on excellent coordination and even better timing.

"*Almost,*" came the reply. "*Stop being so impatient. I had farther to fly. Just a few seconds more and we'll be in position.*"

Instead of being annoyed by the response that he had received, Bryen smiled. Prickly. Just like she usually was right before a battle. He should have anticipated no less. Twisting around to look behind him, one hand always holding tightly to Banshee's feathers, Bryen took in the Griffons who flew behind him, their large wings extended, dipping to the left and right as they glided through the air and sought to maintain their position in the wide circle.

He nodded to himself. They were ready. Or at least appeared to be. Maybe a little anxious. But that made sense. They would deal with it when the time came. The gladiators had all faced worse on the white sand. Then he reached down, rubbing beneath the feathers of Banshee's neck and earning a grumble of pleasure for his efforts.

Almost fifty of the animals, all of them much larger than a draft horse, had appeared at the Sanctuary in Bryen's time of need. He had reached out with the Talent to Banshee right before he started climbing the sandstone pillar, requesting her assistance and that of as many other Griffons who might be willing to help.

Her response had overwhelmed him. He was both shocked and grateful that so many of the usually reclusive animals had deigned to answer his call for aid.

Several soldiers of the Blood Company rode on the backs of each one. Some of the gladiators clearly weren't comfortable, only agreeing to get on the Griffons' backs because they had no other choice.

Bryen had mastered creating a portal for himself. He had yet to perfect doing it for a larger group. So with time passing much too quickly, enlisting the help of the Griffons was the only way to get the entire Company from the Trench to the Winter Pass swiftly.

A few of these hardened gladiators turned green as they soared through the air, losing whatever was in their stomachs, which thankfully wasn't very much, frightened because they were several thousand feet above the mountains. They didn't enjoy the constant buffeting by the tempestuous wind playing off the peaks, disliking how their stomachs lurched when the Griffons swooped and dove ... and those were just a few of the reasons their ride from the west had been less than pleasant for them.

Most of the gladiators, who had thrived on the rush of adrenaline that they had experienced every time they fought in the Pit, took to the experience like a fish in water, loving the thrill of flying. The familiar and welcome surge of adrenaline flowed through their veins when the large animals dove through the air, wings pulled in, wind blasting back into them, hurtling through the sky at an incredible speed, making them feel more alive than they ever had before.

Bryen had no doubt that some of his friends would be offering him a few harsh words once this was over. He could manage that. It was a small price to pay for the edge that he had gained on the Ghoules, who from what he could tell had no idea what was circling far above them. He had been careful not to be seen during his brief reconnaissance of the gorge before returning to where the Griffons waited just to the west of the Winter Pass.

The Ghoules were pushing the Caledonians south, the soldiers reluctantly giving ground in the face of the beasts' onslaught. But it wasn't because of the Ghoules themselves that they gave way.

The Ghoules were strong and deadly opponents, that couldn't be denied. Yet if it was just the Ghoules the Caledonians had to worry about, they'd be able to hold for quite some time no matter how many of the beasts came at them. Duchess Stelekel had selected a good location for the fight, the sides of the gorge pressing in on both sides to narrow the battlefield.

No, the problem came from the several dozen beasts who had arrayed themselves behind the attacking Legions, most atop the snowdrifts. The Elders. The servants of the Ghoule Overlord in both body and spirit.

Victory in the battle now was being determined by a simple mathematical calculation. There were too many Elders and too few Magii.

Bryen hoped that he could rebalance the equation.

When he had told Declan how they were going to attack the Ghoules from the air, his friend had stared at him for several long, incredulous seconds, and then burst into laughter, thinking that he was making a joke. When Bryen didn't laugh, Declan's humor died away, his expression becoming grave, the Master of the Gladiators realizing that he was actually serious. Bryen wanted the Blood Company to attack the beasts from the backs of the Griffons with their spears and swords.

Declan had argued that it would never work. There was no time to train. There was no time to practice. None of the gladiators had any experience riding Griffons. Besides, the animals were temperamental and often overly aggressive. Several had balked when some of the gladiators tried to hop onto their backs as if they were no more than horses.

So what Bryen was thinking was completely distinct from a cavalry charge. Only archers might stand any chance of success, and even then the Griffons couldn't be moving at more than a slow glide for them to have any hope at hitting their targets.

After Declan finished offering his argument against what he believed Bryen wanted to do, Bryen had agreed with him. Then he explained what he really had in mind. The proposal made Declan think for a bit longer, his friend finally nodding his head after he had considered the suggested approach from every angle.

"That could work," he had agreed.

And thus their delay in reaching the Winter Pass until after the Ghoule Legions had begun their attack. Bryen needed the extra time to pick up a critical ingredient that would determine their success.

"We're in position," Aislinn finally communicated, her flight of Griffons having reached the eastern side of the Winter Pass. *"Coming back around now."*

Bryen waited a few seconds more, until Banshee had finished her curl in the air and was turning back toward the Winter Pass, the other Griffons still lined up behind her.

"Shall we get started, Banshee?" asked Bryen. The large animal squawked in reply, her muscles bunching beneath Bryen as she prepared to attack the beasts far below them. Knowing that his friend was ready, Bryen turned his attention back to Aislinn.

"We're diving ... now."

"We'll meet you in the Pass," replied Aislinn.

Banshee tilted on her wing and swooped down at Bryen's urging, the other Griffons in the flight following right behind her. On the other side of the Winter Pass, Bryen glimpsed the same thing happening, Aislinn leading her squadron of Griffons in a plummeting dive that with a quick twist of the animals' wings allowed them to fly right through the canyon, Bryen from the north and Aislinn from the south.

As the rush of air struck him, Bryen smiled broadly, the speed of the dive sending a jolt of exhilaration through him. Then, in just seconds, the rough ground of the canyon and the huge snowdrifts along the edge rearing up in front of him, Banshee opened her wings and turned her shoulder so that they leveled out and soared no more than a few dozen feet above the Ghoule host.

But it wasn't the Blood Company that attacked the beasts from the air. Declan had been right. Employing spears and swords from that height and at that speed was too much to ask of even the most skilled fighters.

Rather, it was the several dozen Magii Bryen had picked up as they made their way toward the Winter Pass. The men and women of the Order of the Magii made their presence known with devastating effect as they focused the full force of the Talent against the Elder Ghoules. Streaks of white light shot down from the sky, along with shards, spheres, and other designs in the natural power of the world that ripped apart the beasts before they even knew what struck them.

The surprise attack caught the Elders napping and sent a ripple of shock through the Ghoules. Many of the beasts halted their assault as they watched in surprise and then dismay as the Magii eliminated almost all of the Elders in a devastating onslaught that lasted only a few minutes, the Magii on the ground adding their strength to the effort and taking advantage of the beasts' chaotic and poor response.

Though the Ghoules were taken by surprise, the Caledonian Army wasn't, Bryen having communicated his plan to Duchess Stelekel. She had been waiting for the Griffons to appear, her soldiers immediately shifting to the attack. Duke Winborne and the Blademaster led assaults from both flanks and added to the momentum that the Magii had stolen so quickly from the beasts.

When Bryen swung back around after his third pass above the Ghoules, having destroyed at least six Elders on his own with the blazing spikes of light that shot from the blades of his spear, he could sense that the battle had already turned.

None of the Griffons had been harmed, although a few had close calls as some of the Elders tried to counter the assault.

No more than a handful of Elders were still alive, so many of the Magii had already turned their focus to the Ghoules since their initial attacks had been so successful.

Because of that, the Ghoules were beginning to waver. Several packs of the beasts were already pushing against their brethren, trying to force their way through the Legions that had become a disorganized mass, trying to escape the white-hot energy of the Talent by escaping to the north.

Bryen let out a rare shout of triumph, punching his fist into the air, the blades of the Spear of the Magii blazing brightly. His cry was taken up first by the Blood Company and then by the soldiers on the ground as the Ghoules began to stream back toward the north.

The Caledonians had won. For now.

But the war wasn't over. No, there were still Ghoule Legions in Caledonia that needed to be dealt with.

And there was one more task that remained for Bryen, likely the deadliest yet.

He had killed the Ghoule Overlord.

Now he needed to destroy the Curse.

THE END

KEEP READING for the first two chapters of Book 7, *The Protector's Victory* — and the exciting conclusion of *The Tales of Caledonia*.

BONUS MATERIAL

If you really enjoyed this story, I need you to do me a HUGE favor – please follow me on Amazon and BookBub. And if you have a few minutes, consider writing a review.

Keep reading for the first two chapters of Book 7 of *The Tales of Caledonia, The Protector's Victory.*

THE TALES OF CALEDONIA
BOOK SEVEN
THE PROTECTOR'S VICTORY
PETER WACHT

1. TIRING OF THE GAME

Bryen stepped to the side just in time, pivoting away, the blackened steel of the Ghoule's spear sliding through the space he'd been standing in just an instant before. He slipped to the side again, avoiding another lunge, staying on his toes, always moving. Then one more time, bending backward so that the Ghoule's spear stabbed just short of his face, Bryen gaining a much too close view of the sharpened tip.

Tiring of the game, knowing that allowing the Ghoule to control the rhythm of the combat would only hurt him in the end, Bryen infused the double blades of the Spear of the Magii with the Talent as he spun away from the beast one more time. Sensing what his opponent was going to do next, he jabbed backward with a short thrust, hearing a pleasing grunt of pain, the sound telling him that he had hit his mark, the spear dipping in his hands as the beast began to droop toward the ground, his life counted in seconds.

Ripping the blazing steel out of the Ghoule's gut, the nauseating yet satisfying stench of burning meat hitting his nostrils, Bryen ducked, a large claw passing over his head. The lethal swing missed him by no more than a hair, one daggerlike finger actually cutting neatly across the side of his brow. Ignoring the trickle of blood that flowed down the side of his face, Bryen jumped over the spear the frustrated Ghoule swung at his knees.

The massive Ghoule – the beast was well over eight feet tall – was fast. Really fast. Almost as fast as Bryen was. Even so, speed rarely compensated for bad decisions.

By allowing his uncontrollable drive to kill Bryen to rule his thoughts, giving little consideration to the need to defend against a counterstroke, the beast had overextended, never believing that he might miss. Bryen was more than happy to show him the error of his ways.

With the Ghoule off balance, Bryen, with an economy of motion, only really having to flick his wrists, slashed swiftly with his Spear, the top blade cutting right through the beast's wrist, a spurt of blood erupting from the wound as the blazing steel sliced through flesh and bone. The sword, claw still holding the hilt, clattered to the stone.

Before the badly wounded Ghoule could even scream, Bryen finished the beast, continuing his initial motion and bringing the lower blade up and then across the Ghoule's throat, the beast's head falling not too far from the severed claw, the body crumpling to the smooth grey rock, a thick black blood bubbling out from the clean cut across his neck.

"You do not belong here, Protector," hissed a voice from just above him. "This is the center of my power. I rule here!"

Bryen stepped back then, finally having a few seconds to get a better look at his surroundings. He hadn't had the chance to do so before.

How he had gotten there was a mystery to him. As soon as he opened his eyes, the massive Ghoule attacked him, the speed of the assault so swift that he gave little thought to where he was or what he was doing, allowing his instincts to govern his decisions as he defended himself.

What was this place?

He had been asleep in a borrowed bedroll behind a tent that had been erected next to one of the snowdrifts lining the Winter Pass.

How had he gotten here, wherever here was?

Had he somehow made use of the Talent while he slept?

Now that he had a brief moment to think, he began to understand. It was all making a strange kind of sense.

It had to be the Seventh Stone. The artifact had done this to him before, seeking to help him learn about the challenges he would need to overcome in reconstructing the Weir by actually taking him to the Sanctuary in his dreams.

But was this a dream or was it something more?

Bryen stood at the very edge of a large square space, what he realized was actually the top of a truncated pyramid. Roughly crafted, worn and chipped steps ran down the four sides to the bottom, which was several hundred feet below. Beyond that, he couldn't see much at all. A wispy grey haze blocked his gaze, though every so often he glimpsed through the swirling mist a sprawling city just beyond the massive plaza that surrounded the ancient structure.

Looking back across the top of the pyramid, a large stone slab sat perfectly centered on the dull grey stone. Carved columns, pitted and worn, stood like silent sentinels around the outside of the summit, a large dome with a hole in the very center that aligned with the stone slab set on top of them.

Right in front of the altar stood three very large Ghoules, much like the two he had just dispatched. Although the beasts held their spears at the ready, strangely, the Ghoules looked at him more with a hint of curiosity than hunger, which was a rare occurrence. Bryen could only assume that these Ghoules had yet to face a human who could match their own martial skills, so he had captured their interest, the beasts likely trying to determine how he had eliminated two of their brethren at the cost of only a scratch.

Behind the Ghoules, twisting in and out of the ancient columns, was a billowing black cloud that seemed to have a mind of its own, the mist failing to obey the demands of the wind that blew steadily across the top of the pyramid from west to east.

He knew where he was now. There was no other answer.

The Temple of the Ghoules.

He had never been here before. Even so, he knew that he was right. This was, indeed, the center of Ghoule power. The fortress of the Ghoule Overlord and, perhaps more important, the source of the Lost Land's Dark Magic.

That could only mean that the swirling black fog was the Curse, the power once contained in the black diamond, the power that had corrupted the people who had once lived in this land and become the Ghoules, the twisted power that had set the beasts on a path of conquest and slaughter.

It seemed so long ago, yet it was only just yesterday that Bryen had defeated the Ghoule Overlord in the Sanctuary, eliminating the Curse's host. Bryen had realized then that even with all the power that the Master of the Lost Land exercised north of the Shattered Peaks, that's all that the Ghoule Overlord was. A physical manifestation of the Curse. A container, a puppet, for the Dark Magic of the Lost Land.

Still, that didn't reduce the peril that he and Caledonia faced in any way.

Bryen had come to understand that even though he had killed the Ghoule Overlord, destroying the Dark Magic's vessel, he had not destroyed the Curse itself. Doing that, removing this corrupt evil from the Lost Land, was the only way that he could ensure the safety of Caledonia.

So he had no choice. His task was not yet complete.

He had to destroy the Curse.

Even with the rebuilt Weir that he had constructed with the help and guidance of the Ten Magii, the Curse could not be contained. If he did not do what was required, the Curse would contaminate Caledonia just as it did the inhabitants of the Lost Land. Bryen was certain of that.

It was inescapable. Because just like its Ghoules, the Curse was insatiable. Its thirst for power, for control, unquenchable and always driving it forward.

"You will die here, Protector," hissed the voice just above Bryen, the black mist punching in and out of the pillars, teasing him, taunting him, coaxing him, "and in your death I will be reborn. I will kill everyone you love. I will take Caledonia and make it mine, and then from there I will take the world. But first I will take you. I will make you mine, what I need you to be." The mist twisted through the columns faster and faster, appearing agitated, angry, unfulfilled, as if its patience was being tested. "You do not have the power to stop me, Protector. Even with the Seventh Stone, you cannot defeat me. In the end, you will have no choice. You will serve me."

Bryen heard the truth in the Curse's words, chilling him to his core, and understanding the grim reality of what would happen if the Curse consumed him.

He thought that he had saved Caledonia. He thought that he had won.

He hadn't.

He had only delayed the inevitable.

So many of his friends, so many gladiators in the Blood Company, so many soldiers in the various Guards, had died for him.

Sirius had died for him.

Yet the true threat, the more dangerous threat, to Caledonia remained.

Bryen had failed them.

That thought almost crushed his spirit, filling him with an angst that threatened to freeze him in place.

He had done what was needed. He had accomplished what was supposed to be impossible.

He had rebuilt the Weir.

Still, it wasn't enough. More was required of him, because he was likely the only one who could challenge the Curse. The only one likely to have any chance at all of destroying the Curse.

Bryen was pulled from his debilitating thoughts when the black mist surged out from between the columns, hovering right above the stone slab. The fog began to take shape, Bryen's eyes widening in disbelief.

Floating above the altar wasn't the Ghoule Overlord as he thought would be the case.

No, it was something far worse.

A terrifying image.

It was him.

A confirmation of what Bryen feared the most. A confirmation of a niggling suspicion that had teased him since he left the Sanctuary.

The Curse wanted him as its next host.

Bryen closed his eyes for just a moment, taking a deep breath, seeking to control his growing fury at this new fate.

He couldn't let it happen. He wouldn't let it happen.

Feeling the need to strike out, his rage mimicking the white-hot energy of the Talent, Bryen drew on the power of the Seventh Stone, the blades of the Spear of the Magii glowing brighter than a bolt of lightning. Two streams of power shot straight at the Curse.

At the image of himself.

At what the Curse wanted to make of him.

He needed to destroy the Dark Magic. He needed to destroy himself.

Before he could determine the result of his efforts, in a flash of blinding light, the Temple of the Ghoules vanished and with it the Curse. Yet right before the dream that wasn't a dream disappeared, Bryen caught a glimpse of his image laughing at him. Mocking him for his naivete, for him believing that he could actually do something about the destiny in store for him.

"You need to be careful, Bryen," said a voice right at his side. "Even with the Seventh Stone, the Ghoule Overlord holds the advantage over you in the Lost Land. Whether you are there in body or spirit, it doesn't matter."

Bryen blinked a few times, clearing the spots from his eyes. He was back on more familiar ground. The Sanctuary. The carved out hollow in which six of the Seven Stones rested on their pedestals, streams of unwavering power shooting from each one -- emerald, ruby, black opal, white pearl, sapphire, jade -- into the air, the kaleidoscope of energy forming the Weir.

"The Ghoule Overlord isn't really the Ghoule Overlord," said Bryen, understanding finally what he was truly up against.

He turned to face the shimmering figure who was just as tall as he was and had a very similar frame, lean, muscular. The only real difference between them was the hair, Bryen's white with a few flecks of brown mixed in, the spirit's a light brown. That and the scars that marred Bryen's cheek and neck.

Bryen lifted his hand to his brow. The trickle of blood had slowed, though still had not come to a stop. Reaching for a thin stream of the Talent, Bryen applied the natural magic of the world to the slash, the flow of blood ending as the wound healed, leaving behind nothing more than a thin scar that would only be visible when the light hit it a certain way. Just another mark on his body to add to all the others.

Courtesy of a dream that was more than a dream.

"He is and he isn't," corrected Viktor Keldragan. "In that you're right."

"Now you sound like Sirius," said Bryen, immediately regretting what he had said as soon as the words left his mouth, a feeling of loss and a pang of guilt surging through him. He could only imagine what Viktor must be feeling. Sirius had been a complicated man, but a good man, and he was Viktor's brother. He had been Bryen's grandfather, although he had never really known him as such. If not for Sirius' sacrifice, Bryen and the Ten Magii never would have succeeded in rebuilding the Weir. "I'm sorry. I shouldn't have said that."

"It's all right," replied Viktor, placing a misty hand on Bryen's arm to convey that he was not offended. "You're absolutely right, nephew. It's exactly something that Sirius would say."

Bryen nodded, silent, thankful for Viktor's understanding.

"It's just unfortunate that he's not here to tease anymore," continued Viktor. "He was always so serious, it was so easy to get him going."

Bryen smiled then. "It was, wasn't it? Sometimes you could set him off with just a look."

Viktor chuckled at that, remembering several instances of that occurring when he and his brother were growing up. "Indeed, you're right. You didn't have to be doing something wrong to raise his ire. He simply had to think that you were doing it." He allowed those pleasant memories to wash over him for a few seconds more. Then his expression turned serious. "Don't feel guilty for his death. It was not your fault."

"Easier said than done," replied Bryen softly.

"Sirius died doing what he knew was necessary. He died doing what he believed was right. He died doing what he wanted to do. In fact, I can't think of a better way for him to go to the other side than to do so in a combat against the Ghoule Overlord. It was his choice. It was his right. Don't take that away from him."

"I'll try," promised Bryen, nodding. He understood what

Viktor was telling him. And, in truth, a small part of him agreed with his uncle. Still, his guilt and grief made it difficult for him to believe and accept what his uncle told him.

Knowing that it would take his nephew time to adopt a more honest perspective on what had occurred during the rebuilding of the Weir, one not colored by remorse, Viktor moved back to the topic that had brought them together in the Sanctuary.

"As I was saying, the Ghoule Overlord is the Ghoule Overlord, but the Curse is much more than the Ghoule Overlord. It is not restricted to the Natural World. Boundaries hold no meaning for that scourge. It runs rampant where it chooses."

"How so?"

"Just as you are the Seventh Stone and the Seventh Stone is you, the Ghoule Overlord is the Curse and the Curse is the Ghoule Overlord. It's easiest to think of the Curse as an essence that's alive, an evil miasma with a sentience all its own, regardless of whether it is constrained by the flesh of the Ghoule Overlord or it is running free. The Curse is the Talent in its worst possible form. No matter how much we hate it, we can't ignore the fact that it's a part of our world. It will always be a part of our world. Though we may be able to restrict the Curse's power, the Curse will always seek a way around whatever barriers we try to place around it, and more often than not it will succeed. It is inevitable."

Bryen thought about what Viktor had said for a moment, watching with a great deal of pleasure as the energy contained within the Seven Stones flowed without a flicker or flash in sight into the barricade that would keep Caledonia safe from the creatures of the Lost Land.

But that wasn't entirely true, was it?

Based on what Viktor was saying, the Weir could keep the Ghoules from Caledonia, but not the Curse. The Curse would find a way past the Weir. It already had in the form of Tetric and the other incidents of Dark Magic that blackened the history of the Kingdom, the several times that the members of the Order of the Magii needed to combat those peers who had chosen a darker path.

The Curse would find a way to take Caledonia, whether through the Ghoules or in some other manner. That meant it would find a way to take him.

"So my work isn't done," Bryen concluded, having already figured it out but needing to say it to confirm it in his own mind.

"Unfortunately not," agreed Viktor, "assuming, of course, that you would want to take on this additional challenge."

"You say it as if I have a choice."

"My apologies," chuckled Viktor. "I was simply trying to soften the blow."

Bryen nodded, accepting his uncle's apology. "So the only way to ensure the safety of Caledonia is to destroy the Curse."

"That's correct."

"Can that even be done?" asked Bryen. "If the Curse is like the Talent, how can you destroy something so powerful? Something so omnipresent? It doesn't seem possible."

Viktor thought about Bryen's question for a time, clearly in no rush to answer, because he wasn't really certain himself. All he could do was offer a mix of fact and conjecture, and even then it was weighted more toward the side of the latter.

"With the Seventh Stone, theoretically, yes. It can be done. You can destroy the Curse."

"Theoretically?" asked Bryen. He really did feel as if he was engaging in a conversation with Sirius, though he kept that belief to himself this time.

Viktor shrugged his shoulders, an apologetic look on his face. "I will speak more with the other Magii. Unfortunately, that's the best answer I can give you at present."

"What about practically? Theory means little when it comes to challenging the Curse."

"I just don't know," sighed Viktor. "I will talk with Mikayla and the others. Perhaps they will be able to share more than I can."

Bryen nodded, thanking him for that. He felt as if he was right back where he had started when Sirius and Rafia had begun badgering him to take responsibility for reconstructing the Weir. An almost impossible task with no clear outcome, other than the likelihood of his own death.

So much had changed in the last few days. Then again, so much hadn't.

Destroying the Curse couldn't be easier than rebuilding the Weir. In fact, based on what he had just experienced at the Temple of the Ghoules, he had no doubt that it was several magnitudes more difficult with the expected outcome much the same and much more certain.

Just as always happened when Bryen was faced with a difficult choice, a choice that wasn't really a choice actually, Declan's words played through his mind. Words that now were beginning to gnaw at him.

"You must do what you must do."

Bryen shook his head in resignation, feeling slightly sorry for himself.

Why was he always the one who needed to do the doing?

Embarrassed, he crushed that emotion immediately. As always, regardless of how he felt, the truth in Declan's words couldn't be denied.

The Ghoule Overlord had wanted him. The Ghoule Overlord had wanted the Seventh Stone so that he could destroy the Weir.

But now as Bryen thought about it, his mind opening to the broader possibilities, the image of himself that the Curse had formed above the altar stuck in his head, he realized that the Curse actually had wanted him for another reason altogether.

Bryen would be the perfect host. Combining the power of the Seventh Stone with the Dark Magic of the Lost Land, the Curse embodied within him would be unstoppable.

But it wouldn't be him.

He would be the Curse, and the Curse would be him. They would be one.

The Curse would rule him. He would be a slave once more.

So just as always Bryen really didn't have any choice at all.

As Viktor and the Sanctuary began to fade away and Bryen slipped back into his fitful slumber, he realized that he was really getting tired of Declan's sayings. And he was really getting tired of these dreams that were more than dreams.

2. MANIFESTATION OF THE CURSE

"Do you have any proof?" asked Aislinn. "Any real evidence? Anything tangible?"

"Nothing substantial. No more than just a belief. Just what I saw and heard in the Sanctuary after I killed the Ghoule Overlord, or rather destroyed his body. And then just what I saw in my dreams."

"In your dreams?" she asked, her tone suggesting a faint hint of disbelief.

"Yes, in my dreams."

"Why would you have faith in your dreams?"

"Because dreams aren't always dreams. Sometimes there's little difference between what's real and what's a dream."

He touched the thin black scar that ran through the larger scars marring his cheek and his neck to make his point, those wider marks a constant reminder of what happened if you allowed your concentration to lapse, even for just a few seconds. A lesson that he had taken to heart in the Pit and beyond.

Aislinn nodded, really not in a position to argue with him. When Bryen finally had told her how he had gotten that burn that never faded, she had believed him. It had made too much sense. Nevertheless, she had been curious, so she had asked Rafia about it.

The Magus had confirmed what Bryen had said, noting that it was a rare skill, to be awake in a dream. A dangerous one as well. Because if you brought so much of yourself into a dream, what happened in the dream would have the same effect as if it was occurring in real life.

You could die in the Spirit World just as if you were in the Natural World. Something that Bryen had escaped by the skin of his cheek when he faced off against the Ghoule Overlord for the first time.

Aislinn and Bryen had just emerged from the medical tents that had been set up for the wounded, finding some rocks off to the side that allowed them to sit for the first time since the sun had risen and rest for a few minutes. They had spent most of the day there, both catching only a few hours of sleep during the early morning. Although Aislinn doubted Bryen had slept much at all the night before if he had entered more fully than he should have the world of dreams.

They were both exhausted, and it showed. They had come straight from the Sanctuary, having no time to recover. Before that they had no rest because of the chase through the tunnel and then across the floor of the Trench to the sandstone pillar upon which the Sanctuary was built. From there they jumped right into the fight in the Winter Pass after flying across the continent on the backs of their Griffons, joining their fellow Magii in their efforts to eliminate the Elder Ghoules from the battlefield.

When that task was complete, they had then turned their attention to the Ghoules. The beasts had held for a time, retreating slowly back up the Winter Pass, only fleeing to the north once they realized that they had lost the only defense they had that could protect them from the Magii's unwavering ferocity.

Then, for most of the late afternoon and well into the night, Bryen and Aislinn had joined the many other Magii with skill in healing to help as many of the soldiers wounded in the battle as they could. This addition of several dozen physicks versed in the Talent to the ranks of the Caledonian Army had proven fortuitous.

The Caledonians had won the battle, in large part thanks to the timely arrival of the Griffons and the Magii. And a great many lives also were saved because of their timely arrival.

Even so, the victory came at a great cost. It had been a bloody encounter, and unfortunately there was little that the Magii could do for some of the soldiers struck by the Curse. It seemed that only Bryen and Rafia had any real ability to heal the worst of the wounds caused by the Elders' Dark Magic, and even that proved to be a struggle for them depending on how far the Curse had progressed.

"Let's think this through," continued Aislinn. "You watched his body turn to ash, yet you think that he may have survived somehow, correct?"

"I'm not sure," Bryen replied, a touch of uncertainty in his voice.

"You're not sure? You're not sure that you killed the Ghoule Overlord?"

"I did kill the Ghoule Overlord, but it's not that simple. There's more to this story than just flesh and blood."

"So what you're saying is that there is the living Ghoule Overlord and then there's the living Curse."

"Yes, that's a good way to put it."

"What do you mean specifically by that?" asked Aislinn, thinking through the ramifications of what Bryen was saying, about what the consequences would be if there was a separation between the two. "If I'm understanding correctly, you're implying that the Curse isn't just a power, a corrupt power, it's also an entity all on its own. Some kind of sentient being."

Bryen raised his hands, asking for patience. It had been a long last few days and nights. He knew that they were both tired and easily irritated. So to avoid the last, he decided to start fresh, hoping that what he said provided the clarity that was required.

"Yes, you're explaining it all better than I am. As you're suggesting, I believe that there is more to the Ghoule Overlord than just his flesh. There is the body and the spirit, and the two can be one or they can be distinct because the body is just a shell for the Curse, just as Tetric became a shell for the Ghoule Overlord during the uprising. The true essence, the true power, of the Ghoule Overlord is the spirit. Even so, the spirit of the Ghoule Overlord isn't the Ghoule Overlord. The spirit of the Ghoule Overlord, the power that drives his thoughts, decisions, and actions, is the Curse. The Ghoule Overlord is simply a physical manifestation of the Curse. A tool to be used, nothing more."

"That's quite a lot to take in and doesn't bode well for us," said Aislinn, her sharp mind working through what her Protector had just told her.

"I know."

"So in the Sanctuary you killed the Ghoule Overlord. The host for the Curse."

"I know I did. I watched it happen with my own eyes."

"But the spirit of the Ghoule Overlord – the source of power, the Curse itself – survived."

"Yes, after I killed the Ghoule Overlord, or rather destroyed the vessel the Curse was using to achieve its objectives, the Curse escaped when the black diamond dissolved."

"Diamonds just don't dissolve," murmured Aislinn, more for herself than Bryen, trying to wrap her brain around what Bryen was explaining to her.

"This one did, just as the Seventh Stone did when it merged with me. Twice."

Aislinn took a moment to think about what Bryen was saying. There was a certain kind of logic to it all, though she really wished they had some kind of proof. She preferred confirmable fact to speculation, but with the Talent and the Curse there was little to be had with either.

Having no choice but to acknowledge that truth, who was she to say what was and wasn't possible? It would be foolish after all that she had seen and experienced in just the last year.

"I want to make sure that I understand. Tell me again what you saw."

"During the combat with the Ghoule Overlord, I broke his staff," explained Bryen. "The black diamond slipped from the top of the black ash and shattered on top of the pedestal."

"Right, but that ..."

"But that doesn't mean anything, I know. What happened next does. When I killed the Ghoule Overlord, or rather when I destroyed his body, or what was actually the Curse's shell, the broken pieces of the diamond transformed into a black mist that blasted through the Weir and back into the Lost Land, probably back to the Temple of the Ghoules."

"The Temple of the Ghoules?" asked Aislinn. What happened with the black diamond certainly was possible -- again, she wasn't in a position to say what could and could not happen, especially not after her Protector's experience with the Seventh Stone -- but she had no knowledge of the Temple of the Ghoules.

"Yes, it's the source of the Curse in the Lost Land. Or it could just be where it resides. I'm not sure entirely. I need to find out more about the Curse before I can say for certain."

Bryen answered with such confidence. She wanted to believe him. Yet, how could he know where the Curse came from? And how could he know about such a place as the

Temple of the Ghoules? No one had ever survived a trip into the Lost Land? No one but ...

Aislinn lifted her head, her eyes widening as she began to understand from where Bryen might be getting his insights. Bryen had said that his conclusion was based not only on what he had seen, but also on what he had heard.

"Bryen, who did you speak with in the Sanctuary when you were crafting the Weir?"

"Viktor Keldragan," replied Bryen, saying it as if it was the most natural thing in the world to speak with a Magus who had died more than a thousand years before.

A small part of Aislinn's mind found it difficult to comprehend what Bryen was suggesting. She ignored it, knowing that she needed a much broader perspective when it came to discussing the Talent and the Curse.

Bryen had explained briefly how the Ten Magii had aided him in rebuilding the Weir, and Rafia hadn't batted an eyelash after he had explained it all. So if the Keeper of Haven believed what her Protector had said, she could try to do so as well.

"What did he say?"

"We were discussing the power that the Ghoule Overlord exercised," said Bryen. "I'll never forget what he said. 'Even with the power he can manipulate, the Ghoule Overlord has lived a long time because of that power, but I expect that he has forgotten that the power that he controls is also controlling him. He is not a master of the Curse. The Curse is the master of him. Just as you are a host for the Seventh Stone, he is a host for the Curse, and right now the Seventh Stone is the stronger master.'"

Aislinn thought about that. There was a symmetry to the statement that her analytical mind appreciated. "What did he mean by host for the Curse?"

"My guess?"

"Yes, your best guess."

"That the Ghoule Overlord is the Curse and the Curse is the Ghoule Overlord. As I said, I believe he is a physical manifestation of the Dark Magic of the Lost Land. However, the Curse itself, the spirit, is distinct from the flesh. The Ghoule Overlord is simply a means for the Curse to achieve its objectives in the Lost Land. The Ghoules don't obey the Ghoule Overlord. They obey the Curse. They just don't know it. Or if they do, they don't care. Or they can't do anything about it."

Aislinn nodded as she mulled his answer. It made sense, too much sense, and it was the direction that her mind had been going as well that led her to one inevitable and frightening conclusion. "The Curse survived and remains a threat to Caledonia."

"Yes, it does. I think that the Curse that was contained within the black diamond and gave the Ghoule Overlord his power returned to the Temple of the Ghoules when I destroyed the body that it had been using for the last however many centuries."

"So the black diamond, which is an artifact of the Curse, did what the Seventh Stone can do. It merged with a Ghoule to create the Ghoule Overlord, essentially an embodiment of the Curse as you explain it, just as the Seventh Stone merged with you."

"Yes, that's the theory that I'm working from right now. It's the only explanation that looking at all the various puzzle pieces gives us a chance to craft a larger whole and understand what has occurred and what could occur."

The more she thought about it, the more what Bryen was telling her made a frightening kind of sense. Then her musings returned to something that Bryen had said that had stuck in the back of her mind. "Wait a second. The Temple of the Ghoules. You said that it was ..."

"It's the seat of power for the Ghoule Overlord in the Lost

Land. It's also the bastion of the Curse. The Dark Magic of the Lost Land is centered there, comes from there."

"How do you even know about the Temple of the Ghoules? I've never even heard of it. I doubt anyone has ever heard of it. Rafia and Sirius certainly never mentioned it."

"There's a good reason for that."

"What would that be?" Aislinn asked, even though she believed that she already knew the answer. All her doubts and concerns were slowly fading away as she, too, began to fit together all the pieces.

"Because only one person has ever seen the Temple of the Ghoules," replied Bryen. "Only one person has even been there."

"Viktor Keldragan," Aislinn murmured, her confidence in Bryen's theory growing.

"Yes, my uncle went there to retrieve the Seventh Stone and steal the black diamond so that the Ten Magii could construct the Weir the first time."

"He told you about all this?"

"In part," Bryen confirmed. "He showed me a good bit of it. He shared some of his memories with me since his essence and those of the other nine Magii remain within the Seventh Stone. Remain within me now. He showed me how he navigated the Lost Land -- the route that he took and its many dangers, escaped with his prizes, and what happened when the Ten Magii built the original Weir."

"So you can retrieve those memories whenever you want?"

"No."

"Why not?"

"Viktor and the spirits of the other Magii will share information with me if they choose. If they believe it's necessary. They don't obey me. We just work together when the need arises."

"And this is all that you're going on?" asked Aislinn, who

struggled to keep the unease that remained within her from breaking free.

What Bryen was telling her made too much sense, and that's what worried her. Just because you didn't understand something didn't mean that it wasn't real. However, her hesitation came from another more personal source. Her concern for Bryen. Because if he was correct, she understood what the next step would be.

Bryen smiled. He knew that Aislinn was reaching the same conclusions that he had already. She just needed more time to digest everything and to get past her fears. But there was no reason not to be entirely honest and perhaps give her a gentle, final push over the edge. "There is something else."

"What would that be?" A tinge of trepidation tainted her voice.

The stresses and strains of the last few days, added to her growing concerns regarding what Bryen was telling her, were beginning to wear on Aislinn. She needed some sleep. This probably wasn't the best time to have this conversation. Nevertheless, it was too important not to have it now. So she took a few deep breaths, trying to control her very short temper, realizing that giving in to it now wouldn't be helpful.

"As I said, I had a dream. Two actually. One on the way here. The other early this morning. Both were very similar."

"About me?" she teased, wanting desperately to feel, if only for a moment, that she was in a normal relationship instead of one that was always colored by death and destruction.

Aislinn's comment made Bryen smile and earned her a wink. "Well, if you want to know about those dreams ..."

"No. No." Aislinn waved her hands in front of her, stopping him before he could embarrass them both, her irritation gone, now replaced by resignation. "Tell me about the other dream."

Bryen took a moment to gather his thoughts. At first, he had thought that it was just a nightmare. He had dozed off while

Banshee flew to the east, away from the Sanctuary after he had reestablished the Weir and the Blood Company had defeated the Ghoules.

He had hoped that the Ghoule Overlord truly was dead. He wanted to believe that he had killed the beast, but Bryen was having a hard time convincing himself of that. The fact that one of Sirius' comments – "Hoping doesn't make it real" – kept playing through his mind didn't help matters.

"Let me do one better," Bryen replied, realizing that giving Aislinn the chance to see it for herself was much better than an incomplete recitation. "Let me show it to you."

Bryen reached for the Talent, then using the trick that he had learned from Viktor, he connected with Aislinn so that she could experience the dream just as he did.

Instantly Aislinn was transported to the Temple of the Ghoules, the stench of sulfur infusing the air, observing everything through Bryen's eyes.

He stood on top of the massive, truncated pyramid that rose several hundred feet into the air, the steps worn and pitted, running down to the expansive square surrounding the structure.

Aislinn was amazed by the clarity of it all as she took in this strange, new environment. The large slab of raised stone in the center. The dome held by soaring pillars covering the summit of the pyramid. The circular hole in the dome.

From where Bryen stood, he stared down at a city of arches and rectangles that stretched on for miles. There were no tall buildings, most appearing to be long communal structures that were separated by dry, winding canals with dozens of bridges spanning the gaps that were no longer needed. By the bridges closest to the pyramid, there were large, dark holes that dropped into the ground reminiscent of the nests of the black dragons that littered the base of the Trench.

Who knew what resided in those burrows, and Aislinn

could tell that Bryen had little desire to find out, gazing upon those shadowy enclaves making her feel distinctly uncomfortable. The temple was kept apart from the rest of the city by a huge square that must have been at least a quarter mile wide and could easily hold a hundred Ghoule Legions if not more.

Scanning beyond the outskirts of the city, the Ghoule metropolis sat in the dormant hollow of a towering volcano, which in turn rose out of a lake, the water of which appeared to steam and boil as it flowed off toward the horizon in all directions, the far shore just a distant smudge. Along the cusp of the crater, a dozen waterfalls fell off the mile-high rim.

Aislinn was taken by surprise when the Ghoule Overlord made an appearance. She almost reached for the Talent, catching herself just in time. She had to remind herself that this was Bryen's dream. She was simply observing, experiencing what he did.

"I see you, Protector," said the Ghoule Overlord. The beast revealed himself atop the pyramid just on the other side of the altar, stepping out from between the pillars. "Again. No matter what I do I can't seem to get rid of you."

"I wouldn't think that you'd want to get rid of me. I thought you wanted the Seventh Stone. You can't take the Seventh Stone until you kill me."

The Ghoule Overlord offered an evil grin, revealing his sharp teeth, his black eyes blazing with the power of the Curse. "You're right, Protector. But you're also wrong." The Ghoule Overlord leaned in closer, his shadow extending across the slab of stone. "I do want you. When the time is right, when I am done with you, I will eat your flesh. I will gnaw on your bones. All your efforts will have been for naught. I will use the Seventh Stone to destroy the Weir you constructed and open the path to Caledonia for my Legions. My Ghoules will hunt and your humans will suffer."

The certainty with which the Ghoule Overlord spoke sent a

shiver of fear through Aislinn. Even though Bryen had defeated this beast, in his dream, it appeared to have never happened at all. It was as if the Ghoule Overlord didn't know that Bryen had killed him or refused to accept that reality.

"That will be difficult for you to do now that you're dead," Bryen said.

The huge beast laughed, a horrible, teeth-rattling sound that drifted out over the dead city. "You didn't kill me, Protector. You can't kill me. You took my flesh, yes, but you did not kill me. You can't kill the Curse."

Aislinn played the monster's words over and over in her mind. All the while, Bryen stared at the Ghoule Overlord, studying the creature, fixing his gaze on the carving of the black diamond in his forehead. She hated the conclusion that she reached, what it truly meant. Nevertheless, she was certain that she was correct, having reached the same conclusion as Bryen did, his words confirming it for her.

"You're not a Ghoule. You use the Ghoules. Tools to be employed and no more than that."

The Ghoule Overlord laughed again, nodding his head. "Correct, Protector. You are smarter than I thought. I am strongest in my flesh form, although I do not need flesh to survive. I am the Curse. I am the Dark Magic that exists in all the realms of this world, more strongly in some than others. And here I am very strong. I made the Lost Land what it is. I made the Ghoules what they are. And when I am done, the human lands to the south of the Shattered Peaks will be mine as well. From there I will expand my rule, spread my Dark Magic, because that is my true purpose. To make all the realms of the world, Natural and Spirit, mine. The Curse can be defeated, though even that is rare. It can never be destroyed."

"And you need me to do that," offered Bryen. "You need to become me to do that. You need the power that only I can give you."

"Perceptive, Protector," said the Ghoule Overlord, nodding his head in agreement once more. "Yes, that's why I need you. You will be my tool for spreading the Curse. The Seventh Stone will make my work much easier. In fact, I can feel it in you right now. It's restless, the Dark Magic within you. You've done a clever job of suppressing it. Still, you won't be able to control it forever. The Curse is chaos. It cannot be restrained. It will find a way to break free. It will find a way to run wild. It always does. That's what it is. That's what it does. That's what I am."

"I've defeated you once," challenged Bryen. "What makes you think you can beat me now? You said it yourself. You're weaker when you don't have your host. You need to be flesh to access your full power. I destroyed your body. I will destroy you in your current form."

The Ghoule Overlord's black orbs flashed in anger, his clawed hand gripping the twisted black staff with the black diamond wrapped within its top just a bit tighter than usual as he struggled to control his building rage.

"You didn't defeat me, Protector. I let you win the combat. Consider it a test of sorts. To find your weaknesses."

Bryen smiled at that. "And what did you discover? What are my failings?"

The Ghoule Overlord grinned evilly then, his eyes now sparkling with delight. "That you care, Protector. About your people. About your land." The Ghoule Overlord shrugged his shoulders, as if what he had just revealed actually was all too obvious. "I don't care. That's the difference between us, and that's what will lead to your death. What will lead you to me. You care about the humans fighting for you. I care nothing for my Ghoules. They are tools just as you said. They serve a purpose. They can be discarded as needed. Not so your precious humans."

"Compassion isn't a weakness," countered Bryen.

"It is the ultimate weakness!" roared the Ghoule Overlord.

"Your compassion will lead to your undoing. It is what in the end will give you to me."

With barely a flick of his staff, a stream of Dark Magic shot from the black diamond straight toward Bryen, who opened himself to the Seventh Stone and crafted a shield of energy to his front that resembled the scuta his gladiators used so effectively against the Ghoules.

Just in time. The blazing white energy deflected the threads of darkness.

Aislinn cringed within herself as the Dark Magic sped toward Bryen, sped toward her. She shouldn't have worried. The Dark Magic flailed uselessly against Bryen's shield, unable to penetrate his barrier.

She realized as well what the Ghoule Overlord was doing. The monster wasn't trying to kill Bryen. Not yet. The beast simply stood in place, studying him, satisfied to keep him pinned where he was for a few moments more.

"That is quite impressive, Protector. But it is not good enough."

The stream of Dark Magic continued to flow toward Bryen, and with another flick of his wrist the Ghoule Overlord adjusted the tainted energy's form, the Curse becoming an inky cloud that descended upon Bryen, covering him entirely so that he could see nothing but pitch black.

Bryen responded instantly by shifting the shape of his defense to a protective dome, the Talent preventing the Curse from touching him. Even in a dream, Aislinn realized that Bryen needed to avoid coming into contact with the corrupt power. Because this dream wasn't just a dream. It was much more than that.

Every so often, a sliver of evil reached out from the surrounding murk toward Bryen's shield, the two distinct energies flashing brightly whenever they came into contact, and then just as quickly the misty black drifted away.

Aislinn saw immediately what the monster was doing. The Ghoule Overlord wasn't trying to break through Bryen's barrier. The beast was trying to determine how strong he was. The Curse was attempting to determine what he needed to do to kill him.

No. Aislinn realized in an instant that she was wrong. The Curse didn't want to kill him. The Curse was trying to determine what would be needed to take ...

Aislinn felt a debilitating pain burn through Bryen, starting in his gut and working its way out to his extremities, the shock of the assault almost making Bryen drop his shield. He suffered through the torment for several agonizing seconds, barely able to hold onto the Talent. She could sense him losing control. The power was slipping through his fingers, until thankfully he was able to lock away most of his suffering just as he did the Curse within him. Bryen was thinking clearly again.

With a shiver of fear, Aislinn realized that the pain Bryen had just experienced wasn't the Ghoule Overlord attacking him. It was the Curse within him, the Dark Magic contained by the Seventh Stone choosing that moment to try to break free and rejoin its Master. How he had managed so much of that blighted evil, she didn't know.

Aislinn felt the Dark Magic slam against the barrier that Bryen had created within himself to protect against the corruption of the Curse. She marveled at his control as the Dark Magic pounded with a fast and regular rhythm against the thin barricade, desperate to gain its freedom, to break free, to claim Bryen for its own.

"As I said, Protector. I am the Curse. I am the Dark Magic of this world. You can challenge the Ghoule Overlord. But you can't challenge me. You cannot fight against the Curse, because I am already a part of you. No matter how much you might deny it, no matter what you might do to prevent it, it's too late. You already belong to me. You just don't know it yet."

Aislinn sensed the pull of the Curse intensify within Bryen, with even greater force the Dark Magic slamming faster and faster against Bryen's defenses much like a blacksmith crafting a new blade.

Aislinn experienced Bryen's rising fear, sensing how close he was to losing this terrible fight. Then she noticed a subtle shift in Bryen, his racing heart slowing, reason returning to battle the fear.

As the seconds passed everything around him, everything within him, faded away, until there was only his heartbeat. It was the only sound that Aislinn heard. An incredible ability, she believed, Bryen able to concentrate so acutely.

Once he regained control over himself, he took the next logical step. He focused on the Seventh Stone, allowing the power of the artifact free rein within him, reveling as the overwhelming amount of the Talent residing within the jewel crushed the Dark Magic, the barrier protecting him from the Curse knitting itself back together and solidifying before its prisoner could do as it wished.

When Bryen opened his eyes once again, Aislinn saw that the Ghoule Overlord had not moved, the stone slab still separating them. The beast was still as a statue, except for the slow shake of his head. His adversary's rapacious grin suggested that he had just discovered exactly what he wanted to know.

"An enjoyable diversion, Protector," rasped the Ghoule Overlord. "But I have what I need. We can continue this at a later time."

"You seem very sure of that," said Bryen. "That we will meet again."

"We will, Protector. Much sooner than you might think. You know my words are true. You can't deny them. It is getting harder for you to control the Curse. I just confirmed that. And as time goes by, it will only become more difficult for you. You want to know why, Protector?"

Bryen didn't bother to respond, simply staring at the Ghoule Overlord. Aislinn knew why, coming to that horrible realization in the blink of an eye. She already comprehended the truth, just as Bryen did. He was just reluctant to admit it to himself.

"Because you can't control me, Protector. Listen to my words, for they are the truth. I am the Curse. I am chaos. I will come for you again, and when I do you will not be able to deny me. You will be mine. You will serve me."

In a flash, Aislinn was ripped from the dream, the action disorienting, making her feel slightly ill.

"After that, the dream faded," Bryen said, locking eyes with Aislinn as he released his hold on the Talent and severed the connection between them.

"That was all of it?" asked Aislinn. "You didn't leave anything out."

"I showed you everything that happened."

"What's the city surrounding the Temple of the Ghoules called?"

"Viktor named it Mertvey Gorod, which he translated as the Dead City. The crater itself and the lake around it are known as the Cauldron."

"Show me the second dream, the one from this morning with your uncle. I want to hear what he said."

Bryen complied, using the Talent to share the memory with Aislinn so that she could listen to his conversation with Viktor. When that was complete, Aislinn reached up to his brow, running her fingers gently over his newest and most likely not his last scar.

"These dreams that are more than dreams certainly support your theory that the Ghoule Overlord is a manifestation of the Curse. That the Curse has a consciousness of its own."

"The black diamond and the Curse are no different than the

Seventh Stone and the Talent. I believe that Rafia would agree with me on that."

"She probably would," admitted Aislinn. "Your dreams are so real, terrifyingly so. But what if you're wrong? What if they were just dreams?"

"Then I'm wrong. Regardless, we still need to find a way to remove the Ghoule Legions from the Winter Pass."

"And if you're right?"

"Then we're not done. The Weir is in place. The Ghoules can't get through. But ..."

"The Ghoule Overlord can. Or rather the Curse. The Ghoule Overlord and the Curse are one and the same. And the Curse already has demonstrated that it can bypass the Weir and work its evil in Caledonia."

"Yes, the Curse, or rather the Ghoule Overlord can since he is the physical representation of the Curse. He will continue to hunt me. He will not rest until he has the Seventh Stone and he can use me as he wishes. Then he will do exactly as he said he would. He'll destroy the Weir and release the Ghoules on Caledonia."

"So if the Curse makes it back through the Weir," said Aislinn, "we don't stand much of a chance."

"Unfortunately ... correct."

"What's correct?" asked Declan, who approached with Lycia and Davin, Rafia stepping out from the medical tent just a few seconds afterwards and coming to stand behind the twins to listen.

Bryen spent the next few minutes explaining what he and Aislinn had been talking about, as well as the conclusions they had reached because of his dreams and his conversations with Viktor Keldragan.

"So let me just get this straight," cut in Davin. "You don't believe that the Ghoule Overlord is just a Ghoule. You believe that he's the corporeal representation of the Curse. A vessel for the Dark Magic of the Lost Land, nothing more. You also believe that the Curse made the Lost Land what it is, made the Ghoules what they are today. When the body of the Ghoule Overlord dies, the spirit of the Curse simply returns to the Lost Land and takes a new host. A new Ghoule is selected to become the Ghoule Overlord so that the Curse can continue its efforts to spread across the realms. Because of that, we can't stop the Ghoules unless we destroy the Dark Magic of the Lost Land. And we can't do that unless we destroy the spirit of the Ghoule Overlord, or rather we destroy the Curse itself, since those are one and the same."

"Yes," Bryen replied, shrugging his shoulders as if to say that it was just a small matter in the larger scheme of things. "That about sums it up."

Davin nodded his head a few times, letting everything that he had just said percolate in his mind.

"Great, the fun never ends," he finally replied with a wink and a nod. "But seriously, can't this monster just die?"

"You trust what you learned in your dream?" asked Declan. He had no cause not to believe Bryen, even though the rational part of his brain found it difficult to lend a great deal of credence to something that was constructed more of belief than reality. "I mean it could have been just a couple of bad dreams, lad. No more than that."

"It was too real for that, Declan," Bryen replied softly, understanding Declan's hesitation. "I've had dreams like these before. Dreams that aren't really dreams. I think they're connected to the Talent ... and also to the Curse." He admitted that last reluctantly. "I don't think I'd have them otherwise. I don't think they're dreams so much as conversations taking place in a different space. That's the best I can describe it. I'm there, and I'm not there. The Ghoule Overlord is there, but he's not there."

"And you believe this is real?" Declan asked again.

Bryen pointed to the thin, black scar on his cheek just above the other scars that ran down to his neck.

"I got this scar from the Ghoule Overlord. We fought in the Sanctuary. That happened almost a year before we actually made it to the Sanctuary to repair the Weir. I talked with him and fought with him in my dream, just as I did last night. I confirmed it all with Viktor."

"Viktor Keldragan?"

"Yes."

"How did you confirm it with the spirit of a dead Magus. That's ..." Declan looked at Bryen, taking in his serious expression, realizing that there was no point in questioning him. He just needed to get used to the fact that strange things always seemed to happen around Bryen, in large part because of the Seventh Stone and the power he facilitated. "Never mind. I don't need to know. I don't want to know."

"How will you know where to go?" asked Lycia.

She appreciated Bryen trying to explain everything to them, but she knew him too well. She understood that this conversation was more for their benefit and not his. Bryen had already decided what he was going to do, and there was no point in trying to dissuade him.

"I just know. I saw it all when I was speaking with the Ghoule Overlord. I've never been to the Lost Land, but thanks to Viktor sharing his memories with me, in my mind I can see the route he took to steal the diamonds. All of it. I know where I need to go. I know how to get there. I can navigate the Lost Land like I can navigate the Colosseum. With my eyes closed."

Declan nodded, willing to accept Bryen's reasoning. "You can't do this on your own, lad. You need help."

"I'll be going with him," said Aislinn, her tone daring anyone to challenge her.

Declan nodded again, considering. "That's a good thing. A Magus and a warrior. Two Magii, I should say, assuming you can escape your father," and before Aislinn could protest that she could do as she pleased, he raised a hand to placate her, then turned his attention back to Bryen. "The Lady of the Southern Marches is a good start, but you'll still need more help. That's why these two are here."

"Davin and Lycia?" Bryen valued what his friends brought to the table, their skills as warriors unmatched. Even so, he didn't want to put them at even greater risk than they already were. Nevertheless, he realized upon looking at his friends that they had already decided. Despite his misgivings, there was no point in trying to get them to reconsider.

"I guess having the best fighters in the Pit with me couldn't hurt. Might even help."

"Thanks for the vote of confidence," said Davin, his sarcasm apparent.

"Then it will be the four of us," Bryen said.

"Five," interrupted Rafia. "I'll be coming with you."

With the stormy look on the Magus' face, not even Declan was going to try to stop her.

I hope you enjoyed the first two chapters of Book 7, *The Protector's Victory*. Order your copy today for the exciting conclusion of *The Tales of Caledonia*.

LOOKING FOR MORE ...

This short story is a prelude to the events in my series *The Sylvan Chronicles* and is free to readers who receive my newsletter.

Join Peter's newsletter and get your FREE short story.
www.kestrelmg.com